SOFIA DE LEON WAS IRON AND LACE.

She was the widow of a man who had shot at Joel Trevor and daughter of a man he had killed with his own hands. In the ruins of her husband's ranch Joel had looked into her eyes—those eyes like embers—and seen the soul of a vulnerable woman, yet in the space of a few hours, she had transformed herself into the *patrona* of the hacienda.

Joel could still feel the fire of her lips on his cheek when she kissed him goodnight. The rustle of her silk skirt echoed in his mind.

From her bedchamber across the courtyard, Sofia watched the window of Joel's room. "Come to me, my love," she whispered into the night air that lay between them. "Come to me."

Fate had brought Joel and Sofia together again, and their lives were forever intertwined. Their blood would mix and their lands join into the greatest ranch in Texas, Lantana,

THE KINGDOM

The Kingdom

by
Ronald S. Joseph

WARNER BOOKS

A Warner Communications Company

WARNER BOOKS EDITION

Copyright © 1978 by Ronald S. Joseph
All rights reserved

ISBN 0-446-81467-9

Cover art by Tom Hall

Warner Books, Inc., 75 Rockefeller Plaza, New York, N.Y. 10019

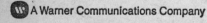 A Warner Communications Company

Printed in the United States of America

Not associated with Warner Press, Inc. of Anderson, Indiana

First Printing: April, 1978

10 9 8 7 6 5 4 3 2 1

For my father

Prologue

In the summer of 1886, an itinerant photographer on his way from Galveston to Laredo strayed from the trail and found himself suddenly surrounded by a band of five Mexicans on horseback. Although they brandished Colts and Winchesters, they did not molest him. Instead, they took his wagon in tow and led him south.

Knowing no Spanish, the badly frightened photographer, whose name was Elmendorf, assumed he was the prisoner of bandits from beyond the Rio Grande. He had no money; he obligingly opened his purse to show them, but they displayed no inclination to set him free. They pressed on, stopping only once at a trickling creek to refresh their mounts.

After about an hour, Elmendorf thought he beheld a mirage quivering in and out of focus in the shimmery atmosphere that sat over the landscape like a bell jar.

There was a tower, a dark minaret against the white sky, surrounded by a building that seemed to be a jumble of roofs.

Elmendorf barely glanced at it, expecting the image to fade like a poorly fixed photograph in the glare of the sun; but when it persisted and sharpened as they advanced, he realized that he was seeing not an ephemeral mirage but a magnificent Victorian mansion set in

7

the middle of the landscape like a city on the moon.

Rising a full three stories above the plain, it had yellow limestone walls and leaded-glass windows which, reflecting the dazzling midsummer sunlight, created a checkerboard of dark mirrors. And above it all, above the gabled peaks and valleys of the gray slate roof, soared the tower.

Elmendorf and his captors were approaching the encircling wall, a low adobe fence breeched on its northern perimeter by a massive oak gate swinging between two tall, square columns that supported a wrought iron arch. Elmendorf saw that something was written in the arch, and he squinted up into the glare of the sky to read the word spelled out in iron: LANTANA.

Of course! he thought. Of course! He had stumbled onto the fabled Lantana Ranch. He should have known it from the grandness of the house!

Then, remembering rumors he had heard of what usually happened to trespassers on the Lantana, he looked about at the armed vaqueros who surrounded him and felt a quiver of both fright and immense relief. He was amazed that they hadn't shot him!

His approach had not gone unnoticed at the big house. For the better part of an hour, almost from the moment he'd been intercepted by the fence riders, a woman had been peering at him through a brass army telescope aimed northward from the lofty tower.

When he drew near, she capped the telescope, closed her rolltop desk over the long lists of accounts she had been studying, and descended the tower's steep, narrow stairs. She reached the porch as Elmendorf's wagon rolled to a stop in the yard below.

Elmendorf, a polite Swiss, managed a bow despite his shock. Nowhere except in sporting houses of Paris had he seen a woman in trousers. It took him a moment to recover sufficiently to study her more closely. She was, he remarked, quite beautiful . . . and taller by a head than most women he knew. Her features were fine but determined, and her stance told him that she was accustomed to giving orders. She wore a blouse of white native cotton, unbuttoned far enough for Elmendorf to see the beginning of what he considered a daring amount of cleavage, and soft doeskin breeches that tapered into her knee-high boots. Her only adornment was a gold wedding band.

"Welcome to the Lantana," she said. "I am Anne Cameron."

So this is the famous Anne Cameron! Elmendorf thought. He had heard about her almost from the moment he'd gotten off the boat at Galveston. Although he'd never expected to meet her, he'd imagined that someone who was the ruler of an empire ten times the size of his home canton of Zurich would be quite different—a woman with the regal mien of a French baroness or the haughty bearing of a German duchess, perhaps. Or, since this *was* the Frontier, she might have been a tough and leather-skinned boss-woman, a pioneer with flinty eyes that had looked too long over the bleached white landscape baking beneath the Texas sun.

Instead, he found her to be an exceedingly striking woman endowed with an unaffected presence that served to accentuate her physical beauty. Her hair, caught in a loose bun at the nape of her slender, graceful neck, was as yellow as the cactus blossom, and her eyes shone as green as prairie grass glistening in the sunlight after a spring rain. And, most interesting of all, he sensed in her an immense strength, an aura of determination and self-assurance.

A Texas woman, he thought to himself. This is what they all should be like.

"Please come in," Anne Cameron said. "My men will take charge of your rig."

She spoke a few quick words in Spanish, softly, but even Elmendorf, who understood nothing of the

9

language, recognized the tone of a command. The vaqueros sprang into action. They swung from their mounts and took over Elmendorf's horse and wagon.

Anne ushered him into a great foyer, and Elmendorf gasped despite himself. He'd seen nothing like it outside the ducal residences of Europe. Directly in front of them rose the grand staircase, wide enough to accommodate twelve men walking abreast. Its handrails of solid brass gleamed the full length like twin streaks of lightning, and on the landing, replacing the entire wall, glowing like a jeweled mosaic, all emerald, jade, topaz, and aquamarine, was the most beautiful stained-glass window he'd ever seen.

"La Farge," Anne explained, sensing his admiration. "There are months on end in these parts when that's the only green we see."

She led him into a parlor, and he sank blissfully into a well upholstered settee facing a fireplace which, he realized, was large enough to burn a small tree in.

As if bidden by a silent command, a young Mexican girl glided into the room carrying a silver tray with a frosty pitcher and two tumblers.

"A julep will cool you," Anne said, filling the crystal glasses, "and relax you from your journey. It's far too late in the day for you to travel on. My husband is due back soon, and I hope you'll do us the honor of being our guest. I've had a room prepared for you, and supper is at sunset. Tomorrow you'll be refreshed, and our men will escort you as far as the western boundary."

"Madame is too kind," Elmendorf said.

"Not entirely," Anne replied, and her smile brought him completely under her charm. "I noticed by the sign on the side of your wagon that you're a photographer. In return for my hospitality, I'd like a photograph taken. I'm thirty-eight years old and have never sat for a portrait."

Elmendorf studied her with admiration, thinking

10

that only a woman of her rare beauty would be so willing to state her age.

When he did not reply immediately, she continued, "I've never had a photograph taken of me before. But I think it's something my husband and I should do. For our children and our children's children to remember us by."

She looked suddenly pensive, as if she were staring into the future. A slight smile crossed her lips. When she next spoke, her words were so soft that Elmendorf barely heard. "And I want the photograph to show us as we really are . . . at this moment. Someday it will be all that they have of us."

The red velvet curtains had been pulled back and the late afternoon sunlight streamed into the parlor. Anne stood beside her husband. Alex Cameron sat in a chair, one leg crossed casually over the other, a thick layer of white caliche dust still coating his boots. His reddish-brown hair had been hastily combed, but there was a band around his forehead where his Stetson had rested. Circles of sweat darkened his armpits, and Anne had not given him time to remove his holstered revolver.

She had not changed clothes either. Still in pants and the same cotton blouse, she was dressed just as she had been when Elmendorf arrived, except that around her neck she now wore a golden lavaliere set with a blood-red garnet. Her half brother, Carlos, had remembered it at the last moment and had gone running up to her dressing room to fetch it.

Now Carlos, with Anne and Alex's two children, stood off to the side, waiting his turn before the camera. Elmendorf paused in his preparations and studied him. Carlos was nineteen years old, a young man who could be described as both handsome and beautiful. No taller than Anne, he was slim but well-built, with hair as sleek and black as a crow's feather. He was clean-shaven

11

with a clear, tanned complexion. His lips were full and his nose was proudly arched; but it was his eyes that arrested Elmendorf's attention. They were gray, but of such lightness and clarity that they seemed to have been cut from flinty quartz. Elmendorf knew that when fixed by the silver on his photographic plates, Carlos's eyes would be mesmerizing.

Waiting beside the young man was Dos Cameron, a flaxen-haired eleven-year-old boy, sturdily built and square of jaw. He wore a battered Stetson, on the crown of which he'd affixed the emblem of the Confederate Army.

Anne had spoken to him softly, saying, "Dos, are you sure you want to wear that? We lost the war, you know."

"I like it, though," Dos said.

Anne had smiled and acquiesced.

Beside Dos was his sister Maggie. At seven, she was already almost as tall as her brother. Her chestnut-colored hair was thick and wavy and reached below her waist. As she grew older, Elmendorf knew, it would turn a rich mahogany. He could see, too, that beneath the plainness of her girlish face was a bone structure that would one day make her a beautiful woman. And he did not fail to notice the color of her eyes: a striking meadow-green that exactly matched her mother's.

Elmendorf returned his attention to Anne and Alex. He positioned himself beneath the folds of the camera's voluminous black hood. The apparatus's glass eye stared at the couple.

"Are we ready?" Elmendorf called.

A thrill rushed through Anne, a sudden grip of excitement, a sort of stage fright. Her fingers darted to her throat and caressed the lavaliere as if it were a talisman. It had belonged to her mother, and to her grandmother before that—a woman Anne had never known but with whom she sensed an almost mystical bond of kinship whenever she wore the necklace. Anne

12

thought of her children, and her imagination conjured up their descendants, generations of her blood whom she in turn would never know.

She bent her head and looked down at Alex.

"This is for them," she said, sure that he could read her thoughts. "I wonder if they will remember us."

Alex took her hand and gazed up into her eyes. His voice was wistful.

"As ghosts, my love. . . ."

PART ONE

1860—1867

1860

1

They had set out on Anne's twelfth birthday. The night before she had prayed for a cloudburst, a broken wagon wheel, news of *bandidos* or an Indian raid, anything to delay the journey—because, more than anything else, she wanted to have a real birthday party, to share sweet cakes and lemonade with her newfound friends, the twin daughters of the hotel keeper and the farrier's little girls. She had hoped for a few presents, a long green ribbon of watered silk to match her eyes, a horseshoe nail ring . . . she even dared hope for a china doll. In her dreams that night she had them all, and she and her friends had eaten cake until they hurt, and afterwards they had played hide-and-seek in the ruins of the Alamo.

But her father woke her before dawn, and since she was still half-asleep, carried her to the wagon that waited outside, loaded and ready to go. So, when the sun rose an hour later and she was wide awake, the buildings of San Antonio were far behind them, and ahead lay lonely miles of rolling hills beneath a cloudless sky.

They stopped at noon beneath a live oak tree and celebrated her birthday. There *were* cakes, after all. Her mother, Martha, had bought them from the bakery the night before, little raisin cakes with bits of lemon peel and drizzled sugar icing. It wasn't the same, sharing birthday cakes with her parents instead of with girls her own age, but Anne relished every crumb. There was a doll, too—a stiff little rag doll stuffed with corn husks that she fell in love with immediately. She still longed for a china doll, but she knew she couldn't have everything she wanted.

Then her father, Joel, scanning the sky, said they'd better get going. Clouds had built up in the west and he sensed a storm.

Her mother had once told her, "You are a frontier child, my darling, not a girl for the cities or the towns. Sometimes life will be dangerous; often it will be hard; but, in compensation, it will always be new. And you should always look to the future."

Even as she listened, Anne had looked into her mother's eyes and had seen Martha's deep longing to settle down, to quit the life of roaming that had carried them piecemeal from Tennessee, west to the North Platte, then south to this vast new state of Texas. And Martha's longing was echoed in the child.

But Joel Trevor had kept his family on the move. He had been born in the Great Smokies, and had been in his time a mountain man, a soldier, a riverboat hand, and a trader. He had the look of a frontiersman, tall and strong with black hair and cautious gray eyes. His face had weathered handsomely, as if it had been cast in bronze. Astride his horse, he rode as if he and the animal were one. On foot, he moved like a cat.

Martha had been the loveliest girl in East Tennessee, a parson's daughter with flaxen hair and eyes like a summer lake.

They met the winter she was twenty, at the home of a friend. And before the evening was over, Martha was in love with the tall, strong mountain man.

Joel courted her throughout the long cold winter of 1846, often walking ten miles through deep snow to

18

spend an hour with her before trudging back again to his trapper's cabin in the woods.

Her mother disapproved; not that she disliked Joel—but, she warned, "He'll break your heart as many times as there are days left in your life, my love. He'll wear you out before your time. He's not a settler. I can see it in his eyes. He's looking far afield, and his home is not in Tennessee."

But Martha was too much in love to heed.

The winter worsened, and finally Joel was snowed in. Martha waited and watched for the first hint of thaw. When it came and Joel again made the trek from his mountain cabin to the parson's house in town, Martha sensed that something had changed. She chattered all evening with a nervousness born of uncertainty, and when Joel invited her out for a walk beneath the first full moon they had shared in months, she was almost afraid to go.

He was mostly silent for the first half hour, and Martha clung to his arm as if to let go would be to lose him to the woods forever. She tried to interest him in several topics, but his replies were brief and vague. Finally, when they reached the edge of the village by the lake hemmed with snow and were about to turn back along the paths to her father's house, Joel took her in his arms and kissed her for the first time.

She pressed close to him, her cheek against the scratchiness of his woolen coat, and tears spilled from the corners of her eyes.

"Oh, Joel," she cried. "What's the matter? Has something gone wrong between us?"

He tightened his arms around her. "I'm restless, Martha. I have the urge to move on. Already this land is too crowded for me."

She took that to mean he wanted to get away from her too, and her voice caught in her throat.

When she didn't reply, he went on: "I want to head west. I've heard a lot about what it's like out there.

19

There's land no man has ever seen, rivers that have never been fished, and more game than a man could ever use. I know it's the place for me. I've got to go."

"But, Joel," Martha said, "what about me? I love you."

He put his hand beneath her chin and tilted her face toward his. For the first time, he saw her tears. With a gentleness she wouldn't have believed possible from his big, rough hands, he brushed the tears from her cheeks and said, "I was kind of hoping you'd go with me."

They were married within a week, and within another week were heading west. For the next dozen years they wandered. Just when Martha had a garden in, when curtains were finally hemmed and hung, when she knew the neighbors well enough to join in their gossip, she would see that roaming look in Joel's eyes again, and she would know that weeds would choke her seedlings. The curtains would be folded and packed along with the pots and the china, the neighbors would be kissed good-bye, and Joel and Martha and their child would set out at dawn for another place where Joel had heard the grass was sweeter, the game more plentiful, and the settlers less numerous.

Then a change came over Joel. Martha never knew what caused it, never realized that it was the longing in her own eyes that finally touched him—but, as surely as he'd once been a restless rover, he became, at thirty-six, ready to settle down. Once he'd cared nothing for money; now he grew frugal and saved his greenbacks. And, when he'd accumulated three thousand dollars, he made a deal for some land in Texas south of the Nueces River—sixty thousand acres of brushland at a nickel an acre.

It was to this land in the heart of the *brasada,* an area that others had warned was too barren, too hostile to be of any use to anything except the rattlesnake, the coyote, and the wild Nueces steer, that they journeyed that mid-summer in 1860.

They had been assured that, except for the scorching heat, the trip would be easy. "Rolling hills," the innkeeper in San Antonio said. "Child's play, I'd imagine, for the likes of you from the mountains of Tennessee. And once you cross the Nueces, there ain't nothin' but grass and sky, and it's flat as a tabletop. You're a lucky hombre if you so much as spot an oak to shelter under outta the noonday sun."

"Four days," they'd been told—maybe five, at the most. "No injuns, no *bandidos,* and no rivers to speak of 'cept the Nueces, and that's tame enough."

Everyone said it would be simple.

They didn't mention that every stunted bush or tree or weed bristled with thorns or nettle. Or that every varmint they saw, from the skittish wild cattle way off in the brush to the pesky horsefly, came armed with horns or fangs or stingers of some sort.

Nor had anyone mentioned the terrible thunderstorms, the July gulley-washers that beat the grass flat against the earth and stung their faces like a thousand tiny whips. Nor the frightening lightning and thunder that left them half blind with a ringing in their ears. Nor the mud, which seemed determined to suck everything into the bowels of the earth, and in which they stood a foot shorter and their heavily laden wagon was mired axle-deep.

Then, too, there were the usually dry arroyos that became racing creeks. And lazy streams that turned into turbulent rivers. And the gentle Nueces, which spread to a wide torrent of churning brown water and cost them a day of travel.

No one had warned them about that.

And now, when by Joel's reckoning they were less than half a day's ride from their destination, another crippling storm was brewing. From the looks of the sky,

21

it promised to be even more violent than the ones that had plagued them earlier.

"We're in for a doozy," Joel said, calling to Martha, who rode on the wagon with Anne by her side.

Martha didn't reply. She'd hardly said a word all day. Looking at her closely, Joel saw how tired she was. Her thin, once pretty face was pinched and pale. Beneath her bonnet, her hair was lank and damp, and clung uncomfortably to her bare neck. Perspiration soaked dark blotches through her mud-stained blue gingham dress. She had rolled up her sleeves, and Joel could see her aching muscles strain as she worked the reins, controlling the six feisty little mules that drew the wagon.

She could take it, he knew. Wherever he roamed, Martha had always traveled by his side, surmounting hardships, never looking back. She had saved his life more than once. There was the time she had nursed him through the terrible fever that had racked his body from November to the following spring. And the time on the North Platte when his rifle had jammed, and the Arapaho brave who was trying to steal his horse had lunged at him with a club. Martha had sprung between them, and flashing the knife she kept in her boot, had slashed the Indian's throat. She had attacked with frightening fury, and Joel had had to pull her away from the dying brave.

She had suffered worse than they were going through now. Of course, she'd been younger then, and stronger. As he looked at her now, he couldn't remember ever seeing her so tired and pale.

He felt the awful pain of guilt, for despite all, Martha had never complained, had never said, "Look what you've gotten me into," even though Joel knew in his heart that all she had ever wanted out of life was to dwell among family and friends, keeping house in a cabin of their own.

And children! She'd said, "Oh, Joel, I want lots of

22

kids! Let's fill the house with them. Let's teach them how to read and write and sing and maybe even play the fiddle. They'll be a joy to us all the days of our lives. Oh, Joel, let's have a big family!"

But all they'd had was Anne, and though the matter was never mentioned between them, Joel knew it was the hardships he had put her through with his restless ways that had caused Martha to lose so many. Sometimes when he caught her looking pensively in the lamplight, he figured she was recalling all the babies she'd conceived but had not carried to term.

I'll make it up to her, Joel swore, watching her struggling with the reins. Once they reached their new home they'd never move again. He'd build her a fine house where she could live in comfort for the rest of their days.

The deep-throated rumbling of thunder broke his troubled reverie. His gray eyes scanned the horizon and spotted a clump of young mesquites in the distance.

"Let's head for those trees yonder," he called. "The storm's going to keep us out another night."

The clouds burst just as they reached the mesquites.

"Climb in the wagon," he yelled above the wind and thunder. "Fasten the canvas. I'll look after the animals."

Lightning danced around the brushland, great bluewhite bolts split the air with their sound like cannon fire, and rain fell in hard, stinging drops. For a time, the raindrops turned to hail the size of acorns, and spooked the animals so that Joel had to stay with them to calm their fear.

When at last he was able to crawl into the tiny wagon, he was drenched through. He rolled up in a woolen blanket and lay beside his wife with Anne between them.

"This is the worst blow yet," he cried above the howling wind.

Adding emphasis to his statement, a lightning bolt crackled from the clouds and split one of the young mesquites in the nearby grove. A flash of fire exploded from the green heart of the slender tree, as if a demon trapped within had been released, and immediately the smell of charred wood filled their nostrils.

Anne had thrown herself into her mother's arms and covered her ears against the thunder. When the booming ceased, the girl sat up and put the palm of her hand against her mother's forehead.

"Mama," Anne said, "you're shaking so bad."

"Are you cold?" Joel asked.

"She's hot as fire," the child said.

"I'm all right," Martha said. "I must be a little scared, that's all." But her voice was wan and thin.

Joel placed his hand where Anne's had been.

"You're burning up with fever!" he exclaimed. "Why didn't you tell me?"

"I knew you'd stop, and I didn't want us to," she said. "I wanted us to get there today."

Joel rummaged on the floor of the wagon for the medicine kit.

"Here it is," Martha said, withdrawing a corked bottle from her pocket. "I've been sipping it all day, and it hasn't helped a bit."

"Here," Joel said, pulling out the stopper, "drink the rest. Then try to sleep. When the storm blows over, I'll make you a dry bed under the trees. It'll be cool there."

The storm raged most of the afternoon. Under the watchful eyes of Joel and Anne, Martha tossed and turned in fitful sleep. Occasionally, nightmares overtook her, and she cried out names from her childhood. From time to time, when she came to consciousness, her arms would encircle her waist and she would double up in pain.

Joel was scared, though he struggled to appear calm, not wanting to alarm Martha . . . or Anne.

As the storm subsided, Martha woke up once more. For the moment she seemed to be free of pain. Her dark eyes sought his as she said, "It's cholera, Joel."

"Don't say it, Martha! It can't be!"

"I've seen it before, Joel. I know it's cholera."

Joel knew it too, but he didn't want to hear it from Martha's lips—as if keeping it unsaid could make it go away. He placed a finger over her lips. "You'll be all right. You just need to sleep. Don't worry." But in his heart, he was unable to take his own advice.

Martha attempted to smile, but the terrible pain gripped her again and her knees drew up against her bosom.

Leaning over her, Joel tried to kiss her; but Martha jerked her face away and said, "No! Be careful! You might catch it too. Think of Anne!"

When the storm was over and darkness fell, Anne took blankets from the wagon and made a rude bed beneath the trees for her mother. Then, using the dry wood they carried with them, the girl built a fire and put water on to boil for coffee.

Joel carried Martha from the wagon and pulled the blankets up over her. The pain was worse, he could tell, although Martha had still not complained, and he realized, finally, with horror, that without help she would soon be dead. The medicine, for all the good it did, was gone. Martha had swallowed the last of the bitter potion during the storm.

"She's terribly sick," Anne said, almost to herself.

"She's going through the worst of it now," Joel lied. "By morning, she'll be better."

"I don't think so, Papa."

"Don't talk like that, child!" Joel snapped.

Anne's eyes reflected a gravity and wisdom far beyond her twelve years, and Joel saw that it was futile to try to deceive her. Instantly, he regretted the harshness in his voice. "I'm sorry, kitten. It's just that I'm tired too. Maybe we should have something to eat."

"I'm not hungry, Papa."

25

Joel was not hungry either, and when Anne made no move to prepare supper, he said nothing.

The leaden grayness of twilight deepened into black, and the locusts sang in the branches overhead. Martha no longer cried out in her sleep, but her breathing was ragged and labored. Joel watched over her and mopped her feverish brow with a damp cloth. Anne sat with her back against a tree trunk and peered into the night.

"Papa!" she whispered. "Look yonder! It looks like the clouds are on fire."

Joel glanced to the south where Anne was pointing. Far in the distance, the underbellies of the last of the storm clouds glowed a baleful orange.

"What could it be?" she asked.

"Strange," Joel said. He stood up.

"Maybe lightning set a grass fire," Anne ventured.

Joel had thought of that. But he was considering something else. "It could be a bonfire. I've seen bonfires make clouds glow like that."

"That could mean there are people there," Anne said.

"And maybe medicine," Joel added. "I've got to find out. They might have something to help your mother."

He groped in the wagon for his saddle. Anne was at his side in an instant.

"Are you going to leave us here all alone?"

"I've got to, kitten. Are you afraid?"

Anne hesitated for a moment. Her eyes searched the surrounding darkness. The locusts cried shrilly, and she thought she heard a rustling in the nearby brush. But then she saw her mother's pale face in the flickering campfire light. "No, Papa. I'm not afraid."

Joel gave her a kiss on the forehead. "Look after your mother. Keep her comfortable."

"I will, Papa."

"I'll be back soon, I promise." Joel swung up in his stirrups. "That fire doesn't look too far off."

26

2

Joel was wrong. It took over an hour of hard riding to reach the bonfire, and by the time he arrived his horse was staggering.

Approaching a large hacienda, he could see, even from half a mile away, that a fandango was in progress. Two large fires roared side by side, and every window in the big house was ablaze with light. The rollicking guitar music that floated out to greet him was mingled with laughter and voices raised in song.

As he galloped near, two horsemen dressed as vaqueros approached, their rifles raised, and called out for him to halt.

"*Quién es?* one cried.

"*Amigo,*" Joel called back, reining up. He knew little Spanish. "I need help. *Ayuda.*"

The two vaqueros barred his path.

"*Qué quiere?*" one asked. He was swarthy, with a full black mustache, and a ragged scar that reached from his left temple to his chin.

"My wife. *Mi esposa . . .*" Joel struggled to remember the words. ". . . *enferma.*"

The other horseman, older, with a big belly and a hooked nose, muttered something in a short, staccato sentence. Then he motioned to Joel and said, "*Venga!*"

Guarding him on both sides, they led Joel to the steps of the hacienda. There Scar Face spoke sharply to a servant girl, who scurried into the house. Inside, the guitars strummed gaily. Through the windows Joel could see dancers stepping quickly to the Mexican rhythms of the music. The dark-haired, dark-eyed women were lovely in ruffled dresses that fluttered as they waved their graceful arms and swung their bodies at the waist. The men wore *charro* attire—dark, tight-fitting suits with embroidery of gold and silver. He could see servants passing among the guests, offering wine in crystal goblets and mounds of *empanadas* and *dulces* on heavy trays of Mexican silver.

The sight of such luxury in this desolate land sent Joel's thoughts flying back to Martha and Anne camped in the brush an hour's ride away.

"I need help quickly," he said. "*Pronto*. My wife is dying."

Hook Nose held up his hand, commanding silence.

Joel thought of the ride back and remembered his horse. "*Caballo*," he said. "*Agua, por favor*."

The men looked at his exhausted horse. Here was something they cared about. They made Joel understand that he was to dismount; then, while Scar Face kept watch over Joel with his rifle at the ready, the other vaquero led the horse to the watering trough.

Inside the hacienda, the servant girl they had met on the steps went in search of Doña Natalia, the sister of Don Enrique de Leon, the owner of the ranch.

At that moment, Doña Natalia was in the family chapel at the end of the corridor on the main floor, but she was not praying. Instead, the large spinster with the heaving bosom and steel-gray hair was sitting on one of the mahogany *bancos* trying to comfort her weeping niece.

"Sofia," she cooed, "you must stop this foolishness and dry your eyes."

But the girl continued to cry.

Doña Natalia pried the girl's hands away from her face and tilted it up to the candlelight.

Even in the chapel's dim illumination, Sofia's beauty was breathtaking. Her complexion was olive, but pale enough to show the noble blood that bespoke Imperial Spanish ancestry. Her glossy black hair was plaited into thick ropes, then wound into buns over each ear. Her nose was straight and aquiline, the shape so prized by the proud Spanish; and her lips, full and provocatively pouty, were naturally pink. But her real loveliness was in her eyes, which even now, red-rimmed from tears, still glowed like smoldering embers. It was said among the young grandees from the Nueces to Saltillo that one look into Sofia's eyes would melt a heart of stone.

Pulling a large lace handkerchief from her sleeve, Doña Natalia dabbed at the girl's tearstained cheeks. "Sofia, my child, you must stop this at once. Your eyes are already red. Soon they'll be swollen, and there'll be no hiding the fact from your father's guests."

Sofia tossed her head defiantly, brushing aside her aunt's handkerchief. "To the devil with my father's guests! They won't see me anyway. I'm not going to the party."

"What nonsense!" Doña Natalia chided, tucking the handkerchief back inside the sleeve of her black silk gown. "Of course you're going to the party. You have to go. Whoever heard of a *novia* not attending her own engagement ball?"

Her words brought a new flood of tears from Sofia, who threw her arms around her aunt's neck and collapsed against her bosom.

"There, there, *niñita,*" Doña Natalia whispered, stroking Sofia's shining hair. "Crying won't help. Besides, it's not the end of the world."

"Oh, but it is, *Tiacita!*" Sofia wailed. "The end of *my* world! How could Papa make me marry Luis? He's fat and old, and I hate him!"

Doña Natalia's eyes softened with sympathy. She couldn't blame her niece for despising Don Luis de

29

Vargas. He was in no way a young girl's dream of a husband—nearly fifty, he was bald and obese with dull, agatelike eyes which were almost lost in folds of fat. His mouth was hard and brutal, giving some credence to the widespread stories of his cruelty. People said he'd fought a score of duels and had sent each of his adversaries to the grave, that he was as quick to use the stinging whip on his vaqueros as he was to dig his needle-sharp spurs into the belly of his overburdened stallion. From the servants, who always know such things, came whispered tales of how he'd tormented his first wife, until as if by act of will (because the doctors could find no trace of illness), she grew more and more frail—ultimately escaping from him through death.

Doña Natalia herself had pleaded with Sofia's father not to arrange the marriage. "He's not for her," she had argued when the subject first came up. "She's young and innocent. He'll make her life miserable."

"Silence!" Don Enrique had commanded. "I know what I'm doing." His hand brushed the surface of a map spread out amid the clutter of his desk. "Look at his holdings! They stretch from San Blas to Arroyo Verde. Thousands of *varas*. Ebonal is much greater than my own Lantana. And Luis de Vargas has no heirs. Study him carefully the next time he calls. His color is bad, yellow like sand. There's a trembling in his fingers, and his breath comes hard. He won't live long."

Doña Natalia's black eyes flashed angrily. "So, you sacrifice your only child for more of this dry wasteland around us."

Don Enrique refused to meet her glare. Instead, his fingers spread over the map until it encompassed all the territory that one day would be his.

Someone scratched at the carved oak door of the chapel, and Doña Natalia, hastily brushing the tears from Sofia's cheeks, said, "Enter!"

The servant girl slipped into the chapel and bobbed a quick curtsy. "Doña Natalia, there's a man outside. A gringo!"

"Don't use that word," Doña Natalia said. "You know I don't like the sound of it."

"*Sí* señora," the girl said, wondering how else to describe the foreigner.

"What does he want?" Doña Natalia asked.

"I don't know," the girl said, shrugging her thin shoulders. "The guard told me to inform Don Enrique."

"Then why pester me?" Doña Natalia snapped irritably. She had already had enough trouble for one evening. "Go tell him yourself!" But when she saw the reluctance on the child's face to approach the *patrón*, she relented and said, "Oh, very well, I'll speak to my brother."

The girl sighed gratefully and quickly disappeared from the chapel gloom.

"Now, Sofia," Doña Natalia said. "Go upstairs to your room. Put cold water on your eyes and pat some color into your cheeks. You're pale as the moon."

She kissed her niece's forehead and, with a great rustle of her silk skirts, was gone.

Rising from the pew, Sofia approached the statue of Our Lady of Guadalupe. A smoky candle guttered at the Virgin's feet. Choosing a fresh taper, she touched its wick to the dying flame. When it caught, she pressed its base into the soft wax of the spent candle. Its golden glow illuminated the tiny features of the Patroness of Mexico.

"Please, Madonna," Sofia prayed, forming the silent words with her lips, "save me from Don Luis."

Her dark eyes implored the plaster statue for a sign, as the candle's black smoke curled above the Virgin's head, but the painted features remained immobile. Sofia's shoulders shook with a sob that racked her body. There would be no miracle. She knew it. Since it was pointless to go on hoping, she dried her eyes and bowed her head in resignation. Then, before rising to go upstairs to her room, she snuffed out the candle.

Doña Natalia found her brother in the midst of a heated conversation in the courtyard around the splashing fountain. "Of course the *americanos* will go to war." he was saying. "The states of the South will never accept Lincoln as their president. They'll leave the Union and Texas will go with them."

"What do we care?" said Carlos Delgado, an *hacendado* from farther south. "It has nothing to do with us. Our loyalty is to Mexico, none other."

"Exactly, my friend," Don Enrique said, a smile creasing his craggy face. "Thus their war will play right into our hands. There'll be no better opportunity for us to wrest the land south of the Nueces away from the gringos and reunite it with Mexico."

"I think not, Don Enrique. I believe Mexico has lost the territory of Texas for all time."

All eyes in the circle turned to look at the speaker. Ramiro Rivas had finally screwed up enough courage to enter the conversation. Unlike the others, he had only a modest ranch. He was not nearly as rich as they, nor was he as arrogant. In fact, he had been flattered and surprised by the invitation to the ball . . . though he knew that, since Annexation, so many *hacendados* and their families had abandoned their Texas ranches and moved back to the mother country, that to exclude any Mexican landholder, no matter how insignificant, was to have a poorly attended party.

"And would that please you, señor?" Carlos Delgado asked. He did not like Ramiro Rivas and trusted him less. He suspected him of being a Liberal, a supporter of the Indian, Benito Juárez.

"I'm certain Don Ramiro's sentiments echo our own," said Don Enrique, more to avoid a confrontation between his guests than to do honor to Rivas.

Ramiro Rivas said nothing in his own defense. It had taken all his courage to speak out in the first place, and now he had nothing left. But his thoughts would have been considered treason by the men in the circle. Younger than the others, Ramiro Rivas barely remembered the defeat at San Jacinto; and half his life had been spent under the United States flag. In all honesty, he had no desire to return to Mexican rule, a country whose people were at least as divided as the gringos north of the Rio Grande.

Don Enrique stepped into the silence. "I welcome the war. May it occupy the *americanos* forever."

"Excuse me, Brother," Doña Natalia intervened. Enrique's incessant posturing irritated her, and she was glad of an opportunity to interrupt.

"What is it?" he asked, annoyed because he had been about to launch into a speech.

But when she motioned for him to step aside with her, he bowed a *con permiso* to his friends and joined her beneath a flowering bougainvilla in a corner of the courtyard.

"Is it Sofia?" he asked. "Have you talked some sense into her head, or shall I go up to her myself?"

"No, it's all right. She'll be down soon."

"*Very* soon, I hope." He glanced around. "People are beginning to wonder, and I won't have her making a fool of Luis. You know his pride."

"I know it well," Doña Natalia said, just managing to keep the contempt out of her voice. "But that's not what I came about."

"Then make it quick. My guests are waiting for my return."

"They'll have to wait a little longer, I'm afraid. A caballero is waiting outside to talk to you. There seems to be some kind of trouble."

Don Enrique frowned with irritation. "Too much, too much. First, there's Sofia with her childish caprices; now someone is on my doorstep with his troubles."

"He's waiting," Doña Natalia repeated.

"Very well. I'll go."

33

As the two of them entered the house and crossed the cool, tiled foyer, Luis de Vargas stepped out of the shadow. "Doña Natalia," he said, bowing. "Enrique." The tune of a lively dance reached them from the ballroom. The breathless laughter of the youthful dancers rang happily above the music. "A lovely party. Everything in such excellent taste. What wine! And such delicious food! Surely you've imported a chef from the *capital*."

"Thank you, Luis," Enrique said nervously, seeing the suppressed anger in his neighbor's eyes. "But you are really too kind. I only wish I could have hired a chef from Mexico City. Unfortunately, we've had to rely on our own untalented cooks to provide what meager nourishment you've seen before you."

Luis demurred. "And the band. Surely the most gifted north of Monterrey."

"Clumsy-fingered vaqueros with badly tuned guitars," Don Enrique countered, following the polite formula that required him to deprecate his considerable efforts.

"You are truly too modest, Enrique," Luis went on. The lantern light shone on the smooth dome of his bald head, his thin, hard mouth attempted, but did not achieve a smile. "It is a lovely party. It could be made more lovely only by the presence of your beautiful daughter, Sofia."

At last it was out in the open. Luis was angry and he had conveyed his feelings to Don Enrique, but with the delicacy that protocol demanded.

"Sofia is taking great care with her toilette," Doña Natalia interjected. "You know how it is with a young girl at her engagement ball. Everything must be just perfect."

"But of course," Luis agreed. Etiquette prohibited him from pressing further. "I shall be waiting for her entrance. I know the delay will have been worth it."

He bowed with exaggerated courtesy and headed for the ballroom.

34

"He's drunk," Natalia hissed.

"Just a bit tipsy," Enrique said. "But did you notice his color? And the hands, how they shake?"

"It's only the champagne."

"On the contrary. He trembles worse when he's sober."

Natalia found the subject and its implications distasteful. She snapped shut her fan, punctuating the end of the conversation, and said, "Don't forget the caballero waiting outside."

"I'm going now," Enrique said. "Go talk to Luis. Keep him company until Sofia comes down."

The wait seemed an eternity to Joel.

"Vaquero," he said, "tell them to hurry. I need help quick. *Pronto!*"

"Silencio!" Scar Face answered, gesturing with his rifle.

Suddenly, the hinges on the massive front doors began to creak and light spilled forth from the foyer, as out stepped the resplendent figure of Don Enrique. The gold-embroidered costume he wore, catching the bonfire glow, gleamed like bright lightning, and his black boots shone like polished ebony. His head was held high, his dark eyes glittered; his hair was white as clouds at midday.

He strode to the edge of the porch beneath the great arch and looked down at Joel, who stood at the foot of the steps.

"And to what do I owe this honor?" Enrique said. He spoke in Spanish, and Joel did not understand.

"Señor," Joel began, "I've come for help. My wife is sick. . . ."

Don Enrique didn't bother to listen further. He was thinking: Natalia tells me a caballero waits outside my door. Some caballero! It's only a gringo. One of the vermin that infest this land. Just look at him. Filthy! And they have the audacity to consider themselves

35

superior. I detest them all, the grey-eyes who over-run . . .

"Please, *señor*," Joel said, thinking the *hacendado* had not understood his English. *"Mi esposa . . . enferma, muy enferma."*

Don Enrique watched with pleasure as Joel struggled to find the words.

"Ayuda, por favor . . ." Joel begged, *"medicina. . . ."* Still Don Enrique had no reply. He was enjoying watching the gringo squirm.

But upstairs, someone else was watching. Sofia had heard voices, and stepping into the shadows of her balcony, had witnessed the scene below. The gringo's voice, which was strong and deep, even as he begged for help, had first attracted her. And, as she studied him in the bonfire glow, she saw that beneath the dirt and sweat and fatigue that lined his face, he was uncommonly handsome. She admired the strength of his jaw and the way he held his shoulders straight, tired as he must be. And she saw that his eyes were gray. "Killer gray," her people said when they referred to Anglo-Texans, but she imagined those gray eyes could be warm and gentle when he held a woman close. He didn't look to be a killer, or a devil—as her father claimed all gringos were.

As she advanced farther onto the balcony, gripping the iron railing with both hands, she wished it were daylight so she could see the stranger more clearly.

"I'm Joel Trevor," he said. "I've bought the Narvaez ranch not far from here. . . ."

So you're the one, Don Enrique thought; the gringo I've been hearing about. Well . . . may your wife die. At least she'll bring no more gringos into the world.

He called in Spanish to his guard, "Bring the foreigner's horse. Send him away."

Joel understood the gesture.

"Señor, por favor! Medicina!"

Sofia watched, horrified at her father's coldheartedness. Don Enrique had turned and was almost through the door when Joel cried out once more for help. Don Enrique glanced back over his shoulder. He said in perfect English, "We have no medicine for you here. We have nothing at this hacienda for gringos."

The heavy doors slammed behind him.

"Wait!" Joel cried. "Wait! You've got to help me!"

He started up the steps, but, before he could reach the doors, Scar Face reached for his bullwhip.

It cut the air and struck like a snake, wrapping four tight leather coils around Joel's midsection, pinning his arms to his sides. Joel teetered for a moment on the top step, not yet aware of what was happening, a look of shock on his face at his sudden paralysis. Then the guard yanked back on the whip, dragging Joel from the porch. He fell hard, striking the sharp edges of the steps one by one, unable to protect his head. Blood spurted from a gash above his right eyebrow and from another on his split upper lip. He rolled to a stop, face down in the dirt at the guard's feet. Blood from his wounds formed dark pools beneath him and filled his mouth with a warm salty taste.

Sofia cried out, but the sound of her voice was masked by the guards' laughter as they watched Joel try to struggle to his knees. He was almost up when a wave of dizziness overwhelmed him and he pitched forward once again, face-down in the dirt.

The second guard knelt over him and quickly bound his hands behind his back. Then, roughly, with the toe of his boot, he prodded Joel until he had him swaying on his feet. The whip loosened and fell away.

Because Joel's hands were tied, Hook Nose hoisted him roughly onto his horse. Joel rocked unsteadily in the saddle, blood and dirt blinding one eye, his upper lip already swelling and throbbing with every racing heartbeat.

"Now, gringo," Scar Face said. "Go! Go like the wind!"

37

Once again, the whip split the air like a pistol shot. Its stinging tip cut across the horse's rump like a branding iron. The gelding bolted forward, nearly throwing Joel. Frantically, instinctively, he gripped with his knees to keep his mount.

Sofia clutched her throat in fear as she watched Joel pitch backward, then forward until his face was almost in the horse's mane. It seemed impossible that he wouldn't fall.

The gelding's hooves struck like thunder as it galloped between the crackling bonfires and out into the darkness of the night.

Below Sofia's window, the guards laughed again as the horse and rider disappeared from sight. The man with the whip cracked it a couple of times in the air, then, carefully, almost lovingly, wound it back into a tight coil and hung it from his saddle.

As Sofia slipped back into her room, her heart was pumping wildly. The color that her aunt wanted on her face was now burning hotly across her cheeks. She paced the room, unable to keep still, the heels of her tiny slippers drumming a tattoo on the hardwood floor.

The guards' brutality had horrified her, but she was even more repulsed by her own father's cruelty. If she had not witnessed it herself, she would never have believed that Don Enrique could send a man away who came begging for his aid. And she realized with revulsion that the guards acted in accord with Don Enrique's wishes.

She fell across her bed, her throat choked with nausea, her breath rapid and shallow, her small breasts heaving against the laced bodice, but she was too angry, too shocked, to cry.

Pulling the down-filled pillow to her, she held it against her bosom. It was several moments before she realized the repeated sound she heard was a tapping at her door and not her own racing heartbeat.

"Momento," she called. Her voice was small and

weak. She sat up and ran her trembling fingers over her face as if she could erase the fires of disgust and horror that blazed on her cheeks. "Enter," she said at last.

A servant girl of not more than twelve slipped shyly into the room. Her hands toyed with her apron and her downcast eyes studied the floor. "Señorita," she said, "Doña Natalia sends for you."

"Tell my aunt I'm coming now."

The girl bobbed a curtsy and departed.

Rising, Sofia crossed the room to the dressing mirror. She tried to examine her face, but her reflection was obscured by the mental image of Joel lying at the foot of the steps, his dark blood mingling with the dirt. In an attempt to shake off the vision, she leaned in close to the glass and stared into her eyes; but his face seemed to float before her, wearing the look of shock that overcame him as the whip whistled through the air and wound itself about him. But worst of all was the memory of the anguished cry she'd heard as he called after Don Enrique's retreating figure: *Wait! Wait! You've got to help me!*

Sofia whirled away from the mirror, kicked off her dancing slippers—sending them skittering across the polished floor—and threw open the door of her armoire. Grabbing her yellow leather riding boots, she pulled them on over her stockings. Finally, she reached up on a shelf and took down a shawl of midnight blue cotton. This she draped over her head, tossing its fringed length over one shoulder.

Entering the empty hallway, she walked on tiptoe so the heels of her boots would not ring out on the floor of terra-cotta tile. Ahead of her was the grand staircase that wound downstairs to the foyer. Dance music and the babble of voices filled the air.

She moved stealthily, only pausing for a moment at the top of the stairs to be sure that no one stood below. Then, quickly, she scurried across the open space to the other arm of the corridor, where there was a door to

39

an inside stairway. Glancing back to be sure she had not been seen, she opened the door and slipped inside.

As she stepped into the darkness, she stopped for a moment to catch her breath and to overcome the brief panic that clutched at her on the narrow winding stairs. Then, cautiously, she began to inch herself down. She did not stop when her probing fingertips told her she had reached the first floor door. That would lead her into the pantry and then into the kitchen. Instead she crept over the uneven stone floor until her boot struck a heavy iron ring.

She knelt, and curling her fingers through the ring, leaned back for leverage and tugged. Again and again she yanked at the ring until her fingers ached and the muscles in her upper arm felt as though they would burst the tight fabric of her sleeve. Beads of perspiration broke out on her forehead and upper lip. Moisture collected in her armpits and bled dark crescents into her dress.

But, just as she was about to give up, the stone to which the ring was attached began to give. The slight movement encouraged her. She tugged once more, straining back on her heels, and the stone groaned and moved again.

She had to rest. Sitting back, she mopped her brow with the fringes of her shawl. Once she had caught her breath, she gripped the ring again and began lifting. Stone scraped against stone. It was heavy, almost too much for her; but at last the big rock slab was free. She shoved it aside and knelt on the edge of a gaping hole in the floor.

Half a century before, when her grandfather, old Don Carlos, had built the hacienda, the warlike Comanche had roamed the *brasada,* attacking, burning, and pillaging the isolated ranch houses. To protect his family against marauding Indians, Don Carlos had caused a tunnel to be built, concealed between two thick adobe walls. From the house, it cut straight underground for nearly a hundred yards, debouching finally through a hard-baked clay pipe concealed behind a dense growth of thorny brush on the bank of a winding arroyo. As far back as anyone could remember, it had never been used except by exploring children of the hacienda.

As Sofia perched on the tunnel's edge, a heavy, dank odor of earth and fetid water filled her nostrils. The darkness was absolute. A tomblike chill wafted upward from the opening. A shiver racked her body. She almost lost her courage, but making the sign of the cross over her breast, she took her last breath of fresh air and lowered herself into the tunnel.

The bottom was slippery. She had to reach out to keep her footing. Immediately her hands recoiled in horror. The walls were slimy and hairy with fine, cobweblike roots. She shuddered and pulled her shawl even more tightly around her.

There wasn't room to stand. Instead, she inched forward, bent at the waist, her eyes searching ahead into the impenetrable darkness. Because she had to hold on to the sides to keep her balance, she forced herself to ignore the creepy feeling of the tunnel's tendril-furred walls.

The passageway seemed unending. She ached from being bent double, and the stench of rotting vegetation and foul water gagged her. But she pulled the scarf up around her nose and stumbled onward. Several times she tripped over thick roots, muddying her ball gown and her face. And twice she froze in her tracks, thinking she heard something scurrying at her feet. She was afraid of rats; she would die if one touched her. But when she stopped to listen, all she heard was the thumping of her heart.

At last, she sensed the end of the tunnel ahead. Not light really, it was more a lessening in the intensity of the pervading darkness. Spurred on by the thought of breaking free into the fresh sweetness of the nighttime

41

air, she started to run, hobbling like a hunchback beneath the tunnel's low ceiling. She could hear the evening breeze rustling the dry leaves in the brush that concealed the exit into the arroyo. She was running now as well as she could, scarcely feeling the repulsive hairy roots and the slime that dripped from them. Breathing through her mouth, she stared ahead to what was now a definite patch of deep blue.

Suddenly she sprawled forward as her boot struck a root and her feet flew out from under her. She threw out her arms to break the fall. Instinct, more than anything else, sent the waves of alarm through her body, for she certainly couldn't see anything, and it would be seconds before she consciously realized what her hands had touched. But she knew it was a snake, tough and sinuous like a thick muscle, as big around as her arm, and coiling swiftly with undulating contractions that coursed the length of its long body.

She screamed, and the echo of her voice rang from the far end of the tunnel like the hellish shriek of a bound demon, a scream that deafened her own ears with its force. Her instincts said: Recoil, back up, get away from it! But she plunged forward, screaming again, trampling over the snake, never knowing how close its venomous fangs came to piercing the fabric of her sleeve as they slashed downward through the fringe of the scarf.

She stumbled through the mouth of the tunnel, through the thorny underbrush, until she was safely across the shallow arroyo. As the echo of her last cry reached her from the tunnel and died away in the night, she fell sobbing to the ground and was sick.

Though she lay there for less than a minute, it seemed an eternity to her. Slowly, painfully, she got to her feet and began to wend her way, following the winding arroyo. Her dress was in shreds, and her hands and face bled from the scratches of a hundred thorns.

From the distant hacienda, carried out on the eve-

42

ning's warm breeze, the dulcet strains of "La Paloma" reached her, six strumming guitars rising to the melody, the tenor's plaintive voice beginning the tale of the lovely young woman called the Dove.

The music grew fainter as she hurried alongside the creek. Finally, all she could hear were random snatches of melody and the occasional long held note of the singer's voice. She checked her position. The bonfires glowed in the distance; she was farther away than she had thought. And when she turned and looked to the east, she could see the dark outlines of the *ranchito*, the village of shacks where the peons lived.

A pack of rangy, underfed dogs howled news of her approach. A lantern sputtered on in one of the shacks, and an old woman peered out into the darkness.

"Quién es?" she called.

Sofia clung to the shadows so the old woman wouldn't see her torn and muddy dress and the scratches that covered her face and hands.

"Quién es?" the old woman called again.

Sofia identified herself. "Send the *curandero* out to see me," she said.

"Would the señorita like to wait in my little house?" the old woman inquired.

"No, I'll wait here," Sofia said. "But send for the *curandero*. Quickly!"

The old woman barked an order to one of the half dozen children who gathered about her legs. A swollen-bellied boy, dressed only in a shirt of rough cotton, broke away from the others and ran to the end of the row of shacks. In another minute, Sofia saw a second lantern appear in the village. It came toward her as the *curandero* approached.

"Buenas noches, señorita," he said as he drew near.

The lantern light illuminated his features. Sofia had known him all her life, and for as far back as she could remember he had never changed. He'd always been old: white hair, white beard, a face as wrinkled as an apple

43

left to dry in the sun. There was more than a little Indian blood in him, and it was said that he could walk without leaving a footprint. When she was a child, she had been afraid of him, with his strange prayers, bitter herbs, and miraculous potions—for like all *curanderos* his ways were mysterious. Part witch doctor, part faith healer, part herbalist, the *curandero* cured the sick, healed the wounded, and eased the pain of the dying. When Sofia was thirteen and lay shivering from the fever, Casimiro had come to her bedside and worked his magic on her. Within days she was strong again, and she was no longer afraid of him, but soon grew to regard him with respect and awed devotion.

"*Buenas noches,* Casimiro," she greeted him. "You are needed."

"Who is sick?" Casimiro asked.

"A woman. Far away. Can you ride a great distance?"

"Yes," he answered. "I am strong."

"We need two horses."

"I will send for them."

An old woman from a nearby shack brought Sofia a sweet mixture of hot coffee and chocolate to drink while she waited. There was a rising moon, and in its pale blue light the woman could see Sofia's torn and muddy dress and the crisscross scratches that covered her face and hands. But her eyes veiled discreetly over and she asked no questions.

Just as the horses were being brought up, Casimiro returned with his leather pouch containing his herbs and medicines.

"You will lead us?" he asked as he was helped into the saddle.

"Yes," Sofia answered.

Although all she knew was that the stranger had ridden away north, she took her reins and spurred her horse into a canter. Casimiro followed, and the two of them hurried off into the darkness.

3

Sofia and Casimiro rode in silence. In the distance a lone coyote bayed soulfully at the moon. All around, the dark shapes of stunted brush and skittish wild cattle kindled Sofia's imagination, and she saw bandits and demons at every turn. Only Casimiro's presence reassured her and kept her pressing onward. She realized suddenly the folly of what she was doing. Surely, back at the hacienda, her absence was already known. Enrique would be in a rage, turning the household upside down, questioning the servants, berating Natalia for having left Sofia alone even for a moment. It would be only minutes before word reached him from the *ranchito: the señorita rode north, far beyond the arroyo, taking Casimiro with her*.

Enrique would know instantly what she was up to and would follow her. Undoubtedly Luis would gallop along with him. When they caught up with her . . .

Sofia shook her head in an attempt to banish all thought of the consequences that lay ahead for her. At the moment, she didn't care. She kept seeing in her mind's eye the battered face of the stranger who had sought aid at her father's feet, and his last cry for help rang in her ears.

"Andale!" she called to Casimiro, and she spurred her horse into a run.

The bonfires had faded to a faint glow behind them when Casimiro's hoarse whisper signaled Sofia to pull up beside him. With a silent gesture, he drew her attention to a dark figure in a motte of mesquite trees. Moonlight through the feathery leaves etched the vague outline of a man swaying on horseback.

It's him! Sofia thought, a sudden chill racing up her spine, as she sensed his great fear across the distance that separated them. Casimiro looked to her for counsel.

She took a deep breath, barely trusting her voice, and called out, "Señor! We mean no harm."

Joel watched from the trees, having suspected for some time that he was being followed. He had sensed it first in the reactions of his gelding; then he heard the galloping hooves themselves closing in on him. Taking refuge in the shadow of the mesquites, he had worked frantically to free his wrists from the rope that bound them. If he were going to die, he would die fighting. He wouldn't be killed strung up like a calf.

But now he was baffled: A woman called out to him, and her voice trembled with urgency. A passing cloud masked the moon, deepening the darkness around them, and, when it slipped away, the moonlight shone more brightly than before, revealing two figures on horseback, a woman and a man.

Still wary, Joel kept his silence.

"Please, señor!" Sofia called again. Her voice carried clearly through the night. "We've come to help you. Trust me!"

At last Joel spoke. "Who are you?"

"I am Sofia de Leon, from the Lantana hacienda. I have brought Casimiro, the curandero. He has medicine to cure your wife."

"Stay where you are," Joel ordered.

Sofia saw a movement in the shadows of the brush,

then, as Joel moved into the moonlight, the glint of his pistol barrel.

"There is no need for that," she said. "We are unarmed. We've come only to help."

As Joel came nearer, he realized how young she was, and he saw that the man beside her was old, stooped at the shoulders, and that his hands held only his horse's reins.

"You've brought no one else?" Joel asked.

"We're alone," Sofia replied. "I swear it on the Virgin and on my mother's soul." She made a swift sign of the cross.

Joel hesitated another instant, then admitted, "I need help bad. My wife is dying."

"Please," Sofia said. "Put your pistol away. You don't need it, and I'm afraid of it."

Joel holstered his Colt and came closer. Sofia cried out when she saw his wounds. Blood still flowed freely from his forehead and covered the side of his face. His lip was swollen to twice its normal size, and blood from that cut had caked in his beard and on the bandanna that was knotted around his neck.

Casimiro leaned close to his mistress and said something in Spanish.

"Casimiro will stop your bleeding," Sofia said.

"No time," Joel said. "We've got to get to my wife." But he swayed in the saddle and Sofia saw how weak he was.

"You'll never make it," she said. "You're losing too much blood."

Joel knew she was right. Already he felt the dark wings of unconsciousness enfolding him. He swayed again and grabbed the saddle horn to keep himself from falling. Sofia swung instantly from her horse and ran to his side. Her sudden nearness reassured him and made him feel secure. The brute determination of will that had kept him alert and in the saddle vanished, and he gave himself over to her completely, as if she could

47

make everything right. He slid from the saddle into her arms, nearly crushing her with dead weight.

"Casimiro!" she cried.

The old man was already there. With strength that belied his age, he caught Joel beneath the shoulders and stretched him out on the ground. Then, reaching into the leather bag, he produced a canteen and swabbed the blood from Joel's face. The lip had scabbed over, but fresh blood poured copiously from the wound on the forehead. Quickly the curandero took a handful of dried moss and cobweb from his bag and pressed it against the cut. Sofia held the compress in place as Casimiro wound a strip of clean cotton around Joel's head.

Reaching once more into his leather pouch, Casimiro brought forth an earthenware bottle. He uncorked it and touched it to Joel's lips.

"Drink," Sofia said. "It will give you strength."

The thick, salty liquid gagged him, and he tried to spit it up. Casimiro expertly pressed two fingers against Joel's throat and the potion went down. But he had lost too much blood, and unconsciousness overtook him.

"He's dying!" Sofia cried. She cradled Joel's head in her lap and ran her fingers through his thick black hair. Tears filled her eyes and she studied his strangely handsome face, still beautiful despite its wounds and pallor. She had never known a man like this and could barely comprehend the emotions that drew her to him. "Oh, Casimiro!" she cried once more, feeling her heart thumping within her breast. "I think he's dead!"

Casimiro shook his head. "It's only weakness, señorita. He will come to in a moment." He soaked a cotton wad in a solution of ammonia salts and wafted it beneath Joel's nose. Almost immediately, Joel gasped for breath and his eyelids flickered open.

Sofia's countenance loomed over him, and in his confusion he believed he was drifting in a dream. He

48

was a child again and afraid of the dark. His mother held him close and he felt safe and secure in her arms. Then reality rushed back on him and he remembered where he was. Immediately his thoughts were of Martha.

"Help me up," he said. "We've got to get to my wife."

The curandero shook his head.

"Not yet," Sofia said. "You still haven't the strength. Here, drink more of this. It will help you."

Joel swallowed the foul liquid and fought to keep it down.

"More," Sofia urged, but he groaned and jerked his head away.

"You must," she said and once more pressed the flask to his lips.

"What is it?" he murmured.

"Ox blood," Sofia said, and he retched despite himself.

Casimiro took a cloth from his pouch and cleaned Joel's face.

"Be still for a moment," Sofia said. "You'll feel better soon."

The moon rose steadily overhead and, with each passing minute, Joel's strength was returning. At last, supported by Sofia, he was able to stand.

"Why have you done this?" he asked her, looking into the wide dark eyes that never seemed to leave his face. "Why did you come to help me?"

Sofia had no honest answer. She was too confused by her emotions to realize that from the moment she saw him beneath her balcony she had lost her heart to him. She believed it was pity . . . and outrage at her father's cruelty that had caused her to act. And she would have denied, even to herself, that she had acted out of love, for she knew that Joel was married, and, in the context of her upbringing and experience, such feelings for another woman's husband were unthinkable.

She simply said, "I felt sorry for you."

49

Casimiro made a motion for silence.

"What is it?" Sofia whispered.

Casimiro silenced her again and cupped his hand to his ear.

By then Sofia and Joel heard it too: the sound of galloping horses in the distance, coming closer.

Joel saw fear flash across Sofia's eyes.

"My father!" she said. "Quick, Casimiro, ride away! If he finds you here he'll punish you!"

"Come," Casimiro said to her.

"No," Sofia said. "I can handle him. But he mustn't find you. Go now! Quickly!"

The old man gathered up his leather bag and struggled into his saddle.

"Fly away, Casimiro," Sofia breathed. *"Vaya con Dios!"* She slapped his horse's rump, and the mare and rider vanished like a phantom into the night.

"Say nothing," she told Joel. "I will take care of my father."

The silhouettes of Enrique and Luis appeared on the horizon. They were upon them in a moment.

Enrique yanked back on his reins. His horse whinnied and reared on its hind legs scattering gravel. Enrique cried in outrage at the scene before him, Sofia with her arms around the gringo.

"Stand away, Sofia!"

But she stood her ground, still supporting Joel in her arms.

"Por Dios, I'll shoot you both if you don't obey," Enrique cried. "Stand away!"

"Father, hear me . . . !" Sofia begged.

"Do as he says," Joel said. He removed Sofia's arm from around his waist and moved away from her.

"So this is the bride you offer me, Enrique!" Luis shouted. His horse was less fleet than Enrique's and he'd only just caught up. "A girl who flees her father's house in the arms of a gringo!"

"No!" Enrique said, thinking quickly. The marriage

he'd maneuvered so carefully to arrange would not be wrecked by Sofia's idiocy. "Just look at the child! See how torn her dress is! See the scratches on her face and arms. It's clear the gringo has abducted her!"

Blind anger overwhelmed Luis. *"Cabrón!"* he shouted, whipping his pistol from its holster.

"No!" Sofia screamed.

The gunshot split the night air.

Joel cried out in pain, reeled backward, and sprawled in the dirt.

Sofia started toward him, but Enrique spurred his horse and blocked her way. He caught her roughly around the waist and dragged her up into his saddle. She struck out against her father, trying to break free, but he held her firm.

"Let me down!" she screamed. "Let me down!"

"Shut up, you fool!" Enrique ordered. "Shut up!" He brought the back of his hand against her cheek so violently that lights flashed before her eyes.

Luis was still staring at the gringo who lay motionless beside a clump of cactus. He took careful aim with his pistol and squeezed the trigger.

Sofia's cry of despair caused him to flinch and the bullet shattered a cactus an inch from Joel's head.

"Andale!" Enrique yelled. "To the hacienda!"

He spurred his horse and they sprang forth in a gallop. Luis reined his gelding about and followed. Sofia, locked in her father's arms, turned back and sought a last glimpse of Joel's inert form in the moonlight.

"Murderers," she cried. "I hate you!"

"That may well be, my little child," Enrique hissed into her ear, "but this is the last fit of insolence I'll have to endure from you. We'll have the wedding tomorrow, and henceforth you'll be Luis's problem."

"I won't marry a murderer," Sofia sobbed.

"I've raised a fool," Enrique said, his lips close to Sofia's ear, his voice barely audible above the thunder of his horse's hooves. "You don't seem to understand. Until tomorrow morning, you'll do exactly as I say. You have no choice. And after the wedding, Luis is your master."

"Never!"

"You think not?" His laughter raised the hair on her neck. "Just wait," he said. "Luis will tame you. You'll see."

Doña Natalia kept a vigil over Sofia throughout the night. From time to time the girl cried out in troubled sleep, bringing Natalia to her bedside with words of solace and a cool, damp cloth for her fevered brow. "Be quiet, my child," she cooed whenever Sofia whimpered and wept, and she held her niece close to her bosom until dreamless sleep once again stilled her torment.

At dawn, Enrique threw open Sofia's bedroom door. He was followed by two maids carrying the elaborate white lace wedding gown that had been ordered from Madrid.

"Wake her and dress her," he commanded Natalia. "We'll meet in the chapel in an hour."

The clanging of the courtyard bell roused both servants and guests. A flurry of excitement and speculation swept the household, as last night's revelers—who had danced until three and whose heads were splitting from too much wine—were dismayed to learn that the wedding was taking place immediately and that they were expected in the chapel before breakfast, and before their eyes were properly open.

Sofia had to be pulled from bed. "I won't! I won't!" she wailed. She snatched the wedding dress from the maids, making them cry out at her ferocity, and threw it in a heap beside the armoire.

"Pick up the gown," Natalia ordered the maids, and she rushed to Sofia and enfolded her in her arms.

"Never!" Sofia screamed. "I'll never marry Luis!"

Natalia rocked her niece to and fro as if she were a squalling baby. "There, there," she murmured over and over. "There, there, my sweet." She could think of no other words of comfort.

One of the maids swung open the shutters and daylight streamed into the room, burnishing the floor and whitewashed walls with gold. The noisy ringing of the courtyard bell assaulted Sofia's ears, taunting her with its message. She broke from her aunt's embrace and rushed to the window, intending to slam the shutters on the sound that seemed to toll her doom.

She stopped suddenly, her silhouette frozen in the window frame. Her dark, swollen eyes had caught an ominous movement far off, just above the horizon, marking the spot where Luis had shot Joel.

"The wings of death," she murmured, her voice just above a whisper.

Doña Natalia moved beside her. "What is it, my darling? What are you saying?"

Sofia did not reply. She let herself slump in Natalia's arms. Natalia scanned the landscape beyond, but her eyes were too weak to perceive what had finally broken Sofia's resistance. Circling in the bright morning sky, just above the place they had left Joel, dark pinpricks traced patterns against the blue— carrion hunters, the hideous black buzzards that rode the rising currents and fed off the dead.

Beaten at last, Sofia permitted herself to be led about like a sleepwalker. The maids stripped off her night dress and reached into the armoire for the first of many petticoats that Sofia would wear beneath her wedding gown. Finally, they slipped the gown over her head and fastened the row of buttons at her back. Sofia stood still and pale in the middle of the room and let them do their work.

As Doña Natalia watched, a frown creased her fore-

53

head and she wondered what it was that had so suddenly taken the fire from Sofia.

From first light, Joel had watched the buzzards circling above him. His horse had disappeared during the night, but he knew he had to keep moving. He stumbled and crawled over the hard caliche, hating the vulturous birds with their rapacious eyes and tearing beaks, hoping desperately that they would fly away and leave him in peace. The pain burned through his shoulder, and he needed to rest. But they followed him, patiently, knowing that he was wounded and that in a little while, when the sun grew hot and blazed directly overhead, he would move no more.

At last he came to an arroyo. He rolled down its sloping bank into the cool green moss of its bed. Pressing his mouth to the muddy flow, he moistened his swollen tongue; then he took the cool water and bathed his forehead. He stayed there until he had drunk enough to slake his raging thirst.

The sky was white hot, and the buzzards, encouraged by his lack of movement, sailed closer overhead, landing, finally, little more than an arm's length away. Joel screamed at them, scooping up the flat rock and hurling it at them. They batted their great wings and took off, but they rose reluctantly, insolently, with the assurance that he would soon be theirs.

Perversely, this gave him the strength he needed to cheat them of their feast. He took his knife and cut his shirt away from the bullet wound that pierced his shoulder; then, using the shirt as a bandage, he wound it tightly around the arm, binding it to his chest as tightly as he could, hoping that the immobility would lessen the throbbing pain that racked him from his fingertips to the middle of his back.

Slowly he got to his feet, reeling as a wave of dizziness swept over him. When it passed, he staggered out of the arroyo and set off across the sun-bleached land-scape.

He was never sure how long it took him to reach the camp. Perspiration blinded his eyes, and the pain had long since grown so intense that a merciful, numbing shock had overtaken him.

It was nearly sunset when he heard Anne's voice calling him. He blinked away the film of sweat that poured off his forehead and saw his daughter running toward him.

"Papa! Papa!" she cried.

He stumbled, too weakened to take another step, and fell to his knees.

Anne was at his side immediately, horrified by his wounds. "Oh, Papa! What happened?"

He slumped into her arms and wept with both joy and pain.

Slowly she helped him rise and supported him as he hobbled toward the wagon. His lips moved and he rasped the question that tormented his brain. "Martha?"

Anne avoided his eyes. "Water," she said. "I'll get you a drink."

She started to move away, but his hand went around her thin wrist and, exhausting his last bit of strength, he pulled her back. "Your mother? How is she?"

Anne tried to answer, but tears welled up in her eyes and her throat tightened, blocking her voice.

Then Joel noticed that she was clutching something in the fist he held. He turned her hand over and she opened her fingers. There, cupped in her palm, was a garnet lavaliere. It had belonged to Martha's mother, who, on their wedding day, had presented it to Martha. Except for the wedding band Joel had placed on her finger, it was the only piece of jewelry Martha had ever owned.

In the dying sunlight, the stone glowed scarlet like a drop of blood.

Anne's fingers closed back over it.

"Mama gave it to me," she said. Now the tears filled her eyes and fell in silver streaks down her cheeks. "She said it was mine . . . to remember her by."

"When?" Joel asked, his voice flat, his mind numb with shock.

"This morning," Anne replied, "just before dawn."

A great sob racked Joel's body as he sank to his knees and wept. Kneeling beside him, Anne put her arms around him; and they gave each other what comfort their mutual grief could spare.

The grave was shallow, but Anne was not strong enough to dig deeply in the sunbaked soil. They wrapped Martha's body in a blanket and covered it with earth and stones. Then Joel opened the family Bible and read, "Yea, the sparrow hath found a house, and the swallow a nest for herself, where she may lay her young, O Lord of hosts, my King, and my God. Blessed are they that dwell in thy house: they will be still praising thee."

"Amen," Anne said. There was a moment's silence, broken only by the sound of a mockingbird high up in the mesquites. Then Anne raised her voice and sang,

"Yes, we'll gather at the river,
The beautiful, beautiful river.
Gather with the saints at the river
That flows by the throne of God."

They camped there the rest of that day and the next. Anne bathed and bandaged Joel's wound, but the pain grew steadily worse; and the following morning, when she changed the dressing, Joel recognized the foul smell of putrejaction.

"The bullet has to come out," he said. Anne watched as he unsheathed his knife and laid it in the coals. "You'll have to cut it out," he said.

"No, Papa! I can't!"

"You have to. I'm too weak to do it myself."

56

"I can't! I can't!" she cried. She shrank away from him.

"It has to be done," Joel shouted, almost in anger, but he saw the horror in Anne's eyes and his voice dropped softly. "I'm sorry, kitten. I wouldn't ask you if there was anyone else. But if the bullet doesn't come out I'll lose the arm."

And probably die, he thought. He could see by Anne's expression that she was thinking the same thing.

"Be brave," he said. "I'll tell you what to do."

He had her fetch a bottle of whiskey from the wagon.

"Half full," he said, holding it up to the light and examining its contents. "I hope it's enough."

He pulled the cork with his teeth and took a swig.

"I'm going to get roaring drunk now," he said. "I'll leave a little bit in the bottom for you to pour over the wound when you've got the bullet out. And, for God's sake, whatever I say, no matter how much I beg, don't stop until you've got the bullet out. Do you understand?"

"Yes, Papa." Anne's eye was on the knife which was beginning to glow red hot.

Joel took another long pull at the bottle. The whiskey burned his gullet and relaxed the knotted muscles in his back and arms. He raised the bottle again and again. And as he drank he explained to Anne what she had to do.

When he was so drunk that the earth spun beneath him, he lay down on the hard ground and mumbled for Anne to begin.

Gripping the knife, now sterilized with fire, she held it in the wind until it cooled. She knelt beside Joel's shoulder and touched the point to the swollen flesh.

"I can't!" she cried.

"Do it!" Joel slurred. "Do it, or I'll die!"

Anne gritted her teeth and cut into the putrid flesh. A moan escaped from Joel's lips and beads of perspiration formed instantly on his forehead.

57

"Do it!" he gasped.

When it was over, Anne hurled the knife away as far as she could. Then she dropped to her knees and was sick.

Later, while Joel slept off the effects of the whiskey, Anne picked up the bottle and put it to her lips. She had cleaned his wound with it and there was little left, not more than a swallow, but she drank it at a gulp, blinking back the tears it brought to her eyes. She wished it would make her drunk; she wished it would knock her out. But it did nothing. It might as well have been water.

She stared out at the sun, which was slipping low in the sky. Something had happened to her, she realized, but she didn't know what. She felt stronger in some way. Soon it would be dark, but she felt no fear at keeping watch alone over her sleeping father. And she believed that if something were to go wrong, if he were to die, she could take care of herself. All the mysteries had been removed. She could bury him, she knew; she had buried her mother. And she could hitch up the team and drive them. And she would! If she had to, she would!

She thought about this for a moment. She could cook for herself if she had to, and she could make a shelter for the night. And she could shoot if necessary. She'd never fired her father's pistol, but she knew how it worked. She could load it and cock it and shoot it if she had to. She knew she could!

Walking around the back of the wagon, Anne hitched herself up onto the tailgate. She picked up the little rag doll that lay nearby and began smoothing out its tangled yarn hair and pressing flat the folds in its gingham dress. She cradled it in the crook of her arm, rocking it back and forth as if it were a baby that needed comforting.

The western sky was swiftly growing crimson. The

land around her was flat and hard and hostile. But she felt she could tame it.

She knew she could!

She knew she could do all these things. And more, perhaps, things she couldn't yet imagine.

But, as the sun dropped below the horizon and the first faint stars winked from the purple sky above, she felt the warm tracks of tears upon her cheeks, and she wished that she didn't feel so strong. She wished she didn't know all the things she was able to do.

4

Two hundred miles north, on a farm near the German settlement of New Braunfels, Rudy Stark waited for his father to pass judgment on him. An ornately carved grandfather clock, the treasure of the family, brought with them on the long voyage from the old country, ticked loudly, counting off the minutes while the old man gripped his stein of beer and pondered his decision.

From his seat at the end of the table, Rudy let his eyes make a swift circuit of the room. His sister Hannah sat stiffly with her husband on a hard bench against the wall. Both wore identical expressions, their faces drawn tight with self-righteousness, as certain of the accusations they had brought against Rudy as they were of their own virtue. Hannah defiantly met Rudy's gaze, and her lip curled with contempt. Her denunciation of him still echoed in the room.

Their brother Peter, still a boy, stood beside the ponderous oak cupboard, arms folded, eyes downcast so he would not have to acknowledge Rudy's stare. He did not know if Rudy had actually taken the money, and he did not care. He only wanted the family council to be over so that he could slip out of the house and steal an hour with his sweetheart already waiting behind her father's barn.

Rudy's mother, Frieda, sat at the head of the table beside her husband. Her face was drawn and white, and she pressed a rumpled handkerchief to her lips to muffle the shallow sobs that rose within her whenever she considered the possibility that her firstborn might be a thief.

It can't be true! she prayed as she looked down the length of the dining table at Rudy, who was sitting quite still, his clasped hands resting on the polished wooden surface. His composure cheered her slightly and convinced her, despite Hannah's allegations, that he was innocent. She closed her eyes and recalled the baby she'd held in her arms during the storm-tossed crossing from Bremerhaven to Galveston nearly twenty-one years before. She would have leaped up now, would have rushed to his side to cradle him once more, but the presence of her husband, Joachim, held her, as it always did, in her place.

Sitting beside Rudy was Emma, his wife of less than a year. Lank brown hair framed her moonlike face. Of all her ordinary features, only her eyes were remarkable —Rudy had discovered them to be the barometer of her spirit, the indicator of her moods, smoldering coals when she expressed her love, flat and black when she was hurt or troubled, and glittering, polished black agates when, as now, she was consumed with anger.

Emma had never grown close to the cold, stern family she'd married into; and regardless of the verdict, she'd already decided to persuade Rudy to take her away. She dreaded the thought of spending another night in this house of spare, joyless meals and cheerless fires, where music was never heard, not even on Christmas Day. The child in her belly was nearly at term, and she couldn't bear the idea of raising it under this roof.

She reached out and covered Rudy's hands with

hers. The touch of his skin sent a thrill through her, and she still couldn't believe her luck in catching him. She'd always known him. They'd gone to school together, and even when she was too young to really know why, she had always chosen a desk behind and to the side of his so she could look up from her slate and steal a glimpse of him. And then one day, when she was barely eighteen, she had looked out of her mother's kitchen window and spotted him in the nearby field, naked to the waist, his skin tanned dark as saddle leather, his fair hair sun-bleached so white it looked as if he wore a cap of silver; and she decided then, even though she was far from being the prettiest or the richest girl in the community, that she would marry him. It had been astonishingly easy. Once she had bolstered her courage enough to talk with him without growing tongue-tied, she found it but a simple further step to flirt. And Rudy was intrigued. Not that he was unused to flirts. All the other girls teased and led him on. He was far too handsome to be left in peace. But gradually he realized that the other girls flirted with all the boys, while Emma had eyes only for him. He was flattered and took her seriously. And one Sunday, after church, he walked with her down by the banks of the Comal and proposed.

Emma sensed him looking at her now, and she gazed up into his eyes, which were as blue and stormy as the clouds of a January norther. Smiling in brave support, she squeezed his hands.

Joachim Stark pushed his stein aside and cleared his throat. He addressed his son in German, for he forbade the use of English in his house.

"The amount that was stolen does not matter. A thief is as guilty whether he takes a pfennig or a crown."

He glared down the long table at Rudy and went on. "You claim that Hannah lies and that she has no proof. But the money is gone, and somehow your gambling debts have been paid. I say that Hannah tells the truth

62

and that it is you who are not only a thief but a liar. And I say that no son of mine can be those things. Henceforth, I have only two children. . . ."

Frieda Stark cried out, "No, Joachim, no!"

Joachim ignored her anguish. "I have only two heirs, my daughter Hannah and my son Peter. Rudy no longer lives in this house, and his name will not be spoken under my roof."

"Joachim!" Frieda begged. "You can't turn them out. Think of Emma! The baby!"

Joachim held up his hand. "Emma has committed no crime. She may remain with us as long as she wishes. She may have the baby here, and we will take it into our hearts."

Emma, who was watching Rudy, saw his face go pale beneath his tan, felt his hands form fists beneath hers. She rose and addressed the family.

"Rudy is innocent. Hannah made up the story because she wants the farm for her children and no others. Be wary, Peter, for your turn will come!"

"Nicht wahr!" Hannah cried, springing to her feet, confronting Emma across the table.

"Enough!" Joachim roared. "The business is settled. We'll hear no more about it. Rudy will go. Emma is free to stay or go as she pleases."

Emma's voice shook with rage and indignation. "I shall go with my husband, as God intended."

"Liebchen!" Frieda pleaded, extending her open arms to Emma. "The baby. It's due. Stay with me at least until after the birth!"

"I would rather have my child in the dirt by the side of the road."

"So be it," Joachim proclaimed. "It is finished." He rose and turned his face to the wall. "I shall wait one minute. When I turn around again, I do not want to see either of you."

The ticking of the grandfather clock marked the fleeting seconds.

"Rudy!" Frieda cried. *"Mein Sohn!"* She reached out for him, aching to embrace him, but fear of her husband kept her fast by his side.

Rudy's eyes met hers sadly, and he whispered, *"Auf wiedersehen, Mutter."*

Joachim counted the seconds. When the minute had expired, he turned slowly around. The chairs at the foot of the table were empty.

Rudy and Emma crossed the farmyard and bedded down in the barn. The animals stirred briefly, scarcely disturbed, then returned to their slumber. Sometime after midnight, Rudy shook Emma awake and declared they were leaving.

"But where?" Emma asked.

"I don't know," Rudy said.

"My father will take us in," she suggested.

Rudy shook his head. "No. I want to get far away from this place."

"But how?" she asked. "I'm in no condition to ride."

"We're taking the wagon. I've worked all my life on this farm. I'm entitled to something."

She watched as he spread saddle blankets to make a pallet for her on the wagon bed. Working quickly, he hitched the plow horse to the wagon and helped her up. Quietly, he swung back the barn door. Outside, a strong south wind rustled the leaves in the trees, and the inky sky was sprinkled with stars. Rudy glanced toward the house, where all was dark and still. He wished he could see his mother once more. Aside from that, he felt no loss.

Peter, returning stealthily from his rendezvous, watched them from the night-cloaked field. He saw Rudy lead the horse slowly from the barn. The wagon creaked, but no more loudly than the rafters of the barn did, strained by the rising wind. They rolled down the path to the gate. Peter shrugged. He did not care.

His head was too full of the neighbor girl's caresses for him to think of alerting the family.

In another minute the wagon reached the road, and Rudy flicked his whip against the horse, sending the wagon lurching forward. Before long, the farmhouse had receded into darkness.

After a while, when they broke into open country, Emma rose from her pallet to sit beside Rudy.

"Do you think they'll come after us when they see we've taken the wagon?"

"We'll be too far away by the time they find out."

"Good!" Emma said, and she locked her arm lovingly in his. "Tell me, Rudy. Did you take the money?"

"It was only a double eagle," Rudy said, "twenty dollars. The old man is rich. I never thought he'd miss it."

"So you did take it, after all?"

"Yes," he said.

"I'm glad," Emma said. Her voice was hard and bitter. "I only wish you'd taken more!"

5

Even before Joel mentioned it, Anne realized she would have to return to San Antonio.

"This is no place for a girl alone," he said.

There was still an hour of sunlight left, and they sat outside a dilapidated shack they'd discovered on their new land. It appeared to be an overnight station, little more than a lean-to which in the past had provided temporary refuge for the occasional band of vaqueros caught out on the range during roundups. A simple rectangle, the shack was made of mesquite branches basket-woven between posts and mortared together with dried mud. On top was a roof of rotting thatch, so low that Joel was unable to stand upright inside.

Where the wood to build it had come from Joel couldn't imagine, for as far as he could see stretched flat, treeless plains, a prairie of waist-high grass that rolled in waves before the afternoon breezes. In the distance, their dun-colored backs rising like shifting boulders out of the grass, grazed a herd of wild cattle.

"Where will I live?" Anne asked, not really caring.

"The sisters at the convent will take you in," Joel said. "They'll treat you well and teach you all the things you would have learned from your mother if she had lived."

"And how long will I have to stay?"

"Until you're grown."

"Don't you think I'm nearly grown now?" she asked, hoping he would change his mind.

Joel looked at his daughter and managed a smile. "Not quite . . . but soon," he said.

Anne rose and approached the campfire. Taking jerky, as she'd seen her mother do, she pounded it into flakes and browned it in a Dutch oven over the coals. Then she added flour and water and stirred. In a while, the mixture would boil down into a meat gravy they could pour over hardtack.

"I don't want to go," she said, laying down the spoon.

"I know. But it won't be long before you're back."

Anne said nothing, but she didn't believe him. She feared that once she left she would be gone for good.

They ate their evening meal in silence, without appetite, thinking the same thoughts but unwilling to share them.

Later, before falling asleep, Anne asked, "When do I have to go?"

"I ought to be healed up pretty good in a week. We'll set out then."

Anne sighed miserably and closed her eyes.

Joel watched over her for a long time, wishing he could keep her with him. He realized that her departure would deprive him of all that remained of Martha. He reached out and gently stroked her golden hair. She stirred in her slumber, turning her face toward his. On her cheeks he saw the dried trail of tears, and he understood that she'd cried herself to sleep, silently, so he wouldn't know.

"Oh, Annie," he whispered. "I'm sorry. But there's really no other way."

The little mesquites were not hard to find in the flat and almost treeless countryside. Neither Joel nor Anne

67

broke their apprehensive silence, but as they approached, both recognized the spot immediately. Joel reined the little mules and brought the wagon to a halt. They descended and walked to Martha's grave beneath the trees. Joel was relieved to see that nothing had disturbed it. They stood beside the mound of rock and dirt where even now green shoots of wild grass were beginning to sprout.

"We ought to mark it," Joel said at last.

"I'll never forget the place," Anne replied. "It will be easy to find. Right here by the tree that lightning struck."

The thin tree had been sheared in two by the bolt. Half lay on the ground, its branches twisted, already dead. The other half still stood, its heart exposed and blackened by fire, its leaves beginning to wither.

Anne left her father beside the grave and wandered out into the field. When she returned, she had in her hand the knife she had hurled into the darkness ten days before.

"It's all rusty," she said, handing it to him.

He turned it over and over, running his fingers along the blade. "It'll come clean," he said.

He gripped the knife and began carving on a piece of wood he had taken from the wagon. When he finished, he stood it in the ground. It read:

MARTHA TREVOR
WIFE & MOTHER
1826 — 1860

"I feel better now," he said, "now that it's marked. It just wouldn't be fitting to let her sleep in an unknown grave."

Pulling the ribbon from her hair, Anne bound together a bouquet of rust and gold lantana she found blooming on a bush nearby. She lay the bouquet on the mound of earth, and then climbed up beside her father on the wagon.

They had covered little more than a dozen miles

when Joel suddenly reined up and said, "Look yonder, Anne. Your eyes are keener than mine. What do you see?"

Following his gaze, Anne squinted in the harsh sunlight. "It's a horse and wagon," she said, "and a man standing close by." She stared harder. "And I see someone else lying on the ground."

Then from the distance came a woman's long, anguished cry of pain. It trailed off briefly then rose again more urgently than before.

Anne's face went white. "He must be killing her!"

Joel wasn't so sure, but he took no chances. "Hide in the wagon," he ordered. "Don't come out until I tell you."

As Anne clambered through the canvas flaps into the wagon's sultry interior, Joel pulled out his Colt and laid it by his side on the buckboard seat just in case. Then he snapped the reins and drove the mules forward.

Kneeling in the back, her heartbeat drumming in her ears, Anne held the canvas flaps together, leaving only a tiny slit between them through which she peered at the figures in the distance. She perceived, as soon as Joel did, that the wagon was an old rattletrap hitched to a weary nag and that the man standing over the prostrate woman was a farmer, a big man dressed in gray homespun with a wide-brimmed, flat-crowned straw hat. The woman lay in the full sun on a horse blanket in the dust. Her cries went unheard, drowned out by the Trevors' noisy approach—the mules' thudding hooves and the wagon's complaining axles—but both Joel and Anne could see that she was writhing in agony, her body rolling from side to side on the blanket.

Then the man who was standing over her became aware of the wagon and he waved frantically, shouting out for Joel to stop, as if he feared Joel and his team would race on by.

Joel pulled up, still a careful distance away, and called out: "What's the matter?"

The man's big hands reached out, an imploring gesture that assured Joel he had nothing to fear from him. "Thank God!" the man shouted. "I need your help. My wife is having a baby!"

The baby came hard, and before it was over, the woman cried out that she would rather die than to endure such pain. Indeed she hadn't thought it was possible to suffer so and still remain alive. Her husband was terrified and he grew paler each time she cried out. Joel soon realized the big man was on the verge of fainting and would be of no help.

So Joel turned to Anne and told her what to do to assist him. Just before dark, as the sun's last rays turned the clouds above to red, the baby's first outraged wail carried forth over the prairie. Anne watched, trembling with excitement, blinking back tears of awe, as Joel cut the cord, washed the blood from the wizened little creature, and handed him, swaddled in a cotton blanket, into the weak but welcoming arms of his mother.

Joel and Anne were forgotten for a time while the man and his wife marveled over their new child. Then a wave of fatigue washed over the woman and she closed her eyes. The man turned to Joel and extended his hand. He was feeling fine now. The color had returned to his face, and his grip was strong. *"Danke schön!* You were a good Samaritan. I don't think I could have . . ."

Joel fended off the compliment. "You would have done just fine. I'm only glad I was able to help. By the way, my name is Joel Trevor. And this is my daughter Anne."

"I am Rudy Stark," the man said. "My wife Emma."

"And the baby?" Anne asked. She had not left Emma's side, and her finger was clasped tightly in the baby's tiny fist.

Rudy looked at Emma, who held the baby close to

70

her breast. Her half-closed eyes glittered serenely in the flickering campfire light. She gazed up sleepily into Anne's face and smiled. "You were so brave and helped so much, my little Anne," she said. "I think you should be his godmother, and so you name him."

Anne gasped. "Oh, no, I couldn't!"

"Please!"

"Papa!" Anne cried, unable to conceal the delight in her voice. "Should I?"

"Of course," Joel said.

Anne glanced to Rudy for confirmation. The farmer nodded in return, asking, "What shall it be, little godmother? What shall we call our son?"

Anne's mind raced. The responsibility was almost too much. Then suddenly her thoughts lit on her favorite book.

"I think," she said, taking her time, finding the decision awesome, almost afraid to put her thoughts into words. "I think . . . his name should be David Copperfield."

"Copperfield?" Rudy said, doubtful.

"It's a beautiful name," Emma murmured.

"He's a beautiful baby," Anne said. "And we can call him Davey for short."

"Davey," Emma whispered, succumbing at last to sleep. Her eyes closed and she hugged her baby nearer.

Joel and Rudy sat up late into the night. Coffee simmered in a pot on the campfire's coals, but the men passed a bottle of Rudy's mother's peach brandy back and forth in celebration of Davey's birth. Emma and the newborn slept soundly. Anne, too, lay sleeping beside them as if it were up to her to protect them.

"You're a German, by your accent," Joel said.

"Ja," Rudy replied, again taking the bottle Joel passed him. "We come from New Braunfels. We were farmers there."

"What brings you down here?"

Rudy took a long swig of the brandy and relished

71

the fiery liquid that seared his throat. The brief, almost imperceptible pause before he answered alerted Joel that he would not be getting the whole truth.

"There was a family disagreement," Rudy said. "Emma and me figured it was best to strike out on our own."

A hell of a disagreement, Joel thought to himself, for them to leave their home just when Emma's baby was due. But he said nothing, reaching out instead to accept the quickly emptying bottle.

"Got any plans?" he said at last.

"Find work somewhere," Rudy answered.

"No farming in these parts," Joel said. "Dirt looks good enough, but I'm told there are some god-awful dry spells."

Rudy nodded, a look of stubbornness settling over his features. "I'll find something. I learn quick and I am strong. I can handle the jobs of two men."

Joel studied him. He looked burly enough to wrestle an ox and win. His forearms were nearly as thick as his biceps, and the horny callouses on his big hands supported his boast.

A sudden thought crossed Joel's mind. His eyes traveled across the campfire and considered Emma, sleeping peacefully with her baby in her arms. Nearby lay Anne, the rise and fall of her regular breathing clearly audible in the silence that stretched between the two men. Then Joel thought again of Martha and of the traveling they'd done and of the babies they'd buried in graves so far away that they would never be visited again. He lingered with his memories a long time, grateful to Rudy for not intruding.

Above them, the stars wheeled in their paths across the nighttime sky. An owl hooted far out in the darkness and a wild cow lowed in response.

Finally Joel spoke. "What do you know about ranching?"

"Nothing," Rudy answered.

Joel appreciated the directness of the reply. "You know cows, don't you?"

"Farm cows ain't nothing like Nueces cattle."

Joel nodded. "These wild critters aren't good for a hell of a lot, but a man can get good money for their hides. And then there's tallow. And from time to time you can even get a price on their beef if you can drive them over to St. Mary's on the hoof. You know about St. Mary's, don't you?"

"I heard the name," Rudy said.

"It's a port town," Joel explained. "Booming, I hear. Lots of skippers from everywhere, buying produce and shipping it by boat up east. I'm reckoning on supplying them with hides . . . and I figure I could use some help."

"Are you offering me a job?" Rudy asked.

"Maybe," Joel answered, "but listen to the rest. . . ." Then he told Rudy about Martha and of the decision he'd made to put Anne in convent school in San Antonio because there was no one to take care of her on the ranch.

". . . Seeing the three of them together over there," he continued, "has given me an idea. I was thinking that maybe Emma could take charge of Anne; help raise her. She could teach her all the womanly things, and in return Anne could help out with the baby . . . and the others of your brood that I imagine will be coming along."

Rudy tilted the bottle again and wiped his lips of the sweet, burning liquor. "And me?" he asked. "What would there be for me?"

Joel raised the bottle but answered before drinking: "I'm going to need someone I can trust. I can hire up any number of peons, but I want a smart man for my foreman."

Rudy started to reply, but Joel held up his hand and went on. "I can't pay a penny right now. Everything I own is tied up in the land. But by fall I could make your salary good . . . back pay starting now. Let's say twenty a month. In the meantime, you'd have plenty to eat and a place for your wife and babe. The shack we're holed up in isn't fit for man or beast, but the two of us could build a good house. . . ."

He paused now and took his pull at the bottle.

The German waited a while before answering. He took a stick and poked the coals beneath the coffeepot, waving away the red-fringed ashes that rose in the blue curl of smoke. He had already made up his mind, but he knew it was better to make Joel wait for his answer.

He poured a cup of coffee, offered it to Joel, and when it was declined, brought it to his own lips. He felt Joel's eyes on him and knew he could prolong the moment no longer.

"It's not a bad offer," he said at last. "But I'm thinking it would be more interesting if you paid twenty-five. My family is growing."

Joel nodded. "Call it twenty-five."

Encouraged, Rudy pressed again. "And you say we will build a house together; yet the house is yours."

Joel saw what Rudy was up to. He leveled his gaze at him and said, "Don't forget, it's my land."

Rudy understood. He had wanted more, but he was pleased with what he had achieved, and in no position to bargain, he'd managed a five dollar increase. He'd work hard and bide his time, at least through the winter, but then . . .

He smiled suddenly and reached across to shake Joel's hand. "It's a deal. Twenty-five a month and a shelter."

Later, as Rudy lay beside Emma and the baby, he thought to himself: All my life I been a farm hand for my father. And I come away from that with nothing but a wagon and a plow horse. Yes, my friend, twenty-five a month and a place to live is good enough for now. But I'm going to do a lot better this time. When I get to know your ways, I'll find the means to get more. I won't be breaking my back to make you rich only to end up drifting again with nothing to call my own but a wagon, a nag, and the shirt on my back. No, by God! When I leave your spread, I'll have me some gold jingling in my pockets. I swear it! One way or the other! No matter what I have to do!

6

The days shortened as the year waned into late autumn. By October, Joel and Rudy had completed two trips to St. Mary's, each time taking with them a wagonload of hides and returning with provisions and cash. Working late into the longer nights, they built a three-room house, dressing soft white caliche stone into blocks one foot thick and two feet long, which they then piled one atop another until the walls were high enough to roof with thatch. They finished just before the first norther blew in wet and cold across the prairie. Then they ripped down the old shack, tearing into it with a vengeful fury that vented the loathing they'd all grown to feel for the squalid hovel. They stored some of the wood for winter fuel, and with the rest they built a rough corral.

On the gatepost, Joel nailed a plank of wood into which he had carved, THE TREVOR RANCH.

Emma and Anne cooked and sewed and tended an autumn garden that had been planted with seed the men had brought back from the coast. The men brought fabric, too, and foodstuffs. And books that Emma and Anne took turns reading aloud to them at night by the warm yellow glow of the oil lamp. They read Poe and Hawthorne, Melville and Thackeray, Byron and Longfellow. And when Joel settled Rudy's back pay, giving him seventy-five dollars in gold, Rudy bought his wife a copy of *David Copperfield*.

Emma had squealed with delight. "Look here!" she cried when she lifted the book from its brown wrapping. "Davey's own book! His very own!"

Taking a pen, Emma dipped it in ink and wrote on the flyleaf in her finest hand:

Für mein Sohn, David
Copperfield Stark, von
deiner Mutter, Emma.

—*30 Oktober 1860.*

The baby was growing fat and healthy. Anne abandoned her rag doll for Davey, playing with him, cuddling him, brushing down the unruly golden fuzz that covered his scalp, and soothing him to sleep with German lullabies she had learned from Emma.

By the middle of November, the cold weather up north was driving more and more wild cattle south onto Joel's ranch. He and Rudy worked from first light to sundown preparing a shipment of hides for another trip to St. Mary's.

"Will you be gone long this time?" Emma asked. She hated being left alone in this wild land while the men did their trading on the coast. The nights were the worst, when darkness intensified every nocturnal sound from far off in the brush and her imagination played havoc with her nerves. At times like those she made Anne sleep with her in her bed with the baby between them, and she woke with a start at every unfamiliar noise, sleeping soundly only in the brief interval from the time the sky began to brighten in the east to Davey's first cry for milk.

"Please don't stay long," she begged Rudy. "I'm so afraid when you're not here."

"Joel says ten days," Rudy answered.

"So long?"

77

"We have a lot to do. We have to stock up for the winter," Rudy explained. Emma's chin was quivering, and he could see that she was about to cry. He averted his eyes and shifted the last bundle of hides from his broad shoulders to the wagon. To distract her, he pulled a folded sheet of paper from his coat pocket and handed it to her. "Look over this again. See if you've written down all you need."

Emma barely glanced at the paper, too upset to care. "Yes, yes," she said, pushing it back toward him. "Everything is there."

As Joel came toward them, leading the team of mules, Rudy called out almost eagerly, "It's all ready!" He gave a final yank to the ropes that secured the hides to the wagon.

"Then let's hitch up and be off," Joel said. He measured his shadow in the ground. "It's still early. I'll wager we make it to Palo Pinto before sundown."

" 'Bye, Papa," Anne said, running from the house to kiss Joel farewell.

"What shall I bring you, Annie?"

"A surprise."

"I have the very thing in mind," Joel said, hugging her again and kissing her on the forehead.

"Hurry back," Emma said, her voice cracking. "Please hurry! I'll keep a light in the window!" She threw her arms around Rudy and held him close.

Joel was already on the wagon. Rudy kissed Emma quickly, ashamed that she should cling to him in front of Joel, and broke roughly from her embrace.

Sudden hot tears stung Emma's eyes. Feeling the abruptness of his movement away from her, her mood changed to anger. She spun on her heel and stormed back to the house, letting him see only her back as the wagon began to move away.

Inside, Davey was crying. She lifted him from his crib, unbuttoned her bodice, and offered a breast to his hungry lips, already counting the minutes until Rudy's return.

Joel liked St. Mary's.

"Think about it," he told Rudy as they rolled down Centre Street, the main thoroughfare, which was paved with crushed oyster shell dredged up from the bay. "Barely three years old and it's already one of the busiest ports on the whole Gulf Coast."

It was exciting to look out over the masts of the schooners rocking at anchor in the dark green waters of Copano Bay, knowing that beyond the islands that separated them from the Gulf of Mexico lay New Orleans, Mobile, and Pensacola, and that around the tip of Florida flowed the watery highway to the big eastern ports. Herds of Texas steers milled and lowed in pens on the bluff waiting to be shipped out. Below, at the foot of the street, traders, merchants, and seamen crowded the elaborate wharf and bustled around the large warehouses that flanked its landward ends. Joel noticed that in the month and a half since his last visit to St. Mary's, another wharf was going up to the southwest, on the edge of town.

"Damned if it isn't growing before our very eyes!" he exclaimed.

They rode down Centre Street, past the lumberyards and stables, past Dr. Simpson's apothecary shop and the two-story wooden hotel known as the Jasper House, where they would put up while they were in town.

"Come on," Joel said, flicking his whip over the mules. "Let's get these hides sold so we can drop in at the saloon and wash down some of this dust we've been eating for the past four days."

A few hours later, bathed and shaved and with the good feel of cash in their pockets, Joel and Rudy sauntered out of the hotel and crossed the oyster-shell street, lured by the jaunty sound of piano music that spilled

79

from the establishment known as the Barrelhouse, a combination grocery and saloon.

Inside the double doors, past the front counters and shelves stocked with flour, sugar, meal, and spices, men stood elbow to elbow at the long, ornately carved mahogany bar brought by sea from Honduras the year before. Poker and dominoes were being played at tables in the middle of the room; and against the other wall, in cramped, high-backed booths, sailors and cowmen traded tales and lies over whiskey and rum.

Joel and Rudy found a place at the bar.

"Name it, boys," encouraged the barkeep, a red-faced beefy man with a walrus mustache.

"Whiskey," Joel said, and Rudy asked for a beer.

Feet perched on the brass rail, elbows resting on the polished mahogany, they drank for a while in silence. Rudy finished his draught quickly and ordered another.

"Hey, Joel. There's a lady over there giving you the eye," he said.

"I know she is," Joel replied. He'd been aware of her from the moment they entered.

The woman, just reaching her prime, was proud of her looks and sure of herself. Her dress was green velvet, trimmed in gold, cut low in the bodice to accentuate her powdered bosom. She wore her hair in tight dark ringlets around her oval face, and her cheeks and lips were redder than any Joel had ever seen.

Catching his glance, she flashed a smile that disarmed Joel with its openness, as if they were two good friends who ran across each other every day.

She was sharing a table by the piano with Homer Post, proprietor of the Barrelhouse, and she twirled a crystal champagne glass in her gloved fingers.

Joel let his eyes drop back to his drink, suddenly shy and embarrassed.

Rudy laughed at his side. "You gonna disappoint a pretty lady like that?"

"You take up with her if you're so interested," Joel said.

"I'd say she fancies you, Joel. It wouldn't surprise me if she comes over here."

Rudy's laughter annoyed Joel. "Quit looking at her. You know I'm a widower only four months gone."

"Ain't nothing says a widow man can't be nice to a pretty lady. In fact, if I was in your boots, I'd be joining her quick."

Joel didn't reply, but an urgent hunger gripped him, as it had not since Martha's death. It's not decent, he told himself; and he wished that he still wore the black armband he'd discarded after only a month—when he decided its constant reminder was bad for Anne.

"Just like I thought," Rudy said, "she's coming here."

Joel swore under his breath. "I expect you're leading her on."

"Never! It's you she likes. She never even looked my way."

In another instant the woman was at Joel's side. She smelled of perfume, a scent of woodland flowers that reminded Joel of his youth in Tennessee.

Placing her empty glass on the bar in front of her, she said, "I've seen you here before. Been a month or two, as I recall."

Her voice was husky and softly accented—Cajun, Joel surmised.

"I've been enjoying champagne," she said. "But I'm not averse to whiskey."

"Barkeep!" Joel called, still not meeting her eyes. "The lady wants champagne."

"Thank you, *chéri*," she said.

He looked up at last and caught her smile, her even white teeth and her unsettlingly red lips.

The hunger within him grew, and he became oblivious to Rudy's presence. To the barkeep he said, "Just leave the bottle here and bring me a glass, too. I never had champagne, but I might as well try it."

The woman shifted her position at the bar so that he could see the fullness of her breasts and the perfumed cleavage between them. She'd figured it would be simple; he'd looked an easy mark. But now, for reasons she couldn't fathom, a haunting cloud moved over his eyes and he seemed to withdraw.

Joel almost told her to go away. He almost said that he'd rather be left alone. But she turned again, to pick up her glass, and, against his will, his eyes caressed the smooth creaminess of her neck and the soft lines of her back. He longed to stroke the soft down on the nape of her neck, to run his fingers through the dark ringlets that reached her bare shoulders.

"To your health," she said. Again that smile! She clinked her glass against his.

The delicately stemmed goblet felt strange in his hand, and the taste of champagne surprised him. It was sweet and fruity, and he wondered how such a drink could make you drunk.

"My name is Lenore," she said. "What may I call you?"

As she gazed up at him, he noticed the blue of her eyes was flecked with gold and green like her dress. Her perfume flooded his nostrils and her bare arm brushed the back of his hand.

He felt his pulse begin drumming in his temples. "My name is Joel."

"I like that. It's from the Bible."

Joel wanted to reply, but his voice caught in his throat.

"Why don't we sit down?" she said. "Old Homer has left his table free."

Joel followed her across the room to a place beside the piano.

"Jorge," she said to the Mexican at the piano. "How about a sweet tune? *Una canción dulce, por favor.*"

The piano player nodded, struck a few chords, and began a ballad.

82

They had another glass of champagne, and Joel asked if she were from New Orleans.

Lenore nodded.

"What brought you to St. Mary's?"

She shrugged. "I wanted to see the world. I wanted to travel. This is as far as I got. You might say that my ship sailed without me."

She smiled again with an air of insouciance that beguiled Joel.

"Oh lá lá!" she said suddenly. "Look at this! We are out of champagne so soon."

"I'll order more," he said, but she restrained him with a hand on his arm.

"I have a bottle in my room upstairs. Very cold, quite delicious; much better than Homer serves down here. Why don't we share it there?"

The strength of the wine had taken him by surprise. He felt its warmth permeating his limbs, relaxing his muscles, and sending a flush to his face as it tightened the skin around his temples.

She raised an eyebrow, inquiring.

He was ready. "Let's go!"

They rose, but she held back momentarily. "There is one little thing, *monsieur*. I hope you understand . . ."

"Don't worry about it," Joel said. "I've got money."

Lenore smiled happily. "Come with me. It's just up the stairs."

Rudy watched them disappear through a door in the back of the saloon. Muttering a curse in German, he drained his mug. "Barkeep!" he called. "You got brandy?"

"Rum and whiskey."

"Rum," he said. He shoved a coin across the bar and took three shots quickly, one after the other. Then he stumbled out of the Barrelhouse onto the street. It was dark already, and a cold wind whistled out of the north. He headed into it, toward the edge of town where he remembered seeing a Mexican cantina. What was good enough for the bossman was good enough for him, he figured. For a moment around the wharf, he lost his way, but guitar music in the distance led him forward.

Soon the yellow light in the cantina's windows came into view, and Rudy staggered up to the door.

"Señor?" a voice inquired. Rudy turned, peering into the shadows. A girl, barely fifteen, wrapped in a rebozo against the chill, stood beside the wooden building.

"You want a woman?" she asked.

Rudy nodded. "Let's go inside," he said.

"No!" she said. "They no like me in there. We go to my house."

Realizing that the man was drunk and that she would have to lead him, the girl came over to Rudy and wrapped her arm around his waist. They walked along the shore until they came to a cabin of oak logs and thatch.

"You wait," the girl said, halting beside the door.

"It's cold," Rudy complained.

"Momento," the girl said, holding up a finger. *"Un momento."* Then, leaving him on the step, she disappeared inside.

Rudy leaned against the rough wall of the shack and waited. He heard a commotion within and soon the door reopened. A man and woman, carrying three small children wrapped in blankets, slipped outside. They averted their faces, giving him not a glance. Then the girl reappeared at the door.

"Now," she said. "You come in."

"Who are they?" Rudy asked, looking after the figures retreating into the darkness of the windswept oaks.

"You come in now," the girl repeated. She dropped the rebozo and brought his hand to her small, warm breast.

Rudy stared behind him. The man and woman settled

84

the children beneath the trees and curled up beside them.

"Your family?" he asked, horrified.

"They wait out there for us," the girl said. She pressed closer to him, her hand working quickly at his belt. "Come in," she whispered. "Close the door."

"No!" Rudy said. "This is no good!"

He tried to break away, but her hand slipped down into his trousers and she held him near.

"Close the door," she whispered.

Rudy swayed and stumbled toward her. Reaching around him, she pushed the door shut. Then she led him to the pallet on the far side of the narrow room.

Rudy was aware of a cold stiff wind and of the gritty wet sand between his shirt and skin. He tried to rise, but the pain in his head sent him reeling. When next he woke, a thin ribbon of sunlight bound the sky to the watery horizon in the east. He did not need to reach in his pocket. He knew his money was gone.

He staggered to the water's edge and let the cold salt spray rinse his face. He was disoriented. He did not know which way to head for town. So he climbed the bluff behind him and looked about until he spotted plumes of smoke rising from chimneys to the south.

As he walked, his anger at being robbed grew, and slamming his fist into his palm, he swore into the wind. At last he caught sight of the cantina, closed and shuttered now. Dropping down off the bluff, he began to make his way back upshore toward the shack where the girl had led him.

Finally he reached a finger of land curling around a shallow cove. There ahead, curtained and locked against the norther's gusting wind, was the shack.

Roaring like a frenzied bull, Rudy charged across the shell-strewn beach. He attacked the house with his bare hands, smashing the window panes, and kicking at the door's rusty hinges. From within came shrieks and cries.

"Come out, you greasers!" be bellowed. "I'll kill you one by one!"

He battered his shoulder into the door again and again until the planks began to splinter, and the frame that held it separated from the wall.

"My gold!" he screamed. "I'll have it back!"

He threw himself once more against the door, feeling it give beneath his weight. He rolled across the floor, springing up into a defensive crouch, ready to protect himself. The girl's parents cringed against the wall, shielding the three wailing children. The girl, dressed only in a long woolen nightdress, knelt on her pallet, her hand within the folds of her gown.

"Get out!" she cried.

"I want my money!"

"What money you talk about?" Her eyes flashed brightly and her long black hair fell in tangles around her neck.

Rudy's hands formed fists. "The money you stole, you bitch! I'll have it back now."

The girl watched him warily. She could see his pulse throbbing plainly in the raised veins in his neck. His fingers flexed, open and closed, and she knew that in another instant he would attack.

"Papa," she said, "give him the money."

"You're thinking smart now," Rudy said.

The man left the small children with his wife and moved carefully to the other side of the room where he crouched down before a wooden chest. Rudy turned to watch him, leaving himself exposed to the girl.

He never heard her move. He felt only the sharp blade of the knife she had concealed in the folds of her nightdress as it passed between his shoulder blades.

Pain kindled lights in his eyes and he heard his own voice wrenched from his throat in a scream. He ran stumbling from the cabin, clawing at his back in an attempt to remove the blade. At water's edge, he fell to his knees and was unable to rise. On all fours, he began to crawl toward town.

How he managed to reach Centre Street, Rudy never knew, but they found him there unconscious and white from loss of blood. Among the crowd that had gathered was a stable boy who remembered him and ran for Joel.

"He's my man," Joel said, when he reached the scene. "Will he live?"

"I reckon so," said a stooped thin man with lank yellow hair and gold rimmed glasses. "I'm Doctor Simpson. If you'll give me a hand we'll haul him over to the apothecary shop where I can treat him properly."

"Who did it?" Joel asked.

"Oh, a little *puta* that lives down the way," the doctor said with an air of resignation. "Damn' jackass ought to have known better!"

Joel stayed over an extra day, waiting to be sure that Rudy would be all right.

"I bought a horse for Anne," he said, "a bay mare. You'll find it waiting at McGruder's stables. Ride it on back to the ranch when you get healed up."

"Nein, nein!" Rudy protested, struggling to rise from his bed. "I can make it."

"You've been fool enough already," Joel said. "Do what the doc says and hang around a couple of days. The ranch won't fall apart without you, you know."

Rudy sank back in his pillow. "Emma's gonna be mad as hell."

"Tell her it was a bar fight."

"It ain't that," Rudy said. "It ain't the knifing. It's the money. She gave me a long list of provisions to bring back."

"Give the goddamn' thing to me!" Joel said, unable to hide the disgust in his voice. "I'll buy what she needs."

"Danke," Rudy sighed.

"Save your thanks," Joel said. "Just get on back as soon as you're able. And try not to be such a damned fool in the future. Ain't nothing that gets a man in more trouble than putting his pecker in the wrong place."

That night Joel returned to Lenore. He had found her to be generous, gentle, and sympathetic. He had discovered in her arms a love unlike the love he had shared with Martha but which was no less satisfying in its own way. And he was glad for the opportunity to see her once more.

"Entrez!" she called when he knocked, and he opened the door carrying a bottle of port the barkeep below had assured him was a favorite of Lenore's.

"Oh, you are a darling! *Merci, créri!"* She was wearing a dress of indigo and lavender with white lace spilling from the neckline. Again he noticed that her eyes were the sort that reflected the colors she wore, for gone were the gold and green of yesterday, and now the blue of her irises was flecked with violet.

She took two glasses from her washstand and set them on the little table for him to fill. "I heard about your man getting cut up and hoped you would be staying over. Was he badly injured?"

"He'll recover. He's strong as a bear."

"I'm so glad. Oh, this port is delicious! It's my vice, you know."

Joel smiled, pleased, and relaxed into the overstuffed chair beside her bed. Lenore sank back in her cushions and rested her feet in his lap. Piano music filtered up from downstairs.

After their second glass, Lenore reached across and pulled Joel to her until their lips met. "I'm happy you came back," she said.

She got up and undressed slowly, letting him watch her, aware of the growing hunger in his eyes. At last, when she was down to her lacy camisole, she held out

88

her arms to him and pulled him close. He found her perfume more intoxicating than the port he had drunk. Their lips met, and Joel felt his body quiver with desire. His fingers found the satin ribbons of her camisole and released them. The lacy garment fell away, and Lenore led him to the bed.

He fell on her, kissing her roughly, running his hands down the silken curves of her body.

Lenore pushed him gently away, and began undoing his buttons one by one. She smiled in understanding. "Don't be in such a hurry, *mon cher*," she said. "We have all night."

His fingers found the oil lamp on the nightstand by the bed and turned it down until the room was nearly dark.

Later, as they lay beneath the covers listening to the surf striking white and foamy against the beach, Lenore ran her fingers through Joel's thick dark hair and said, "You are the best thing that's happened to me since I arrived in St. Mary's I wish you didn't have to leave tomorrow."

"I'll be back in a month or two." He wished it could be sooner.

Lenore sighed, rolling over and moving her arm across his bare chest. "Oh, but, *chéri,* I won't be here."

"You're moving on?"

She nodded, her chin on his shoulder. "I've been talking to the skippers in town. I see almost every one of them that drops anchor in Copano. They tell me that war is coming, and when it does, the North is going to lock up every southern port, including St. Mary's. I want to return to New Orleans before it's too late."

"Blockade?" Joel asked.

Lenore nodded again. "That's what they say. The Yankee gunboats won't let anyone in or out. And, you can imagine that I have no desire to be a prisoner in St. Mary's. Who knows, the war might last a year . . . maybe more."

"A blockade would ruin my business," Joel said somberly.

"I fear it," Lenore replied. "There will be no place to sell the hides."

"Not unless there's a way to get around the blockade," Joel said, "—a safe way with no risk."

Lenore sighed and closed her eyes. "If you devise a way to do that, *mon cher,* you will become the richest man in Texas."

7

Emma was nervous and edgy. Hoping against hope that for some reason the men would cut short their trip and return early, she took to scanning the horizon for sight of them over the waves of golden grass. And when the days dragged on and on, she took out her apprehensions and loneliness on Anne, scolding her for the slightest transgression. She blamed Anne for being too noisy whenever Davey woke bawling, accused her of laziness when the girl took time out from the chores to play with the dog, castigated her for inattention if she dropped a stitch or sewed a crooked seam.

Anne tried to avoid Emma and to keep her silence, but Emma's face would darken and her eyes would glitter like polished stone. "Don't you go sullen on me now!" she would order. And Anne dared not even sigh with resignation for fear of irritating Emma further. She found herself longing, even more than Emma, for the men's return.

On the tenth day, Emma ignored her chores and spent the afternoon sitting on the steps of the house, holding Davey in her arms, staring out over the prairie for sight of the men. After sundown, true to her word, she placed a lamp in the window, tending it hourly, refusing to sleep.

The next morning, Anne found her still sitting on the hard bench by the window, her face drawn from fatigue and her eyes flat and lusterless.

"Something bad has happened," Emma muttered. "Rudy would never be late. He knows how I worry."

"Maybe the rain . . ." Anne began, trying to comfort the woman, but Emma cut her short.

"What do you know?" she snapped. "And what do you care? You slept like a baby last night! You're no help to me at all."

Anne couldn't see how doing without sleep would have benefited Emma, but she knew better than to argue.

As she'd done the day before, Emma assumed her position on the steps and kept her vigil. The day was clear, with a high bright sun warming them for the first time since the rainy norther had struck. Anne prepared lunch, but Emma refused to eat and watched with resentment as the girl ate her stew.

In late afternoon, a stiff wind picked up, raising dust and rustling through the fields of grass. Anne brought Emma a shawl, but the woman seemed not to notice the change of weather.

"It's getting cold again," Anne said. "You ought to cover Davey."

Without a word, Emma accepted the shawl and wrapped the baby in it. Her eyes never left the horizon.

Then from far off in the wind-bowed grass, the dog began to bark.

"It's them!" Emma cried, rising to her feet, straining to catch sight of the men. "Anne! Quick! Do you see them?"

Leaning from the doorway, Anne peered out and saw that the horizon was empty. But the dog kept barking, its high, shrill yaps punctuated with low, nervous growls, which put Anne on guard, sending a sudden warning chill through her that raised the hair on her neck.

Ignoring the dog's peculiar behavior, Emma left the steps and ran out into the yard.

"Emma!" Anne called, her voice a husky whisper. "Emma, come back!"

But Emma ran farther into the yard, rising on tiptoes for a better look.

"Emma!" Anne cried. "Come back! It might be someone else!"

Emma heard at last and she turned, suddenly very frightened. Her eyes grew wide, and Anne saw her face turn pale. Emma was staring past her, past the house, behind it to the west.

"Emma!" Anne cried again. "What do you see?"

Emma seemed unable to answer. She clutched Davey close to her breast and, turning her back on Anne, broke into a run headed away from the house toward the tall grass.

"*Emma!*" Anne screamed. "Come back! Don't leave me! Please don't leave me alone!"

But Emma kept running. Anne watched, wild with fear, as Emma reached the edge of the tall, waving grass and vanished into its camouflage.

Anne's heart flew into her throat as she heard the sound of horses' hooves in the distance. Turning she raced to the back window and pressed her face against the pane. Two men in wide sombreros astride huge black stallions were riding out of the west. They were already at the corral, two Mexicans in leather coats and leggings with rifles at their sides.

Anne stared in horror, realizing with a shock that Emma had abandoned her.

As the men reached the corral, Anne ran back to the door, slammed it shut, and straining, shoved the heavy wooden beam across it. The beam jammed in its brackets, but Anne took a deep breath and, gritting her teeth, forced it into place, barring the door. She looked about wildly, her eyes falling, finally, on one of Joel's pistols hanging in a holster beside the fireplace.

Outside there was the crash of splintering timber, and Anne realized that the men were knocking down the corral. She snatched the pistol from the wall and hurried to the back room. Kneeling on Emma's bed, she pulled the weapon from its holster. Its weight astonished her, and she hoped she would be able to fire it.

A rifle shot split the air, jarring her, and she heard the frightened cattle stampede out of the corral. She pulled six bullets from the cartridge belt and began pushing them with trembling fingers into the chamber.

Be calm! she ordered herself; but her breathing was ragged and she was sure the men outside could hear her racing heart.

She had four shells in place when the men tried to open the door. They cursed in Spanish at finding it barred. Then came the sound of breaking glass.

The window! she gasped, horrified. I forgot to close the shutters!

She imagined the scene in the other room: the men reaching through the shattered window, grasping the wooden bar and sliding it back through its iron brackets. She heard the bar fall heavily to the floor. Then the latch scraped in its track and the door creaked on its hinges. Boot heels rang out on the stone floor of the front room; a voice said something in Spanish; another answered.

The pistol grew heavier. Anne had it aimed at the doorway, clutching it in both hands, its hammer cocked, but she feared she wouldn't be able to hold it much longer. Already its long barrel was beginning to trace an ever-widening wobbly circle.

The men were prowling about, and she realized it would be only a moment before they discovered her.

Shoot straight! she warned herself. If you miss, they'll kill you!

Then she saw him! A tall sombreroed Mexican with a drooping black mustache and fierce dark eyes. His leering smile at finding she was only a young girl vanished as he caught sight of the pistol in her hands.

"Get out!" Anne shouted suddenly. "Get out or I'll shoot you!"

But the Mexican stood frozen in the doorway. In another instant his companion appeared at his shoulder, and seeing her pistol, he murmured, *"Cuidado!"*

The sound of his voice alarmed Anne. She squeezed the trigger, and the first man spun around crying out in pain. She fired again, and another bullet struck him in the back, sending him sprawling into the front room. The kick of the pistol was too much for Anne's weakened grip, and the weapon went tumbling to the floor. She didn't hear the other man sprint from the house and gallop off on his black stallion; but when she recovered from the immediate shock, she realized he was gone.

She dropped to the floor in a crouch and grabbed the pistol, waiting there for a long time, trembling too violently to move. Finally she became aware of the spreading pool of blood from the dead Mexican who lay in the doorway.

"Emma!" she yelled, and, receiving no answer, called again.

She surprised herself by getting to her feet and being able to stand. She was further amazed that she could look at the man she had killed, but she stared at him with detached fascination. She hadn't known that a bullet could do such damage. He lay face down, a gaping hole in his back, his blood seeping over the stone floor like dark oil. She had to step in it to get around him.

At the doorway, she looked out toward the windswept grass and called again for Emma. This time there was a response, and soon she spotted Emma, carrying Davey, making her way into the cleared yard.

Emma was shouting to her, but fright had caused her to lapse into German.

"Make sense, Emma!" Anne ordered. "Talk English!"

Emma reached the house and took in the scene behind Anne.

"You killed him!"

"I had to," Anne answered. She looked again at the body. "Emma, we have to get him out of here."

"No!" Emma exclaimed, recoiling. "I don't want to touch him."

"You have to help me."

"Leave him there! Rudy and Joel can take him out. We can stay outside till they get back."

"No!" Anne said, glaring at Emma. "I don't want him in the house."

She took Davey from Emma's arms and put him in the crib.

"What if he's not dead?" Emma protested.

"Of course he's dead," Anne said. Her voice was sharp, and she was suddenly tired of arguing with Emma. "Grab one of his arms. I'll take the other. We'll drag him out by the corral."

"I can't look at him!"

"Then close your eyes. I'll lead the way."

Together they hauled the body through the front door and across the yard, concealing it in the high grass beside the ruined corral.

"We ought to bury him," Anne said, leaning against the broken fence for support. "But I'm too tired."

"Good," Emma saaid. "Rudy and Joel will take care of it."

"Oh, why don't they come home?" Anne cried out, breaking down at last. She longed for Joel to be back with them, taking charge of things. Her sudden weakness seemed to restore Emma's strength. She took Anne by the hand.

"Come," Emma said. "Let's go back to the house and wait. They'll be home soon. I know it."

But the afternoon waned. Leaden clouds once again

filled the sky, and sunset was but a deepening of the purple shadow that blanketed the land. Anne withdrew into herself, sitting alone and silent on a bench in the front room.

Her mind kept returning to the afternoon's events. It dawned on her that Emma had never once thought of her safety, that she had run for cover with Davey, leaving Anne to fend for herself—perhaps to be killed—and she understood that it would always be that way. Her heart grew heavy: this realization filled her more with sorrow than with anger.

She was unable to take her eyes off the dark stain that covered the stone floor in the doorway.

It wasn't really murder, she reflected. He would have killed us all if I hadn't done it. But still . . .

The thought was too much for her, and she dropped her head into her arms and wept quietly.

Darkness rekindled Emma's fears. She grew agitated, frightened that Joel and Rudy would be gone yet another day. Her attempts to talk to Anne brought only silence. She nursed Davey and sealed the broken window with a blanket nailed into place.

At last, distracted and nervous, she turned on Anne.

"You shouldn't have done it," she said. "You should have run into the grass with me. They would have left when they saw there was no one here and nothing for them to take. Now you've caused us more trouble. You think the other one is going to stay away? You think he will just ride off and leave us alone after you killed his friend? He'll be back, I know. With others. And then what will become of us?"

She waited, expecting a reply from Anne, and when she got none, she grew angrier still.

"You were stupid!" she said. "And what you did was wrong. You did murder!"

"No!" Anne cried. "It wasn't murder! They would have killed us!"

"You don't know that. You'll never know. And all your life you'll have to remember that you did murder!"

Joel crossed the dry creek two miles to the east of the ranch house. He could see its dark outline against the purple horizon, but the absence of light in the window filled him with dread. He popped his whip over the mules' backs and drove them forward.

Anne and Emma heard the heavy thud of hooves and high-pitched squeal of the wagon's axles.

"It's them," Emma announced, racing for the door. "They're home!"

She ran out into the darkness of the yard, straining to catch a glimpse of the wagon coming through the prairie grass.

"Rudy!" she called. "Rudy!"

Joel caught sight of the lighted doorway and Emma's figure silhouetted against the house.

"Emma!" he shouted. "'Anne! Is there anything wrong?"

Emma was running toward him now, and he saw Anne appear in the door.

Thank God, he thought, they're safe! And he reined back on the mules to slow the wagon.

Emma, crying Rudy's name, kept running toward Joel.

He stopped the wagon.

"Oh, Rudy, you're home!" he heard Emma say. But when she reached the wagon and realized that Joel was alone, she let out a cry and covered her mouth with her hands.

"It's all right, Emma," Joel said quickly. "He's all right. He's coming on a little later, that's all."

He slapped the reins lightly and the mules pulled the wagon forward. Emma walked alongside, holding on to the harness, unwilling to accept that Rudy was not with Joel.

"What has happened?" she demanded. "Why is Rudy not with you?"

"Nothing to worry about, Emma," Joel said. He had decided to let Emma hear the story from her husband, not knowing what excuse Rudy would dream up.

"He's in trouble," she cried. "He's ill or hurt!"

"No! Don't worry, Emma," Joel said again. "He'll be home in a couple of days. He's bringing back a horse I bought for Anne."

As they entered the yard, Joel called out to his daughter, who still hovered in the doorway: "Annie, I'm home! Come give your papa a hug!"

But she did not respond. When she made no move to greet him, he realized there was trouble. He stopped the wagon and jumped off.

"What's the matter, Anne?" he asked, as he joined her in the doorway. Anne raised her face toward his, and he saw the tears that stained her cheeks.

"Annie, honey, what is it?" He turned to Emma. "What's happened?"

"She better tell you," Emma said.

"Anne?" Joel asked again.

"Tell him, Anne," Emma said. The cold, hard edge again crept into her voice. "Tell your papa what you did!"

Anne tried to speak, but the words caught in her throat.

"Annie! Annie, what is it?"

"Come with me," she managed to say. She took the oil lamp from the table by the door and led Joel back out into the yard. The pool of light guided their footsteps until they reached the tall dry grass beside the corral.

As they neared the corral, Joel saw the barricades were down and that the cattle had escaped.

"Oh, Annie, a few wild cows . . . that's not worth crying over."

She shook her head miserably. "No, Papa. It's worse. Look!"

And he followed her gaze into the grass.

"Oh, my God!" he murmured, seeing the body lying face down on the ground.

"I did it," she said. "I shot him and killed him."

Joel bent over the body, which was cold and already growing stiff.

"Emma says I did murder," Anne said, her voice weak and tired. "But I was afraid he would hurt us. I was afraid he would kill us."

Joel turned him over and stared at the dead man's face in the yellow lamplight. A shock of recognition jolted him.

"You did right, Anne," he said gravely. "This man *would* have killed you. You saved your life *and* Emma's! Don't ever think different."

So, we meet again! Joel thought, addressing the dead man silently. And he continued to study the swarthy face with its ragged scar running from the left temple to the chin.

8

For the first time since their marriage, Luis de Vargas brought Sofia back to the Lantana. The few servants who witnessed her arrival late one night were shocked by what they saw.

"*Nombre de Dios!*" one exclaimed. "He must beat her! Look at the bruises around her eyes!"

"Those aren't bruises," another said. "They're dark circles. She must be too unhappy to sleep."

"And look how thin she's grown!"

"Oh, the poor *princesa!*"

And though the news of her return spread quickly among the servants, that was the last they saw of her. Sofia found herself a virtual prisoner in her father's household, incarcerated in the same upstairs bedroom that had been hers as a girl, held under lock and key, and chaperoned every moment by Doña Matilde, a wizened, sharp-eyed widow who was a cousin of her husband. Sofia saw almost no one else, not even her beloved Natalia. She was visited only occasionally by her father and every night by Luis, who would stumble heavily into the bedroom, bloated with the evening meal and reeking of wine and brandy.

These were the times she dreaded the most, when she prayed fervently to the Virgin to release her, to let death free her from the gross caresses of the man her father had given her to.

She still could not accept or endure the horror of his lovemaking; and when, inevitably, she swooned and fell limp beneath him, Luis would take this for passion, and rolling off breathless and satiated, would congratulate himself on his ability to handle his young wife.

Sofia was forced to dine alone. Her meals were delivered on trays left outside the locked door by silent, unseen servants. The trays were returned, barely touched, to the kitchen where they'd been prepared. As the cool, bleak days passed in the joyless company of Doña Matilde, Sofia's only diversion was to observe the view beyond her iron-barred window: the flat grassy prairie, the unmarked horizon, and the great canopy of sky, its leaden grayness matching her mood and spirit.

"Why can't I see my aunt?" she pleaded.

Doña Matilde barely looked up from her sewing. "You know that Natalia is sick. She's allowed no one."

"I don't believe you," Sofia said. "I heard her voice only yesterday in the corridor. She sounded strong and well."

Matilde's jaws tightened, but she didn't reply.

"I'm a grown woman now, a married woman," Sofia insisted, her voice rising with defiance. "There is no reason for me to have a *dueña*. I demand that you unlock the door and let me walk free in my father's house."

"You must take that up with Luis," Matilde said evenly, knotting the thread and holding up the chemise she'd been hemming. "I have no say one way or the other."

Sofia studied the old woman for a moment, hating her sharp features, the sparse gray hair pulled severely over her skull-like head, and the bloodless lips that always seemed drawn into a tight, stern line, as thin and white as the thread with which she sewed.

Sofia tried another tack. "This can't be pleasurable

for you, Doña Matilde, sitting all day in this room with only your needlework and your prayers."

Matilde shifted her bony hips on her stool and shrugged, rearranging her shawl over her stooped shoulders. "I am a widow. What else is there for me?"

"If that is a widow's fate, even though I'm young, I still would prefer widowhood to my marriage to Luis."

This brought Matilde's gaze to Sofia at last. "There, Sofia, you have your answer to the locked door."

Sofia averted her eyes, hiding from the woman's stare and said, "I hope I die young!"

"Blasphemy!" Matilde said. "Our time on earth is left to God."

"May He take me then! I am ready."

Matilde crossed herself and uttered a quick prayer.

Sofia paced the room, stopping now and then to peer through the window at the unchanging scene beyond. "How I long for summer! I prefer its heat to the dullness of the winter months."

"To everything there is a season . . ." Matilde began.

"Be quiet, old woman! I don't want to hear any more of your platitudes!" Sofia snapped.

But Sofia didn't hear Matilde's indignant reply, as she was distracted by the sight of a man on horseback riding through the tall grass toward the hacienda. She leaned against the window, her hands gripping the sill.

It can't be! she thought, and blinked, unbelieving. No! It can't be!

But the man was quite close by now, and she recognized his features, the fine line of his jaw, the strong good-looking face, the straight and easy way he rode in the saddle.

"It *is* him!" she cried, startling Matilde. "I thought Luis had killed him, but he's not dead after all!"

"Who?" Matilde demanded, rising from her stool and scurrying across the room to the window.

"Gracias a Dios!" Sofia breathed, making the sign of the cross. "He is alive!"

103

"Who is that man?" Matilde questioned. "A *norte-americano!* How do you know him?"

But Sofia did not answer. Silently she watched as Joel galloped up to the hacienda's steps and reined back. A commotion began below as the front doors flew open and Joel was challenged.

"Send for your *patrón*," she heard Joel saying; and then she noticed the body strapped to the back of his horse.

Ignoring the chill blast of air that gusted through the iron grillwork, Sofia opened her window to listen as Enrique, roused from his siesta, appeared in slippers on the threshold. He recognized Joel immediately, and his face darkened.

"Señor," Joel said. "I know you speak English and I know you understand. So listen to me and listen good. I once tasted your brand of hospitality. Now here's a sample of mine. If any more of your *bandidos* come marauding on my place, they'll be served up more of the same!"

With that, he released the straps that held the vaquero's body and let it fall to the ground at the foot of the steps.

Sofia gasped as she saw the dark wound in the dead man's body. She was horrified, but she couldn't deny the thrill of vindication that swept through her as she recognized the corpse as the man who had horse-whipped Joel and dragged him in the dirt.

"Murderer!" Enrique shouted.

"Leave me in peace, señor! That's a warning!" Then Joel spurred his horse and broke away.

Sofia's heart leaped in her chest. She gripped the iron bars and leaned out into the wind. *"Adios, señor!"* she cried before Matilde could drag her back inside. *"Adios! Vaya con Dios!"*

Joel recognized the voice. He spun his horse about and scanned the side of the building until his eyes caught sight of Sofia's pale face behind the grille of her window. He raised a hand in greeting. Though he knew it was dangerous to linger, he waited until he saw hers lifted in reply. Then, digging his heels into his horse's flanks, he took off, galloping fast toward the east.

Matilde tightened her thin arms around Sofia's waist and pulled her back into the bedroom.

"You know the gringo?" she gasped, scandalized.

"I've only seen him once," Sofia answered, breathless with excitement and joy. "But I thought he was dead."

"And dead he soon will be," Matilde swore. "Enrique and Luis will not stand for this."

"He'll defeat them," Sofia said. "He's done it twice. He'll do it again if he has to."

"Silence!" Matilde shouted. "You're an impudent fool. I curse the day Luis took you for his bride."

"I do too, Matilde. I do too."

Luis, faint patches of purple tinting his sallow cheeks, burst into the foyer. "We must go after him, Enrique! Let's finish the job we started."

"Calm yourself, Luis," Enrique said, restraining the man with a hand on his shoulder. "We need no more bloodshed."

"Are you saying you intend to let the gringo go? He killed one of your men."

"I'm aware of what he did, Luis," Enrique said evenly. "It's just that I have other plans for taking care of him. Now, put away your rifle and join me in a glass of wine."

Luis was aghast at Enrique's coolness. He followed him into the *sala* and accepted a glass of port.

"I received good news this morning from San Antonio," Enrique said, taking a chair before the blazing fireplace and urging Luis to do the same. "The telegraph reports that Mr. Lincoln has been elected."

Luis sighed impatiently. He had no desire to talk politics, particularly gringo politics.

"The Southerners will not stand for it," Enrique added. "They hate this man Lincoln. They call him the Illinois Ape. It means war."

"What do we care?" Luis responded, calmed somewhat by his port, concentrating instead on the dancing amber lights the burning logs kindled in his glass. "It's all so far away. It won't touch us."

How dull-witted you are, Luis! Enrique thought. How utterly stupid! But he arranged his face pleasantly and smiled over the rim of his glass. "The gringos will fight. Even here in Texas they will fight. It's their duty. Trevor will not be able to avoid it. While he is gone, I'll find a way to take his ranch. And, if he survives the war, he'll find on his return that he is as landless as a peon!"

1861

9

Among the boys seeking supper and a night's lodging, only one was over twenty. They were rawboned but healthy and could barely contain the exuberance they felt in anticipation of their great adventure ahead.

Stonyfaced with displeasure at the extra work it took to feed them, Emma knelt before the stove and pulled out two more pans of cornbread from the oven.

"At least we could get an hour's work out of them," she muttered in German to Rudy. "It galls me to feed them for free. This is the third band of vagabonds in the past week."

"Careful, Emma," Rudy cautioned. "They may not know what you're saying, but they can understand your tone."

"I don't care," Emma said obstinately, but she served the rest of the food in silence.

The boys ate ravenously, devouring the first real meal they'd had since leaving Brownsville on horseback three days before. Joel watched them with a divided heart. At thirty-eight, he was already too old to comprehend their boyish lust for war; yet he could understand their excitement at being let loose in the world, unbridled for the first time.

The initial group of lads had come knocking at the

ranch house the previous Sunday. The one thing Joel and Rudy had learned from that first encounter was to keep silent about their opinion of the war. Rudy, like most of the newly settled Germans, considered himself an out-and-out Unionist. Joel wouldn't have gone that far. Nevertheless, he *had* ridden sixty miles to register his vote in the February election, and he *had* cast his lot against secession. But he was in the minority. Texas quickly departed the Union she had once fought so hard to join; and old Sam Houston, defeated at last, left the Executive Mansion in Austin and retired in sorrow to the family home in Huntsville.

Joel dreaded war. Though he had no love for Abe Lincoln and his "Black Republicans," he loathed slavery. And he believed the South was too weak and ill-prepared to defeat the industrial North.

He and Rudy had never been so busy. In anticipation of a blockade, there was a frantic commerce in hides, and Joel had to construct a bunkhouse and hire on a dozen vaqueros to assist in cow-hunting. At least three wagons a week left the ranch for the port at St. Mary's. For the first time in his life Joel was getting rich, but he realized his newfound prosperity would cease the instant the Yankees instituted their threatened blockade.

"Joel also feared a draft. For the moment, Texas was only calling for volunteers like the ragtag bands of lads who had begun trailing through his ranch on their eager way to enlist at the garrison in San Antonio. But conscription was inevitable—and he and Rudy would be called up.

He watched the boys heaping their plates with fried steak and greens and thick wedges of cornbread drizzled with molasses, and he kept his opinions to himself. He had no wish to repeat the mistake he'd made with the first group who had straggled through. Feelings had run high. They had been insulted by his

108

views and had risen as one, leaving their meal un-
finished, declaring that they would rather starve than
break bread with a Unionist.

Tonight, Anne watched them too. She was thirteen
now, and the strong, handsome boys fascinated her.
She hardly dared speak to them—not that she was
shy, but she couldn't imagine that anything she had
to say would interest these daring youths who looked
forward so fearlessly to whipping the Yankees. So
she sat at the table, too spellbound to eat, listening to
their talk. She listened in particular to the eldest, a
boy named Jim with curly dark hair and the faint
shadow of a mustache above his upper lip. He was
by far the handsomest, she decided, glancing only
cursorily at his companions—two boys who claimed
to be twins but who looked nothing alike, and a lad
with red hair, freckles and a cowlick that no amount of
bear grease could tame.

Her attention returned to Jim. He was burly and
bronzed and his eyes were nearly as green as her own.

"I just hope we ain't too late," he was saying. "I'm
scared that by the time we get into the fracas the
Yankee cowards will be hightailin' it back up to ole
Abe's doorstep."

"There's talk they're 'bout to give in to Jeff Davis
already," one of the twins agreed.

"I reckon there'll be plenty of time for you to see
action," Joel said.

"And plenty of time to grow sick of it," Rudy added.

"Not me," the redhead said. "I'm hankerin' to fight
so bad I can taste it!"

"Me too," the twins said.

"War 'ud have to be powerful bad to make me want
to go back to Brownsville any time soon," Jim said.
"I done had my fill workin' on them steamer boats up
and down the river."

"You mean there's a river down there big enough

for steamboats?" Anne asked, astonished at the idea of so much water anywhere in that arid land.

"Biggest river you'll ever see, girl," Jim said.

"I've seen the Red and the Colorado and the Nueces," Anne said cooly, miffed at being addressed as "girl."

Jim laughed. "I'm talking about the Rio Grande. Why do you think they call it that if it ain't somethin' special? *Grande* means big—or don't you talk Mexican?"

"I know what *grande* means, and I know what *rio* means too," Anne replied. She was quickly growing disenchanted with Jim and his superior air. "I reckon I speak Mex as good as anyone. And I talk German too."

"Well, you got me beat there, girl," Jim said, laughing again, unruffled by Anne's boast.

Joel had sat silently musing through all their chatter, but now he interrupted the contretemps to ask a question of Jim. "Tell me about the boats," he said. "What do they carry?"

"Oh, everything," Jim answered. "Everything a person needs. People too, and livestock. They steam back and forth from Mier to Reynosa and Bagdad. Ever heard of Bagdad?"

"I heard the name," Joel answered.

"It's a Mexican port, right smack on the Gulf. Every now and then a big ship sails in carrying goods from far away . . . places like Havana and London. If the war had'na come, I'da signed on with one of them schooners and sailed off for adventure. Still aim to, only I guess it'll be a while now."

Joel fell silent again and listened to the boy talk about the ships from Europe and the Caribbean and their cargoes of linen and cotton goods, of silverware and china and rum. And an idea grew in his head. . . .

Later, Joel offered the boys a place to sleep in his bunkhouse with the vaqueros. Jim declined for them, saying, "If it's all the same to you, we'll bed down in the barn. We'd rather sleep with the animals than with a passel of Mexes. Leastwise we won't have to keep watch over our wallets all night."

Joel, who had no desire to argue with them, let them sacrifice comfort for their prejudices and bade them good night.

In the dark silence of midnight he strolled out beneath the stars, his mind buzzing with the scheme he'd just devised. The plan was filled with risk. It could rob him of everything he'd worked for if it failed, but the way the war was certain to go, he was afraid he stood to lose everything anyway, so he had to risk it. And he had to act now, or it would be too late.

At dawn the next morning he woke the boys, shared breakfast with them, and saw them on their way. Then he packed his own wallet with grub for four days and strapped it behind his saddle.

"I'm going to Mier," he told Rudy. "Take care of everything here. I'll be back soon as I can."

Rudy watched him ride off to the south. Joel had kept his own counsel, but Rudy, remembering Jim's conversation the night before and piecing it together with Joel's destination, realized Joel's intent.

A smile of admiration came to his lips as he stared after Joel's retreating figure. I got to hand it to you, boss, he thought. You're one damned smart man.

Don Enrique de Leon had been in Mier for a week. The little Mexican town on the Rio Grande provided the closest marketplace to his hacienda, and he journeyed there every other month to purchase the necessities and luxuries deemed essential for the Lantana. His caravan of half a dozen two-wheeled *carretas* was already loaded and waited under guard in the stable at the *fonda,* where he occupied the finest suite. As usual, he had finished his shopping early and was enjoying the rest of his stay by gambling during the

111

day and at night sharing his bed with a fresh young country girl provided by the proprietor of the *fonda*.

The peasant beauty had proved to be a demanding lover for a man his age, and Don Enrique was considering cutting short his visit in order to preserve his health. But one of the guards that he had stationed at the stable to watch over his *carretas* came to him at the gambling table with the news that the gringo from the neighboring ranch had taken a room at the inn.

His curiosity piqued, Don Enrique abandoned the game, despite the fact that he was five thousand pesos behind. "I'll be in my quarters," the *hacendado* told his servant. "Learn what the gringo is up to and report to me later."

Don Enrique was sharing an early dinner with the peasant girl when the servant returned with the information that Joel had spent the afternoon around the docks on the Rio Grande and then had paid a call on the *Banco de Mier y Saltillo*.

Enrique dismissed him and finished his leisurely meal. Then he pulled on his coat and adjusted his cravat in the mirror.

"Where are you going, *querido?*" the peasant girl asked.

"I must see a friend of mine," Enrique answered, reaching for his hat and dusting it with the cuff of his coat.

"Don't go, *corazón!*" the girl begged. "I will be so lonely."

Don Enrique smiled, flattered that the girl so desired his company. "Don't fret, *mi linda*," he said, consoling her with a kiss on the forehead and a gentle pat on her buttocks. "I won't be long."

He strolled out of the inn and crossed the plaza to the line of mule-drawn hacks in front of the cathedral.

"Take me to the house of Don Felipe Rodriguez," he instructed the driver as he stepped up into the seat.

"Si, *señor*," the driver said, and he snapped the reins, so the rickety hack jounced forward into the dusty street.

As befitted a prosperous banker, Felipe Rodriguez lived in one of the town's finest dwellings, a two-story house of white stucco, adorned with blooming bougainvillea and hibiscus. It held within its walls a spacious patio, paved in blue and white tile and boasting in its center a dancing fountain that even in the summer gave the courtyard an illusion of coolness.

Don Felipe came to the courtyard to greet his unexpected guest and lead him inside.

"Don Enrique!" he said. "I had not seen you for several days and had assumed that you had already journeyed back across the river."

"Not yet, Felipe, not yet, as you can see. There was . . . eh, another little matter remaining that required my attentions."

Felipe Rodriguez caught the impact of Enrique's words. "Ah, yes, my friend," he said, smiling conspiratorily. "I quite understand. I often find such business myself whenever I travel to Saltillo."

He clapped his hands and a servant appeared out of the shadows with a bottle of *pulque* and two small glasses.

"You will do me the honor, señor?"

"With pleasure," Enrique answered, reaching for a glass.

They toasted each other and tossed back the liquor. As Felipe refilled the glasses, he said, "I can see you've something on your mind, my friend. Tell me, what can I do for you?"

"A little information," Enrique said. "You were visited today by a *norteamericano* by the name of Joel Trevor. He happens to be a neighbor of mine, one with whom I've had some considerable trouble. I was wondering if you could tell me what his business is here in Mier."

"Yes," Felipe said. "He came to the bank this evening with a very interesting proposition. I tell you this because we're longtime friends and he is a complete stranger. Besides, he is a foreigner."

"Yes," Enrique said. "Go on, please."

"He wants to buy some riverboats—two to begin with and more later on. He told me that the war in the United States will force the government in Washington to blockade all southern ports. He seems to think that by buying these boats and reregistering them under the Mexican flag, he can outwit the Yankees. It is his plan to transport cotton from the Confederate States through Texas into Mexico, then down the Rio Grande to European vessels docking at Bagdad."

He paused and waited for Enrique to comment.

Enrique arched his eyebrows and said, "The man *is* clever. It sounds like a promising idea to me."

Felipe went on, "He contends that the American flag will protect his enterprise. He claims the Americans will refuse to molest a Mexican vessel, for fear of creating strife on this border while contending with insurrection at home."

"A very reasonable assumption," Enrique commented. "I suppose you lent him the money."

"Not at all," Felipe said. "And we don't intend to."

Enrique was surprised. "But, why not?"

"There is a serious flaw in his proposal. For his plan to work, and in order for him to make back the very large sum that it would take to put it into operation, the American navy will *have* to institute the blockade he is counting on. What if they don't? What if the Gulf ports remain open? Without a blockade there will be no reason to divert shipping from New Orleans or Galveston to such a minor port of call as Bagdad. *Dios mío,* have you ever been to that place? A hole of pestilence in the middle of a marsh. Malaria abounds and not six ships a year drop anchor there. And for security, Trevor has nothing . . . nothing but

114

his *ranchito*. Now I ask you, what do we want with a few thousand acres of American soil?"

Enrique's brow was furrowed and he toyed with the glass in his hand. "He was willing to put up his ranch as collateral?"

"Of no use to us," Felipe said, reaching again for the bottle of *pulque*.

"But I wouldn't mind having it," Enrique said. "I'm opposed to gringos owning property south of the Nueces. As long as the land remains in Mexican hands, there is hope that one day we can return it to the *patria*."

"Then go to him. He's staying at the *fonda*. I'm sure he would be glad to strike the same bargain with you."

"No, no," Enrique said. "As I told you, there's been bad blood between us. I don't want him to know I'm involved in any way, but I have an idea. If you lend him the money, I will guarantee it in gold. Then, if his enterprise should fail, you will be repaid in full, and I will add his land to the Lantana."

Felipe nodded. "That means there is no risk to us."

"None at all. I will sign whatever papers you need."

Felipe brushed his hand through the air. "I need no signature from you, Enrique. I've dealt with you for so many years that your word is quite sufficient."

"You have my word."

"Then we have a bargain. Tomorrow, when the foreigner returns to the bank, I'll give him whatever sum he needs." He poured a drink to seal the contract. "There's one thing I'm curious about, my friend," he said. "It's obvious you desire his business to fail."

Enrique nodded. "It's critical that it should fail."

"Then what happens if the Americans *do* institute a blockade?"

Enrique shrugged and held up his glass in salute. "If that should happen, then I'll find another way to deal with him!"

115

10

In July, Joel again accompanied his wagons to St. Mary's. When they reached the bluff, he held up his hand and halted his teamsters. The green waters of the bay were almost deserted. Gone was the forest of masts he had grown accustomed to seeing. Only two schooners floated at anchor just off shore and an old skow was all that lay moored beside the wharf.

He knew immediately what had happened.

"Dónde están?" one of the Mexican drivers asked.

"They're gone," Joel answered. "They've slipped out. The Yankees must be on their way."

Hitching his horse outside the Barrelhouse, he pushed through the swinging doors to find that, except for four old men huddled over dominoes, the place was empty and forlorn. A sheet covered the piano; shadows hung like curtains from the corners.

Among the men at the game table, Joel recognized Homer Post, the proprietor.

"Where'd everybody go?" he asked.

Homer chalked his score and answered, barely glancing up. "Who knows? Brownsville, Havana . . . the captains didn't even know where they were headed. Soon as word got here that the Yankees had bottled up Galveston, they all skedaddled. Damnedest sight you

116

ever saw. Looked like a goldurned race to get out of the bay. The *Santa Cruz* and the *Zephyr* sideswiped each other in the cut and didn't even bother to turn back for repairs. So, who knows where they went? Go on, pour yourself a shot. There's a bottle on the bar. Take what you want, it's on the house. Ain't nobody around to sell it to."

Joel accepted the offer and then, pulling up a chair, joined the men at the table.

"What about Lenore?" he asked.

Homer Post shrugged. "She lit out a couple of weeks ago."

"New Orleans?"

"Naw," Homer said, shaking his head. "It was way too late for that. She scared up a skipper heading for Mexico—Vera Cruz I think. Smart girl. She'd be starving to death if she'd hung around St. Mary's." He stopped shuffling the dominoes and looked up at Joel. "I know you, don't I?"

"I've been here before."

"Sure. You trade hides, don't you?"

Joel nodded.

Homer gave a short, bitter laugh. "Well, good luck to you."

"You're saying the price is down."

"Down?" Homer struck a match and lit up a cigar, squinting at Joel through the blue haze. "*Down* ain't the word for it! Hell, if I can't sell whiskey, who do you figure is gonna buy them hides?"

"Bad as that?" Joel said.

"Couldn't be worse."

Joel nodded, pensive. He poured himself another shot and drank it slowly. At last he said, "Well, I guess this marks the end of the cow business."

The men were engrossed in their game, and no one responded.

In the weeks that followed, Joel moved quickly. He

117

traveled alone to East Texas through thick pine woods and marshy bayou land, visiting every plantation he came upon, offering two cents a pound for its cotton. When the planters balked, as they inevitably did, he asked: "Where else are you going to sell it?"

He didn't return home until he was down to loose change.

"I must've bought up every bale from here to the Sabine," he told Rudy. "Now I've got to figure out a way to haul it down to the Rio Grande."

"The vaqueros told me about a fellow by the name of Rivas," Rudy said. "He's not much of a rancher, they say, but he has his hand in the transporting business. Seems he's done some overlanding between San Antonio and Laredo."

"So he's got wagons . . ."

"Chihuahua carts—those two-wheeled wagons the Mexicans call *carretas*. The vaqueros claim those two-wheelers roll better over this terrain than the four-wheeled wagons we've been driving to St. Mary's. Maybe you can hire him."

"I'm down to pennies," Joel said. "I'll have to see if we can strike a bargain. Find out where this man Rivas lives, and I'll ride over and talk turkey with him. "

Ramiro Rivas lived a day's ride away on horseback. Accompanied by Santos, one of the vaqueros, Joel reached his destination an hour before sunset. The house could hardly rave been called a hacienda. It was larger than Joel's by several rooms, but it was built of the same caliche blocks, and its roof was also of thatch. Nearby, attesting to Rivas's semi-prosperity, was a stable stocked with oxen, and in the yard below stood a dozen or so carretas.

Perfect, Joel thought. Between his carts and my wagons we ought to have nearly twenty vehicles, which will give us a train large enough to make the trip back and forth to the Rio Grande worthwhile.

Having been alerted by his men to Joel's approach, Rivas met Joel and Santos on horseback some distance from his house. He was a slender dark man with lank black hair and bright, intelligent eyes. Joel figured his age at about thirty.

"*Buenas tardes*," Rivas said in greeting, but he was wary and waited for the two men to identify themselves.

Joel held up his hand to demonstrate his friendliness. "My name is Joel Trevor. I own the old Narvaez ranch some distance from here."

A look of recognition passed over Rivas's face. "Ah, yes, I know who you are. I was told about you by Enrique de Leon."

Joel's hopes of dealing with Rivas plummeted. "So you're a friend of de Leon?"

Rivas hesitated. Then he shrugged and said, "I know him quite well . . . but a friend? No, I wouldn't say we two are friends."

Thank God, Joel thought, and his hopes revived.

Rivas smiled, reading Joel's mind, and said, "From what I hear, you are no friend of his either."

"We've had our differences."

"So I've been told," Rivas said. Then he smiled again. "Welcome, señor. My house is your house. Come. My wife will make you something to eat."

Petra Rivas couldn't have been much more than twenty-three or -four, but already she had a brood of six and another on the way. She prepared a hearty meal of *carne asada* and frijoles. Later, as she crooned her babies to sleep, Joel and Ramiro Rivas sat outside in the cool evening breeze and talked business.

The next morning when Joel saddled up and headed back to his ranch with Santos, he carried with him Rivas's promise to supply carts and drivers for the cotton train, in return for a tenth of Joel's profits.

A month later, the first cotton shipment reached

the Rio Grande. Joel and Rivas stood on the river bank and watched deckhands load the bales on the boats. As the carretas were emptied, they were lashed aboard rafts and ferried back to the Texas side.

"Those carts will be going back full next time," Joel told Rivas. "Now that the blockade has bottled up the South, there's going to be plenty the Confederacy needs. I plan on doing a little wheeling and dealing when I get to Bagdad."

The first of the riverboats, the one called *Azucena,* emitted a shrill whistle and prepared to get under way. Fluttering from the stern was Joel's guarantee against trouble from the Yankee fleet: the red, white, and green tricolor of the Mexican republic.

The whistle sounded sharply again. Deckhands stood by, ready to haul away the gangplank, waiting only for Joel to come aboard.

He turned to Rivas to say good-bye. "When I was a boy, I worked as a riverboat hand. Now I'm back at it. I guess that's what you call coming full circle."

"There's just one difference," Rivas said.

"What's that?"

"Now you own the boat."

Joel thought about it for a moment, then added, "Me and the bank. I suppose if any Confederate was listening he'd have me up for treason, but I'm grateful as hell for the Yankee blockade."

Rivas shook his hand. *"Buen viaje,* Joel."

"Hasta la vista, Rivas." He stepped onto the deck, and the gangplank was hauled aboard.

At that moment Felipe Rodriguez was leaving his office at the bank and entering his carriage to head homeward for lunch and a three hour siesta. When he heard the riverboat's whistle, he diverted his coachman to the dusty road that ran along the river. From his shaded leather seat, he watched the boat steam eastward toward the port of Bagdad with cotton bales

120

stacked high on its two decks, and he saw Joel standing beside the captain on the bridge.

When the boat had passed, he tapped his cane on the isinglass and directed the coachman to take him home.

This should be of interest to Enrique, he thought as the carriage jostled over the rutted dirt road. I must remember to write him a letter when I return to the bank.

11

Bagdad! The name itself conjured up in Joel visions of a wild, wicked city—bustling wharves lined with gambling dens, opulent dance halls, and noisy saloons. He imagined the harbor would be choked with schooners flying flags from countries he had never even heard of, and the streets would swarm with sailors from England, France, and South America. There would be Portuguese, Spainiards, and coolies, as well Joel imagined all this and more. He couldn't wait to reach Bagdad.

But when the *Azucena* whistled notice of its arrival and rounded the bend where the wide, muddy river debouched into the Gulf of Mexico, his heart fell.

Bagdad was a sleepy village floating on marshland. By Joel's reckoning, there couldn't be more than a thousand inhabitants living in the flimsy *jacales* that lined the river bank and bunched around the market-place. The wharf was a ramshackle affair, and Joel saw not a single warehouse. Anchored in the bay was a solitary ship, a three-masted schooner that heartened Joel somewhat by displaying the Union Jack.

Joel waded ashore knee-deep in the swirling brown water, past the algae-bearded pilings of the ruins of what had once been the village's only river dock.

Clouds of mosquitos, buzzing noisly, attacked him, raising welts on his face and hands before he reached dry land. It took him half an hour of inquiring and false leads before he wandered into a filthy cantina and found the captain of the British boat.

"I'm Captain Jack Amberson." The man nodded to Joel and, attempting to rise, succeeded only in knocking over the bottle of tequila in front of him. He was half-drunk and happily signaled to the proprietor for another bottle and a glass for Joel. Amberson was a stocky, barrel-chested man with eyes as blue as the Atlantic. A frosting of gray subdued the deep auburn of his hair and beard, and his skin showed the effects of years of burning tropical suns and icy ocean gales. "Delighted to meet you . . . uh, what was the name again?"

Joel told him.

"Ah, yes! Here, Trevor, have a glass with me. This is some bloody drink, what?" he said, filling Joel's glass to the brim. "I'd say the Mexicans had found a way to distill the very fires of hell."

Taking a lick of salt, he threw down the tequila and bit into a quartered lime. His face turned alarmingly red and beads of sweat glistened on his forehead.

"*Aaaaah!*" he exclaimed and slumped in his chair. "It doesn't take much of that to get one quite pickled!"

He filled his glass again, but waited before drinking for the furnace within him to cool.

"What brings you here, Mr. Trevor?" he asked, trying to steady himself by locking both hands around the table's edge. "Why are you seeking out an old drunk Liverpool skipper?"

"I've got cotton to sell," Joel answered.

Captain Amberson's lower lip protruded and his shoulder gave a great shrug. "A damn fine cargo. Your bloody civil war caught our English mills by surprise. They're begging for the stuff."

"Do you want it?" Joel asked.

123

"I do indeed, sir," Amberson said, gazing hungrily at the oily liquor that filled his glass.

"How much will you give me a pound?"

"Ah, would that I could, sir," Amberson said, "would that I could!" He went through the ritual of salt, tequila, and lime again. "But I've fallen on hard times and haven't a farthing. Happen I was caught short in the melee at Galveston and had to move out with only half my crew and without my return cargo. Already paid for, it was, too. That's the sad state of affairs as brings me destitute to this hell hole. And what brings you to this tropical Garden of Eden, Mr. . . . uh?"

"Trevor," Joel said. "As I told you, I've got cotton to sell."

Amberson shook his head. "Ah, yes, I remember. It's these spirits that becloud the memory. I ask you, Mr. Trevor, why is it that the hotter the country, the hotter its food and drink? Now take England, for example. Nowhere on that misty isle can a bloke find so much as a chili pepper . . . not a single, solitary one. One would think that the good Lord in His infinite wisdom would have endowed the place with a bit of something that could set a fire in your belly and raise a sweat on your face. It would be an immense comfort in the bloody dead of winter. But, no! He bestowed peppers on lands where they're bloody well not needed. The farther south you sail, the more peppers you find. I quite imagine the bleedin' equator is ringed with them. Now what do you say to that?"

Joel had nothing to say. He made a move to rise, since he desperately needed to unload his cotton, and he could see he was getting nowhere with the drunken captain.

He had reached the cantina door when he heard Amberson calling his name.

"Come back, Mr. Trevor. Please dally a moment

longer. Perhaps . . . just perhaps, we can strike a bargain."

"What have you got in mind?" Joel asked, returning to the table.

"Let me have your cotton. I've an empty ship and I don't fancy staying in Bagdad forever. Let me have your cotton shall we say on consignment . . . on speculation. I'll take it to Liverpool and sell it."

"You mean just turn it over to you and wait for payment?"

"Aye," Amberson said.

"And what guarantee do I have that you'll be back?"

"My word."

Joel shook his head. "No deal. I can't take that chance."

Amberson nodded slowly. His bloodshot blue eyes estimated the remaining drinks in his bottle.

"Thanks anyway," Joel said.

Amberson poured himself another shot. "I don't blame you, my friend," he mumbled. "I wouldn't take the chance myself. But you'll be back. I'd bet my bleedin' life on it. You'll . . ."

The liquor overwhelmed him in mid-sentence. His eyes flickered twice, then closed. Slowly, very slowly he seemed to fold up as his head came to rest on the table top. In another instant, the cantina reverberated with his hoarse snoring.

Joel heard a sound behind him and surmised it was the proprietor approaching to throw the captain out but when a voice—husky, accented, familiar—called him, he turned and saw her in the doorway.

"*Lenore!* My God, I can't believe my eyes!"

"So it *is* you, Joel," she said, smiling with delight. She wore the same green and gold velvet dress Joel had first seen her in back in St. Mary's. "I heard gossip there was a gringo by the name of Trevor in town, and I prayed it would turn out to be you."

125

She slipped her arms around his waist and kissed him lightly on the lips.

"You're supposed to be in Vera Cruz," Joel said. "Homer Post gave me the word."

"We *were* supposed to be in Vera Cruz," she replied. "I waited too long to return to New Orleans; so I hitched my wagon to this falling star." She indicated the snoring captain with her fan.

"Amberson?"

"The same," she said. "This is as far as we got. A year ago I set out to see the world. In that time I've enjoyed the pleasures of St. Mary's and Bagdad . . . and not the legendary Bagdad, as you can see. It's getting to the point that I'm afraid to go on."

Joel laughed. "Well, I'm glad you put in here. You're the only bright moment in an otherwise god-awful day."

"You're so sweet, *chéri*." She stood back at arm's length. "Well, let me look at you. You look marvelous, still handsome."

"And you're more beautiful than ever," Joel said. Then he laughed again. "Listen to us! Talking as if we haven't seen each other in years, and it's only been a couple of months."

"It seems like eons!" Lenore said. "The captain and I sailed right here from St. Mary's. I keep watching the bay for another ship to take me away, but there's been nothing, nothing at all. Just our own *Aeolus* lying out at anchor. And you, Joel? What brings you here with all that cotton? I saw two steamboats down at the river."

"It's a long story, Lenore."

"Well, don't tell me here. Let's go somewhere for dinner. There's a café down by the river. The food isn't *haute cuisine*, but it won't kill you either, and that's more than I can say for other places in this town."

"What about Amberson?" Joel asked.

Lenore shrugged. "Let him sleep, *pauvre bête!* He has a great sadness."

126

"What's that?"

"An empty ship and no place to go."

Joel put his arm around Lenore's waist, and she led him off to the café, where they had an acceptable, if not exactly sumptuous, meal.

"How I long for a glass of cold champagne!" Lenore mused as they toasted their reunion with raw *pulque.* "Even a *ballon de rouge* or a taste of absinthe would do. This Mexican poison will kill you in the end."

But she drank the liquor neat and let Joel pour her another glass.

"Now tell me, *mon cher,* why you have come to Bagdad?"

As Joel recounted his story, Lenore listened and nodded in sympathy. "*Hélas,* the captain is correct," she said at last. "From what I've heard, you may be here months before another ship sails in."

"Amberson wants me to turn the cotton over to him. He says he'll sell it in England and bring the money back to me."

"Have you any other choice?" she asked.

Joel shook his head. "It appears not."

"But you don't trust the captain?"

"I don't even know him."

"But you know me . . ."

Joel studied her without replying. He could see she was up to something. Her eyes were bright and alive.

". . . and you trust me, do you not?"

"Of course I do," he said, understanding at last.

"*Mervilleux!* Then *I* shall be your agent!"

"I'll be goddamned, Lenore. It's loco, but I believe it would work!"

"It's not loco at all, *mon cher!* I'll sail with the captain and keep him honest!"

Joel jumped up from the table. "Come on, Lenore. Let's sober up Amberson. I want to get that cotton loaded and on the high seas by the next tide."

Arm in arm, they hurried down the rutted street toward the cantina where Amberson slept.

"And I'll see that he gets the best price," Lenore said, breathless at the pace Joel forced her to match.

"And don't come back with an empty hold," Joel instructed. "Buy things I can sell across the border . . . weapons, ammunition, medicine—whatever you can get."

"Like laudanum, morphine?"

"Exactly! And don't forget luxuries. They're going to be in short supply. Laces, silks, shoes. I'll be able to sell all that at a good profit."

"Oh, Joel! This is so exciting! England! At last I'm going to see the world!"

12

*. . . to inform you, my dear Enrique, that the
Señor Trevor, was seen here this very day by my
own eyes loading a vast quantity of cotton aboard
his riverboats, the Azucena and the Estella, These
boats then departed for Bagdad, where, I feel certain, their cargoes will be transferred to ocean-
going vessels.*

*Because of your interest in the matter I thought
it my duty to write . . .*

Enrique didn't need the letter from Felipe Rodriguez
to alert him to Joel's actions. The day before, he had
ridden out to see for himself what the vaqueros had
called the trail of snow.

From north to south, along the path traveled by
Joel's train of carts and wagons, stretched a line of
fleecy cotton lint clinging to the brush and grass.

"They passed this way several days ago," one of
the vaqueros informed him.

"And they'll be back again," Enrique predicted.
"But this time we will be ready for them."

When Joel returned home from Bagdad, he sat with
the others in the lacy shade of a lone mesquite and

sipped lemonade that Emma had made. Rudy lounged against the tree trunk, braiding four strands of rawhide into a reata, as the vaqueros had taught him. Emma shelled beans into a basket on her lap. Anne lay on a blanket on the ground entertaining Davey with a *bolita* Joel had brought back from Mexico.

Joel had already informed Rudy of the risk he'd taken in Bagdad, and the tense silence that fell between them extended to Emma and Anne.

Lighting up a stogie, Joel gazed out over his ranch, feeling satisfied that he had done quite well in only a year. The caliche-block house had been joined by another a short distance away, built by the vaqueros to house Rudy, Emma, Davey, and the new baby that was on the way. A bunkhouse for the hands stood off to the back. A dozen head of domestic cattle were in the corral, and there were chickens and goats, and a flourishing garden. In the last month the men had dug a new well, deep enough to assure them a constant supply of sweet water.

Suddenly, the enormity of his gamble struck him, and rising, Joel left the group, uncomfortably aware of their eyes on him. He just might have thrown all this away, he realized, and he felt guilty at chancing the well-being of those who depended on him. But he had had no time to consult them, to warn them, to ask their opinions. He'd had to act; there was no other way. Still, he felt blameworthy and somehow underhanded. Recalling Rudy's stunned disbelief when he told him he had entrusted the entire cargo of cotton to Lenore and an English skipper he'd only just met, he wished he'd kept the details to himself.

Davey began to fret, and Anne picked him up and walked around with him in her arms. Pointing to a butterfly that flitted above a clump of sage, Anne tried to quell his cries.

Emma waited until she considered Anne out of earshot. Then, putting down her basket, she asked Rudy what was the matter.

Answering in German, Rudy gave Emma the details of what Joel had told him.

Emma's amazement matched Rudy's. "Has he gone mad? What will become of us?"

"I don't know," Rudy answered.

"He'll lose the ranch for sure."

"I think so," Rudy said. "But we must bide our time. Perhaps the next owner will need a foreman and we won't have to move."

"I always thought him shrewd," Emma said. Her voice was laced with scorn and indignation. "Imagine! Entrusting everything to a dirty whore!"

Anne continued to walk Davey back and forth, but her ears had picked up the conversation, and her German was keen enough for her to understand.

Later that evening, when Rudy and Emma had retired to their own house, Anne asked Joel, "Papa, what is a *whore?*"

Joel looked up, surprised. "Where did you hear that word?"

"It's bad, isn't it?" Anne said. "I thought so."

"Who told it to you?"

"I heard Emma say it. She said it in German. *Hure.* But I looked it up."

"It's pronounced *hore,*" Joel said, "and it means 'harlot.' "

"Oh," Anne said, and she nodded. She knew that word from the Bible.

Joel waited a moment. When Anne didn't pursue the point he asked, "What was Emma talking about?"

Anne shrugged. "Oh, nothing. I just heard her say it."

"Annie, you're not being completely truthful."

Anne chewed her bottom lip. "If I tell you, you won't think I'm a tattletale, will you?"

131

"I can see something's bothering you, and I think we ought to talk about it; that's all."

"Well," Anne began, "Emma said you had entrusted everything you own to a . . . a *Hure*." Somehow, it sounded better to say it in German.

"I see," Joel said. "Well, come here and sit down beside me. I think we ought to talk it over."

He explained it to her as well as he could, about the loan, the cotton, the skipper, and about Lenore.

"So she really is . . . one of those," Anne said.

"I suppose," Joel said. "But she's also a lady, . . . a lady who's been very kind to me and who is trying her best to help us out of a fix. I trust her and like her, and you will too if ever you meet her."

"Can I someday?"

"We'll see."

I'd love to meet a *Hure,* Anne thought, but she did not say it aloud.

"But I want you to remember something, Anne: People are what they are, and not what others say they are."

"I'll remember."

"See that you do. Someday, when you're older, it may comfort you."

Once again Ramiro Rivos's Chihauhau carts inched their way southward through the brush country scattering their trail of snow.

The drivers lubricated the wheels and axles with the thick succulent leaves of nopal cactus, but the shriek of wood turning on wood carried for miles. For over an hour, Enrique de Leon and a score of vaqueros had been listening to that sound growing louder, coming nearer.

The day was sultry. A strong south wind caught the dust raised by the carretas and billowed it high into the air, where it formed a hovering hazy yellow cloud that trailed them across the prairie.

132

Enrique studied the cloud and the wheels' ear-splitting squeals and decided the time had come.

"Cover your faces with bandanas," he ordered his men. He would not be riding with them, and he wanted the deed carried out exactly as he'd planned. "I want none of you recognized. It must look like the act of *bandidos*. No one must know I am involved."

The men nodded and masked themselves. They re-checked their rifles and each one soaked a torch in a cask of coal oil.

"I want as little bloodshed as possible," Enrique said. "But the carretas must be completely destroyed."

He sat high in his saddle and peered past the vaqueros, waiting for the moment when the lead wagon would lurch into view.

The men watched Enrique. A spark of excitement flashed among them as they saw him nod. One torch was lit, and from it the others.

"*Ataca!*" Enrique shouted.

The mounts sprang forward. Rifle shots rang out above the wagonwheel's cry.

Enrique tightened his reins to control his nervous stallion. The dust was so thick he couldn't see the action, but soon the hazy yellow cloud changed hues, turning white with puffs of gray and black. The stench of burning cotton reached his nostrils, as bright orange flames leaped high into the air.

A smile of victory curled Enrique's lips. "I've beat you, Mr. Trevor!" he cried. "Soon your little pocket of land will be mine!"

He jerked his stallion about and spurred him back toward the Lantana hacienda.

When Joel heard the news, he and Rudy rode out to survey the tragedy. The wagon train was utterly destroyed. It stretched along the prairie like the charred bones of a giant serpent. A few remaining cotton bales still smoldered. Three men had been killed; four

133

others had been wounded, including Ramiro Rivas, who had been carried back to his ranch and was being tended by his wife. The other drivers had scattered, some to Rivas's ranch, others to safety in the concealing brush; but one had walked all night to bring word of the disaster to Joel.

"Poor Rivas," Joel said as he scanned the length of the burned-out wagon train. "This has wiped him out. I'm going to have to find a way to make it up to him."

"It wasn't your fault," Rudy said. "It was bandits."

"Bandits, hell!" Joel muttered. "I know damned well who it was."

"Enrique de Leon?"

"It had to be," Joel said, his voice dark with anger.

"What do you aim to do about it?"

Joel shrugged helplessly. "What can I do? I've got no proof it was de Leon. Even Rivas's own drivers think it was bandits. Besides, de Leon's got enough men to supply an army. What could the few of us manage against him?"

Rudy was secretly relieved, but he was anxious to find out how the destruction had affected Joel's finances.

"I reckon this has put you in a fine spot too," he said.

"That's not the half of it," Joel said. "I've got more cotton warehoused up in East Texas. Lots more. But now there's no way to get it down to the Rio Grande. And the worst part is that goddamned bank note I've got staring me in the face down in Mier. The first payment comes due the middle of September . . . a month and a half. If Lenore and the captain don't come through on time, I'll be selling my saddle."

You'll be selling, Rudy thought; but he kept silent and let Joel ride on down the line alone.

"Well, let's go see Rivas," Joel said when he rejoined Rudy. "We'll see if there's anything we can do for him. Then I'm going to mosey on down to Bagdad and wait for that boat to come in."

13

Bagdad had changed. The boom had begun. On his arrival, Joel counted eight ships at anchor. At the water's edge, laborers perched on scaffolding were laying a roof beam of a sizable warehouse, and streets that only recently had been dusty and deserted were now busy with people.

Joel managed to find a room behind the cantina where he'd first met Amberson. Stowing his gear, he rode down to the dock. A British schooner had just unloaded, and Joel joined the haggling traders examining its cargo. Under the blazing Mexican sun, bolts of cotton cloth lay side by side with cases of rifles and boxes of amunition. He saw medicines and silks and hundreds of pairs of shoes. There were pots and pans and beribboned Paris hats. The traders were swarming over the cargo, fingering the fabrics and examining the rifles. They bid furiously against each other, and when a purchase was made, watched carefully as their men packed the goods into waiting carretas and hauled them away.

"Here you go," a broker said, catching Joel's eye. "Cloth from Nimes, strong and durable. It'll wear like iron. I'll let you have it cheap."

Joel shook his head.

"You're making a mistake, my friend," the broker said. "A bolt of this will bring you fifty dollars across the river."

Joel had no doubt. Fifty dollars at least. He desperately wanted to get into the action, and he cursed his lack of money.

"Don't pass it up," the broker advised, but already he was looking past Joel for a more promising customer.

"Do you know anything about the *Aeolus?*" Joel asked.

"What's that?" the man asked, annoyed at the interruption.

"The schooner *Aeolus*. Captain Jack Amberson is the master. Have you heard any news about her?"

"Don't go waiting for her," the broker advised. "She won't be carrying anything we don't have here. How about shoes? Is that what you're after? Or morphine?"

Joel shook his head and moved on.

Again and again he asked about the *Aeolus* and Amberson as he wandered about the waterfront. The reply was always the same. Finally, an English sailor overheard his inquiry.

"Aye, I know the ship," he said. "A three-master out of Liverpool, is she not?"

"That's right," Joel answered. "Do you have any news of her?"

"I saw her myself," the sailor answered. "She'd run aground just off Land's End."

Joel's heart sank. "Are you sure it was the *Aeolus?* Maybe it was another ship. . . ."

"It was the *Aeolus* all right," the sailor said. "I recognized her master, Amberson, bawling orders from the bridge."

"Was she damaged bad?" Joel dreaded the sailor's answer.

"She was listing to port," the sailor said, shrugging. "More than that I can't say. Could be she sailed free

137

in the next tide. Could be she broke up in the gale that was headed her way. All I know is that I last saw her helpless as a beached whale."

Joel left dockside in misery. He knew he should be trying to drum up business for his riverboats, which were due in the next day. He figured he could recoup some of his losses by persuading the traders to ship their wares at least as far as Roma, if not Laredo. But his heart wasn't in it. He didn't care if the riverboats stood empty. Perhaps it would be better if they did, since he didn't have the money to pay the crews, and they would be deserting him soon.

Well, let 'em! Joel thought. Let 'em take the god-damned boats too! If they don't, the Banco de Mier will!

Suddenly, a violent trembling shook his body, and staggering, he clutched a nearby cart to keep from falling.

"Borrachín," the owner of the cart said knowingly, and he and a companion laughed at seeing a gringo drunk so early in the day.

The shaking ceased as abruptly as it had struck, but Joel was left with an odd lightheadedness. Drifting back to the center of town where old men and boys passed the time in the meager shade of the dilapidated plaza, he looked about for a vacant bench where he could rest. A cold sweat had covered his body, and he felt overcome by an intense lethargy.

I'm tired, he thought . . . tired of scrambling, tired of worrying. And for the first time he regretted his decision to move to Texas and settle down. It had brought only misery: Martha was dead and Anne was growing up motherless—and fatherless most of the time, he admitted. Now all his grand schemes were slipping down the drain and he was powerless to prevent it.

He tried to empty his head of his worries, but they crowded in on him like insistent voices whispering in

138

his ear as he circled the plaza looking for a bench. The benches were all occupied. Old men sitting cross-legged and silent watched him as he passed. Gone was his silky, feline grace; he moved like an invalid, his face ashen beneath his tan, and his hands shaking uncontrollably.

I'll go to the cantina, he thought. I can rest there. I'll get something to drink. I hope I have enough money to get drunk. Maybe that'll make me forget . . . at least for a while.

He awoke on his cot and saw, through the window, that the sun was at high noon. The room was stifling and smelled of sickness, and his body was drenched with sweat. He tried to rise but was too weak to lift his head from the hard little pillow. He had drunk his share of liquor in his time; and he'd often paid the price, but never had he suffered as much as now. A hammering in his brain sent white lights of pain across his eyes, and his bones ached as if he'd been bucked by a horse.

Gradually he became aware of another presence in the room.

"Who's there?" he managed to murmur.

An old woman in black raised her heavy body from a stool in the corner and approached his cot. She soaked a rag in a bowl of water and draped it over his forehead.

"What happened to me?" he asked. His voice was thin and weak.

The woman held a finger to her lips, signaling him to keep quiet. "Malaria," she said.

"How long have I been here?" he asked, and when she didn't respond, he asked in Spanish: *"Cuánto tiempo?"*

"Tres días," the old woman replied, extending three fingers for him to see.

"Three days!" he breathed. "Malaria!" He realized he'd been unconscious all that time.

Again the woman motioned for him to be silent. She changed the damp rag on his forehead and resumed her vigil from the stool in the corner.

He slept the rest of the day and all the following night. The next morning, after drinking the thin soup the woman brought him, he felt strong enough to leave the cot. Despite her protests he staggered to the door. The overhead sun dazzled his eyes and the heat of midday nearly overwhelmed him. He stepped out into the street, moving slowly, gingerly, for every movement threatened to exhaust him. Checking his pockets, he came up with four cents—enough for a lemonade on the corner. He stumbled uncertainly toward the plaza where the vendors set up their carts.

From across the street he heard someone shout, "Hey, mate!"

Joel ignored the voice and moved on slowly toward the plaza.

Again: "Hey, matey, it's you I'm calling! The one who was asking after the *Aeolus!*"

Joel stopped and looked up. Squinting against the blinding noonday glare, it took him a moment to realize the man across the street was the sailor he'd spoken to the day he arrived in Bagdad.

"You *are* the same bloke, ain't you?" the sailor asked. Seeing Joel's ravaged face now made him unsure.

"Yeah," Joel answered in a voice that was husky and ragged. "Yeah, I'm the one."

"Well, she's heading in," the sailor said.

"She what . . .?" Joel began. His aching brain was too befuddled to comprehend.

"She must have floated off that bar right nice," the sailor said. "The *Aeolus* is sailing into port like the beauty she is."

Joel's heart drummed in his chest, and forgetting

his weakness, he began hobbling toward the shore.

They've come back! he thought. They didn't skip out and they didn't sink! They've come back just as they said they would!

He reached the low bluff above the wharf. Beyond stretched the green waters of the sea. And there, slipping into harbor, her sails billowing like the white Gulf clouds behind her, was the *Aeolus!*

Joel threw back his head and bellowed a roar of victory. Sailors and tradesmen stopped what they were doing and gaped in astonishment at the wild man doing a feeble Indian war dance on the bluff, waving his Stetson in the air and shouting at the top of his lungs at the docking schooner.

Lenore was appalled by the sight of him. Over his protests, she made Joel return to his cot in the little room behind the cantina.

"There's time enough for business later," she said, dismissing the old woman and taking her place on the stool beside Joel. "Now you must rest. You look weak as a kitten."

Joel watched her as she squeezed out the wet rag and laid it on his brow. She had never been more beautiful. England and the sea air seemed to have deepened the blue of her eyes; and Joel realized the color of her cheeks and lips was natural, not painted. She wore her hair in loose waves now, and it fell about her bare shoulders with an abandon that made him want to take it and crush it in his hands. Her blue silk dress was, she assured him, the "height of Paris fashion," and her yellow leather boots "fit for a duchess."

He fell asleep with her image in his mind. When he awoke he was afraid it had all been a fever dream, but as soon as he opened his eyes, Lenore was again at his side.

"How do you feel?" she asked.

"Better. Much better."

141

"You slept soundly and your fever is gone." Her fingers lightly stroked his forehead, brushing his thick shock of hair out of his eyes. "Here is some cold tea. Can you sit up?"

"Yes," Joel answered. "I feel much stronger."

She helped him up and brought the glass to his lips. He drank greedily, feeling that he'd never been so thirsty in all his life.

"You look stronger, too," Lenore said. "I think I see some color in your face again."

"Hell of a way to welcome you back," Joel said.

"Don't worry about it. Just get well."

Later, Lenore brought him some soup and coffee. Joel sat on the edge of his cot to eat the soup and talk to her.

"I was afraid you and Amberson wouldn't make it back," he said.

"Poor goose," Lenore replied. "I promised you we'd return."

"A sailor told me you'd run aground."

Lenore pursed her lips in disapproval. "The captain was, shall we say, in his cups. He made a slight error. It was nothing, really. We sailed free on the next tide. After that I kept his rum from him and made him promise not to touch another drop until we reached Bagdad."

"Where *is* Amberson?"

"He's supervising the unloading. He's desperate for a bottle of tequila, but I've forbidden it until the cargo is on the dock. I'm sure he's being a perfect tyrant to the stevedores."

"You're a powerful woman, Lenore."

She smiled proudly. "I know how to get my way."

Joel finished the soup and sitting back against the pillow, sipped his coffee.

"Eh bien," said Lenore, "don't you want to know how we fared?"

"I've been afraid to ask."

142

"Never fear, *chéri,* we couldn't have done better! The captain drives a hard bargain. He had cotton brokers kneeling at his feet. Thirty cents a pound!"

Joel closed his eyes in relief.

"And we didn't return empty-handed," Lenore went on in a voice bright and happy. "We loaded on such a cargo I'm astonished we didn't sink beneath the waves. Oh, Joel! Just wait till you see! There's fabric, hundreds and hundreds of bolts; guns and ammunition for the whole Confederate army, it would seem. Opium, quinine, bandages. And we even found room for a bit of silk and lace."

Joel caught her hand and held it. "We're rich, Lenore!"

"*You're* rich, Joel. The captain and I only want our fair fee. What does a skipper want with money? And I . . . I've never been so happy. I'm seeing the world!"

Joel's strength returned rapidly. Whether it was because of his good fortune, his delight at seeing Lenore again, or his own robust constitution, he didn't know; but before the week was out he was able to go across the river, where he haggled with the quartermaster at Fort Brown. He managed to sell him all of the arms and medicine the *Aeolus* had brought in at prices he would not have imagined possible.

Despite protests by Lenore and Amberson that he was giving them too much, he paid generously for their efforts. He placed an order with a wagoner in Bagdad for a dozen carretas to replace those lost by Rivas. And still he had the silks, the cottons, the shoes, and laces to haul back across the border to sell for top dollar in San Antonio.

Throughout the week, Amberson had stayed blissfully drunk in the cantina. On his own last night in town, Joel took Lenore to a little *fonda* beside the river where they dined on quail and beans and rice and warm tortillas.

143

After dinner he reached across the table and took her hands. Her eyes sparkled in the candlelight, and he smiled to see that the Spanish wine they'd shared had brought a flush to her cheeks.

"We could get a room here, Lenore," he said. "Would you stay the night with me?"

"I'd love to, Joel. I've dreamed of you every night I was away." And taking his arm, she accompanied him as he went to rent a room.

Upstairs, in the room lit by soft glowing candles, Joel stood behind Lenore and unlaced her corset. It fell along with her petticoats to the floor. Gently he turned her around. His fingers caressed the creamy flesh of her breasts, and he bent to kiss her on the eyelids, the lips, and the neck. His arms circled her waist as he pulled her close to him.

"Men adore undressing women," Lenore whispered in his ear. "But they never seem to realize that women would enjoy undressing them."

Her fingers traced the outline of his chest beneath the rough fabric of his shirt. Carefully, as if picking violets, she unfastened his buttons one by one, teasing him, tantalizing him with her slowness until his shirt fell open. She pushed it back over his shoulders, brushing his bare skin with her fingertips.

Her hands went to his belt and released the buckle. Then, kneeling before him, she undid the buttons of his trousers.

When he stood naked before her, her lips touched his inner thighs and set him aflame. He picked her up then, to carry her to the bed, and she was soft against him, pliant and willing. Her perfume—the scent of woodland flowers, of damp moss and sweet grass— enticed him. He was a youth again, lying naked on a river bank in a Tennessee valley. There was sun in his eyes, and a spring breeze, cooled by a distant mist, wafted over him.

Moaning with pleasure, he took her to him. Lenore's

eyes fluttered and closed as she let her head sink deeply into the pillow and abandoned herself to him.

A mockingbird sang from a branch in the morning air outside their window. The Gulf breeze was still cool at that early hour, and Joel and Lenore sat together side by side in their bed sipping hot chocolate brought to their door by a servant girl.

"I wish you would stay with me, Lenore," Joel said. "By the time this war is over, I'm going to be a rich man. I could give you everything you ever wanted."

Lenore smiled wistfully. She moved closer to him, resting her head lightly on his chest, and said, "If there was ever a man I thought I could settle down with, Joel, it is you."

"Would you come with me?" Joel asked. "Would you try it . . . at least for a while?"

Lenore sighed. "I love you, *chéri*, really I do. And I wish I were the kind of person who is happy to stay in one place. *Hélas . . .*"

Joel stroked her dark hair and spoke softly. "I used to be restless too. I used to think that roaming was the only life for me."

"Maybe some day, *mon cher*," Lenore said, but her voice lacked conviction, "after I've seen the world . . ."

"Do you love Amberson?"

"No . . . but he's promised me Paris, Marseilles, Rio, and Venice. I can't pass it by. Please don't hate me for that."

Joel drew her to him. But her eyes already reflected the look of the sea, and he knew it was useless to try to change her mind.

Later, Lenore watched as Joel's boat steamed away up river. She stood on the bank and waved farewell until it rounded the bend and disappeared. Then she dried her tears and turned back toward town to rejoin Amberson.

145

Within a week a messenger on horseback had delivered a letter to Enrique de Leon's hacienda. It began:

Yesterday the norteamericano, Señor Trevor, arrived in Mier and satisfied the obligations of his loan. I thought you would be interested in this news . . .

Enrique read no further. Cursing, he crushed the paper in his fist.

1864

14

"You look like a general!" Anne said, admiring Joel in his uniform of Confederate gray.

"Only a captain, Annie," Joel told her, as she made a final adjustment to his sash of yellow silk, "And I feel foolish in this getup. I don't know why I can't fight the Yankees in leggins and vest like I'm used to."

"Quit bellyaching, Papa! You look wonderful."

When Joel turned to study himself critically in the mirror, he hardly recognized his own reflection. He shook his head and muttered, "A goddamned tin soldier! I never thought I'd be wearing this uniform. And I wouldn't be either, if the Yankees hadn't taken to raiding all the ranches in these parts. What do they expect to gain? We got nothing of any use to them . . . just wild cows and mustang horses they can't get within a mile of. I heard they burned the Sanchez place not fifty miles south of here."

"Do you think they'll ever attack up this far?" Anne asked.

"That's the reason I'm in this cornball uniform," Joel replied. "And that's why I'm rounding up that sorry lot of ragtag soldiers. Poor sons of guns! There isn't a man among 'em between fourteen and sixty. All the ablebodied men left these parts when Rudy did. And half of them have been wounded, killed, or captured. I've been beating the bushes all the way from the Nueces to Laredo, and all I can scare up is boys and grandpas. Some army!"

"Well, at least they're willing," Anne said, trying to appease him.

"Willing, hell! I had to threaten to string 'em up if they even thought about deserting."

"You wouldn't, really—would you?"

Joel shook his head. "No," he said quietly. "Most of them are the last menfolk left in their households. I can't blame them for slipping off now and then to see how their women are doing."

"Well, you don't have to worry about Emma and me while you're gone," Anne said.

Joel looked at his daughter and smiled. Anne had grown up fast, he realized. At sixteen, she was already a young woman, tall and strong with long limbs and the grace of a lynx. And she was beautiful, with hair that was thick and fair. She wore it loose, and when she galloped along beside him, with her blond mane flying in the wind, catching the sparkle of the sun, she made him think of a fine, high-spirited palomino. Her face had taken on an angularity not unlike his own, with a determined chin and prominent cheekbones; and the tanned darkness of her complexion seemed to accentuate the vibrant green of her eyes.

Over Emma's objections, Anne dressed in pants—leather breeches, the kind Mexicans wore; and she was happier in a peon's humble *camisa* than in the fine silk blouses Joel imported from France. Her boots—made in Mexico, fine-tooled, and the color of ox blood—were an extravagance. She owned a dozen pair.

She was strong-willed and stubborn. Joel had long ago learned, as had Emma, that he couldn't make her bend to his wishes. So he sharpened his powers of persuasion and hoped for her cooperation. Still and all, she was a constant comfort to him, and as she matured he grew to rely on her more and more.

Since Rudy's departure, Emma had become more nervous and irritable than ever. Rudy, who had been gone a year, was serving under Taylor in Louisiana. His infrequent letters told of hardship and deprivation, of southern soldiers fighting among themselves for clothes and boots off dead Yankees, of maggoty food, and of disease that had to go untreated because there was no longer any medicine. And he wrote of how much he longed for home.

Rudy hadn't wanted to go, but in the end it had been a choice of serving the Cause or taking off for Mexico. A band of Germans from the hill country had camped one night on the ranch. They had urged Rudy to join them on their trek to the other side of the Rio Grande. They planned to found a community and to stay in Mexico at least until the war was over . . . perhaps forever. Rudy had been tempted. But Emma was pregnant and could not travel. Reluctantly she had agreed that he should go on alone; she would join him later, after the baby was born. Still Rudy had hesitated, fearing her tears and wrath—until, in another week, he had been called on by a recruiting team. There was no way out; Rudy had been forced to don Confederate gray.

Rudy had never seen the son that was born the day after he left, and in his absence, Emma had grown fat and slovenly. With three babies to care for, she found little time to devote to Anne. Anne, in consequence, had grown independent and self-confident.

"You'll take care of things?" Joel asked, reaching for his rifle.

"Don't worry," Anne said. "I can handle the vaqueros."

"I want a new corral built . . ." he began.

"I've already got the men started," Anne said. "And I think I'll have them build a bigger bunkhouse. They're about to bust the walls out of the the old one."

Joel studied his daughter for a moment; then he smiled. "I won't worry about a thing."

She walked with him to his horse. He swung up into the saddle, and leaned down to kiss her good-bye.

"See you soon, Annie."

"Don't get shot," she said, pretending to scold when she felt like weeping.

Joel laughed. He spurred his stallion and led his army of children and old men toward the southwest where he'd heard the Yankees were camped.

Joel's gray eyes scanned the horizon and picked out the thin ribbon of black smoke rising high into the still air.

"Moreno!" he called to a stoop-shouldered Mexican corporal, old enough to be his father.

Moreno rode up to his side. *"Mande, Capitán,"* he said. He was native to the area of their encampment and was serving as Joel's guide.

"Whose land is this?" Joel asked.

"It belongs to an *hacendado* named Luis de Vargas. It's called the Ebonal," Moreno replied.

"From the looks of that smoke, I'd say the Yankees have been at work."

"Sí, Capitán," Moreno agreed.

"Take Salinas and Willard," Joel said. "Scout ahead and find out what that smoke's all about. We'll lay low here till you report back. Be careful, don't let yourselves be seen. The Yankees may still be around."

Two hours had passed before the men returned. In the interval the smoke turned pale gray, then vanished from the sky altogether.

"A burned-out house," the private named Willard reported. "Nothing but rock walls and ashes."

"Outbuildings?" Joel asked.

"There was a few still standing," Willard answered.

150

"Mostly shacks. The others was burned along with the house."

"Any sign of life?"

"Not that we could see. 'Course we didn't venture too close."

Joel nodded. "We'll ride on over. Maybe there are provisions in those outbuildings we can use."

He ordered the men to break camp. They mounted and formed up behind him.

As they rode up to the Ebonal, thin wisps of smoke still curled up from the embers of the hacienda's ruins. A motherless calf bawled beside the body of a dead cow in what had once been a pen. Except for the calf Joel's men could see nothing living—not a dog, a pig, or a goat. An ominous silence hung over the place.

Joel was on edge, wary. He sensed something wrong. "There must have been a lot of people living here . . . a place this size."

"Maybe they got away before the Yankees hit," one of the scouts suggested.

"I hope so," Joel said.

But a shout from one of his men alerted him that a body had been found in the charred remains. In the next few minutes the troops discovered seven more, all men, three in the ashes and four in the high brush beyond the outbuildings.

Joel watched from his horse as his guide, Moreno, rolled one of the bodies over. A shock of recognition jolted Joel as he stared into the lifeless face.

"Who was that man?" he asked.

"The *patrón*," Moreno replied. "The owner of the hacienda, Luis de Vargas."

Although he'd seen the man only once, Joel remembered him well: the bald head, the heavy jowls, the thin lips that had curled cruelly as he raised his pistol and fired a bullet through Joel's shoulder. And the eyes! The dull agate eyes that now stared, unblinking in death, at the cloudless sky.

151

"But for you, my wife might have lived," Joel murmured.

"What's that, Capitán?" the scout asked.

"Nothing," Joel answered. "I was just thinking out loud."

As Joel continued to stare into the dead face, he did not attempt to suppress his feelings of vengeance and vindication.

You tried to kill me once, you bastard! Joel thought. And you thought you had! I ought to leave you to the buzzards and coyotes!

But, reining his horse away, he called out to his men and ordered them to dig a trench to bury the bodies.

The marauding Yankees had left several outbuildings untouched. Already the men had broken into the larger ones and were dragging out bags of corn, salt, and sugar; and a cheer went up when a couple of young privates rolled out a barrel of rum.

"Load those provisions on the chuck wagon," Joel commanded. "We'll ration out the rum tonight. I guess there's none of you so young and so feeble that you wouldn't benefit from a little nip."

Then he dismounted and made his way over to another of the outbuildings, the heavy oak door of which sagged on rusty hinges. He gripped the well-worn wooden handle and tugged. The door resisted. When he pulled again, applying all his weight, the door cracked an inch. Giving another yank, he swung the door wide open.

He flinched with alarm, for even as he peered into the darkness, he knew that he was in danger. There had been a sound, a tiny click of a hammer being cocked, and he saw the dull glint of a pistol aimed at his face.

He thought he was a dead man. In the space of a heartbeat he dropped to his knee and whipped out his

152

revolver. Then he heard a cry, a woman calling his name.

"Señor Trevor! No! Don't shoot!"

But his reflexes had taken command and he fired. The report of the revolver filled the small stone building. He heard a scream, then the sound of someone falling as a pearl handled pistol skittered harmlessly in the dust at his feet.

From all over, his men came running to his aid, but Joel already knew that the danger had passed—that there had, in fact, never been any danger at all. He rushed into the building and knelt before the prostrate figure. He turned her over and gazed into her face.

"Oh, my God!" he breathed, recognizing her pale features.

Putting his arms around her, Joel lifted her gently from the stone floor. He carried her out into the daylight, leaving a trail of blood as he walked.

"Who is she?" one of the men asked.

"Her name is Sofia," Joel answered grimly. "She saved my life one time."

He laid her out in the shade of a lone oak tree.

"Is she dead?"

Joel didn't answer. With trembling fingers he cut away her blood-soaked blouse, searching for the wound, terrified of what he might find.

Then her eyes fluttered and opened. Once again she uttered his name. "Señor Trevor!"

"Thank God!" he murmured in relief. The bullet had creased her side, just below the armpit; but the wound, though bleeding profusely, was superficial.

"Get some alcohol! And bandages!" he shouted. "Quick!"

A private ran for the medicine kit.

"You'll be all right," Joel said, holding her close, trying to stanch the flow of blood with his hand.

But Sofia had fainted again and lay limp in his arms. The private sprinted back with the kit, and Joel

153

cleaned the wound and bound it tightly with clean cotton bandages. Then he removed his shirt and wrapped it around her.

Sofia was fully conscious now, though her face was white with pain.

"I'm sorry," Joel said again.

She tried to smile, to reassure him.

"Don't try to move," he told her. "You'll be all right. It's only a flesh wound."

She nodded her understanding and lay quietly in his arms beneath the oak. One of the men brought her a cup of rum. Joel held it to her lips as she drank. Slowly color returned to her cheeks. Though she was still in pain, she managed to sit up and talk with him.

Recalling the time she brought the curandero to him, Joel said, "This is a hell of a way to show my gratitude."

"It wasn't your fault," she said.

"I saw the pistol barrel. I shot without thinking."

"Don't blame yourself. How could you know?" She smiled at him again, letting her eyes linger on his face, the face she'd dreamed of constantly ever since the first time she'd seen it. His deep gray eyes seemed beautiful to her. The phrase "Killer Gray" was a term her people used for all gringos, referring to their eyes. But even in the brief instant when he had dropped to his knee and fired his revolver, she had seen no trace of killer in his eyes. She remembered once thinking how inappropriate that appellation was, with regard to him; and she had often imagined how warm his gray eyes would be as he held a woman he loved.

"I thought it was the Yankees," Sofia explained. "I thought they had come back."

She looked away toward the trench the men were digging to receive the bodies.

"How many dead?" she asked.

"Seven."

"My husband too?"

154

"Who is your husband?" Joel asked.

"Luis de Vargas. This is his hacienda."

Joel was stunned. Sofia saw the shock on his face.

"We were married the day after he shot you," she said. "It was my father's doing. I had no choice."

Joel stared at her dumbly. He couldn't imagine her in Luis's arms, and hated the man even more for having possessed her.

"Is he among the dead?" she asked again.

Joel nodded.

A bitter smile crossed her lips. "I'm glad," she said. "I hope he is in hell!"

A pallet was prepared for Sofia in back of one of the wagons.

"We'll take you to your father's," Joel said. "There's nothing left here for you."

"There never was," Sofia replied. "I was a prisoner—Luis's prisoner, my father's pawn. When word reached us that the Yankees were near, everyone fled—everyone except Luis and a few of his men. I begged him to let me go with the others. But he was afraid that once I got away from the Ebonal I would never come back. And he was right. I would have gone to Monterrey, where I have relatives who would have hidden me. I would never have returned. So he kept me with him to the end. And when the Yankees came, he locked me in one of the granaries—even in the face of death I was his prisoner. How I loathed him! And how happy I am to be free of him forever."

The journey to Don Enrique de Leon's hacienda took a day and a half.

When they arrived at the Lantana, Sofia, who still lay in the wagon, asked, "Is everyone dead here as well?"

Joel was riding beside her. "The house is standing," he told her. "And the little shacks behind it."

"Do you see anyone?"

Joel was about to answer no when he saw a movement, a man with a rifle running between the house and the stable. Joel barked "Halt!" to his troops.

"Sofia," he said, "you've got to call out to them. They're armed and probably think we're Yankees. Call out and tell them who you are, otherwise they'll start firing at us."

He reached into the wagon and helped her to sit up.

Her eyes searched the landscape. They were quite close to the hacienda and it looked strangely deserted and vulnerable. The stables beyond were empty of horses. Even the dogs that ordinarily roamed the dusty paths between the collection of *jacales* where the peons lived were nowhere to be seen.

"They're gone," she said.

"No!" Joel said. "They're here. They're just hiding. I saw one of your father's men a moment ago. Call out to them before they start shooting."

Sofia cupped her hands and shouted. *"Oiganme! Soy Sofia! No tiren!"*

Silence greeted her call.

"Again," Joel said.

But before she could speak, a fusillade broke out from the hacienda and the stables. Bullets cut the air between them.

"Is he crazy?" Joel cried. "Letting them shoot at his own daughter!"

Sofia screamed and huddled in the wagon bed. Joel's men dropped to cover.

"Fire!" Joel yelled to his men, jumping from his horse and scrambling behind the wagon.

Rifle answered rifle from both sides. The burning smell of gunpowder filled the air. The sound of gunfire deafened Sofia.

Inside the house, behind the grillwork of a first-floor window, Enrique emptied his rifle and reached out for another one, freshly loaded.

156

"But, señor!" his aide protested. "Your daughter is there! I heard her call."

Enrique, who had recognized Joel, tore the rifle from the man's hands and took aim.

"Señor! Your daughter!"

"She has taken up with gringos. She must take her chances with them!"

He fired toward the wagon where he had seen Joel take cover. Wood splintered an inch above Joel's head.

Joel dropped to the dirt behind a wagon wheel and balanced his rifle on one of the spokes. He saw Enrique now, a shadow behind the grillwork.

Enrique's gun barked twice more, striking the wagon in a close pattern. Sofia screamed again, her cry rising above the sound of rifle fire.

"You son of a bitch!" Joel shouted. "You'd kill your own daughter for a chance at a gringo!" He squinted down his barrel and took aim.

Inside the house, Natalia ran screaming into the room where Enrique was barricaded. *"No, Enrique! Por Dios!"*

She tried to wrest the rifle from him. He wheeled about and struck her savagely, sending her flying against his heavy mahogany desk.

Joel saw Enrique move, saw him twist and turn. His finger squeezed the trigger.

Inside the hacienda, Enrique doubled over. His rifle clattered to the floor, as he slumped to his knees and finally sprawled at Natalia's feet in a spreading pool of blood.

She stared at him aghast, as if she were seeing a monster. His eyes, glassy in death, turned sightless to the ceiling.

Natalia looked away abruptly. "Command them to stop!" she told the aide. "There must be no more killing!"

The man ran from the room, and in a few moments, the gunfire ceased.

157

Joel waited warily, not sure if the battle were over or if Enrique's forces were merely pausing to regroup.

Finally, there was a shout from the lower window, and Sofia recognized Natalia's voice, calling her name.

"Tía Natalia!" she cried back, raising her head above the wagon's side. *"Soy yo, Sofia!* I've come home! I'm with friends. Tell the men not to shoot!"

After a moment, the heavy front door swung open, and Natalia burst out, followed by three of her servants. Raising her long black skirts, she ran toward the wagon. Tears streamed down her cheeks and she cried Sofia's name over and over.

Already a handful of Enrique's men appeared from their hiding places behind the hacienda. Their rifles were held at their sides to assure Joel and his troops they would not shoot.

As Natalia reached the wagon, she extended her hands and touched Sofia's face. *"Mi vida, mi corazón!"* she wept.

Her arms went around Sofia in an embrace, and Sofia cried out in pain.

"You're hurt!" Natalia shrieked. "They attacked you!"

"No!" Sofia said. "It's nothing. I am well."

Natalia turned to one of the servant girls and ordered: "Go find the curandero. Tell him Sofia has need of him."

"Take her to the house," Joel said to the corporal in charge of the wagon.

Natalia walked alongside the wagon, still clutching Sofia's hands.

"Why did they shoot?" Sofia implored. "Did no one hear me?"

"It was Enrique," Natalia replied. "He must have gone mad!"

"Where is he now?"

Natalia's silence told her everything.

Joel watched Sofia carefully. Her pale face was a

mask, revealing little. Her somber dark eyes remained dry as, slowly, they studied the facade of the hacienda, then drifted over to the stables, the granaries, the storehouses, and the cluster of rude shacks where the peons lived. They took in the slaughterhouse, the pigpens, and the corrals. They lingered briefly over the gardens, then swept the horizon from east to west.

Joel saw Sofia straighten her shoulders and admired her for suppressing a wince despite the pain in her side.

At last Sofia spoke. "Then, I am now *la patrona?*"

Natalia nodded sorrowfully.

Sofia extended her hand to one of the vaqueros. "Help me down."

With his aid she left the wagon and climbed the steps of the long arched porch, where she stood, proud and beautiful. "Now stable the horses. See that they are curried and fed," she told the man. "Señor Trevor, you and your men are welcome in my house. Please enter as my guests. Come, Tía Natalia! We must see that a meal is prepared."

She waited until Joel had climed the steps and stood beside her.

"Once you were turned away from this door," she said. "It will never be so again."

She took his arm and led him into the foyer.

That night Joel lay in a great canopied bed. The mattress was soft down and the sheets were scented with the fragrance of sunlight and spring air. He watched the dancing circle of light cast on the ceiling by the oil lamp at his bedside, and his thoughts were of Sofia.

Who is this woman? he wondered. She seemed to be made of both iron and lace.

In the ruins of her husband's ranch he had looked into her eyes—those eyes like embers—and had seen

159

the soul of a vulnerable woman, one who had lived in helpless sorrow, used by Enrique and tormented by Luis. She'd seemed so frail—as fragile as a china doll with her pale, transparent complexion and thin shoulders. Yet he had also seen her temper and her bravery —when she had ridden to his aid with her curandero on that terrible night long ago. And he thought about the look on her face when she had learned that Enrique was dead and that she was now the mistress of the hacienda. In the space of an instant she had transformed herself from wounded refugee to empress— capable of holding the reins of her father's vast estate. She had issued orders coolly and confidently. Throughout dinner her aunt—so recently her *dueña,* now her subject—looked to her for decisions and advice.

But, most of all, Joel remembered the slight gesture Sofia had made before descending the wagon to assume her role as *patrona* of the Lantana: the squaring of her shoulders as if to better accept the burden, and the effort she made to hide the pain from the bullet wound, even as it clouded her eyes and whitened the corners of her mouth.

While she was showing Joel to his room after dinner, Sofia had said, "I hope you will be comfortable here," and handing him the oil lamp, had added, "Thank you for everything." Then she had kissed him quickly on the cheek and had stepped back into the shadows of the corridor.

He could still feel the fire of her lips on his cheek, and the rustle of her silk skirt echoed in his mind. He had felt the impulse to reach out for her, to take her by the hand and draw her back to him, but she had vanished into the darkness without looking back.

Joel leaned across to the bedside table and blew out the oil lamp.

From her bedchamber across the courtyard, Sofia watched the window of his room until the light behind the louvered shutters went out. "Come to me, my love," she whispered into the night air that lay between them. "Come to me!"

15

Joel confessed to Sofia that it was he who had shot her father. She accepted the information without a word, and when he tried to tell her he was sorry, she pressed her fingers to his lips, silencing him.

"You saved my life," she said. "There is no reason to be sorry."

Joel and his men were about to depart, and Sofia's heart was heavy. She found herself praying that God would intervene to prevent Joel from leaving. But after only three days, Joel ordered his men to saddle up. They were setting out for the Rio Grande to join forces with the already legendary Colonel John Ford and the Cavalry of the West.

Joel knew as they rode away from the hacienda that his fever was returning, for he had awakened before dawn in a cold sweat. His bones were aching already, and the sun felt like coals on his head. But he hoped that the bout would be mild and that he could hold out at least until they met up with Ford. By noon, however, he realized he could go no further.

He called his sergeant over to him. "Murray, the malaria's coming back. I can feel it."

"We got no quinine, Captain," Murray said.

"I know. I'm going to have to ride back to the

hacienda. They'll take care of me there. I want you to take the men and join up with Ford."

"You want someone to go along with you?" Murray asked.

"No, I can make it on my own if I ride fast."

"You're looking pretty flushed."

"I know," Joel said. Sweat streamed from his forehead and soaked his bandanna. "I think the fever's already hit me."

Calling for his orderly to bring him pen and paper, he scrawled a message to Ford, turning his men over to the colonel. Then he signed it and handed it to Murray.

"I'll rejoin you when I get my strength back," Joel told the sergeant. "Till then, may God be with you." And he began to ride back to the Lantana.

The *brasada* seemed limitless. Time and again Joel thought he saw the dark shape of the hacienda shimmering on the horizon, only to have it vanish like smoke at his approach. The fever weakened him, and in the end he had to tie himself in the saddle to keep from falling. Long before the sun dropped low in the west, he emptied his canteen of its last drops of tepid water. Once he came upon a twisting arroyo. He stopped and let his horse drink from the brown trickle that moistened its muddy bed. His throat was parched and his lips were swollen; he yearned to lie on his belly and drink alongside his horse, but he dared not untie himself and drop down out of the saddle, for he knew he would never have the strength to climb back up.

He rode on, shaking with fever, nearly delirious with thirst. His mind wandered. For a time he thought he was back with his troops. He imagined Sergeant Murray and the guide, Moreno, were at his side.

"It's cold, Murray," he said. His teeth were chattering and he had to grip the pommel to keep his balance. "I'm shivering all over. Don't we have a blanket?"

But Murray's specter merely stared at him with its good eye.

Joel imagined he heard Moreno say, *We are lost, Capitán. I do not know this terrain. The hacienda is not here.*

"Ride on," Joel said. "We have to find it."

It's too late, Capitán. We must turn back. Look! Darkness is coming.

Joel stopped his horse. The fevered delirium left him suddenly. The sun was setting, turning the sky above to copper. He shook his head to clear his thoughts.

Then he saw it! Just breaking the flat horizon was the red-tiled roof of the Lantana hacienda. His spurs dug feebly into his horse's flanks. The horse walked slowly forward until, finally sensing a barn up ahead with hay and water, it broke into a trot. Joel swayed in the saddle, gripping the pommel with weakened fists. As the house loomed before him, Joel saw lights in the windows and heard the clang of the dinner bell. His horse was galloping now, out of his control, its hooves thundering over the hard ground. Joel pitched forward up against its mane. The reins flew from his hands and over the horse's head, dangling free for a moment before snaring one of the front hooves. Joel heard the bone in the horse's foreleg snap—a loud crack like a pistol shot. Then he and the animal plunged headlong into the chaparral.

"I know this man," Casimiro said.

"You have a good memory," Sofia replied. "He is the one I took you to on a dark night long ago."

"I remember," Casimiro said. "His wife was sick and he had been wounded."

"Can you help him now?" Sofia asked. Holding a lamp beside the bed, she watched as the aged curandero raised Joel's eyelids and gazed into his unseeing eyes.

"He is very sick," Casimiro replied. "Feel how he burns with fever."

"Please cure him, Casimiro," Sofia whispered.

The curandero reached into his leather pouch and withdrew a bundle of dried herb. "Brew this as a tea. When it is cool, give him one cup in the morning and one again in the night. And let him drink one glass of well water every hour. Do this for three days."

He closed his pouch and headed for the door.

"*Gracias,* Casimiro," Sofia murmured.

"*A sus órdenes; señora,*" the curandero replied. Then he bowed gravely and hobbled from the room.

Sofia turned to a servant girl. "Take these herbs and make tea as the curandero said."

Then, alone with Joel, she sat beside his bed and bathed his fevered brow with cool water from a bowl on the night table.

He slept, but his sleep was troubled. She could see his eyes flickering beneath closed lids, and she wondered what tortured dreams played out their scenes within his brain. She wished she could get through to him, to calm him, to reassure him that he was safe in her house, that he was secure in her care. She wanted to take him in her arms and comfort him as a mother would a child, as a lover would a beloved.

Once he cried out the name Anne. Her heart felt the stabbing pain of jealousy and she wondered who Anne might be.

Then, in his sleep, he extended his hand. She took it in hers and gripped it tightly. It seemed to comfort him, for his breathing became regular and a look of calm came over his face.

She stayed with him, did not leave his side, even for meals, for three days, and tended to him as the curandero had instructed.

At last the fever broke. Sofia summoned her maids and had them dress the bed with fresh sheets. She called two of her men up to the room and waited outside in the corridor while they sponged Joel's body and dressed him in a clean nightshirt. Then she sent for Casimiro.

The old curandero knocked quietly at the door. Sofia bade him enter. "Look," she said. "I think he will recover."

Casimiro bent over Joel, putting a hand to his forehead. Joel's eyelids fluttered and he found himself looking up into the old man's bearded face. In the lamplight the curandero's hair glowed like a white halo.

"How do you feel, my son?" Casimiro asked.

Too weak to answer, Joel merely nodded.

Casimiro straightened and turned to Sofia. "He will be strong again, señora."

Sofia sighed with relief; tears welled up and wet the dark circles under her eyes. *"Gracias a Dios!"* she exclaimed. "And thanks to you, Casimiro."

She knelt at his feet and pulled a ring of turquoise and silver from her finger.

"Here, Casimiro! Wear this and remember my gratitude."

Casimiro bowed to his *patrona* and slipped the ring onto his finger.

"Now give me your blessing," she asked.

Casimiro laid one hand on her head and drew a cross in the air with the thumb and forefinger of the other. "May God grant you happiness, my daughter. Go in peace."

Of his illness Joel remembered very little, but he recalled regaining consciousness from time to time and seeing Sofia's face hovering above him, her dark eyes clouded with concern, her brows knit with worry. Her lips appeared almost bloodless, and her cheeks were pale as ivory. Then one day, feeling the sun streaming across his bed, he raised his lids and saw her smiling down at him. Her eyes were lively and bright. The sunlight striking her cheeks intensified their rosy glow. And he felt his hand clasped in hers.

"You're going to be well," she said. "My curandero has saved you."

"How long have I been here?" he asked. His voice was weak and she had to lean close to his lips to hear.

"This is the fourth day," she said. "You were terribly sick. I was so afraid . . ."

"I'm obliged to you," he whispered; and once again she had to lean close to hear, so close that a wave of her dark hair brushed his cheek and he could feel the warmth of her skin near his.

Releasing his hand, Sofia rose and glided across the floor to the window. As she stood looking out, she was silhouetted against the light, and Joel saw once again how incredibly beautiful she was. His emotions were stirred—gratitude and appreciation, but there was more. . . . He lay against his pillow and watched her, saying nothing, grateful for her presence, delighting in her beauty and grace.

After a moment she turned and said, "It will be evening soon and the air will be cool. If you feel strong enough, we can have tea in the courtyard."

"I would like that," Joel said.

"I'm going to change for evening," she said from the doorway. "If you need anything, there is a bell beside your bed. You have only to ring and I'll be here."

With a rustle of silk she was gone, and the room, though it was filled with sunlight, seemed suddenly gloomy and vacant. Glancing at the beside table he saw the little silver bell. He reached for it to examine it, but his grip was weak and it fell from his fingers. It rang out as it clattered to the tiled floor.

Instantly Sofia reappeared.

"I'm sorry," he said. "It was an accident."

She stooped to retrieve the bell. Then, at the door

167

once again, she said, "I won't be long." And she hurried off to oversee the tea preparations.

Joel's strength grew with the passage of days. Soon he was able to join Sofia on short walks around the Lantana.

"My great-grandfather was granted this land by the King of Spain," she told him. They were strolling through a carpet of daisies and pink buttercups on the bank of a nearly dry creek. "In those days it was terribly dangerous here. The heathen Comanche killed my great-grandfather, but his son remained and built the house we live in now. Slowly he acquired many vaqueros, and when he died my father inherited it. Now the Lantana is mine. My father had no sons, you see."

"I have no sons either," Joel said. "There's only my daughter, Anne."

"Anne!" Sofia whispered. So, it was his daughter he had cried out for in his delirium! She felt greatly relieved. There wasn't another woman, after all!

Joel's eyes swept the scene from the grand hacienda and the cramped *jacales* to the far horizon. "Someday I hope to build a ranch like this," he said.

Sofia fell silent. As they had paused beneath the yellow blossoms of a *huisache* tree, Joel studied her face. Once again she had donned her mask. Her face was like an ivory carving.

"A penny for your thoughts," he said.

Sofia looked startled, breaking the mask. Then she laughed. "Nothing! I was thinking of nothing!"

But she had been wishing he would sweep her into his arms. She wanted desperately to hear him say that he loved her and wanted her to be his wife. If only he would ask her, everything she had could be his— the hacienda, the ranch, all of the Lantana's riches. And most of all, she herself would be his—forever! If only he would ask!

But Joel was silent.

"And you?" Sofia asked hopefully. "What are you thinking?"

Joel frowned, his gray eyes looking south. "About the war. About my men and how I'm going to have to be rejoining them soon."

"No!" Sofia cried, and Joel saw that she had suddenly turned pale. "Not yet!" She was immediately ashamed of revealing her emotions. "I . . . I mean you have not yet fully recovered. You need more rest."

"I'll be strong enough in a couple of days. Then I'll have to go."

A terrible ache gripped Sofia's heart. So little time! Why couldn't he forget the war? He was not well. Couldn't he just stay on with her and let the rest of the world take care of itself?

But when she looked up into his eyes, she saw the determination that filled them, and she knew that nothing she could say would persuade him to stay.

The sunlight fell in a golden haze about them, but for Sofia the day had turned leaden and cold.

16

"You must've dropped twenty pounds," Sergeant Murray told Joel, surveying him with his one good eye.

"I've never been trimmer in my life," Joel said.

"Trim, hell! Downright skinny I'd say. Hey, Cookie, bring the captain some chow! We gotta put some meat on them bones if he aims to fight the Yankees!"

"What's the situation?" Joel asked. They were sitting outside a canvas army tent about ten miles upriver from Brownsville. The July day was hot and humid. A strong breeze swept inland from the Gulf, pushing blue-bellied clouds westward. All around them soldiers camped, stripped to the waist, huddling in what meager shade could be found.

"Well, the Yankees are holding Fort Brown tight," Murray informed Joel. "We've been skirmishing off and on ever since we joined up with the Cavalry of the West. Hell, it's been a goddamned tug of war. Old Rip Ford thinks one more effort oughtta do it. The Yankees are tired and we seem to be getting our second wind."

"How are things down at Bagdad?" Joel asked.

"*Así así,*" Murray replied, indicating ambivalence with a wave of his hand. "I'd say they're trading pretty good. Ever' once in a while the Yankees bottle up the river, but between us and the Mexicans it's been pretty much open. I see your boats making regular runs—cotton one way, Lord knows what all the other. How many you got on the river now?"

"Eight," Joel said. "Had one more, but it blew up off Roma."

The cook brought Joel a tin pan of steaming stew with hard biscuits on the side.

"It ain't fancy fare," Murray said, "but it's hot and it'll keep you from starving."

"Texas beef," Joel said, sampling a spoonful.

"Tough as shoe leather," Murray agreed.

"Tell me about John Ford," Joel said.

"In the first place, they call him Rip," Murray said. "Kind of funny how he got that nickname. It seems he'd send in his casualty lists signed at the bottom 'Rest in Peace, Ford.' Then casualties started coming so hot and heavy he got rushed for time; so he started abbreviating. He signed 'em just plain 'RIP Ford.' Well, the men at the other end of the line read that and took it for his first name, and Rip it became."

"Tall tale," Joel laughed.

"Puredee truth," Murray swore. "Anyway, he's a helluva man, a helluva leader. I know men who wouldn't follow no other but him."

It turned out that Colonel Rip Ford and Joel had a couple of things in common: Both had gone to cabin schools in Tennessee and both suffered from bouts of malaria. But Ford was also a medical doctor and a lawyer to boot. He had been in his time a journalist, a state senator, a mayor of Austin, and captain of the Texas Rangers. And he was one of the profanest men Joel had ever met.

He sat across the campfire wearing a black fedora sporting the emblem of the Confederacy. His boots were scuffed and dirty, and the shoulders of his gray tunic carried the insignia of a colonel, although no-

171

where was he carried on official Confederate rolls, a snub that didn't bother him at all.

Ford was a big, handsome, ruddy man of about fifty, with a gray beard and sharp blue eyes that glittered in the campfire light.

"Things would look a goddamn' sight rosier if the fucking Mexicans would get their house in order," he bellowed. "Any damn' fool knows one civil war on a hemisphere is plenty enough. Naw, they got to go and start one up themselves. Them and the jackass French with that German emperor they set up in Mexico City. *Maximilian!* Now ain't that a high-tone' name, I ask you!"

He laughed heartily and readjusted his battered cavalry fedora on his head.

"So you're the Captain Trevor who so generously provided me with another group of snot-nosed boys and palsied baldheads to fight the goddamn' Yankees? Well, I won't hold it against you. Matter of fact, I'm pleased to meet you."

He reached across and gripped Joel's hand.

"I've heard a lot about you, Colonel," Joel said.

"Lord, I don't doubt it!" Ford exclaimed. "And I've heard a lot about you. Damn' smart of you to get in on the riverboat trade when the getting was good. Made you a rich son of a bitch, I imagine."

"It's a good business."

"That's the only way to get through a war. Though I have to admit, I do relish the smell of battle."

"Do you reckon we'll be hitting at the Yankees again soon?" Joel asked.

"Hell, I hope so! My butt ain't used to camp stools. I'm aching to get back in the saddle. Besides, that horse's ass General Herron and his bluebellies are making deals with that greaser Cortinas to shut down river traffic again. That ought too piss you off right smart, Captain Trevor!"

172

The Cavalry of the West pushed toward the coast. Whooping the rebel yell, Ford's ragtag troops tore into the Union forces, sending them fleeing in disarray back into Brownsville. The Texans were eager for pursuit, champing at the bit for the opportunity to drive the Yankees once and for all into the Gulf. But Ford held them back.

"What the hell do they expect to fight with?" he asked Joel. "We've outrun our supply line again, and that *Cabrón* Cortinas won't sell me ordnance this close to Union guns."

"How about upriver?" Joel asked.

"Oh, he's willing to do business upriver, but then it'll take a week or more to haul the supplies down here—time enough for the Yankees to get their backs up again."

"I can do better than that," Joel said.

Ford's blue eyes studied Joel. "What have you got up your sleeve, Captain Trevor?"

"Not up my sleeve, Colonel—on the river. I've got eight steamers plying between Bagdad and Roma. Your supply sergeant and I ought to be able to track down one of them in no time."

"Do you reckon you can get back here with the ordnance in a couple of days?"

"With any luck," Joel answered.

"Luck's a fickle whore, Captain," Ford said. "Don't trust her. Go on—take my sergeant and get back here with the goods as fast as you can. I feel the fever coming on again. It won't be long before I'm too goddamn' sick to fight."

Joel and Sergeant Wentworth left within the hour. Traveling light, they caught up with the *Estella* before sunset. They hailed the boat, which was carrying a shipment of cotton downriver, and waited on the shore as the captain reversed the paddle wheel, bringing the steamer to a stop mid-river. Leaving his horse with Wentworth, Joel waded into the muddy water and

173

swam to the boat. Deckhands reached over and hauled him aboard.

The skipper, Caleb McCann, met him on the lower deck. "Mighty neighborly of you to come a-calling, boss."

"This is all business, Caleb," Joel said.

"Didn't figure you caught up with us by chance. What's up?"

Joel explained that since Ford and his men needed supplies, he had offered to take his boat upriver to get them. "That means we've got to turn this tub around," he concluded.

"Ain't no way we can do it here, boss," Caleb said. "The river's too damn' narrow. It widens up a bit about ten miles down."

"It'll be dark by then," Joel said, studying the river around them. "That'll kill another day. We've got to come about here."

Caleb's face clouded. "It's your boat, Mr. Trevor. But I'm against it. The wind's too strong. It'll push us on the bank, sure as shootin'."

Still, Joel was determined. "How much line have you got aboard?"

"Plenty," Caleb answered.

"Good. Now first of all, let's dump this cotton."

Caleb stared at him as if he were crazy. "You know what this load is worth?"

"Last I heard, about a dollar ninety a pound. But Cortinas isn't interested in cotton. He won't take anything short of silver pesos. Now tell your men to dump it."

"Maybe we can float it to shore . . ." Caleb suggested.

"We don't have time. Dump it!" Joel ordered.

Then Joel stood at the stern and watched thirty thousand dollars worth of cotton sink beneath the swirling waters of the Rio Grande.

"That's the last of it," Caleb said, joining Joel. He

174

looked mournful enough to cry. "Most expensive meal that river ever ate."

"All right now, here's how we're going to turn this boat around," Joel said, and he explained his plan.

Having briefed Caleb in what was to be done aboard the boat, Joel returned to his horse and swam it back across to the Mexican side of the river, where three deckhands were waiting on shore. Sergeant Wentworth remained on the Texas bank with another three hands. Eight long ropes stretched from the *Estella* to each of the men. Another eight lay slack at water's edge.

The sun had set and Joel estimated they had perhaps another half hour of twilight.

"Let's go!" he shouted impatiently to McCann, but it was a long several minutes before the skipper sounded the whistle signaling he was ready.

The paddle wheel began churning slowly, roiling the brown river water. Almost immediately the lines jerked tight, zinging through the gloves of the men who struggled on shore. For a moment, Joel feared they couldn't hold on, but his men dug their heels into the bank, making deep ruts in the mud, and gripped the rope. On the other side, Wentworth and his crew worked in opposition.

Shouting orders, Joel reined his horse backwards, pulling until he was afraid that the rope connecting him to the boat would snap.

"Stop the wheel! Stop the wheel!" he yelled, almost ready to concede that McCann was right, that the operation couldn't succeed. But just at that moment he saw the boat slip sideways in the middle of the river—a slight movement, but perceptible.

The men worked the lines, pulling on one side of the river, holding taut on the other. The boat slid further sideways, moving more easily now, impelled by its own inertia. Then the wind caught it.

Its drift quickened, sending it toward the shallow water of the Texas bank. Joel spurred his horse backward, urging his men on. The ropes pulled tight, lifting high out of the water. But by now the wind had caught the boat broadside.

"She's going aground!" Wentworth shouted across the river. "She's going!"

Cracking like a whip, Joel's own line snapped and curled high into the air like a flying snake. His men who had been dragged waist-deep into the river, felt their ropes break one by one as the boat slid into the bank. The hull struck bottom and the decks shuddered with the impact.

It's over! Joel thought. She's crippled! She'll lie there in the mud until the next rain raises the river . . . if the current doesn't tear her apart first. He was heartsick and disgusted. McCann had been right. He should have played the sure thing. One day wouldn't have made that much difference after all; and it was a damned sight better than never getting through.

But then he heard a cheer from the boat. He looked across and saw that the impact had caused the *Estella* to rebound. McCann had engaged the paddle wheel, turning it violently in reverse. Slowly the steamer was inching away from the bank, back out toward the middle of the river.

"Grab those slack lines!" Joel shouted, swinging low in his stirrup to retrieve one himself.

On the other side, Wentworth and his men were doing the same. Working against each other, they pulled and held taut. The *Estella* continued to come about; and as the last of the violet light left the evening sky, her bow pointed upriver.

Joel took his bandana and wiped the sweat from his face. McCann was tooting the boat's whistle furiously. Using the lines, the deckhands pulled themselves hand over hand through the water back toward the *Estella*.

Joel slumped in his saddle, exhausted. He breathed

176

deeply, trying to still his racing heart. Again, McCann signaled triumph with the whistle.

Joel smiled, closing his eyes with a weary happiness. "Well, Rip Ford," he murmured softly, "what do you think of that fickle whore now?"

17

With the supplies Joel provided, Rip Ford and his Cavalry of the West pressed on toward Brownsville. The Yankees fled before the Confederate troops, crossing the Boca Chica to Brazos Island, where Union ships waited at anchor to carry them away.

Ford and his men entered a strangely quiet Brownsville to find the town securely in the hands of Confederate civilians. Joel sat in the saddle and saluted as the Stars and Bars were raised aloft, but his thoughts were far away: with Anne and his ranch, and with Sofia. He was weary of war and longed for life as it had been before secession.

That evening, gripped by a return of malaria, Rip Ford collapsed, but in the days that followed, by sheer force of will, he continued to command the cavalry from his sickroom. Joel waited until Ford was on his feet again before he asked for leave.

"You deserve it if any man does," Ford replied. "Hell, without those goddamn' supplies you pried out of Cortina upriver, we'd still be camped out in the brush. Anyway, I don't reckon we have much to fear from the Yankees anymore. Word has it there's only about a thousand of 'em holed up on Brazos Island.

Naw, the Yankees don't bother me. So, pack up and go home for a while."

Joel thanked Ford and left the headquarters. He stuffed his belongings into his wallet and strapped it to his saddle.

"Will you be gone long, Captain?" Sergeant Murray asked.

"I don't know," Joel said simply.

An hour later, he rode away north.

On the afternoon of the third day, he faced a decision. Up ahead, not six hours distant, lay his ranch. He longed to see Anne again. Her frequent letters had reached him regularly in Brownsville, and he knew that everything was well with her. She and Emma managed to work together; the vaqueros were giving her no trouble. "In fact," she wrote in her latest report, "they jump at the sound of my voice. They know I can outride, outshoot, and outcuss the best of them!"

So there was no urgent demand for his presence there—he might be missed, but he wasn't really needed.

On the other hand, if he took the turning to the left and headed northwest, another day's hard riding would take him to the Lantana and Sofia.

He knew she loved him. Her eyes had declared it. Every gesture had spoken clearly. But he was unsure of his own emotions. Was it mere loneliness, he wondered, that now made him long to see Sofia? Was it the forlorn sadness in the eyes of the whores in Bagdad that set him to thinking about his own solitude? Or was it Lenore—the absence of Lenore?

He honestly didn't know.

There were still a good number of sunlit hours remaining in the day, but Joel dismounted and made camp. He ate a meager supper and waited for the long, warm night to end.

At dawn, he saddled his horse and took the turning to the left.

179

18

Sofia wore a dress of taffeta, as gray and sleek as the feathers of a dove. Somewhere, a servant had found for Joel a black *charro* suit, heavily embroidered with silver thread. Sofia's dark hair, plaited and worn close to her head, was crowned with a wreath of yellow daisies. Joel was hatless and he too wore a band of flowers. A garland of lavender verbena, woven by Sofia that morning, had been wound about their waists and bound them together in a love knot.

Kneeling in the chapel of the hacienda, with Natalia and the servants looking on, they were married by the priest from the mission at Palo Pinto.

The couple dined alone that evening on silver plates —the servants had retrieved the dinnerware from the tunnel that ran beneath the house, where they had hidden it from the Yankees. There was quail and white wing, saffron rice, and cheese. Red wine from Bordeaux filled their crystal goblets, and a sweet peach brandy waited in a decanter surrounded by snifters of blown glass as thin as soap bubbles.

The servants swept in and out, elusive shadows on silent feet. In the courtyard a single guitar strummed softly, sweetly. Sofia sat across from Joel, the candlelight burnishing her face and reflecting as a thousand golden sparks in her dark eyes. Her pink lips glistened. Her cheeks were rouged only by the headiness of the wine.

Joel raised his glass to drink, but paused with its rim to his lips, captivated by her loveliness. He set his wine down untouched and slid his hand across the damask tablecloth. His fingertips brushed hers, feeling fire. She clasped his hand and pressed it to her lips.

They rose, abandoning the meal, forgetting the brandy, and together they climbed the stairs. Arm in arm they walked the length of the long corridor.

The bridal chamber had been readied for them. Perfumed candles flickered on the tables, casting soft, dancing lights on the walls and ceiling. The curtains surrounding the bed had been pulled back and tied with bows of yellow silk. Two crowns of pink roses rested lightly on the pillows.

Joel put his arms around Sofia and drew her gently to him. She offered her lips to him, but when they kissed he felt her body shudder. The stiff taffeta dress rustled like dry leaves as it fell to the floor. The silver in Joel's suit glittered momentarily before it joined the discarded dress. Sofia's flesh was warm against his. His fingers traced the curve of her back. Bending, he kissed her neck, tantalized by the gardenia scent she wore.

His lips found hers again and he kissed her hungrily. It had been so long! So long! He needed her urgently. He felt his heart race in his temples, his breath grow shallow and ragged. Quickly, he caught her in his arms and lifted her onto the bed.

Kneeling beside her, Joel caressed the silken flesh of her breasts, her belly, and her thighs. His fingers touched the soft mound of dark curls and stroked her.

Suddenly Sofia cried out and rolled away from him, leaving Joel to stare in confusion. A great sob shook Sofia's body and tears darkened her pillowcase.

Joel left the bed and knelt on the floor at her side.

Her face was pale with fright. Her bloodless lips trembled.

"Sofia! Sofia! What is it?"

She didn't answer. Instead she began to weep violently, covering her face with her hands. As he pried them away, he could feel the iciness of her fingers.

"What is it, my love?"

She opened her eyes and looked at him in desolation.

"Oh, no!" he whispered. "Sofia, surely I'm not the first?"

She shook her head miserably, tears still streaming down her cheeks. "No. No, of course not. There was Luis. But . . . but it was so . . . horrible!"

"Oh, Sofia!" he murmured softly. "Sofia!" He ran his fingers through her long dark hair.

"I love you so," she sobbed. "But I am afraid."

"Don't cry," he said. "Don't be afraid. I wouldn't do anything to hurt you." He dried her tears with the back of his hand. "Be calm and don't be frightened. We'll just lie here together side by side."

And he slipped back into the bed, pulling the sheet over them. Neither spoke for a while. Sofia's breathing grew regular, and for a moment Joel thought she had fallen asleep; but when he turned to look he found her eyes on him.

"I'm sorry," she said.

Joel smiled. "Don't be. I understand."

Then he felt her fingers touch his chest, tentatively, with the weight of a butterfly. He lay still while she explored his body. She brushed the dark curly hair on his chest and rested her palm there for a moment, sensing, in the rise and fall of his ribs, the increasing rapidity of his breathing. Then she traced the thin, silky line of hair down his midsection to his belly, pausing briefly before placing her hand between his legs.

182

A groan escaped Joel's lips and his back arched beneath him.

"Oh, Joel! *Mi querido!*" she whispered, and he recognized the breathlessness of rising passion in her voice.

Now she rolled over against him and her arms encircled his body.

"Please make love to me," she breathed. "I'm not afraid."

Joel was slow and gentle. He moved at her pace, revealing to her for the first time the sweet tenderness of love.

Later, in the deepest cavern of the night, Joel lay sleeping in her arms. The cry of an owl broke the silence of darkness and a soft breeze ruffled the gauzy curtains that surrounded the bed. Outside, heat lightning flickered across the sky, waking Sofia. She opened her eyes and studied Joel, whose body was illuminated by the silvery bursts of light.

Again hot tears streaked her cheeks, but they were tears of joy and happiness.

"Please God," she whispered, "bless us! Give us a long, long life together!"

19

Anne spun her horse to block a young steer that was trying to break loose.

"Alfonso!" she shouted to a vaquero standing by the cowpen. "Open the gate!"

The steer feinted to the left, then to the right, seeking its way clear, eyeing free pasture farther on, while Anne's horse danced back and forth trying to keep the steer in check.

"The gate!" Anne shouted again, but the vaquero's attention had wandered to the doorway of a nearby *jacal* where a young woman stood combing her long black hair.

The steer doubled back, then saw its escape. Anne jerked her horse to the left a split second too late, and the steer thundered past and charged into the high grass.

Anne's eyes flashed in fury. "Goddamn you, Alfonso!" she cried. She was barely able to restrain herself from bringing her whip down across his shoulders. "You son of a bitch! You let him go!"

Already two other vaqueros were riding off into the brush to try to retrieve the recalcitrant steer.

Anne's anger subsided as quickly as it had risen. They had been working hard all morning. It was time for a break. Walking her horse over to the house, she dismounted and headed toward the door. Emma stood on the porch holding Klaus, her youngest child, while Davey and his sister, Luisa, played at her feet.

Emma's lips were pursed in disapproval, and Anne tried to brush past her, sure of what was coming. But Emma's heavy bulk barred the door.

"It's not seemly to talk like that," Emma hissed, shaking her head and fixing Anne with a reproving stare. "A lady does not curse!"

"I only do what has to be done," Anne replied wearily, finding her way around Emma and reaching for the door. She had been in the saddle since before dawn trying to round up the cattle that had escaped during the night, for a sudden thunderstorm had spooked them into battering down a section of the newly built corral.

Emma followed her inside and continued to nag. "Such words! I don't know where you learned them. Never have I heard such language from the lips of a woman!"

"You've never seen a woman work cattle either," Anne retorted. Stripping her leather gloves from her hands, she dipped a cup into the bucket of water and drank thirstily.

"It's shameful to say such things," Emma harangued.

Anne wheeled about, anger and impatience bringing a flush to her cheeks. "Go home, Emma! Tend to your own house! I'll take care of mine!"

Emma's back stiffened. She gathered her skirts and flew from the room onto the porch. In an instant she was back. Her air of self-righteous hurt had vanished, and was replaced by a look of excitement.

"A coach, Anne! Heading this way! Come look!"

Anne put down the cup and followed Emma to the door.

A dark, enclosed coach drawn by six mules was lumbering through the brush and heading directly for the house. The two women stood side by side on the porch and waited with fascination.

A coach in this country! Who could it be?

The driver, a peon in dusty cotton pants and shirt, yanked on the reins and halted the coach a few feet from the porch. He swept his sombrero from his head and bowed from the waist, smiling broadly.

"Señorita," he said, addressing Anne. "I bring a message from your father."

"Papa!" Anne cried. Bounding down the three stone steps, she rushed to the coach.

The man delved into a brown leather box behind him and withdrew an envelope. Seizing it, Anne broke the wax seal. The paper inside was smooth and rich with the feel of real vellum.

This can't be from Papa, Anne thought. Where would he find paper like this?

But she recognized his handwriting immediately and began to read:

My dearest daughter Anne,

I have the best of news for you but want to tell you in person. I assure you it is a cause of joy.

I have sent this coach for you to carry you to the hacienda where I am staying. It will be a day's journey, so wear traveling clothes. But bring several of the fancy dresses I bought for you from the French traders at Bagdad, for this is a time for celebration.

I love you and am most eager to see you again.

Your devoted father,
Joel.

"Oh, Emma!" Anne cried, looking up from the letter, completely forgetting her previous anger at the woman. "It's good news! Papà writes of celebration! He must mean that the war is over!"

"Gott sei Dank" Emma shouted. She sank to her knees, clutching her baby close to her bosom. "Rudy will be home soon!"

186

"Papa sent the coach for me," Anne said. "I must go to him right away!"

She packed quickly in a flurry of excitement. Emma chose two Paris gowns for her, one of yellow silk with white lace and bows, the other a fine stiff taffeta that matched the green of her eyes.

"And shoes," Anne said. "—dancing shoes! I'll take the ones with silver buckles."

Emma wrapped them carefully and added them to the trunk.

"Oh, Emma, I'm so happy. The war is over! Soon we'll have Papa and Rudy back with us and everything will be the way it was before!"

Setting aside their dislike for each other, the two women embraced and kissed each other's cheeks.

"I'll be home soon," Anne promised, tears of joy glistening in her eyes. "I'll be home . . . with Papa."

The trip was long and hot. But shortly before sunset Anne felt the mules slacken their pace and heard the coachman call out that they had arrived. She leaned from the window and looked around. A large hacienda appeared before them, its windows thrown open, a crowd of peons and servants already gathering at the foot of the steps.

The heavy oak doors swung back, and Anne caught sight of Joel as he emerged from the shadows onto the wide, arched veranda.

Even before the coach rocked to a stop, Anne had the door open and stood on its running board. "Papa! Papa!" she shouted.

He looked marvelous, she thought, more handsome than ever! There was a look of happiness on his face that she'd not seen there since she was a child and had forgotten long ago. He waved at her and smiled.

The coach lurched to a halt in a cloud of dust. As Anne gathered her skirts and prepared to descend, a movement behind Joel caught her eye.

187

Sofia, dressed in midnight blue, wearing a lacy mantilla that cascaded like froth about her shoulders and reached to her waist, glided through the door and joined Joel. She slipped her arm through his. Joel looked down at her and smiled again. Then looking back at Anne, he pulled Sofia closer to his side.

Anne stood frozen on the running board. Suddenly, she knew the reason for his joy.

The war was not over! That wasn't what he meant at all!

Joel left the porch and greeted Anne beside the carriage. She let him hug her, but all the while she was staring over his shoulder at the woman who waited at the top of the steps.

"Anne," Joel said. "I'm married again."

"Why didn't you tell me first, Papa?" Anne asked.

"There wasn't time, my dear. But come. I want you to meet Sofia."

Joel led her up the steps and introduced the two women.

"My daughter," Sofia whispered.

Anne suppressed a flinch. She wanted to pull away and shout, "I'm not your daughter! My mother lies dead and buried, and I'll not have another." But Joel's eyes were on her, and she let herself remain in Sofia's embrace.

I won't have it! Anne vowed silently, breaking at last from Sofia's arms. I won't let her tell me what to do! or make any changes in my life!

Sofia and Joel both turned to enter the house, but Anne remained rooted to the spot, lost in her thoughts.

"Come, Anne," Sofia said. "Come into your new home."

"No!" Anne blurted. "The Trevor Ranch is my home. I won't live here!"

"Anne!" Joel said, frowning, perplexed. "What a bunch of nonsense! Of course the Lantana is your home now—as much yours as mine."

188

"No, it isn't," she said. "My home is on *our* ranch, the one we built together."

"But this is our ranch now," Joel said. "Sofia's and mine—and yours."

"Come, *mi vida*," Sofia said, extending her hand in welcome to Anne.

Troubled, confused, and hurt as she was, Anne realized it was futile to resist. She couldn't undo what her father had done. Nor could she turn on her heel, as she wished, and fly back to the little stone house she considered home. She began to fear that the freedom that had been hers for the past several years had suddenly slipped away, that her status had shifted from that of partner to subservient daughter once again. It would be a long time, she feared, before she was her own mistress again.

Sofia waited to escort Anne inside. But Anne ignored her outstretched hand and crossed the threshold on her own.

Late that night, unable to sleep, Anne roamed the long, dark corridors of the hacienda. She had the uneasy feeling that she was being watched. Time and again, as she rounded a corner or entered another of the vast, night-shrouded rooms, she thought she heard a sound, but when she turned her head and looked over her shoulder, there was no one there.

Finally she entered the courtyard and sat beside the splashing fountain. From the shadows of the arches she heard the rustle of skirts.

"Who's there?" she demanded, straining her eyes to peer into the darkness.

Doña Natalia appeared from the arches. A mantilla covered her head and she clutched a rebozo about her shoulders.

"You're restless, child," she said.

Anne recognized the old woman and rose in defer-

189

ence. "I found it hard to sleep. I'm used to my own bed."

Natalia approached and sat down beside Anne. All the while, her dark eyes were studying the girl's face, half-concealed by night.

"I've been followed," Anne said.

"It's only the servants," Natalia explained.

"I'm used to privacy," Anne continued. "In my own house, there's no one to watch me."

"Pay them no mind," Natalia said. "They are only there in case you should wish something."

The very idea astonished Anne. "Don't they sleep?"

"Like watchful dogs," Natalia said, "—with one eye open."

"I don't like it," Anne said.

"You will grow used to it," Natalia promised. Then she clapped her hands together lightly, and a young girl with long, thick braids appeared on soundless feet from the shadows.

"Hot cocoa," Natalia ordered; and in a few minutes the girl returned with a tray carrying two steaming mugs.

Natalia watched Anne closely. "You see? Anything you want. You have only to ask."

Anne took the cocoa from the tray. Anything she wanted—at the clap of her hands! How different life was within these walls! How strange and foreign! The idea appealed to her, despite her misgivings and the stirrings of homesickness she already felt for the house she had so recently left.

"I suppose one could grow used to it . . ." she murmured.

"Easily," Natalia said, a slight smile crossing her lips.

"But I'm used to doing things for myself."

Natalia nodded in understanding. She set aside her cup and took Anne's hand in hers. "My child, I know what you are suffering. My own mother died when I was a child. And when my father took a second wife, I felt betrayed, abandoned. I felt my father loved me less. My life was changed. Rules I had lived by were suddenly altered. I withheld all kindness from my stepmother. I spoke to her only when it was demanded. In my mind, I called her a usurper, and nothing she said or did pleased me. Only when I grew older—much older—and experienced the inconsolable pain of loneliness did I appreciate the happiness and comfort my stepmother gave my father. Alas, it was a lesson learned too late. They were both dead."

A silence fell between the two women. Anne was thinking, It's not the same at all! You can't possibly know what I'm thinking or how I feel!

Anne rose abruptly, ready to leave her cocoa untouched, prepared to declare that she was sleepy now and was going to bed. But she saw that Natalia was weeping silently. Tears filled the old woman's eyes and glistened on her cheeks. Unnerved, Anne sat back down and took Natalia's gnarled hands in her own.

"Please, Doña Natalia, don't cry . . ."

"Forgive me," Natalia whispered. "But the memory and the guilt are so great. How I wish I could have begged my father's forgiveness for the way I behaved! How I regret not having fallen on my knees before my stepmother to thank her for the joy she brought to his last years!"

Natalia regained her composure and dried her eyes. She rose, smiling down at Anne, and patted the girl on the cheek.

"I'll leave you alone, my child," she said sweetly. "Drink your cocoa while it's still hot. It will help you sleep."

She kissed Anne gently and vanished into the shadows as silently as she had appeared.

But Anne did not sleep. She lingered in the courtyard until the first streamers of dawn unfurled across the morning sky. All the while, she was aware that she was being watched over—but her irritation at being followed, at being spied upon, had evaporated. She found herself strangely comforted by the thought that she was not alone, that the clap of her hands would bring a servant to her side. And by the time she left the bench near the splashing fountain to find her way back upstairs, her feelings toward Sofia had changed. Natalia's tears had revealed to her the bitter harvest she would reap if she did not try to love her father's new wife. She thought about her father, how he had been in the years since Martha's death, and now she understood his restlessness. It was suddenly clear to her how desperately lonely he must have been.

Kneeling beside her bed to say her prayers, as she had done when she was a child and Martha was still with her, Anne recalled the Book of Genesis: "And the Lord God said, It is not good that the man should be alone. . . ."

Anne crawled into bed and pulled the coverlet up to her chin. A weight seemed to be lifted from her shoulders. As bright morning light filled the windows, and a flight of white wing cooed soothingly from the branches just outside, drowsiness swept over her, and she fell into a peaceful sleep.

Joel didn't know—and he didn't ask—what had changed Anne's heart; but when she joined them later that morning, she went directly to Sofia and kissed her on both cheeks. Then, taking Sofia's hand, she slipped it into Joel's and held them in her own.

"If a daughter may give a blessing, please accept mine," she said. "My hopes and prayers are for your happiness forever."

Later, when she had gone to change for the midday meal, Joel said to Sofia, "I was afraid she wouldn't accept you. I was afraid there would be trouble."

192

Sofia, looking pleased but surprised, said, "I wonder what it was that reconciled her heart?"

Doña Natalia, who sat in a nearby chair, appeared to be dozing, but a wily smile played across her lips.

1867

20

The visitor waiting in Joel's office noticed a framed map hanging on the stone wall above the fireplace, and he crossed the room to study it. On the map, which detailed the lower half of the state, a thick red line traced the boundaries of Joel's holdings—three adjoining sections that occupied much of the region south of the Nueces. The smallest block was labeled in script "The Trevor Ranch." To the west, perhaps twenty times larger, was the Lantana. Next to it, and largest of all, was the Ebonal.

The visitor, leaning closer for a glimpse at the scale of miles so he could judge for himself exactly how large the combined ranch really was, heard the door behind him swing opened and turned to see Joel enter the room.

"Mr. Wallace," he said, extending his hand. "I'm Joel Trevor. Welcome to the Lantana."

"Pleased to meet you, Mr. Trevor," the visitor said. "I was just examining this interesting map. You seem to own most of South Texas."

"The ranch belongs to my wife and me," Joel said.

Wallace could not keep his eyes from returning to the map. "There must be more than half a million acres there," he said in awe.

194

"Something like that," Joel agreed. Actually there were more than a million and a half, but Joel preferred to let visitors come to their own conclusions.

"I see there are three sections," Wallace went on.

"That's right," Joel said, "but we call it all the Lantana. It's simpler that way."

Wallace's eyes swept the room. It was elegantly furnished in dark mahogany. Two long, leather sofas faced each other on either side of the stone fireplace. An enormous French chandelier glittered above, and the tiled floor was carpeted with Oaxacan rugs.

"Beautiful place," Wallace complimented. "You don't seem to have suffered much from the war."

"We were damned lucky," Joel said, leading Wallace over to a chair beside his desk. "Of course, a hacienda, traditionally, is completely self-supporting. The whole idea is to survive no matter what hell breaks loose in the world outside."

"Well, I've been traveling around quite a bit," Wallace said, "and a whole passel of others haven't fared quite so well."

Joel nodded pensively. After defeat had brought the Confederacy to its knees, the harsh rule of Reconstruction was dragging it in the dirt. The scalawags and carpetbaggers who had taken control of the government in Austin were determined to get their share of the spoils of war. In the *brasada,* south of the Nueces, scores of landowners with ancient grants dating back to the kingdom of Spain found their ranches taken from them, to be sold for mere pennies an acre, when they couldn't pay the heavy taxes levied by the Republicans. Ramiro Rivas was one of these. His beloved Agarita was delivered at auction into the hands of a New York carpetbagger named Kendall. Time and time again, Joel had advised his partner to bank on gold, but Rivas had saved Confederate script— paper that was worthless even before the surrender at Appomattox Courthouse. Joel learned of the tragedy

195

too late. When he rode to Rivas's side with the money to pay his taxes, he found Kendall already in possession. And Rivas, the one-time *hacendado,* was now only the *caporal* of the ranch he had owned.

"Well, then, Mr. Trevor," the visitor said. "Shall we get down to business?"

"You want to talk cattle, don't you?" Joel asked.

"That's right."

"Well, hold up a minute. I've got a couple of others I want to sit in on this."

He went to the window and shouted for Rudy and Anne.

Rudy arrived first. A small white scar high on his left cheek was the only reminder of his part in the war. He was as strong and burly as ever. During his years beside the southern boys, his German accent had been softened by a slight drawl. His clear blue eyes were still sharp and keen, and his blond hair shone like silver. He shook hands with Wallace and dragged up a chair.

Then the door swung open and Anne entered.

"My daughter, Anne," Joel said.

As Wallace rose and bowed, his eyes never left her face.

Rudy watched the visitor carefully. He knew exactly what was going through Wallace's mind. In the years he had been away, Anne had grown up. He had returned from the war to find her one of the most beautiful women he had ever seen. While Emma had grown fat and sloppy, Anne had become tall and graceful, radiating health and strength. She had never minded the sun, and her complexion was tanned and clear. Her hair was nearly as blond as his, and whenever he was in her presence, he found it next to impossible to take his eyes from hers. They glittered green with an inner fire—two emeralds that only hinted at the damped passion within her.

Rudy lay awake nights thinking of Anne. Though

inwardly recoiling from Emma's touch, he grudgingly bestowed on her the attentions she demanded, but his thoughts were always of Anne. And he wondered, even as he held Emma in his arms, what Anne would do if he suddenly approached her, drew her close to him, and kissed her with the ardor that he felt.

Now, as Anne crossed the floor, she scarcely glanced at Rudy. She greeted Wallace and let him kiss her hand.

Rudy watched hungrily. How he, too, would like to kiss that hand! But that would be only the beginning. He wouldn't be able to stop there. He would want to kiss her eyes and her lips. He would have to cup her breasts in his big, rough hands and feel the soft curves of her body against his. He would have to take her, and the fact that it was forbidden only made the desire more enticing.

Anne walked behind the desk and stood beside her father.

"Now we're all here," Joel said. "Rudy is, of course, my foreman; and Anne knows as much about this ranch as either of us—probably more. She ran it single-handed during the war.

"Then you're not only a lovely woman," Wallace said, "but a strong one."

Anne smiled, and he saw steel behind her beauty.

"Now, what's the deal?" Joel asked.

"Beef," Wallace said. "The North is clamoring for it. A cow worth four dollars here will bring an easy forty up there."

"I'm aware of that," Joel said. "We've tried shipping by boat to New Orleans, but by the time we're through there's not enough profit to worry about."

"I'm talking about overland," Wallace said.

"We've been that route too. Ask Rudy."

Rudy nodded. "It was pure hell. We drove a herd up the Sedalia Trail through Indian Territory and Arkansas. Them Arkansas hills ain't no place for mustang cows. And then there were the farmers, all up in arms, trying to run us off. And when we weren't fighting them, we were dealing with road agents who were out to murder us and steal the cattle. *Nein, danke!* The Sedalia Trail is too damn' dangerous."

"I ain't talking about the Sedalia Trail," Wallace said. "I'm talking about a new route—one that goes straight up, right through the heart of Texas to Abilene, Kansas. They got a railhead there now—just built— where they can ship the cattle direct to the East. I ain't saying the trail drive will be easy—hell, moving a herd never is. But there won't be any farmers to rile up, and you won't run into those thieving road agents."

Joel pondered this new situation for a moment. Then he asked, "So what's your proposal?"

"I'll be your man in Abilene. You bring me the cows and I'll find you a market."

Joel nodded.

"Do you have a map?" Wallace asked. "I'll show you the route."

Joel pulled a roll from his desk and spread it out before them. Anne leaned forward and watched Wallace's finger trace a line from near San Antonio to central Kansas.

"See!" Wallace said. "Straight as an arrow with nothing in the way."

"It looks good," Joel said. "There might be some profit in the business after all. What do you say we get down to details?"

"One thing," Anne interrupted. "Does this route have a name?"

"Yes it does, Miss Trevor," Wallace said. "It's called the Chisholm Trail."

21

"Where are you going, *querida?*" Sofia asked.

It was a warm spring afternoon, and the days were growing noticeably longer. Daisies, bluebonnets, and wild verbena brightened the prairie like strewn confetti. The grass was lush, a rippling green sea under the steady Gulf breeze.

Anne paused on the bottom step, looking into the courtyard where Sofia sat with her Aunt Natalia. Both women held embroidery in their laps, their golden thimbles flashing in the sun as they deftly sewed designs on a new altar cloth for the chapel.

"It's such a beautiful day, I thought I'd go for a ride down to Bitter Creek," Anne said. She smiled and left the step to enter the courtyard. She leaned over Sofia and kissed her upturned cheek. Sofia replied with a squeeze of the hand.

"You look so beautiful this afternoon, Sofia," Anne said.

"All women do, in my condition," Sofia replied.

"Nonsense!" Natalia contradicted her gruffly. "I've seen some who were ugly as sows, sick every morning, complaining all day, with swollen red eyes and puffy white faces."

"You were just not looking into their souls," Sofia

told her aunt. "If you had, you would have seen every woman who is carrying a baby glows with God's own beauty."

Natalia gave a crusty harumph in reply and concentrated on a tiny white cross she was embroidering into the cloth.

"I can't wait," Anne said. "I hope it's a boy. I've always wanted a baby brother."

"Well, you'll *have* to wait, I'm afraid," Sofia said. She had set aside her sewing and her hands went to her still small waist. "By my judgment, he will be born in December."

"On Christmas Day!" Anne said.

Sofia smiled happily. "Wouldn't that be lovely?"

A servant brought tea and set it before them. Sofia poured and passed the cups.

"I do wish you wouldn't wear those leather trousers, Anne," she said. "You have so many pretty dresses."

"I wasn't made for dresses, Sofia," Anne said. "I think I was born in boots and pants. If I could look like you in a dress, I'd wear them all the time—but I'm just not comfortable in corsets and petticoats."

Sofia shrugged. She didn't know why she still pursued the matter, since it had been a losing battle from the beginning. And she had to admit that Anne wore her leather breeches and cotton *camisa* with more flair than most other women brought to satin gowns.

"Anyway," Anne went on, "can't you just see me riding my mare all gussied up like that? I'd really be a sight!"

"Not if you rode sidesaddle as a proper lady should."

"It would embarrass the daylights out of me to ride sidesaddle. It's so prissy!"

Sofia laughed. "*Pues,* no one could ever accuse you of being prissy!"

"I hope not," Anne said, rising and giving Sofia another peck on the cheek. "I ought to be off while the sun's still high. See you at supper."

"Enjoy yourself," Sofia called after her.

Anne ran into Joel on the outside steps. He studied her, frowning slightly.

"Take care where you go, Anne," he said. "I'm not too keen on you hanging around the cowboys so much. I know those men and I know what they've got on their minds."

"Oh, Papa, they don't pay me any attention."

"I reckon they pay you more than you imagine."

"They're all so shy—I think they're afraid of me."

"Not too afraid to try something if they think they can get away with it," Joel said. "I've always given you a lot of freedom, but that's one place I draw the line. I don't want you taking up with some good-for-nothing cowboy."

"But, Papa, you're a cowboy yourself!"

"I'm a cowman, Anne," Joel said. "There's a difference. A cowman owns cattle. A cowboy only works them."

Anne smiled reassuringly at her father. "I know what you're saying, Papa. You don't have to worry about me."

Joel nodded, frowning still, as he watched her descend the steps and stride across the caliche yard toward the farrier's shack, where her mare was being shod.

He was aware of the eyes following her, eyes that belonged to young men who had fled the Deep South after the war. They had drifted into Texas—tough, rough, battle-hardened veterans without two pennies to rub together, owning only a saddle and the clothes on their backs. Joel had hired scores of them to work side by side with the vaqueros—a word the newcomers promptly corrupted to "buckaroos." The two cultures, southern and Mexican, didn't clash. Instead, their mingling produced a new breed of man: the cowboy.

Joel liked them. He worked well with them and admired them for their spirit and daring, but he knew they were drifters at heart, rootless and restless. And he didn't want Anne to get involved with them. His gaze moved past his daughter toward the corral and the breaking pens, where the cowboys, attracted by Anne's appearance, had abandoned their work. One of them spotted Joel and barked a warning to the others. They went back to their tasks, for they were aware that Joel's disapproval could send them packing in an instant.

Anne neared the farrier's shack and shouted a greeting to the smith.

"Howdy, Miss Anne," Gil Varner replied. "I got your mare nearly finished. Nice day for a ride. First really hot day we've had this year."

"Feels good, doesn't it, Gil?" Anne said.

He hefted his mallet and began driving nails into the last shoe. In the corner sat a young cowboy sipping cold cider and waiting on a pair of spurs.

"This here's Kelly Moore," Gil said indicating the boy. "Where's your manners, kid? Don't you know enough to stand up for a lady? This is Miss Anne, the the boss's daughter."

Kelly unfolded his long legs and rose slowly. "Pleased to meet you, miss."

"Thanks, Kelly," Anne said. "I haven't seen you around before."

"Just signed on yesterday. I been working around Refugio up till now."

Anne liked what she saw—a tall, handsome man, around twenty-five, with curly chestnut hair down to his shoulders and a sandy blond beard. His eyes were brown, his lips full and red, his complexion fair and smooth with a sprinkling of freckles across the bridge of his nose. The thin shirt he wore stretched tightly over his muscular shoulders and tapered to his flat, hard waist.

He was conscious of her eyes on him and returned the stare with a boldness that Anne had seldom encountered in other cowboys on the Lantana. She felt a blush on her cheeks and turned away to examine the shoe that Gil Varner was just finishing.

"Where're you headed, Miss Anne?" he asked

"I thought I'd ride out to Bitter Creek. With all that rain we had last week, the water ought to be running high enough to fill the pond." Suddenly she realized she wasn't really talking to Gil, but talking through him to the cowboy who still stood nearby watching her. "It's so warm," she found herself saying, "that I thought I'd take a little swim. The creek water'll be chilly, but it'll feel good on a hot day like this."

Her eyes darted to Kelly, then dropped away quickly when she saw his gaze still on her.

"Here you go," Gil said as he finished his work. "Do you want me to saddle her up for you?"

"I can manage," Anne said. "See you later."

She left, leading the mare from the shack to the tack house.

Gill picked up Kelly's spurs to see what repairs he'd have to make.

"Where's this Bitter Creek?" Kelly asked.

Gil's eyes flashed a warning. "You don't really want to know."

"Let me be the judge of that."

"You'd only be asking for trouble. She's the boss's daughter, and he don't have any great hankerin' for her to get tangled up with one of the hands."

Kelly didn't pursue it, and when Gil told him he'd have his spurs ready in a couple of hours, he thanked him and left.

Anne pulled off her leather trousers and draped them over a mesquite branch next to her shirt. The sunlight was warm on her bare flesh, and her toes felt the delightful chill of the dark green water as she stood perched on the bank. She took a deep breath, bracing

203

herself for the shock, and plunged in head first. She came up in the middle of the pond, sputtering, trembling with cold, but feeling her body respond with vitality. With quick choppy strokes to warm herself, she circled the pond several times until the water no longer felt cold, but streamed over her flesh like smooth silk. She flipped over onto her back and floated with the sun in her eyes. All was peaceful. The only sound was the whisper of wind in the branches of the encircling trees. She lifted her hand and stroked her breasts before slowly reaching down between her thighs. Instantly she felt her heart beat faster, thumping in her ears. Her fingers probed and found their mark. She groaned and pressed her legs tightly together.

Just then a bluejay shrieked and fluttered in alarm from a low branch overhead. Anne opened her eyes and let her legs drop, treading water. She scanned the bank. Nothing. Then she heard a twig snap.

"Who's there?" she called. The water seemed suddenly terribly cold, and her whole body shivered.

Out of the brush, Kelly appeared. He strolled up to the bank, grinning, thumbs hooked in his trouser pockets.

"You peeping tom!" she shouted. Her heart was beating just as fast as before, but in anger now, not passion. She crossed her arms over her breasts and treaded out into deeper water.

"How's the water?" Kelly asked.

"None of your damned business," Anne replied. Her voice was cold, with a cutting edge.

"I think I'll come in and find out for myself."

"Don't you dare!" Anne said. "Now go on, get out of here!"

But instead of leaving, he grinned lazily again and sat down on the bank beside the bush where her clothes were hanging. She watched him from the middle of the pond. She knew she had lured him there—she

204

had wanted him to come. But now, inexplicably, she was afraid and angry: afraid of his boldness and daring, that he'd spied on her and caught her caressing herself.

"I'm warning you to leave," she said. "My father will kill you if he finds out you followed me."

"I ain't gonna tell."

"Well, *I* will if you don't leave!"

Kelly winked at her conspiratorially. "I bet you won't."

Anne changed her tone. Speaking sweetly, she said, "Look, Kelly. The water's cold, and I'm getting all shriveled up. Why don't you leave so I can get out?"

"I ain't stopping you from getting out," he said, still grinning.

"You know perfectly well what I mean."

"I reckon I do," Kelly answered. "But I'm mighty comfortable here and don't rightly feel like moving on."

Anger took hold of her again. "Well, I'm coming out anyway. What do I care if a low-life cowboy looks at me!"

She swam for the bank. When her toes touched bottom, she stood up and began walking toward him, her hands modestly covering her breasts.

The smile fell from Kelly's lips. He hadn't expected this. He'd only intended teasing her a little longer.

"Oh, all right," he said, rising and turning his back. "Come on out. I won't look."

He heard her leave the water and pull her clothing from the branch.

"Are you dressed yet?" he asked.

"Hold your horses," she replied.

Then suddenly he felt something hard and cold pressed against the middle of his back.

"Start walking, cowboy," Anne hissed. "I've got my Colt on you, and if you try any funny business, I'll blow a hole right through you."

She steered him toward the pond.

205

"Wait a minute . . . !" he protested.

"Hush up and keep walking!" Anne ordered, and gave the gun a little nudge.

"Are you going to shoot me?" he asked.

"I feel like it," she said. Instead she marched him to the edge of the bank. Then, lifting her leg, she kicked him hard in the seat of his pants, to send him sprawling belly-first into the pond. He came up flailing, spitting water.

Anne laughed, spun her revolver, and dropped it into its holster. She turned and swung up onto her mare. Then, looking back over her shoulder at the surprised cowboy standing neck-deep in the chilly water, she called: "Enjoy your swim, Kelly!"

She spurred her mare and galloped off toward home.

Rudy was just descending the steps of the hacienda when Anne rode up. She tossed her reins to one of the Mexican children who had run to greet her, but Rudy's big hand reached out above their hands and snared them. He held the horse still while she dismounted. As she brushed past him, he caught the clean scent of creek water about her and saw that her curls were still dark and damp from her swim.

"Thank you, Rudy," Anne said. She touched his arm lightly, and the gesture, though brief, sent a wave of passion through him.

Muttering a reply, he watched after her hungrily as she bounded up the steps and vanished into the shadows of the house.

After he dropped her saddle off at the tack house, he headed toward the corral, where he heard a group of cowboys gathered together, ragging one of their compadres.

"What's up?" Rudy asked, pushing into their circle, intending to disperse them.

" 'Pears we done had a freak cloudburst," one of the laughing cowboys replied, "and only Kelly got wet!"

206

The crowd opened up to reveal Kelly, grinning happily and enjoying being the center of attention, drenched to the skin.

It took Rudy only a moment to make the connection.

"Pack your gear, Kelly!" he barked, his face clouding, growing red beneath its tan. "I want you off the Lantana by daybreak!"

The smile dropped from Kelly's face. The other men backed off, no longer wanting to be associated with him.

"Hey, wait a minute, boss!" Kelly protested. "What've I done wrong?"

Rudy reached out, grabbed Kelly's collar, and yanked him to him. "You know damned well what you done! If you ain't making tracks by sunup, I'll have your no-good hide!"

He flattened his palm against Kelly's chest and sent the cowboy sprawling in the dirt. Kelly scrambled to his feet, clenching his fists, ready to fight, but some of the other cowboys grabbed him and held him back.

"Cool down, Kelly!" one of them shouted. "He can beat the tar outta you."

Rudy stared at Kelly with hatred, then spun on his heel and strode off.

Kelly struggled to break free, aching to charge after Rudy's retreating figure, but his companions held him down.

"I'll get that mean son of a bitch one of these days," Kelly vowed. "I'll make him sorry for what he done!"

Around the mahogany dining table that night, Rudy announced that he'd had trouble with one of the hands and had sent him packing.

"Who's that?" Joel asked.

"A fellow named Kelly," Rudy replied. His eyes darted to Anne's.

She said nothing. But after dinner, she caught up

with him as he was heading home with Emma and the children.

"No need to fire him, Rudy," she said, pulling him aside. "He didn't do anything."

"You know how your papa feels about cowboys longing after you."

"He's not longing after me. I never laid eyes on him till this afternoon at the farrier's."

"So how come both you and him turn up at the same time wet with creek water?"

Anne shrugged. Her bright green eyes were wide and innocent. "I went swimming at Bitter Creek. All alone! I don't know how *he* got wet."

Rudy studied her carefully. "For sure, you're taking a big interest in some cowboy you say you don't even know."

For some time now, Anne had been aware of Rudy's feelings for her. It had amused her because she'd thought of Rudy as nothing more than a close family friend—perhaps an uncle—and she had never even considered that it would come to anything more. But now she recognized the specter of jealousy and possessiveness in him, and it annoyed her.

"Oh, back down, Rudy," she said sweetly. "He's nothing to me and I'm nothing to him. Cross my heart! Besides, roundup's just around the corner, and then the trail drive. You're going to need every hand you can get."

Rudy arched his neck stubbornly. "There's plenty of cowboys drifting around. I won't have no trouble hiring up another one."

"Why, Rudy!" Anne said tauntingly. "I believe you really do think there's something going on between this man Kelly and me. And I think you're jealous!"

Rudy flushed. "I ain't jealous! Why should I be jealous?"

"I don't know, Rudy," Anne said, her guile sheathed

in innocence. "But I bet Emma'd be mighty unhappy if she thought that was the case."

Rudy's blue eyes went cold and hard. "I ain't never given you cause to think such a thing."

"Why, you're doing so right now, firing that boy when he never did a thing but show up wet. You're putting two and two together and coming up five."

"You swear that's the truth, Anne?" he asked somberly.

"On my honor, Rudy."

He stared into her eyes, searching for deception. But Anne held his gaze and didn't falter.

"All right," he said, breaking contact. "I believe you."

"Then he can stay on?"

"*Ja!*" he said gruffly. "But he better keep his nose clean."

Alone in her bed later that night, Anne thought about what she'd done. At first, she told herself that she'd only acted to save a poor cowboy's job, but even as she considered it she knew it to be untrue. She had lured Kelly to the pond, making it clear where she was headed after leaving the farrier's. She had liked his looks and wondered what it would be like to be held in his arms. But her own intact innocence, and Kelly's boldness, had frightened her at the last moment.

Snuggling against her pillow, she conjured up his face, pretending he was with her.

If only he'd been nicer! she thought, and her lips curled in a smile. Then I might have let him come swimming with me. I might have even let him touch me!

22

Roundup began, and for several days the area around the hacienda seemed strangely deserted while the cowboys rode out in separate squads to the far-flung reaches of the ranch to gather up the herd. Occasionally, one or another of the outfits would come in from the range with a group of cattle to be road branded and set out to pasture to await the drive up the Chisholm Trail.

Anne found herself looking and longing for Kelly. Whenever she heard the bawling of a newly arrived herd, she would dash to her window or fly onto the porch hoping to catch a glimpse of him striding long-legged across the yard.

She began to worry that perhaps Rudy had fired him after all or that he'd been scared off and had hightailed it to some other ranch. She was afraid that she'd never see him again.

Her nights were spent in restless sleep, dreaming of Kelly, waking with the image of him on her brain, the long chestnut hair, the warm brown eyes, the full, ruddy lips that had smiled so boldly.

Sofia noticed Anne's distraction and analyzing it correctly, tried to keep her occupied. But Anne's mind wandered. She'd forget the task at hand, and before

Sofia knew it, Anne would disappear, only to be found later on the porch, leaning on one of the arches, staring out across the range as if she expected a visitor.

Then, nearly two weeks after the roundup began, and only a few days before the men were due to take the cattle north, Anne spotted Kelly.

There had been an afternoon rain, and Kelly and his squad came riding up off the range still wearing their slickers. Beneath his wide-brimmed sombrero, his hair was damp and dark; in contrast, his beard had become even more sun-bleached until it was now a shining reddish-blond.

Anne's heart raced in her breast. She thought she'd never seen a more attractive man. An inadvertent cry escaped from her lips, and she dashed from the porch across the yard to the corral where Kelly was headed. Caliche mud, sticky as paste, covered her boots, and cowboys were watching and laughing all around, but she didn't care. It wouldn't have mattered if Joel and Rudy themselves were witnessing the scene. All she wanted was to be near Kelly, to welcome him back, to tell him how much she'd missed him.

She grabbed his reins and looked up into his smiling face, trying to speak; but his eyes seemed to bore into her soul, stripping her bare, and she was tongue-tied.

"I . . . you're . . . I was so afraid you weren't coming back," she stammered.

Kelly didn't speak, but his smile grew broader, and he let his gloved hand brush hers on the reins.

"Can you meet me tonight?" she breathed.

"Where?"

"At Bitter Creek—after the hacienda is asleep . . ."

She didn't wait for him to accept. Afraid that he would turn her down, she released his reins and hurried back through the mud, wanting desperately to turn around for another glimpse of him, but not daring for fear that he might be laughing at her, mocking her forwardness.

She needn't have worried. For the rest of the day, Kelly was worthless. Several times the *caporal* had to speak sharply to him, warning him finally that if he didn't straighten up, he'd have to draw his pay and move on.

That night, after he slipped away from the bunkhouse, Kelly bathed in the cold clear water of Bitter Creek, combed his hair and beard, and rode downstream to the pond.

Anne arrived a quarter of an hour later.

She floated dreamily on her back in the middle of the pond, while images of the full moon flashed like bright coins tossed upon the water, and a gauzy blue haze settled over the sage that ringed the clearing.

Sitting alone on the bank, Kelly had almost given up trying to lure her out of the water. He blew a cloud of cigar smoke at the moon and decided to try once more.

"What'd you ask me here for, if all you want to do is swim by yourself?"

Anne didn't respond. Even the coldness of the pond had failed to calm her racing heart, and now that they were alone together—as she had dreamed so often while he was away—she wasn't sure that she could go through with it.

Her toes, her breasts—pink nipples looking like rosebuds balanced on each creamy mound—and her upturned face were all that showed above the water's satiny surface. Kelly looked away, trying hard to imagine the rest. She had stripped and plunged into the pond so quickly that he'd caught only a fleeting, tantalizing glimpse.

That had been half an hour ago, and he was growing impatient. He was almost of a mind to saddle up and ride back to the bunkhouse. That would show her! But like a skipped stone, his glance skittered back over the pond's dark surface to where she floated. He sighed and tried another tack: "Better watch out for water moccasins."

This brought a response at last. Anne gave up floating and began treading water. "I'm not afraid of moccasins," she said.

"Then maybe you're afraid of this old one-eyed snake of mine up here on the bank," he said.

Anne didn't answer, but she started swimming slowly back toward the water's edge. When she got to where the pond was hip deep, she stood up and began walking toward him.

Kelly couldn't remember ever seeing anyone so beautiful. She was tall and tanned, her body shining like polished bronze, with sparkling droplets glittering on the rounded flesh of her small, firm breasts, and her dark nipples velvety as dusky roses.

A sudden hot rush of blood throbbed in Kelly's temples as his eyes followed the silvery trails of water that trickled from her shoulders, between her breasts, and over her belly to disappear in the darkness between her legs.

Seeing his features abrupty contort as if he were in pain, Anne paused, alarmed, suddenly desperately afraid of what was about to take place.

Kelly discerned her hesitation, and fearing that he was going to lose her, quickly ripped off his shirt and threw it atop a mesquite bush behind him. Then he tugged off his scuffed boots and faced her, barefooted and bare chested. His chestnut hair glowed flame red in the moonlight.

Anne studied him. His body was firm and hard. His chest was covered with fine coppery hair that met in a dark line down his middle and disappeared into the waistband of his breeches. She felt the blood begin to course through her body, felt her knees weaken.

Deftly, Kelly flicked open his trouser buttons. Anne watched, spellbound, as his dark line of hair descended into a thick mat covering the base of his abdomen.

213

Then, with an almost careless jerk of his thumbs, he pushed his trousers down around his ankles and stepped out of them. He laughed—a clear, almost childlike laugh—in his delight to be standing naked in front of a lovely woman.

My God! she thought, he's beautiful!

He poised for an instant on the bank, then stepped into the ankle-deep water to meet her. She was wet and slick in his arms. There was a green mossy smell of pond water in her hair, and her upturned face shone in the moonlight. When his lips covered hers, she tried to pull away, but he grabbed her hair and forced her mouth back against his. She felt his tongue probing between her lips, and with a gasp of delight and surrender, she opened her mouth and let him kiss her as he wanted.

His hand slid down and caught her between the buttocks, reaching deeper underneath until his fingers found what they were seeking. She cried out now with fear and pleasure.

"No! Stop, Kelly! Please!"

But he silenced her with anothed kiss. Then his lips brushed her eyes, her temples, and her throat. Without lifting his lips from her skin, his mouth slipped down to her shoulder, then over the creamy mound of one breast and across to the other. His tongue ran over her skin, now fiery and prickly with the heat of passion. Then slowly, tantalizingly, as if it were a tiny whip, the tip of his tongue found her right nipple. He tortured it, flicking it with a delicate touch that made her cry out.

His glistening muscles tensed as he lifted her out of the water with one arm and carried her to the bank, where he settled her on the thick green grass.

"Now," he whispered urgently. "Now!"

But she pulled away from him and held him back. "No, Kelly! I'm afraid!"

Pushing her back down, he crushed her mouth with

his until she thought she was going to smother. She gasped for breath as he released her, and was barely aware that he was gently stroking her belly with the curls of his beard. Despite herself, her hips began to roll from side to side, and a moan escaped from deep inside her throat. With her skin blazing at the touch of his lips, she squirmed and locked her legs behind his back, pulling his face close against her belly. His hands reached up and fondled her breasts, kneading the erect nipples between his fingers. Then his tongue traced the curve of her abdomen, down into the curly dark thatch that she raised toward his mouth.

She cried out again as his tongue found her. Lights flashed behind her closed eyelids and the earth seemed to open up beneath her.

Then, with agonizing slowness, he inched his way back up her body until his face was even with hers.

"Now?" he asked with the breathlessness of passion. "Now?"

"Oh, yes! Now!" she cried.

And he reached beneath her buttocks and brought her up to meet him.

23

The next morning Anne stayed in bed, sending one of the maids to bring breakfast up to her instead of going downstairs. She was sure that no one had missed her during the night, and she was equally certain that if any of the servants had seen her stealing into the hacienda just before dawn, they would keep it to themselves. But she was afraid to face Sofia, afraid that the older woman would be able somehow to discern in her face, by subtle changes that may have taken place, what had happened the night before.

But when her bedroom door reopened, it was Sofia who brought in her tray and set it on the table beside the bed.

"Querida," Sofia murmured solicitously, her pale, lovely face looming over Anne's, her dark brows knit with concern. "Are you unwell?"

Anne slipped deeper into the covers, grateful for the concealing darkness of the room behind closed shutters.

Sofia touched her forehead with a smooth palm. "You don't feel feverish."

"I'm fine, Sofia," Anne said. "Just a little tired. You didn't have to bring my breakfast yourself. I didn't mean to trouble you."

"It was no trouble," Sofia said. "Nothing I do for you is any trouble. I love you as if you were my own daughter."

Sudden hot tears welled up in Anne's eyes. She took Sofia's hand and squeezed it. Sofia bent over her and kissed her cheek, then glided silently from the room.

Anne left her breakfast untouched, too miserable to think of eating. Why can't I be more like Sofia? she thought. She's so good, so pure, so honorable. I would love to tell her what happened between me and Kelly, but she would never understand. Never!

Anne groaned and pulled the coverlet up under her chin.

I won't see him again! she vowed. I did wrong and I know it! I'll speak to Rudy. I'll tell him Kelly has been bothering me and have him sent away!

But the memory of the night before swept over her, and against her will, she found herself reliving every moment of their act of love.

No! she railed against herself, struggling to banish her thoughts, but his smiling face seemed to hover over hers. She could almost feel his hot breath on her cheek as if he were in the room with her—in bed with her. She had only to reach out to touch him. . . . .

They met again that night—and then the following night. It was to be their last rendezvous, their last time together for four months at least. The chuck wagons were stocked; the cattle were gathered in one huge herd; the trail boss and the cowboys were ready. At dawn the next morning, the long, slow drive up the Chisholm Trail would begin.

Anne clung to Kelly, unwilling to leave him, too heartbroken to let him go, desperately afraid she would never see him again.

"I'll be back, Anne," he said. "I promise."

"It'll be so long," she murmured miserably. "All

217

summer. I don't know how I'll live without you."

"Please wait for me."

"I will. You know I will!"

The waning moon was still high when she slipped along the shadowy corridors to her room. She ached all over as if gripped by a fever. She had never known such pain. It went beyond her physical senses, and she wondered if this was how it felt to die. She stood at the window, holding herself in her arms, trying to stop the trembling, and looked out at the watery blueness of the predawn landscape. Soon the men would be stirring. They would breakfast, one last hearty meal, then saddle up and set out, driving the huge herd northward. Imagining their departure, she could almost hear the chuck wagons creak as they started on their journey; could almost hear the cowboys calling to one another above the bawling cattle. And she pictured the cloud of dust that would be raised. By noon it would all have settled once again. The surrounding pastures would be empty. The horizon would be clear. The men would be gone, already far away. And Kelly would be with them!

She saw the scene as vividly as if it were actually taking place. And she imagined herself left behind at the hacienda, facing a desolate succession of long, hot summer days, standing vigil at her window, waiting . . . waiting for a man who might never return.

Suddenly she wheeled away from the window. She threw back the bedspread and ripped from the bed a thin woolen blanket. Reaching into her wardrobe, she snatched a pair of trousers and two flannel shirts, which she tossed into the blanket; then she rolled it up and secured it with a leather belt. She tucked the roll under her arm and started from the room. At the doorway, she paused, remembering one more thing.

She crossed the tiled floor to her dresser and slid

back the drawer. Reaching inside she withdrew a pair of scissors. She gave one long look at her reflection in the oval mirror, then quickly lifted her long tresses away from her head and began cutting.

The curls fell like spun gold at her feet. Her booted toe kicked them away, and she continued snipping until the scissors had encircled her head. Only then did she allow her eyes another glance in the mirror.

She gasped with shock and the scissors clattered noisily to the floor. Her hair barely covered her ears, a blond cap with ragged edges.

Oh, God! she thought. I'm so ugly!

She began to doubt the ruse would work. Her blouse was tight, straining against her heaving breast. She would never be able to fool anyone with her tiny waist and rounded hips. So she turned again to the wardrobe and rummaged among the clothes until her eyes lit on a woolen poncho. She dropped it over her shoulders and examined herself in the mirror.

Not bad! It hid her figure at least.

Then she dragged out a black sombrero and set it squarely on her head.

The effect reassured her. From a distance at least, she was sure no one would recognize her. Turning back to the door again, she grabbed the blanket roll, and slipped into the corridor.

It was nearly midday before she was missed. The excitement of sending off the cattle drive distracted everyone, and it was only after the household returned to normal that Sofia thought of Anne and went looking for her. The disheveled clothing in the wardrobe and the stripped bed alarmed her, but it took the sight of Anne's shorn tresses on the floor beneath the dresser to make her cry out for Joel.

Rudy arrived first. He took one look at the room and realized what had happened.

219

"There's a cowboy she fancies," Rudy said when Joel came up behind him. "A new boy named Kelly. I'm thinking she rode off with him."

"No!" cried Sofia. "It's not possible!"

But Joel was grim-faced. "Was he on the drive this morning?"

"*Ja,*" Rudy said.

"Then let's go after her!"

They saddled up and galloped north, catching up with the slowly moving herd in less than an hour. The trail boss, Ben Talley, spotted them in the distance and rode back to meet them.

"Bring me Kelly!" Joel ordered, and the cowboy was shouted for.

Kelly, who was at the far side of the herd, had to circle round to join Joel and Rudy.

"All right, Kelly!" Joel demanded. "Where is she?"

"Who?" Kelly asked.

Joel's gray eyes were hard. "Quit playing games! You know damn well who I'm talking about."

"Honestly, Mr. Trevor, I . . ."

"Answer straight!" Rudy shouted, his face red with rage and secret jealousy.

"Leave it to me, Rudy," Joel said quietly. Then turning to Kelly once again: "My daughter Anne has disappeared, and I have good cause to think you're involved."

"I swear it, Mr. Trevor," Kelly protested, and Joel couldn't help but recognize the look of honest surprise on the young man's face. "I don't know nothing about it!"

"You lie!" Rudy accused him.

"Hold on, Rudy," Joel warned.

"I ain't seen Miss Anne," Ben Talley intervened. "I've been up and down the line. I woulda seen her if she'd run off with us. 'Sides, I'da sent her packin' right back home with an escort. You know me well enough, Mr. Trevor. I wouldn't allow no cowboy to kidnap your daughter."

Joel frowned. "I know you wouldn't, Ben. I wasn't accusing you of anything."

"I'm innocent too, Mr. Trevor," Kelly said. "I don't know nothing of her whereabouts."

Joel stared at him again, long and hard. He considered himself a good judge of men, and he believed, from the look on Kelly's face, that the cowboy was telling the truth.

"Well, she's gone," Joel said at last, "and I'm going to find her. And when I do, if I learn you're in any way involved, I'll have your hide."

Joel motioned for Rudy to rein around and follow him back to the hacienda.

"You can't let the boy get away with this!" Rudy protested. His hand was aching to unfurl his whip and crack it down across Kelly's back.

"He's done nothing wrong as far as I can see," Joel said.

"He's lying! I can tell it!"

Rudy's rage astonished Joel. He'd never seen the man so worked up before. "Drop it, Rudy," he said quietly. "Let's go back home. Anne's not here. You can see for yourself."

Anne held her mare in check. Hiding in the brush nearly a mile from the herd, she watched as Joel and Rudy turned their horses back and headed south. She saw Kelly linger for a moment beside Ben Talley before riding back around the moving cattle, losing himself finally in a veil of dust.

She waited, scarcely breathing, until the herd departed the area. She waited until the last of the cattle vanished over the horizon. And still she waited, until all that could be seen of them was the dust kicked up by their hooves. Only then did she leave her cover. She would follow them that way for several days, she

221

decided, keeping their dust trail in sight, until she was convinced they were too far away from the ranch for Ben Talley to send her back.

24

Anne pursued the herd by day and camped in the concealing brush by night. She built no fires and ate only the hardtack and jerky she'd swiped from the kitchen as she slipped away from the hacienda. By the morning of the fifth day, with the herd some eighty miles north of the Lantana, she consumed the last of her meager provisions and realized the time had come for her to reveal herself to Kelly.

That evening Ben Talley bedded the herd on the bank of the San Antonio River. Anne could see the roaring campfire beside the chuck wagon and smell the broiling beef of a fat yearling that had been killed for supper. Saddle weary and hungry, she longed to ride straight into camp. But she held back, not wanting to be seen by the others until after she had met up with Kelly.

Night fell quickly, with the setting sun obscured by an ominous wall of purple clouds sweeping toward the camp over the western hills. Lightning flashed in the distance, and soon Anne heard the first low growl of thunder.

As the night watch patrolled the edges of the herd, Anne recognized Kelly's plaintive tenor singing softly to soothe the restless cattle. She swung up into her saddle and rode toward his voice.

Kelly heard her horse's hooves and broke off his song. "Is that you, Ben?" he called.

Anne didn't answer but continued in his direction, filled with trepidation at what his reaction would be when he discovered that she had followed him. The anticipation of feeling his arms around her once more, of looking into his eyes and tasting his lips on hers, overcame her fear.

"Ben?" Kelly called again, speaking quietly so as not to disturb the animals.

The night sky was now half covered by the canopy of the approaching storm, and a streak of lightning jumped from one towering cloud to a distant hill. In the momentary blue-white dazzle, they saw one another.

Anne's heart leaped with excitement. "Kelly!" she cried.

She was at his side immediately. "Kelly, don't be mad! I couldn't help it! I couldn't stand being separated from you."

Lightning crackled once again and he looked at her as though she were an apparition. He knew by the voice that it was Anne, but the figure in the bulky poncho, with cropped hair beneath a black sombrero, bore little resemblance to the woman he had thought he'd left behind.

She jumped from her horse and reached up to him, encircling his waist with her arms. Thunder crashed about their ears and the herd began to bellow. Finally, Kelly swung down from his saddle and embraced Anne.

"Are you crazy?" he asked. "What are you doing here?"

Anne didn't answer. Tears of joy and relief filled her eyes. She pressed close to him and kissed him wildly.

He broke away from her. "You can't stay here!

224

You've got to go back home. Your father will kill us both if he finds out what you've done!"

"I don't care!" Anne cried. "I only want to be with you. Let's run away, Kelly! We can start our own life, just you and me!"

Lightning cracked savagely overhead and the bellow from the herd grew louder. The animals began drifting restlessly, and in the distance, Ben Talley called out an order, but his voice was drowned out in the deafening crash of thunder.

Kelly looked up in alarm, realizing at last that they were encircled by frightened cattle.

"Anne! Get back on your horse!"

But she was oblivious to the danger the cattle presented, and clung to him when another bolt cracked out of the clouds, setting a nearby tree aflame. As the sky filled with light, and thunder boomed continuously, a quickening, violent wind swept over them, kicking up dust.

Kelly realized it was too late to save themselves by riding clear of the herd. The animals were pressing close against them, snorting, pawing, staring with wild eyes at the flashing lightning all around.

"Stampede!" someone cried, and the roar of hooves joined the raging thunder.

"Stampede!"

Kelly grabbed Anne and dragged her with him behind an enormous tree.

"'Hold on!" he shouted above the storm. "Whatever you do, don't let go!"

She hugged the trunk in terror, and he stood behind her, his arms around her, spread out to also touch the tree. Hail began to pound down from the clouds, bruising their shoulders and arms. The frenzied herd was charging past them, so close the cattle actually scraped the bark from the other side of the tree.

The tree shuddered before the onslaught. Anne

screamed in panic, certain that they would be overrun and trampled beneath the pounding hooves.

"Kelly! We're going to die!"

"Hold on!" he shouted and pressed her closer to the trunk.

Lightning, thunder, blinding rain—the cacophony of the clattering horns and drumming hooves: It was a nightmare that seemed to last an eternity.

But the last of the maddened animals eventually passed, leaving Anne dazed and deafened. Kelly slowly released his hold on her, and letting go of the battered trunk, she turned to follow him. They ran through the field of mud to their frightened horses and climbed into their saddles.

"Come on!" Kelly shouted. "We've got to overtake the herd!"

Spurring her horse, Anne galloped after Kelly, who rode toward Ben Talley and a group of other cowboys that had already caught up with the stampeding cattle and were turning the leaders back. The animals began wheeling in a giant circle, racing at top speed but going nowhere. Kelly and Anne joined the others, shouting and waving their sombreros at the wild-eyed steers, driving them more tightly into the churning wheel.

"Don't let 'em bolt!" Ben Talley shouted. "Keep 'em circling!"

Soon the cattle began bellowing to one another, and the cowboys knew they had won the battle. Gradually, the herd slowed, the turbulent front of the storm passed on to the east, and the pelting rain gave way to a gentle drizzle. At last the weary cattle were quiet enough for the cowboys to leave the herd and collect around the chuck wagon.

"You did a good job, boys," Ben Talley said, greeting each of the horsemen as they rode up to the wagon. "Good thing we caught up with 'em before they piled up in the river. They'da been goners for sure!"

Kelly and Anne rode side by side; he was silent

226

and worried, she still breathless with excitement and lingering fright.

"Good job, Kelly," Ben Talley called. "I saw your loose horse and was afraid you'd been . . ."

He paused, trying to account for the other person riding at Kelly's flank.

"Who's with you? Who's the other hand?"

In the flickering campfire light, the face was oddly familiar, but it was streaked with mud and the black sombrero was pulled down close over the eyes.

"You ain't gonna like it," Kelly warned.

"Who are you, fellah?" Talley asked.

"It ain't no fellah," Kelly said. Then turning to Anne, he added: "Go on! Tell him who you are!"

Anne hesitated. Then reaching up, she took off her sombrero and shook her cropped hair free.

"I'll be goddamned!" Talley breathed. His face collapsed and he shook his head in disgust. "So you brung her with you after all, huh, Kelly?"

"I came on my own, Ben," Anne said. "Kelly didn't know anything about it."

"Your paw's gonna raise hell when he finds out," Talley said.

"I don't want him to know," Anne said.

"What do you mean, you don't want him to know?" Talley said, anger rising in his voice. "I'm sendin' you back first thing in the mornin'."

An icy composure settled over Anne's face. Her green eyes glittered in the campfire light. "I wouldn't do that if I were you, Ben."

"And what do you expect me to do?"

"Let me ride with you on the trail drive."

"You're talkin' crazy, Miss Anne. I can't allow no female along—least of all the boss's daughter."

"I won't be any trouble. I can ride with the best of your boys."

"You're missin' the point, Miss Anne," Talley said. "I'm sendin' you back, like I said."

227

Anne paused a moment. When she finally spoke, there was a hard, threatening edge to her voice. "If you send me home, I'll say I was with you all along, that you knew all about it from the beginning. I'll tell my father that you hid me away when he and Rudy came looking for me."

"You're a hard woman, Miss Anne. I never figgered you this way," Talley said at last, when he could see she would not give in.

Anne couldn't believe herself either. She scarcely understood what had given her the courage to stand up and bluff Talley. She knew that if he sent her back to the hacienda she would never be able to carry out her threat. Though Joel might believe her lie, Rudy never would But she stood her ground and faced up to Talley, waiting for his decision.

He spit on the ground as if he had tasted something foul. "Kelly," he said at last. "I reckon you're the reason she's here. So, from now on, she's your piece of baggage She's your responsibility, and I don't want no trouble from either of you! One more thing, Kelly, whether or not you had a hand in this, you ain't never workin' for me again."

Anne and Kelly lay in his bedroll, sharing the few short hours before dawn.

"You should'na done it, Anne," Kelly said.

"I wish you'd quit saying that, Kelly. What's done is done. Anyway, everything'll turn out all right."

"I don't think it will," Kelly said. "In the first place, I won't be able to work at the Lantana no more."

"Don't worry about Ben. He'll keep you on. I know he will."

Kelly shook his head. "No, he won't. When Ben Talley gets mad, he stays mad. Anyway, after all that's happened, I won't be able to work around the other boys. They'll all be talking, you know. They'll be saying that I ran after you 'cause you got the dimes."

"But that's not true!"

"Of course it ain't. I know it and you know it. But the boys'll say it just the same, and my life won't be worth spit. 'Sides, one fine day, someone's gonna spill the beans to your paw, and I'll have to get up and dust right quick."

"If that happens, I'll dust with you—just like I did this time."

"No, you won't," Kelly said. "'Cause I won't let you. I don't want you to end up being one of them girls of the line, chasing after some drifting cowboy."

"We'll get married, Kelly."

He nodded. "Yeah, maybe someday we will—but not as long as your paw is alive. You know as well as I do what he'd think of that."

They were silent for a moment, holding each other close.

Finally Kelly spoke again; his voice rang with regret. "Oh, Anne, why couldn't you have waited? It would'na been for long! And then I'da been back on the Lantana and everything woulda been just fine."

"I just couldn't, Kelly," Anne said. "I just couldn't have waited."

Anne never got to see Abilene. A day's ride away, Ben Talley paid off Kelly and told him to take Anne back to the Lantana.

"Abilene ain't gonna be no place for a young girl," he said. "Four months on the trail can make a cowboy hungry for more than just home cookin'—if you get my meanin'."

Anne did and made no protest. She was surprised to find that it didn't seem to matter either. She didn't care if she saw Abilene or not. The trail drive had been arduous, and—when she wasn't in Kelly's arms—she had found it tedious and dull. True to her word to Talley, she had worked alongside the men, sometimes riding flank or drag, but most often wrangling—taking

229

care of the horses in the remuda. They had set out in April; now it was nearly the end of August, and she found herself longing for the sight of the hacienda. More and more frequently, her thoughts returned to Joel and Sofia. She couldn't erase the guilt she felt at the worry and grief her disappearance must be causing them. And she knew that Sofia, with a baby on the way, would be needing her.

So when Talley told them both to go back home, she readily agreed.

"What you tell your paw is your own business," Talley said, as she and Kelly prepared to depart. "As for me, I'll keep my mouth shut, and I'll see that the boys do the same."

"Thank you, Ben," Anne said. "And thanks for letting me come along."

Talley shook his head. "Don't thank me for that, Miss Anne. If you remember right, you had my hands tied. I didn't do it freely."

Anne looked away. There was guilt for that too. She was a bit ashamed of herself—of her impetuosity and arrogance. Now that it was over, she wondered if it had really been worth it—the worry and the trouble she had caused so many others. Shaking her head as if trying to clear her mind, she looked up again, prepared to apologize to Ben Talley, but he had turned and was walking away from her.

Reading her thoughts, Kelly laid his hand on her arm. "Forget it, Anne," he said. "It's too late."

She watched as Talley swung up into his saddle and rode off. He didn't look back.

"Let's go," Kelly said. "Let's go home."

25

They lay in each other's arms beneath a canopy of oaks. There had been a storm somewhere upriver, and the Nueces was high and green. Its water churned between the banks and boiled in eddies around the tangles of submerged roots.

"What are you going to tell your paw?" Kelly asked.

"I haven't decided yet," Anne answered. "Maybe I'll say that the Indians took me."

"He won't believe a word of that."

"I know. But he won't believe anything else either—except the truth. Nothing else makes any sense."

He raised on one elbow and kissed her lightly on the lips. "It's time for me to be going. It's a long ride to the Agarita."

"Ask for Ramiro Rivas," Anne reminded him. "He was my father's partner and used to own the Agarita until some carpetbagger cheated him out of it. But he's the foreman now, and I'm sure he'll hire you on. Just tell him I sent you—he'll remember me."

Kelly rose and saddled up. Anne flew to his side and into his arms.

"I wish it weren't over so soon!" Anne cried. "'I wish it were just beginning."

"We'll meet as often as we can."

She looked into his warm brown eyes once more and, with her fingertips, traced the contours of his face.

"Don't forget me, Kelly."

"Never."

He kissed her gently and swung up onto his horse. She held onto his hand as if to release it would be to lose him forever.

· "Kelly!" she cried, her heart breaking. "Take me with you!"

He shook his head sadly. "You know I can't."

She *did* know. She knew their adventure was over, that there was nothing left for her but to go home again, and face Joel and Sofia, to try to survive the loneliness of each coming day. But she would wait for the time when she and Kelly could be together again.

"Good-bye, my love," Kelly said. He leaned down from the saddle and kissed her for the last time.

Anne couldn't speak. She released his hand and stepped back. Kelly spurred his horse and started off. Through tears Anne watched him make his way through swells of golden grass. His figure grew smaller as he put distance between them. For what seemed like an eternity, his dark silhouette balanced on the western horizon. Then he vanished.

Slowly Anne moved, as if in shock, saddling her horse and tying the bedroll behind it. She mounted the horse and set off at a walk toward the Lantana.

The landscape was familiar now, her home terrain. She felt it tug at her heart, beckoning her, welcoming her back into its breast. She hadn't realized how much she'd missed it, how much she really loved it. But now the fields of waving grass, the stands of oak and lacy *huisache* reached out for her like old friends, and she felt an unexpected happiness welling up inside her.

And for an hour or so as she galloped southward, toward home, she was able to forget the troubles she would have once she arrived.

Then she reached the site where Martha lay buried. Reining her horse, she dismounted. It had been ages since she last visited the spot. She went to the lightning-struck mesquite whose blackened heart was exposed to the elements, and her fingers traced the epitaph that Joel had carved into the piece of wood.

"Oh, Mama!" she cried out loud in her solitude, and tears flooded her eyes. "Would you be ashamed of me? Would you hate me for what I've done?"

The lantana shrub had flourished through the years and was festooned with tiny nosegays, rust and gold. She picked a few and laid them on the mound of stone covering Martha's grave.

"If you had lived, what would I be like today?" Anne whispered. "Everything might have been different. I'd still be your little girl—as good and gentle as you were. And you'd have no cause to be ashamed of me!"

Her eyes were filled with sadness, and her heart was heavy in her breast.

But it's too late, she thought, too late for all that now. I am what I am. And there's no turning back.

She returned to her horse and set out to finish her journey home.

Sofia's black eyes glittered like polished stone, as she paced back and forth, trembling with anger, her leather heels beating a tattoo on the tile pavings of the foyer.

"You dare to come home with no explanation, turning up on the doorstep as if you'd been gone for minutes instead of months and expect to be welcomed into loving arms with no thought of the grief and worry you've caused!"

Anne recoiled as if she'd been slapped. She'd expected anger, and had steeled herself for it, but Sofia's fury overwhelmed her.

"I'm sorry, Sofia, truly," she said, her voice breaking.

"And you should be!"

"I want my father," Anne said, almost pleading. "Where is he?"

"Upstairs," Sofia said coldly. "With the fever again— brought on, no doubt, by concern and despair over your disappearance."

Anne gasped and flew past Sofia, heading for the stairs, but Sofia's hand reached out to restrain her.

"Wait!" she said. "He's very weak. Let me go first and prepare him."

She brushed by Anne and preceded her up the stairs. Anne waited outside Joel's doorway until Sofia reappeared.

"Don't stay long," Sofia cautioned. "Don't tire him."

Anne entered the darkened room and closed the door behind her. Joel lay on his back on the four-poster, his head deep in the pillows. He raised his hand from the coverlet when he heard her and called out for her in a feeble voice.

Anne hurried to his side. "Oh, Papa! It's Anne. I'm home."

"Annie," Joel said, his voice a whisper.

Anne was appalled at the sight of him. His cheeks were hollow, his complexion waxen, and his hair was shot through with gray. She bent over and kissed his forehead. His skin was dry and papery.

Anne knelt beside the bed and took his hand, horrified to discover that he was too weak to grip hers in return.

"Oh, Papa, please get well soon! I'm home now and I'll take care of you."

"I—I worried, Annie." Every spoken word was an effort of will.

"I'm sorry, Papa. I was a fool. I never meant to hurt you."

His voice had sunk to a hoarse rasp. In the dim light, Anne could see tears forming in his hollow eyes, and she had to bite her lips to keep from weeping herself.

This couldn't be her father. Not the strong, vital

234

man she'd last seen! He was so thin! His form, beneath the coverlet, was so wasted that she realized she could lift him as if he were a child.

Please God! she prayed silently. Don't let him die! I know it was all my fault. Please make him as strong as he used to be! I'll never do wrong again.

An angry Sofia was waiting in the corridor for Anne to reappear. Sofia wanted to take the girl and shake her savagely until Anne acknowledged the extent of the grief she had caused. But when she saw Anne's face and realized how much she was suffering, her own kindly instincts compelled her forward. She extended her arms and Anne fell into them, surrendering at last to the sobs that she'd contained within her breast. Sofia found herself comforting Anne, stroking her hair, holding her close, supporting her.

"He's better, Anne," she murmured. "He was much worse, but Casimiro has been tending him. He'll make him well again. I know it."

He's so weak . . . so thin and weak!"

"Having you home again will help him," Sofia said. "I dread to think of what might have happened, had you not returned when you did."

Anne pulled back her head and looked imploringly into Sofia's eyes. "Oh, Sofia, I've been so wicked. Too wicked to even ask for your forgiveness!"

"There, there, *querida*," Sofia said, pulling Anne back to her. "There is no question of forgiveness—only rejoicing that you are back among us once again!"

Anne wept bitterly in her stepmother's embrace.

"I'm not worthy of you, Sofia—of either of you. I'm sorry, so very sorry!"

Sofia kissed her on the cheek. "Come now, *mi vida,* come with me. I'll take you to your room. You look hungry and tired. I'll tuck you in bed and have dinner brought up."

Anne's return did seem to help Joel. In a few days he was sitting up, and within a week he was able to be carried downstairs to the courtyard to sit with them for an hour or so in the early evening. He was taking solid food again, and Anne imagined she saw color and fullness returning to his cheeks. But he tired quickly, and one of the vaqueros always had to be summoned to carry him back upstairs to his bed because he could not make it on his own.

Neither Joel nor Sofia ever mentioned Anne's absence again. It was clear they preferred to know nothing of what had taken place. But Rudy was a different matter. Whenever he called at the hacienda, his eyes probed Anne's as if he were looking into her very soul.

Does he know? she wondered. Does he simply surmise, or has someone told him?—maybe one of the cowboys who've just returned from Abilene?

Anne tried to avoid Rudy, to look past him; but he had a way of always being near, of always standing where she would have to pass him. And then one evening, when she tried to brush by him in the foyer after everyone else had filed into the courtyard, he caught her by the arm and pulled her back. His lips curled in a lascivious smile, and he tried to draw her close to him.

Anne broke away, eyes flashing. "Are you crazy? What do you think you're doing?"

Rudy backed her against the wall, caging her in with his arms. "Don't play coy with me, Anne! I know all about you."

"Get out of my way, Rudy, or I'll scream for help."

Rudy's smile turned into a mocking laugh, "So you're still pretending to be the virgin princess? Well, someday, *Liebchen,* you'll come to me."

"I'll be damned first!"

A look of anger and lust crossed Rudy's face. "Don't you think I've been watching you for a long time? Don't you know I've seen you when you've glanced in wantonness at this cowboy or that as you rode by like a queen on a pony? Don't you know how long I've wanted you to look at me with that same look?"

"Get out of my way, Rudy!"

When she started to move, he caught her in his powerful arms and pulled her to him. His mouth met hers hungrily. She tried to break from his embrace, but he held her firmly. His lips crushed hers, his tongue sought entrance—probing, craving until she felt her whole body shiver in resignation. And despite her loathing for him, she gave in and let him kiss her until her legs grew weak and she thought she would faint.

At last he released her. His eyes were steely blue as they swept her face, and as he backed away, his hands lingered on her breasts beneath her blouse.

"So, Anne, I *do* have the power to move you, after all!"

"You have the power to disgust me!" She wiped his kisses from her mouth with the back of her hand, then lashed out at him, slapping him across the face.

His eyes narrowed and his mouth formed a snarl. "Someday, Anne, you will not be so ready to rebuff me. Someday you will beg for my kisses."

"Someday I'll see you in hell, Rudy Stark!"

She turned and ran from the foyer toward the courtyard where she knew he would not follow.

26

Joel's strength did not return as it should have. The fever hit him again, and for three days he lay in a delirium, drenched with sweat, unable even to swallow the quinine and herbal teas prescribed by Casimiro.

Anne, Sofia, and Natalia took turns keeping vigil at his bedside, bathing his brow with cool, wet towels; and, always, the old curandero hovered nearby.

The third night was the worst, with Joel's temperature soaring. Time and again he cried out for Martha, and each time he did so Sofia's eyes would cloud over. Sofia was heavy with child and weary from worry and sleepless nights, but her love did not waver.

At last the fever broke, and Casimiro assured the women that Joel would not die. Sofia and Natalia descended to the chapel to recite a rosary of thanksgiving. Anne stayed with Joel and was able at last to slip a few spoonfuls of cool broth between his lips.

"I'm here with you, Papa," she said, not really knowing if he heard her or not. "I'm here and I'll never leave you."

Anne meant what she said. She blamed herself for his illness. His fevered nightmares, his tossing and turning, his wasted body accused her, and she believed that if she had not run away with Kelly, he would never have gotten sick.

"I promise, Papa," she said fervently, cradling his head. "I'll be good and stay by your side forever."

In the days that followed, Joel seemed to be recovering. Once again he was allowed brief intervals downstairs in the courtyard. But he was listless and tired quickly. After only a few minutes, Sofia would have to summon servants to lift him onto his litter and carry him back upstairs to bed.

Joel hated his disability—his life as an invalid. And more than once Anne found him with his face turned to the wall weeping bitterly. He did not seem to share her embarrassment when she caught him with tears in his eyes. It was no longer important to him—no longer a duty—to appear strong and invincible.

There was no question of his returning to work. More and more, Anne assumed the burden of running the ranch. As distasteful as it was to her, she found herself working with Rudy. Though he continued to look at her as if he could fathom her very soul, he advised her wisely and carried out her orders.

Joel's big mahogany desk soon reflected more of Anne than it did of him. A vase of fresh wild flowers adorned its polished surface every morning. The clutter of papers were now stacked tidily in wooden boxes. Ledger books stood in order between heavy onyx bookends, and Anne's neat handwriting began to fill the blue-lined pages, succeeding Joel's labored scrawl.

The work was difficult. There was so much for her to take care of that she often labored far into the night and was back at her desk before dawn. It was a common sight for the midnight crew to see her oil lamp burning in her office window when they left the bunkhouse for work and again when they returned at sunrise. And the yellow glow became a symbol for them for her devotion and dedication. Bunkhouse jokes about the "Boss Lady" ceased, and the cowboys began to look on her with respect and admiration.

Anne had little time to dream of Kelly, but in the stillness of the night, when she doused her lamp and crept upstairs to bed, his presence would suddenly seem almost palpable. She would conjure up his face, hear his voice and his laugh. And when she slipped between the sheets alone and hugged her pillow tightly, she could pretend for a few brief moments that she was holding him close. Then sleep would come, dreamless sleep that numbed her tired brain and stilled the passionate longings in her breast.

At last, Anne could bear their separation no longer. She wrote to Kelly begging him to meet her at Agua Verde, a stagecoach station between the Lantana and the Agarita. His reply, which came within a week, was an almost illiterate letter, printed childishly on a torn piece of brown paper. But Anne didn't care, because Kelly wrote that he would be there on Sunday as she had proposed.

Five days! She didn't know how she would live until Sunday. She threw herself into her work, making arrangements for fall roundup, supervising the construction of a new bunkhouse and better quarters for the families of married cowboys. She drew up plans for a school to be built in the little village that was growing on the ranch, and she wrote letters to San Antonio, Galveston, and New Orleans seeking a teacher for the children. She visited with Joel as often as she could, reporting on the activities of the ranch but taking care not to tire him with detail. And when she had a rare moment, she mounted her horse and rode—rode hard and fast over the prairie land with the sun in her face and the wind in her still short hair—until she was out of sight of the hacienda and utterly alone with herself. Only then could she escape the pressures of the ranch, of Joel's illness and Sofia's constant worry. Only then could she find an interval of peace—and that in itself was all too brief, for almost immediately her thoughts would turn to Kelly.

Nevertheless, the five days that seemed like forever inevitably passed. Then, all at once, it was Sunday!

Sitting beside Sofia and Natalia in the chapel while the visiting priest celebrated Mass, she mouthed the responses at the appropriate times but was oblivious to what she was saying. And afterward, taking her place on Sofia's right at the breakfast table, she somehow got through the meal, although her mind was distracted and her nerves were on edge.

When they finished the last of their *café con leche,* Sofia rose and signaled for the maids to clear the table. Then, turning to Anne, she asked, "Would you like to walk with me? The morning is cool and fresh." Her hands moved over her swollen belly, stroking the baby growing within her. "I'm tired of sitting, and the exercise would do me good."

"I can't, Sofia," Anne said, trying to avoid her eyes. "I have to go somewhere. I have . . . something to do."

Sofia caught her hand. "Anne. Please . . . no!"

"It's nothing to worry about, Sofia," Anne lied. "I just . . ." She could think of no excuse.

"I know what you're planning, Anne. I can read it in your face. Please listen to me. It's no good. Forget him!"

Anne bit her lip. "I can't help it, Sofia. I wish I could, but I can't."

"I will help you!"

"No . . . no! It's no use!" She pulled her hand from Sofia's. "I've got to go now. I'm going to be late as it is."

She turned and ran from the room.

A few minutes later, Sofia heard Anne's boots clattering across the foyer tiles and down the steps of the porch. Hurrying to the window, she caught a glimpse of Anne, who had changed into leather breeches and a fleece-lined jacket, as the girl ran to the remuda.

Anne saddled Ebony, Joel's coal black stallion, and swung up into the stirrups.

"Giddap!" Anne commanded, and her voice carried clearly across the yard and through the window where Sofia stood. The horse reared back, pawing the air, then shot forward, galloping over the prairie toward the west.

Sofia's expression was a mixture of disapproval and sorrow. She wished desperately that she had been able to find the words that would have dissuaded Anne; but she knew her stepdaughter's stubborn will, and she doubted that there was anything she could have said to keep her from her rendezvous. So, as Anne disappeared over the horizon, Sofia simply breathed a prayer that God might keep her stepdaughter safe.

There was a knock behind her and a maid slipped through the door.

"Señora," the servant said. "Señor Trevor calls for you. He is feeling ill."

A look of fright and worry swept over Sofia's face. "I'm coming," she said, gathering her skirts. "I'm coming."

Anne arrived at Agua Verde in mid-afternoon. The daily stagecoach had just departed and the station keeper and his wife were cleaning up. But they were kindly people and strove to make her comfortable.

"Them travelers just about et me out of house and home," the woman said, wiping her work-hardened hands on her greasy apron, "but I reckon I can scare up some vittles for you. You look parched and famished."

The station keeper remained silent and continued to work, stealing glances at Anne every now and then. He wondered who she was and what she was doing there all alone; but no one ever asked those questions in this territory.

"Here you are, dear," the woman said, setting a plate of steaming vegetables and a slab of tough gray meat before Anne at the table. A rotund woman with lank brown hair and sallow cheeks, she smiled cheerily. "If that ain't enough, there's a mite more where it came from."

Anne thought of Kelly—he too would be hungry when he arrived—and said, "I'm obliged, ma'am, but I'm sure this will be plenty."

She ate ravenously, surprising even herself with her appetite; and when she finished, she longed for more but knew she must leave the rest for Kelly.

The man and woman were tired and excused themselves to take a siesta. Anne sat on a hard wooden bench in the shade of the porch and kept an eye on the horizon. Once she thought she heard a horse's hooves and stood up on the bench for a first glimpse of him—but no one appeared.

The sky was blue and cloudless, and a gentle breeze wafted out of the north. Silence surrounded her. Even the mules in the corral behind the station seemed to be drowsing. Anne waited, and the sun dropped lower in the western sky.

What if Kelly didn't come? What if he had mistaken the place? Or gotten the date wrong?

She reached into her jacket pocket and pulled out his letter, unfolding the creased brown paper to reread it once again.

Anne's eyes studied each word. He knew the place and the day they were to meet; he had repeated them both back to her. Then why had he not arrived?

Suddenly she grew afraid. What if he had changed his mind? What if he had decided that he didn't want to see her again?

Impossible! she thought. He loves me—as much as I love him!

But when she read the letter once again, she saw no hint of it. Unlike her own long letter which professed her love for him over and over, his note was brief—friendly, but far from ardent.

Her heart went cold. She shoved the crumpled letter back into her pocket. The sun, now a round red ball, balanced on the horizon.

The station keeper and his wife had been up for some time. She could hear them tending the mules in the corral. After a while the woman came around front and asked Anne, "Will you be staying for supper?"

"I'd like to," Anne replied, looking past her to the west. "If it's not too much trouble."

"None at all, dear," the woman said. "I'm glad for the company."

But Anne was a dismal supper companion, picking at her food, listening for Kelly's horse, jumping at every sound, then slumping down depressed when she realized it wasn't he.

She helped the woman clean up after the meal, but resumed her vigil on the porch when they finished. The night was moonless and spangled with stars.

The woman came to the door. "We're turning in, dear. Can I make you a bed?"

"No thanks," Anne said. "I'll be all right waiting here. It won't be much longer, I'm sure."

The hours passed, and the constellations wheeled their westward course, and she heard the clock inside strike midnight, then the half hour, then one. The woman had awakened and reappeared in the doorway, carrying a lamp.

"Come on inside, dear," she said. "The night air has turned cold, and I've prepared a bed for you."

"No," Anne said. "I've got to wait."

But the woman pushed open the door and held it for Anne. "You best forget him and get some sleep," she said. Her voice was understanding and comforting. "I got a feeling he ain't coming, honey."

Sofia was frantic. Joel had lapsed into a coma, and even Casimiro's efforts—his special magic that had never failed her in the past—were unable to revive him.

"Oh, Joel!" she cried, hot tears streaming over her grief-twisted face. *"Mi vida, mi corazón!* You must get well! You *must!"* She raised her eyes to heaven and begged: *"Dios mío, Santa María!* Save my husband, please! We have had so little time together!"

She clasped his hand and held it tightly in hers. She gazed through tears into his face, hoping desperately for a miracle.

But Joel was far away. He was wandering in a well-lighted place where the winds were gentle and cool. He heard someone call him, and recognizing Martha's voice, felt himself impelled toward her. She seemed to be just behind a glowing mist. He slipped into the brightness, feeling comforted, calm, and well again. Martha spoke his name once more, welcoming him to her side. He felt himself enveloped by the mist. But Joel's almost perfect peace was troubled.

"Anne!" he called out loud. *"Anne!"*

Anne scarcely slept. She rose before the sun and, declining breakfast, resumed her wait on the porch. At noon, the stage from Laredo passed through on its way to San Antonio. The male travelers ogled her and tried to engage her in conversation, but she ignored them. At last, after they departed and the station quieted down again, she admitted bitterly to herself that Kelly was not coming.

Finally, Anne paid for her lodging and her food and set off on her journey back to the Lantana. The station keeper and his wife stood on the porch and watched her disappear in the distance.

"Now what do you think that was all about?" he asked.

"A broken heart," the woman said. Then she turned and went back inside.

Anne rode along in a state of shock, unwilling to believe the truth.

He can't have jilted me! He just can't have! He loves me as much as I love him! I know it!

But then she thought back over their romance and realized that it had been she, not Kelly, who had done the pursuing. She had lured him to Bitter Creek. She had ridden after him up the Chisholm Trail and talked him out of sending her home. And she had been the one to arrange this reunion at the stagecoach station, not he.

Now her misery changed into fury. She cursed Kelly and vowed never to see him again. But another mile farther on, her heart grew heavy and ached in her chest, and she found herself missing the cowboy and making excuses for him.

Maybe he's sick—or in trouble! Maybe his horse threw him or went lame! He wouldn't jilt me! I know he wouldn't!

She almost turned around, almost returned to the stagecoach station with the intention of taking the trail from there to the Agarita in search of Kelly. Visions of him lying injured in the brush beside his hobbled horse filled her head, and for a few moments she was sick with worry.

But again the fury returned, and she knew she was being foolish. He hadn't come because he hadn't wanted to. He hadn't the courage to tell her he didn't love her. He had let her wait and find out for herself. She dried her tears and straightened her shoulders.

It's over, she thought. Maybe I've learned something from all this—but whatever it is, it isn't worth the pain! All I know is that I'll never trust a man again. Never!

And as she dug her spurs into her stallion and galloped toward home, she believed it.

She heard the wailing long before she saw the hacienda. At first she thought it was a wounded animal dying in the brush, but soon she recognized the sound as human, a collection of grieving voices rending the cool twilight air.

When the lights of the big house came into view, the protracted, high-pitched cries grew louder. Anne knew, before she admitted it to herself, what they signified. Her blood turned icy in her veins, and her breath caught in a gasp in her throat.

She raced toward the house, beating her stallion furiously with her whip. She leapt from the saddle and bounded up the stone steps only to be caught by Rudy just inside the double doors.

"Wait, Anne, wait!" he shouted, but she struggled out of his grip.

"*Papa!*" she cried.

The foyer was choked with veiled women, wives of the men who worked on the ranch. They clutched rosaries to their breasts and wept out loud, expressing their sorrow. Their lamentations deafened Anne, frightened her.

"Papa!" she cried again, not knowing which way to turn.

Suddenly she saw Sofia in the doorway to the chapel at the end of the corridor. Sofia, too, was veiled with a black mantilla that reached nearly to her ankles. Behind her, the chapel was ablaze with candlelight. Anne moved like a sleepwalker toward her.

"Where's Papa?" Anne asked, her voice weak and trembling.

Sofia stood very straight, very still, as stonelike as one of the statues of the saints that adorned the chapel walls. A rosary laced through her fingers. Behind her veil, her face was a pale oval, a mask of pain.

"He's dead," Sofia said.

"No!" Anne screamed. She felt her legs grow weak beneath her and reached out to Sofia for support. Sofia backed away, and Anne crumpled at her feet. *"No!"*

"He called for you," Sofia said. Her tone was cold and hard. "He called out: 'Anne! Anne!' But you were not here. You were off somewhere behaving like a ten-peso whore."

Anne sobbed uncontrollably; her eyes flooded with tears; her shoulders shook. "It's not true, Sofia! Believe me!"

But Sofia said nothing. Instead she turned her back on Anne and returned to the chapel.

Getting to her feet, Anne stumbled forward, until she reached the chapel door. There, in front of the altar, on a bier banked with flowers, lay her father.

Anne took one look at his body, wasted, thin—now pale and waxen with death. Suddenly the scene swam before her eyes. A gathering darkness swirled around her. She thought she heard the screams of a thousand winds, thought she saw the chapel candles snuff out one by one. Then she pitched forward with a moan of grief and pain and fell unconscious.

They buried Joel the next day in a grave beside Martha's. Anne shook so badly that Rudy and Emma had to stand next to her and hold her up.

The priest spoke in Spanish about the frailty of the flesh and the immortality of the soul. Anne scarcely listened. After the droning prayer for the dead was over and the priest had sprinkled holy water on the mound of freshly turned earth, Anne moved shakily forward to plant a flowering sprig of lantana on Joel's grave.

She turned and faced the mourners. Her cheeks were chalky white, and the circles under her eyes looked as if they had been drawn with charcoal. She spoke in a trembling voice that nevertheless carried to the friends and neighbors who stood silently with downcast eyes just behind Sofia, to the cowboys and ranch hands who huddled in groups, and to the grieving, black-clothed servants who hovered on the periphery of the great crowd that had assembled to pay their last respects.

"My father is gone. But he was such a man that his memory will live on within us all the rest of our lives. It's God's will that man was born to die—and one by one we too will go, until there are none of us living who stand here now. But there is something that will live on. My father dreamed of it and loved it. He worked for it and fought for it. I'm speaking of this land on which we stand. It will endure—as will his dream!"

Later, Anne sat by herself on the porch of the hacienda. Her eyes swept the horizon from east to west, and she took its measure. The words of her eulogy rang in her ears.

This land! This dream! Yes, it would live on. She swore that she would see it did. That would be her parting gift to Joel!

PART TWO

1868—1875

1868

27

Death, with its companions pain and grief, were familiar to Anne, but in time, sustained by the comforting memory of Joel's unending love for her, she was able to accept the finality of his passing. The loss of Kelly was another matter. Because the first romantic love in her life had abandoned her without explanation, without a word of farewell, even her fondest memories of him were clouded by the remembrance of the long, lonely night she had spent at the Agua Verde stagecoach stop. She would never forget waiting in vain for the sound of his horse's hooves, staring with the last spark of hope and excitement dying within her breast for a fleet shadow across the landscape that would turn out to be Kelly. But he had not come.

And so, as winter settled over the land, Anne bundled up her emotions within her as tightly as she clutched her sheepskin coat about herself. Never again, she vowed, would she allow herself to be so vulnerable, so open to being hurt.

The following spring, Anne traveled to San Antonio to a meeting of ranchers who gathered to discuss the threat of a Mexican rustler named Valdez. The hard winter had driven huge numbers of wild cattle deep into South Texas, and Valdez and his bandits were making forays across the Rio Grande, decimating the ranchers' herds.

Anne found herself seated next to William Kendall, the carpetbagger who had taken advantage of Reconstruction to steal the Agarita from Joel's old partner, Ramiro Rivas.

Before the meeting began, Anne screwed up her courage and asked Kendall point-blank about news of Kelly. His answer froze her blood and drove her even more deeply into herself.

"Oh, Kelly. I had to let him go," Kendall said, his northern twang contrasting sharply with the drawling voices all around them. "He took up with a squaw, a sorry creature ugly as sin. They drifted off west—who knows where? She'd filled his head with tales of Indian gold buried in a mountain cave. He had visions of striking it rich, I believe."

That was the last Anne ever heard of Kelly, the last she ever wanted to hear.

Her childhood had ceased the day her mother died, when Joel had returned to the camp wounded and almost dead himself, and Anne had had to dig the bullet out of his shoulder. The interlude of her youth was even briefer, having vanished abruptly in the old wood and mud shack when she had raised her father's pistol to blow the life out of the intruding vaquero. And now her time as a romantic, trusting young woman came to a sudden end in the dining room of the Menger Hotel, its epitaph spoken in the harsh Yankee accents of her distant neighbor.

When Anne returned to the Lantana, she threw herself into her work. Although Joel had left the combined ranches to her and Sofia equally, the task of running the business fell completely to Anne. Less than two months after Joel's death, Sofia had given birth to a son. He was born, as Anne had hoped, on Christmas Day. And in the intervening months, Sofia's every waking thought, and her fondest dreams, were of the child. She had named him Carlos, after her grandfather, and she seemed to find no time for anything but her baby.

He was doted on and spoiled outrageously by Sofia, Natalia, the servants—and even Anne herself. They adored him equally and without jealousy. They rocked him and played with him and called him *El Rey*.

His birth had saved Sofia. She had mourned so deeply for Joel that Anne was certain that without the baby—this new life that seemed to fill the hacienda with joy—Sofia would have gone mad. Anne had seen the madness coming, had seen it haunting Sofia's eyes, and had seen it displaced when on that Christmas Day, Natalia had wrapped the newborn infant in a blanket of blue satin and lace and placed him in Sofia's arms.

Anne, then, stood alone at the head of the ranch— knowing that while she acted as boss, she must also be custodian, for now there was Carlos, who promised to outlive them all, and who would inherit this domain which they had carved out of the rough *brasada*.

The range was still free and open. The cattle drives were increasing in size, and Anne planned to send two herds that year up the well-traveled trails to Kansas. It seemed a boom that would never end.

A town had sprung up less than ten miles from the hacienda at a place where Bitter Creek took a bend and trickled on toward the Gulf. The settlement was rugged and boisterous, with more saloons than churches, its houses little more than shanty shacks. Rudy complained to Anne, arguing that the people should be forced to move because they occupied Lantana land; but Anne took an interest in the town, feeling that its presence would be good for the ranch. And she named it Joelsboro.

She built a traveler's hotel to attract drummers and a general store to supply the community. And she built a school and tried to attract a teacher.

"The peon children don't need to learn," Sofia objected. "It will do them no good."

"I don't agree," Anne said; and she wrote another long letter to the normal school in Nacogdoches, trying her best to make the territory and the position seem attractive. But she held out scant hope of success. Little more than a month before, the rustler Valdez and his gang had attacked the southern reaches of the Lantana in an attempt to steal a herd of longhorns that were watering at a pond called Ojo del Toro. A crew of Anne's cowboys who were patrolling the area discovered the bandits and ambushed them, killing seven and driving Valdez and the rest away.

Not that there had been any real danger to the hacienda itself. The battle had taken place more than twenty-five miles south. Nevertheless, when word reached Anne, she sent Sofia, Natalia, and Carlos to safety at the hotel in Joelsboro for the night. Somehow, news of the attack escaped the boundaries of the ranch, and Anne was upset to see it reported in the next week's newspaper from San Antonio. Undoubtedly, the information would be picked up in Nacogdoches too, and would frighten away any young teacher who otherwise might be tempted to take the position Anne was offering.

At the moment, Anne had other worries. Sofia was insisting on a trip to Monterrey—to visit relatives she hadn't seen in years. Anne tried to discourage it, claiming it was an unnecessary journey through dangerous territory. But Sofia was not to be dissuaded. For weeks she and Natalia had kept their seamstresses busy creating lavish gowns for them to wear during the six months they intended to stay.

"I think you should leave Carlos here," Anne said. "He's really too young to make that long trip."

"Nonsense, Anne," Sofia replied confidently. "He's strong and healthy. Besides, he's the main reason we're going. I want to show him off to my cousins."

256

"I'm worried about *bandidos*," Anne said.

Sofia smiled placidly. "The men you call *bandidos*, my dear, are actually great Mexican generals and important *hacendados* from the other side of the Rio Grande. And don't forget that I am Mexican, too."

Anne remained unconvinced. Her stepmother had never become used to the reality that this part of Texas, the land below the Nueces, was United States territory. To Sofia it was still part of Mexico, perhaps temporarily in American hands. She even found it difficult to take umbrage at the attacks and rustling from across the border. Sofia felt she understood, as Anne did not, that Valdez and his kind considered gringos and their cattle fair game.

Sofia went on, "And since I am Mexican, they will not harm me. What's more, it wouldn't surprise me if they conducted me safely through the *brasada*."

Anne decided not to press the point. There's time to change Sofia's mind, she thought, time to convince her to call off the trip—or at least to leave Carlos behind.

But in the weeks that passed, nothing that Anne could say, no argument she raised, had any influence on Sofia. If anything, Sofia's excitement over the coming journey mounted as the departure date approached. At last, in the final week of August, everything was ready.

The day they departed Sofia and Natalia were up before dawn, checking and rechecking the contents of their well-stuffed trunks before ordering them loaded aboard the waiting coach. Servants hauled baskets of food from the kitchen to sustain the travelers on their trip. The coachman and his brakeman led the team of six mules from the stable and hitched them to the rig. Going to Carlos's room, Anne took him from his bed and lovingly bathed and dressed him.

"We'll return the end of February," Sofia said as she climbed into the coach beside Natalia.

"That's so long from now," Anne said. She had picked Carlos up and continued to hold him, unwilling to give him up. "I hope you'll change your mind and come home sooner."

Sofia held out her arms to receive Carlos. "A shorter stay wouldn't be worth the trouble of the trip."

Anne delivered the cheerful infant to her reluctantly. "Now, do as I said, Sofia. Drive to Agua Verde and wait for the coach to Laredo. Then follow it. I know it will make the journey longer, but it's safer that way."

"Of course, *querida*," Sofia agreed.

Anne leaned inside and kissed Sofia lightly on the cheek. "*Buen viaje*," she said. Then she kissed Carlos good-bye and, stepping back, closed the door.

The coach jogged forward in the direction of Agua Verde. Anne watched after it until it was out of sight.

After about an hour, Sofia called out the window to the teamster. He halted the coach and swung down onto the running board.

"I've changed my mind," Sofia told him. "I've decided not to go by way of Agua Verde after all. Turn the coach south and head for Roma. We'll save at least two days that way."

"But Sofia!" Natalia said. "You promised Anne . . ."

"She worries too much," Sofia said. "I was only trying to ease her mind. My way is better."

"I would rather follow the stage."

"I'm only thinking of Carlos," Sofia said. "The trip will be hard for him. The shorter the better."

Natalia's eyes fell on the baby, asleep in Sofia's arms. "I suppose you're right."

Sofia smiled happily, knowing that Natalia's concern for Carlos's welfare would win her over to anything.

"So head south," she told the driver. "We'll be in Roma before we know it."

Their coach lumbered over the rugged *brasada*. By

Sofia's reckoning they were no more than a few hours short of Roma and the Rio Grande.

"You see, *tía*," she said to Natalia. "We're nearly there, and all has gone smoothly."

Natalia, who was holding Carlos now, nodded in agreement and adjusted the curtain to keep the wind and dust off the baby's face. As she worked with the window, she spotted a solitary figure on horseback halfway to the horizon.

The driver must have seen him too, because the mules slackened their pace, and the coach began to slow.

"What is it?" Sofia asked.

"Look! A horseman," Natalia answered.

Sofia leaned across and peered out. "Alone, thank God!" she breathed. At the sight of the rider, all Sofia's previous bravado immediately left her, and her heart began pounding in her breast. She reached into her reticule and withdrew her small pearl-handled revolver. "*Cuidado!*" she called out the window to the driver and his companion. "He may be a bandit!"

The horseman had ridden swiftly through the brush and blocked the rutted trail ahead. There was nothing for the driver to do but bring the coach to a halt.

"*Qué pasa?*" he called to the horseman.

"*Buenos días,*" the man replied. He was lean and rangy with a dark sombrero and a drooping black mustache. He carried a holstered rifle next to his saddle but appeared to have no inclination to use it. Nevertheless, Sofia sat looking out of the coach window and kept her revolver pointed at his chest.

"I bring a warning of *bandidos*," the man said to the driver.

Natalia gasped audibly and hugged Carlos closer to her bosom.

Sofia's face had grown quite pale, but she called out boldly from the window. "Who are you, señor? Identify yourself!"

259

The man swept his sombrero from his head and bowed in his saddle. "I am Juan Chapa, señora. I am a vaquero for Don Pablo del Bosque."

"You are far from home."

"I have been to Mier to see my widowed mother."

Sofia was skeptical, but the man was suitably deferential, and something about him reassured her.

"What is this news of *bandidos?*" she pursued.

"I saw them," he replied. "On this trail—not five miles from here. They did not see me, and I was able to ride around them without being molested."

"Let's turn back, Sofia!" Natalia cried.

"Then we are in danger," Sofia said to the man, ignoring Natalia and her plea.

"Sí, señora," he said. ". . . if you continue on this course, you will surely fall into their hands."

"Yet you found a way around them," Sofia said. "Will you guide us safely in the direction you came?"

The man seemed to contemplate this for a moment.

"I will pay you for your trouble," Sofia added. "We are in a hurry and have no time to turn back."

The offer of money appeared to persuade the man. "I am at your service, señora. I will lead you around the bandits."

"Diego!" Sofia called to her driver. "Follow this man."

The coach gave a lurch and journeyed forward, off the rutted trail and into the brushland.

"Oh, Sofia," Natalia whimpered. "I'm afraid. We should have done as Anne said and followed the coach to Laredo. Let's turn back now."

"Don't worry, *tía.* Everything will be all right. This man belongs to Pablo del Bosque. He can be trusted."

"How do you know?" Natalia asked.

Sofia didn't know, but she believed the man.

The going was slow and rough. The two women had to grip the leather hand straps to avoid being pitched

260

onto the floor between the facing seats. Carlos, who was tired and hungry, began to cry.

"Hush, hush, my little prince," Sofia cooed, taking him on her lap and cradling him in her arms. "We'll be in Roma before long."

But no sooner had she spoken than Diego cried out in alarm from his seat atop the coach.

"What is it, Diego?" she called from the window, but she needed no answer, for she saw that the man who called himself Juan Chapa had suddenly spurred his horse and was galloping off at top speed toward a low rising hill in the distance.

"Trickery!" she cried. "Quick, Diego, turn the coach around!"

Diego was in the process of doing so, but the rough terrain and the denseness of the surrounding brush impeded them. The mules, frightened by Sofia's shouts began to balk, oblivious to the sting of Diego's lash.

"*Dios mío! Santa María!*" Natalia screamed, crossing herself. "We are done for!"

From behind the low hill, a band of horsemen had suddenly appeared, brandishing rifles and riding fast toward the coach. In a moment, they were upon them. Two shots rang out and Diego and his companion fell from the coach into the brush. The mules ran wild, pitching the coach dangerously from side to side, tossing Natalia onto the floor. Sofia clutched Carlos and tumbled in a heap on top of her aunt. Both women, weeping uncontrollably, called on the saints to save them, and Carlos cried in fright and sympathy.

The man called Juan Chapa caught up with the coach. Hauling himself from his saddle onto the driver's seat, he wrenched on the reins and began steering the mules into a circle. The other horsemen galloped alongside. Sofia felt the coach whirling. Her body absorbed every shock as the wheels struck rocks and cactus. Certain that they would capsize, she cushioned Carlos between her and Natalia.

But the circling mules began to tire, and before long Juan Chapa brought them to a halt.

Almost immediately, the door was thrown open, and one of the horsemen leered in at the cowering forms of Sofia and Natalia.

He was brusquely shoved aside and replaced by another man, a tall swarthy figure with deeply set dark eyes and a hard, cruel mouth.

"Spare us!" Natalia cried. "Take our money! Take everything! But spare us. We have a baby with us!"

"Silencio, abuela!" the man barked, and Natalia flinched as if he'd slapped her.

"Who are you?" Sofia asked between clenched teeth. Her anger was almost as great as her fear.

"I am Emilio Valdez," the man replied.

As Natalia cried out in recognition of his name, Valdez threw back his head and laughed, his teeth strikingly white against the darkness of his skin. "So, you know me?" he said.

"Everyone knows of you, señor," Sofia replied, struggling to appear brave, trying another tack. "However, you may not realize who I am."

"But of course I do, señora," Valdez said. "You are the *viuda* of Joel Trevor, and you come from the Lantana."

"Then you will certainly let us go in peace," Sofia challenged. "You must know that I am Mexican, like you. There is no cause for bad blood between us."

"Don't talk to me of blood!" Valdez shouted, his white teeth flashing beneath his mustache. "Your vaqueros shed the blood of seven of my friends!"

"And what did you expect, señor? We did not invite you to trespass. Our men fought only for what was ours."

"You speak sharply, señora," Valdez said. "We'll see how long you will continue that tone."

He glanced up at Juan Chapa on the banquette of

262

the coach and barked an order for him to set the team in motion.

"Where are you taking us?" Sofia demanded.

"You are not the only one with a grand hacienda, señora," Valdez replied. His voice was filled with mockery. "I too have a place of my own, and it would please me to extend my hospitality to you."

He slammed the door in her face and set off in a trot beside the rolling coach.

"We are doomed," Natalia lamented, hauling herself up off of the floor. "He will kill us."

"I don't think so," Sofia murmured, trying to still Carlos's cries. "If he meant to take our lives, he would have done it here. I'm afraid he has other plans for us."

Natalia saw the ominous shadows in her eyes and began wailing miserably. "I am too old—I have lived too long for this to be happening to me."

The coach did not return to the rutted trail that led to Roma. Instead, it stayed in the brush, wending its way slowly over the rugged land. Sofia and Natalia were thrown about until their arms and legs were bruised and sore. Mercifully, Carlos fell into an exhausted sleep. Sofia held him tightly while Natalia slipped her rosary beads between her fingers and prayed for rescue.

They rode all afternoon and into the night. Chapa used his lash on the weary mules, driving them onward. Near midnight, they forded the Rio Grande and lumbered up the bank on the Mexican side.

An hour later, they halted at a watering hole, and the mules were allowed to drink. After a few minutes they set out again, and it was nearly dawn before they arrived at their destination.

Valdez yanked open the coach door and ordered the women out. Their bruised limbs ached, and they hobbled painfully from the steps to the ground.

Sofia saw in the dim morning light the outline of

263

a stone house built in a square around a courtyard. Corrals extended to the south and the west, and in the distance, breaking the horizon, were the flat roofs of perhaps a dozen peon shacks.

"Inside!" Valdez ordered, and the women stumbled toward the house.

It was comfortable, but far from luxurious. The main room was sparsely furnished with rude, wooden furniture. There were no carpets, and only a single oil lamp glowed in the center of a plank table.

Valdez led them to a room off the courtyard. "In here," he said.

They had no light, but the predawn glow through the barred window revealed a narrow cubicle with two beds and a table in between. Natalia fell exhausted onto one of the cornhusk-filled mattresses. Sofia turned to face Valdez, holding Carlos between them as if to remind him of his brutality.

"We are hungry," she said. "Or do you intend to confiscate all the food we had aboard the coach?"

"I'll send something for you to eat."

"And milk! Have you any milk for the child?"

"I'll send milk too," he said, and he turned to leave.

"What do you want of us?" Sofia cried, halting him at the door.

"Later," Valdez responded. "That comes later."

"If it's ransom you want," Sofia said, "you have only to demand it of my stepdaughter. She will pay anything. Anything!"

Valdez's lips curled in a smile that chilled Sofia's bones. "It's not money I desire," he replied.

He slipped through the door and bolted it from the outside.

The hot August sun rose in the cloudless sky. For the first few hours the cubicle's stone walls held the preceding night's coolness; then the temperature began to rise. By noon the two women were sweltering. They took turns walking the baby in front of the narrow, barred window, so that Carlos could feel the meager whiffs of warm air that drifted in.

By three, Natalia had collapsed from heat and thirst. She lay prostrate on the hard mattress, gasping in a pool of her own perspiration. Sofia spotted a peasant woman and called to her from the window. The woman approached warily, but when Sofia begged for water, she nodded in understanding and disappeared. A short time later, she returned with a dripping gourd and passed it through the iron bars. Sofia held it to Carlos's lips and let him drink his fill. For herself, she took only enough to alleviate the intense dryness of her mouth. The rest she doled out to Natalia, reserving a little to bathe the woman's fevered brow.

The day was torture. Sofia had never felt such scorching heat. Natalia tossed and turned feebly on her mattress, muttering prayers between periods of delirium. Amazingly, Carlos seemed not to suffer. Sofia had stripped him of his clothing, and he slept through the hottest part of the afternoon.

At last the sun set behind the mountains to the west. A dry, fresh wind picked up and cooled the cubicle. Sofia nearly wept in thanksgiving. Food was finally brought and Natalia seemed to recover. Her ravings ceased, and after a while, she was able to sit up and help Sofia feed Carlos.

Suddenly, at the door, they heard the rasp of the iron bolt sliding back. The door swung open, revealing Valdez on the threshold. He was dressed in leather breeches and a cotton shirt open to the waist. His eyes glittered, piercing the darkness.

"Come with me," he ordered.

"Have you decided to set us free?"

"Not yet . . . I have other plans."

Sofia felt too tired to argue. All she could think about was being released from the prison of their tiny cubicle. She turned to the bed and reached for Carlos.

"Leave him here!" Valdez commanded.

"Never!" Sofia cried.

"It's you I want—not him or the old woman!" He grabbed her roughly around the waist and pulled her to him.

Sofia lashed out, raking her fingernails over his face, drawing blood. Valdez bellowed and wrenched her arm behind her back. White lights flashed before Sofia's eyes, and she felt herself grow faint with the pain.

With the last of her strength Natalia raised herself from her bed and clutched Carlos to her bosom. She watched in horror as Valdez picked up Sofia and strode off, carrying her across the courtyard.

Valdez carried Sofia to his bedroom and tossed her on his bed. He reached behind him and bolted the door.

"Now, my pretty señora, I'll have my revenge for the seven who were killed on your ranch!"

Sofia ignored the intense pain that still gripped her arm. Fear and anger boiled up in her. She sprang from the bed and attacked Valdez with both fists, hammering his chest.

His eyes went flat. His lips tightened with fury. He raised his hand and struck her violently across the cheek. Sofia heard her jaw crack, and her nose filled with blood. Again pain overwhelmed her, and she staggered backwards, sinking to her knees. Valdez dragged her across the floor and threw her once more onto his bed. His fingers clawed at her dress, ripping it to the waist. He tore away the thin cotton of her camisole, exposing her heaving breasts. His eyes glazed with lust at the sight, and his big hands covered her breasts, kneading them roughly.

He was on top of her, crushing her with his weight. She continued to struggle feebly, too racked with pain to fend him off. Now she felt him throwing back her

266

skirts and tearing off her underclothing. With his powerful legs, he spread her thighs apart. She tried to scream, but no sound emerged—only a gasp of terror that was drowned out by his ragged breathing.

Then suddenly she felt him enter her, violently, all at once, until she thought that surely she would be ripped apart. Now she screamed—a long tortured wail that echoed and reechoed off the stone walls. He thrust inside her again and again with the fury of a madman. Sofia's eyelids fluttered and she fainted.

He took her over and over throughout the night—always as brutally as the first time. Once, in a moment of consciousness, she heard Carlos crying from somewhere on the other side of the courtyard—his wailing punctuated by horrified screams from Natalia.

For a moment Sofia realized what atrocities her aunt was suffering at the hands of the other *bandidos*, but her mind refused to let her think about it. It deafened Sofia's ears to Natalia's cries, and it erased from her memory the knowledge that she had ever even heard them.

At last, when Valdez's savage lust was satisfied, he rolled off her. He unbolted the door and strolled outside into the courtyard. Sofia stirred on the bed in agony. She lifted her head in time to see Juan Chapa enter the doorway.

"No!" she managed to murmur.

But Chapa was already lurching toward her, his fingers fumbling with the buttons on his trousers.

"No! *Por Dios, no!*"

But he was now on top of her, and over his shoulder she saw the doorway filling with the other *bandidos*.

28

It was a week before Anne learned of the abduction. When Sofia's coach had failed to arrive in Monterrey on schedule, her relatives there had telegraphed an inquiry to Joelsboro, and the message was sent by rider to the Lantana.

"Valdez!" Anne said, crushing the telegram in her fist. Rudy stood beside her at her desk.

"It must be Valdez," he agreed. "He's the only one bold enough to do such a thing!"

"Goddamn the radicals in Austin!" Anne swore, rising from her desk and pacing the floor in front of the empty fireplace. "If it weren't for those Republican scalawags, we'd still have the Rangers to help us."

"They couldn't help anyway," Rudy said. "If Valdez has taken Sofia and Natalia, he'll be holding them at his hideout across the Rio Grande."

"Oh, the Rangers would do just fine," Anne said. "They wouldn't let a little stream of water get in their way!"

"Well, they've been disbanded—so it's not worth talking about," Rudy said.

For a moment, Anne's fury had been diverted to the Reconstructionist legislature at the state capital;

but almost immediately, her attention returned to the fate of Sofia and her family.

"We'll get no help from Mexico," she declared. "You can count on that. They're probably erecting a statue to Valdez at this very moment." She ceased her pacing and paused before the window. "It's in our hands, Rudy. It's up to us to free them."

"What shall we do?"

"I want you to organize twenty-five or thirty of our best horsemen and keenest shots. Arm them with our finest rifles and plenty of ammunition. We're going to pay a call on Valdez!"

"We?" Rudy asked, astonished. "For sure you're not thinking about riding with the men!"

"Of course I'm going," Anne snapped, suddenly irritated with Rudy and his stolid lack of imagination. "As a matter of fact, I intend to lead the group!"

"You can't do that!"

"I certainly can! You know me better than that!" She saw herself suddenly on horseback at the head of her private army. "And I'll make a damned good general too!"

Sure that no argument would prevail against Anne's determination, Rudy left and within an hour, he had rounded up the men. More than half were Mexican vaqueros, who had been born and raised on the Lantana and who had served Sofia with utter devotion. The rest were gringo cowboys—battle-wise Confederate veterans who had earned their laurels at Vicksburg, Bull Run, and the Wilderness. They massed outside the hacienda to draw their Winchesters and ammunition from Rudy. Then Anne joined them, atop Ebony, the coal black stallion that had belonged to her father.

She wore a new dove-gray Stetson ringed with a headband of pheasant feathers and tight-fitting leggings over her trousers. Her blouse was coarse Mexican cotton, dyed indigo, and her freshly shined oxblood boots gleamed in the sun.

"Let's raise dust," she told Rudy. Digging her spurs into Ebony, she sprang forward at the head of her little army.

They rode all day and at sunset made camp in the brush a few miles west of Roma. Anne singled out a vaquero named Dominguez and gave him orders to slip across the Rio Grande and ride into Mier.

"Be on guard," she cautioned. "Don't trust anyone. But find out the location of Valdez's hideout." Then she handed him a pouch bulging with silver pesos. "This ought to be enough of a *mordida* to get the information we want."

Dominguez smiled, weighing the pouch in his palm. "A *mordida* like this would set any mouth to singing."

When Dominguez returned shortly before midnight, Anne was still awake, waiting for him. He handed her the empty pouch.

"What news?" she asked.

"The *rancho* is five hours from here near a village called San Andrés."

"Was there word of my stepmother?"

"A rumor only—that Valdez had taken two women and a child."

"Cabrón!" Anne swore. She looked off toward the south to the dark hills of Mexico silhouetted against the midnight sky. "Get some rest, Dominguez. We'll ride at dawn."

They crossed the river as the first rays of sunlight broke over the eastern horizon. Anne rode the lead with Rudy and Dominguez beside her. Dominguez had drawn a crude map of the territory, and from time to time, Anne took it out to check their progress. At last, when the sun was nearly at its zenith, she signaled for her troops to halt.

"San Andrés lies on the other side of that pass," she said. "If our map is in order, we should find Valdez

270

just south of here over that low range of hills. Rudy, you and Dominguez scout it out. We'll wait here for you."

They returned shortly to report that they had seen the hacienda with its neighboring *jacales*.

"There was a remuda of perhaps a hundred horses," Rudy said.

"That means he's got at least twenty-five men with him," Anne calculated.

"Almost the same number as us," Rudy said. "We should have brought more men."

Anne looked about at her troops. They showed no sign of nervousness. They sat easy in their saddles, checking their Winchesters, arranging their cartridge belts. "We have enough," she said.

"The hacienda is well made," Rudy went on, "— built around a courtyard. The windows are big, but deep-set. The roof is flat with a high wall around it. At the corners there are narrow slits where riflemen can shoot through. It's from there that they'll defend themselves."

"Surprise is our ace in the hole," Anne said. "We've got to storm the house before they know what's happening."

"One more thing, Anne," Rudy said.

"What's that?"

"I saw Sofia's coach."

Anne merely nodded. That was something she didn't want to think about—not at the moment. There would be time enough for that later. First they had to win the battle.

Anne turned and faced her men. *"Listos?"* she asked. "Are we ready?"

They nodded.

"Anne!" Rudy said quickly. "Let me lead them. Stay here and wait for us."

"These are my men, Rudy," she said, leveling her green eyes on him. "I'll not abandon them now."

271

"But there's great danger."

"I know that," she said. "And I'm scared to death. But I led them here, and I'll be damned if now I'll turn tail and run."

Rudy saw that his plea was futile. "You're a hell of a woman, Anne," he said. "Where do you get your strength?"

Anne gazed past him, ignoring his question. "Let's go!" she said.

"May God give us luck," Rudy prayed.

"May God help us shoot straight," Anne added.

Ebony sprang forth, carrying Anne toward the rise of low hills ahead of them. Her men spread out, flanking her on either side. They cleared the brow of the hill and charged the hacienda. Their surprise attack was effective. Except for the startled cries of a few peons laboring in the distant fields, their appearance seemed to rouse no response. For a moment, Anne thought they might be able to seize the hacienda without a battle.

But as they galloped near, a shot rang out from the fortified rooftop. Then another—followed by a fusillade. Anne saw two of her men fall.

Rudy and Dominguez had already reached the house. They jumped from their saddles and pressed themselves against the wall.

Anne spurred Ebony and headed for the archway that gave onto the courtyard. She was in the open, reining her stallion right and left, zigzagging through a hail of bullets.

"Go back!" Rudy shouted. "Go back!"

From a perch on the roof, Valdez squinted down his rifle barrel and took aim. Anne cut sharply to the left, as Valdez fired, and the bullet sang past her ear. Then he squeezed off another shot, and Anne felt it strike Ebony beneath her. The horse whinnied in pain, reared up on its hind legs, and fell over backwards. Anne was thrown from the saddle and landed hard in the dirt. The fall stunned her. Lights flashed before her eyes and she gasped for breath. But as another rifle shot kicked up dust beside her right shoulder, she shook her head, clearing the cobwebs and began to scramble toward the safety of the wall. Rudy reached out to grab her hand, dragging her toward him. She flattened herself against the house between Rudy and Dominguez.

"They're too much for us!" Rudy shouted. "Look! They're driving our men away!"

Anne saw that her troops had dropped back, scuttling for cover in the brush beyond.

"We've got to get inside," Anne cried. "We've got to get the snipers on the roof."

She ran through the archway into the courtyard. A bullet zinged past her, shattering tile on the well that stood in the center. Spinning, she fired up from the hip. One of the men on the parapet pitched forward and tumbled to the paving stones below.

Rudy and Dominguez burst through the entrance into the courtyard. They fired, reloaded, and fired again, sending two more men to their deaths. Gunfire could also be heard from outside where some of Valdez's men had encountered her troops.

Anne crouched for cover behind the well. Overhead, Valdez and Juan Chapa had flattened themselves against the red roof tiles. Chapa took a bead on Dominguez and fired, striking him in the shoulder. Dominguez's rifle flew from his hands, and he fell back, stumbling through the archway.

Rudy dashed across the courtyard to Anne's side behind the well.

"There're only two left up there," she told him quickly. "They're hiding behind the chimney."

She glanced around her. The courtyard was empty except for the well. There was no place for them to take cover. Then she spotted a wooden door at the entrance to one of the rooms opening onto the courtyard. It swung back and forth in the breeze that swirled around them, creaking on rusty hinges.

"I'm going over there," she whispered to Rudy. "I can get a shot at them from that door. Start firing! Keep them busy!"

"No, Anne!" Rudy protested, trying to stop her. "You'll never make it!"

"I've got to, Rudy! We're nearly out of ammunition. There's no other way!"

She took a deep breath. Her heart drummed in her breast. This could be it! she thought. She had never been so frightened in all her life. Yet through the fabric of her fear ran a thread of cool, dispassionate courage.

She drew on it now. Clutching her rifle, she sprang from behind the well and sprinted for the open doorway. Behind her, Rudy's Winchester cracked again and again, drawing return fire from the roof. As she neared the doorway, Valdez spotted her and fired, but too late. The bullet ricocheted off the stone wall an inch behind her head.

Anne rolled to the floor. She shoved her rifle between the crack in the door, resting its barrel on the bottom hinge, and fired, shattering one of the tiles at Valdez's elbow. He backed up, forcing Juan Chapa back around the chimney.

"We've got 'em, Rudy!" she shouted. "We've got 'em in a crossfire!"

Rudy pulled the trigger. His bullet caught Juan Chapa and slammed him against the roof.

Valdez froze, his back against the chimney. Carefully, he allowed himself a quick glance into the courtyard. His eyes caught the flash of sunlight off the gleaming barrel of Anne's Winchester pointing up at him from the door.

"Surrender!" she shouted. "You can't escape!"

"Never!" he cried. "Valdez would never surrender to a woman!"

So that's Valdez! Anne thought. The dangerous Valdez—and we have him cornered!

For the first time since the attack began, all was quiet. Then suddenly, from behind the closed door of one of the nearby rooms, came the sound of a child wailing.

"Carlos!" Anne breathed.

Valdez took advantage of her momentary distraction to swing around the chimney and draw a bead on her. His swift movement alerted Anne and her finger squeezed the trigger sending a bullet ripping through the sleeve of Valdez's shirt. He threw himself backward, grasping for the parapet. Anne reloaded and took aim, firing off another round just as Valdez swung himself over the edge and dropped to the ground on the other side.

"Rudy!" she cried. "He's escaped! After him!"

Jumping up from behind the well, Rudy sprinted through the archway. Anne left the doorway and flew after him. Outside, Rudy braced himself against the wall and fired. But Valdez had grabbed a horse from the remuda and was galloping off through the brush toward the southwest.

Anne raised her rifle and pulled off a final shot, but Valdez was lost in a trail of dust. Two of her men fired, but they were as wide of the mark as she.

Her fury rose full measure within her. She raised her Winchester with both hands above her head and hurled it in the direction Valdez had fled. "The bastard! The dirty goddamned bastard!"

For a moment, Rudy thought she was going to break down and cry. But Anne swallowed her fury, straightened her shoulders, and broke into a run— back through the archway in the direction of Carlos's cry. She yanked on the rusty bolt and flung back the door.

She stood on the threshold, rooted to the spot, unable to move. Inside, on a hard, filthy mattress, Sofia lay naked, holding a weak and whimpering Carlos in her arms. Her hair was disheveled and hung in thick, dirty strands about her face. Even in the room's dim light, Anne could discern the bruises that covered her stepmother's body and the angry dark swelling that disfigured her jaw.

"Oh, my God!" she cried to Rudy who had run to her side.

"Here," Rudy said, quickly unbuttoning his shirt. "Take this and cover her."

Anne rushed into the room, draped the shirt over Sofia's nakedness, and crooned to her, "Oh, Sofia, my darling! We're here. Everything will be all right. We've come to take you home."

"Home . . ." Sofia murmured. Her voice was weak and shaky.

"Oh, yes, my dear! Home! You're safe again with us at last!"

Stepping inside, Rudy gasped at the overpowering stench of sweat and excrement. "Let's get her out of this place!" he said. Carlos stopped crying as Anne took him from Sofia, and Rudy bent over the bed to lift Sofia in his arms. They moved across the courtyard toward the shade beneath the archway.

When Anne saw Sofia in the full light of day, she cried out again. "Rudy! Look what they've done to her!"

"The swine!" he swore, setting Sofia down gently on the stone floor.

"Where's Natalia?" Anne remembered.

Sofia's lips silently formed her aunt's name.

"Natalia?" Anne repeated. "Where is she?"

"In her room," Sofia murmured.

"Where's the room? I'll go for her," Rudy said.

"Upstairs," Sofia replied.

Rudy and Anne exchanged glances.

"But Sofia, there *is* no upstairs . . ." Anne began.

"Upstairs in her room," Sofia continued, "dressing for dinner."

"What do you mean?" Anne asked, a frown creasing her forehead.

"I should be dressing too," Sofia said. "After all, Father will be angry if I'm late. He's always angry when I'm late for dinner."

Anne looked away, tears stinging her eyes. "Oh, Rudy . . ."

Sofia reached out for Carlos and, taking him once more into her arms, began to chant a nursery rhyme to him:

"One is for sorrow,
Two is for joy,
Three is a letter,
Four is a boy . . ."

"What's she saying?" Rudy asked.

"A poem little children recite whenever they see buzzards circling in the sky," Anne replied. "They tell their fortune by how many birds they count."

Sofia went on:

"Five is for silver,
Six is for gold,
And seven's a secret
That will never be told!"

Sofia finished with a wan smile and kissed Carlos on the forehead. "I should be upstairs dressing for dinner," she said, "but I'd much rather stay down here and play with my doll."

Anne stared at her miserably, realizing the truth at last. "Oh, Rudy, the ordeal was too much for her. She doesn't know where she is. She thinks she's a child . . ."

Rudy tried to silence her with a hand on her shoulder, but Anne concluded in an agonizing voice, ". . . and she thinks Carlos is her doll."

Rudy bent over Sofia and asked, "Do you know us, Sofia? Do you know who we are?"

Sofia looked up at him, her lovely dark eyes nearly hidden by the bruised swelling surrounding them. "Are you friends of my father? Have you come for dinner?"

As Rudy straightened up and met Anne's gaze, he said, "Maybe it's better this way . . . better that she doesn't realize what she's gone through."

Anne clasped her hand to her mouth. "Oh, Rudy! It's too horrible!"

"Stay here with her," he said. "I better go find Natalia."

He left them, and Anne could hear him throwing open the doors of the rooms surrounding the courtyard. After a few minutes, he reappeared.

"I'm afraid to ask," Anne said when she saw his stricken face.

Rudy nodded. "Don't go look, Anne. It's not a sight you should see. I'll have the men dig a grave and bury her."

The remnants of Anne's army were straggling back to the courtyard. Dominguez showed up in the archway, his shoulder already bandaged with his bandanna.

"What are our casualties?" Rudy asked.

"We lost four," Dominguez replied.

"And you?" Anne asked.

"The pain is not bad," he said. "I'll be all right."

Rudy strode outside to greet the returning troops. After a few minutes, he reappeared with a blanket from the coach, and wrapping Sofia in it, he lifted her from the stone floor.

Sofia made no protest except to be sure that Anne followed them with Carlos in her arms. The men had already hitched the mule team to the coach and had the door open to receive them.

"But Natalia . . ." Anne said, hesitating on the running board.

"I'll say words over her," Rudy said, easing Anne inside. "It's too late for anything else—the heat . . .

278

You and Sofia must go on ahead—Sofia should have medical care as soon as possible. I'll send a dozen men back with you. The rest of us will catch up before dark."

He closed the door on the coach.

Anne leaned out and caught his arm. "You're going after Valdez, aren't you?"

Rudy's eyes narrowed, but he didn't answer.

"Don't do it, Rudy! There're too few of you! He'll certainly have more men hidden in the hills!"

"I'd like to kill him with my own hands," he said.

"No, Rudy! Don't try to find him! There's been enough death!"

Rudy stepped back in silence and nodded to the driver atop the coach.

The whip cracked through the air and the mules strained forward.

"Rudy . . . !" Anne cried, but he'd already turned away and was walking back toward the men.

The journey back toward the Rio Grande was a nightmare. A scorching wind off the arid hills seared their faces. The interior of the coach was stifling; it rocked and pitched cruelly, tossing them from side to side. Anne longed to climb out and ride a horse alongside the coach, free and comfortable in the saddle, but she knew she could not leave Sofia alone.

She watched her stepmother with macabre fascination. Sofia never complained. She ignored the heat, the scratchy wool blanket that covered her nakedness, and the brutally rough ride. From time to time, whenever Anne caught her eye, Sofia would smile—but it was no more than a gesture she would have exchanged with any stranger who, through fate, had come to share her coach.

Anne tried to talk to her—tried to breech the barrier between them. But Sofia seemed either unwilling or unable to reply. Her eyes would linger momentarily on Anne's, then return to Carlos whom she cradled and rocked in her arms.

Anne tried to conceal her distress, but inside, her heart was breaking. She couldn't begin to imagine the horror Sofia had suffered, the atrocities she'd been forced to endure; but her battered appearance, her swollen jaw, her nakedness, and the derangement of her mind spoke only too eloquently of her ordeal.

Maybe Rudy is right, Anne pondered. Maybe it's best that Sofia is this way, unable to remember what torture she's been through. But Anne's heart cried out for the woman she'd known before. And she found it intolerable to believe that Sofia would never be the same again.

Rudy and his men caught up with the coach before sunset. Anne was relieved to see him safe—and delighted, after being cooped up in the coach with Sofia, to be able to talk to someone again.

"Did you find Valdez?" she asked as he rode up.

"Nein," Rudy replied. Disappointment and anger still clouded his face. "He vanished like a shadow. We followed his trail to the Rio San Nicolás. After that—nothing!"

"I'm glad you're back, safe."

Rudy nodded in acknowledgment. "We'll hear from him again," he prophesied. "He's not one to accept the licking we gave him."

"We'll be ready," Anne replied. "And next time he won't get away."

Rudy nodded again. "No," he agreed, "next time we'll be waiting."

Although they were only a few miles from Mier, where they could have found comfortable lodging for the night, they made camp where they were. Anne prepared a pallet for Sofia and Carlos and lay down beside them.

The stars were close and unwinking in the inky sky overhead. Anne recognized Scorpio glittering in its arched path across the heavens.

I'm all alone now, she thought. Mama and Papa are gone. And now Sofia—she's gone too—just as if she were dead. There's no one left but me.

Her mind was too troubled for sleep. After an hour of tossing and turning, she rose and strolled out into the brush. Yucca blossoms glowed like ivory in the starlight; their pointed leaves were black daggers poised against the sky.

It was a moment before Anne realized she wasn't alone. Turning, she saw the figure of a man behind her, and her heart jumped in her breast as she opened her mouth to scream.

Then she heard him softly call her name, and she recognized Rudy's voice.

"You scared me to death!" she whispered.

"I'm sorry." He was by her side now.

"I thought you were Valdez!" Her voice was harsh.

"I thought you were too," he said. "When I heard someone walking out here, I thought he'd come after us. I'm sorry I scared you and made you angry."

"I'm too relieved to be angry," she said. Then suddenly all the emotions of the day—her anger, her fear, Sofia's tragedy, and her own desperate loneliness—welled up in her. She began to shake uncontrollably, and hot tears spilled from her eyes.

Rudy's arms went around her shoulders, and she fell against him. He held her tightly, comforting her.

"Don't cry, Anne," he breathed in her ear. "Everything will be all right. Don't cry."

Looking up at him through her tears, she tried to smile. "How different people are," she said. "You Germans say, 'Don't cry, don't cry!' A Mexican would hold you and say, 'Cry, cry!' Sometimes it's the best thing—the only thing—to do!"

"Then cry, if you must," he said gently, and she buried her face in his shoulder and sobbed. His fingers stroked her hair and rubbed the back of her neck.

"I'm so alone, Rudy . . . so alone."

"I'm here, Anne. I'm with you—at your side . . . always."

She welcomed the strength of his arms around her and found comfort in his quiet words. He tilted her face, and his lips brushed hers so lightly that she scarcely realized she'd been kissed. But she felt herself melting against him. Her mouth parted and she waited breathlessly until his lips met hers again.

It seemed to her that tonight there was nothing in the world that she needed more than to be held and kissed.

They sank to their knees, still locked in their embrace, and Rudy kissed her again, rekindling within her the fires she'd kept damped for so long. Like a ghost, the image of Kelly flickered across her memory, then vanished without a trace. She saw only Rudy, his hair shining with the quicksilver of starlight. She felt his hard, muscular body pressed urgently against her own. She tasted his lips on hers and heard the insistent beating of his heart.

His hands found her breasts and released them from her cotton *camisa*. She closed her eyes and gasped as he fondled her, first with his hands, then with his lips. Her nipples grew like maturing buds, nurtured by the warmth of his tongue.

Deftly, Rudy unbuttoned Anne's trousers and pulled them away. She lay down on the ground, and he knelt beside her, caressing her breasts, her belly, and her thighs. The faint starlight tantalized him, revealing only the barest hint of her beauty. He'd dreamed of her so long—had hungered for her so long. And now . . .

He wanted to take her at a rush—immediately,

completely. But he came to her slowly, determined to prolong every moment of this intimacy he'd feared Anne would never allow him.

Anne felt her body tingle with desire. She slipped her arms around his neck and brought his face to hers. They kissed with growing passion. His tongue found hers, and she longed for him to be inside her. She wanted him to fill her, to possess her, to occupy the void of loneliness that seemed to pervade not only her spirit but her body as well.

At last he slipped within her and drove away the demons that tormented her soul. She cried out with pleasure and pulled him closer. His chest heaved against her breast, brushing her nipples, setting fireworks exploding behind her eyelids.

She gasped again and again. She thought she would faint. Indeed, her mind reeled, and she was oblivious to everything except the tempestuous rhythm of his manhood within her.

At last, Rudy himself cried out and fell against her. His body was slick with sweat and his breathing was hoarse and ragged.

They lay side by side for a long time, drifting in and out of sleep. Occasionally, Anne woke to find his arms around her or his head resting lightly on her breast. At last, rising quietly so as not to wake him, she dressed and moved away.

She walked slowly through the brush back toward the camp. With every step, the reality of what lay ahead imposed itself on her, erasing the passions of an hour ago, crowding out the sensations of her body, and filling her mind with old memories, present worries, and the barren landscape of future loneliness—for what had just taken place could not be allowed to happen again.

And by the time she reached her blanket, Anne was horrified at what she'd done. There was Emma to think of, and although Anne had no real affection for her, she had no intention of taking her husband, or even of being the vessel of Rudy's infidelity. Moreover, she did not love Rudy—no more now, even after what had happened, than she had the year before when she had wiped away the kiss he had forced on her lips and had slapped him, telling him she would see him in hell.

Her mind spun as she sank down beside the pallet she'd laid out for Sofia and the baby.

I only did it out of loneliness, she confessed silently, as if Sofia were awake and aware of what had taken place. Sofia's specter stood before Anne, accusing her, her black eyes glittering like agates. "A ten-peso whore," Sofia had once called her. Sofia had always known whenever Anne had done wrong, and she'd always disapproved—but her anger was tempered by love, and her forgiveness was never long in coming. And now, although her stepmother's mind was deranged and she would never know the truth, Anne felt Sofia's censure weighing heavily on her shoulders.

"I'm sorry Sofia," Anne whispered to the sleeping form nearby. "I was so desperately lonely. Everyone I've ever loved has gone—Papa, Mama, and now you, Sofia . . . now you! Everyone has left me . . . and now there's no one left but me!"

Then she felt Carlos stirring at her side!

"Oh, Carlos! There's you! How could I have forgotten!"

She leaned over, kissing the sleeping infant on the cheek. His flesh glowed in the starlight, and his breath was sweet and gentle. A tear fell from her eye and splashed onto his shoulder. She kissed it away and pulled the blanket up snugly around his chin.

"Carlos! You're part of Papa—just as I am. As long as we're together, neither of us will really be alone. And you'll live on to carry on Papa's name."

She bent over to kiss the little boy again. "Carlos! You're our future!"

Then she closed her eyes and slept.

1874

29

The desk clerk at San Antonio's Menger Hotel looked up and smiled. "Good afternoon, Miss Trevor. A pleasure to see you again."

"How are you, Frank?" Anne asked, reaching for the pen to sign the register.

"Just fine, Miss Trevor. Fine and dandy," the clerk said.

"Is my regular suite ready for me?" she asked.

The clerk arranged his face apologetically. "I'm afraid not, Miss Trevor. There's been a slight misunderstanding. A British gentleman is occupying the rooms you requested. We thought he'd be gone by now, but it seems he figures to stay another few days."

A frown of annoyance creased Anne's forehead. "You know how I hate to stay anywhere but in my usual suite."

"I'm terribly sorry. But I've arranged for you to occupy the Governor's Suite—if that's agreeable to you. It's much nicer and quite a bit larger—there'll be no extra charge, of course."

"Well, I don't suppose there's anything to be done about it," Anne said, her annoyance not a bit assuaged by being given the Governor's Suite, even if it did come as a bargain.

"A Britisher, you say? Those Englishmen are scouring the state like buzzards, picking the bones of any poor ranch that's fallen on hard times. I'm here to tell you, they'd better not come scouting around the Lantana!"

The clerk smiled knowingly. "I don't reckon they'd find good hunting on your spread, Miss Trevor."

"You're right, Frank. Anybody who comes hunting on my place gets hunted himself."

"So I've heard," the clerk said, almost to himself. Then he quickly added, "Now I'll have a boy show you up to the Governor's Suite, and I'll send someone to fetch your trunk from the coach."

As Anne climbed the stairs to the second floor, the clerk dropped his fixed smile and turned to his assistant. "Lord, I was afraid she'd cause a scene, but she took it quite well."

"Who *is* she?" the assistant asked. Having come to the hotel only a month before, he didn't know the ranch owners by name.

"That's Miss Anne Trevor. Probably the richest woman in the state. You heard of the Lantana Ranch, haven't you?"

"She owns *that?*"

"She does. And runs it single-handed. Story has it she won't have no truck with men. Seems she was jilted some time back."

"Fellah'd have to be loco to jilt a woman like that. Think of all that money!"

"And them eyes!"

An hour later, Anne left the hotel and strolled out onto Alamo Plaza. She felt uncomfortable, attired as she was in a green silk bonnet and a long taffeta dress, even though beneath her skirt, she still wore her favorite oxblood boots.

As she strolled, she looked at the scene about her. The plaza was teeming with vendors hawking sliced watermelon, sweet cakes, brown sugar candies, and hot buttered corn on the cob. A stonemason chipped noisily at a block of pink granite, and a scattering of beggars sat here and there in the scanty shade, their palms out, soliciting pennies. Fashionable women darted in and out of shops while their canopied buggies waited in the crowded streets, and unyoked oxen lay about the place like huge brown boulders.

As always, when she stood on this spot, Anne's thoughts flew back to the summer she was twelve, when she and Martha and Joel had prepared to make their wagon journey south to claim their new home.

Her eye picked up a group of squealing children engaged in hide-and-seek around the Alamo. She watched them for a moment, almost reluctant to leave. I wonder whatever happened to the farrier's daughters I used to play with, she thought . . . and the innkeeper's twin girls. I wonder if they're still here. Are they married, with children of their own?

The idea crossed her mind that one of these children—scampering around the old mission as she herself had once done—might belong to one of her long-ago playmates.

The town still looks almost the same, she mused. Oh, it's a bit bigger—more people, more noise. But other than that, nothing's really changed. Nothing . . . but me! I'm twenty-six, and I no longer travel in the back of a wagon.

She smiled, almost wistfully, for her past. Then she hailed a carriage and rode off to meet her bankers.

When Anne descended from the carriage and strode into the bank, Mr. Farley and Mr. Wallace were just emerging from their office at the rear. They were bidding farewell to a tall, auburn-haired man in a fawn swallow-tail coat and dark blue trousers. Anne's entrance caught Mr. Wallace's eye. He smiled broadly, as he always did in the presence of great money.

"Well, well, Miss Trevor! We've been expecting you."

"How do you do, Mr. Wallace?" Anne inquired. "And you, Mr. Farley?"

"Can't complain, Miss Trevor," Mr. Farley repiled. "I hope your trip up here was pleasant and you're comfortably installed at the Menger."

"The trip was easy enough," Anne said. "But I'm not too pleased with the hotel. I reserved my usual suite more than a month ago only to find when I arrived that they've given it over to one of those scavenging Englishmen we're plagued with from time to time. I allow, if we're not careful, every blessed acre of Texas will be owned by English capital."

The sudden stricken looks on her bankers' faces nonplussed her, and she paused.

"Miss Trevor . . . I, uh . . ." stammered Mr. Farley.

"Why, what's the matter, Mr. Farley?" she asked, looking from him to Mr. Wallace and back.

"It's that, uh . . . that, uh . . ."

"That's quite all right, gentlemen," the stranger standing with them broke in. "I sympathize completely with the lady's sentiments. We have the same problem in my own bonny country."

Turning, Anne looked at the stranger. The color of his hair stirred vague memories within her: chestnut, like Kelly's. His forehead was wide and smooth, with thick dark brows above eyes bluer than a summer sky. His complexion was fine, with highly colored cheeks, and an almost mischeivous smile played on his full red lips.

"Allow me to introduce myself," he said. "I'm Alex Cameron, from Edinburgh, Scotland. We true Scotsmen are in complete accord with your opinion of the English, Miss Trevor."

The bankers' faces brightened, and Anne smiled happily, relieved that she had not committed a gaffe.

"I'm very pleased to meet you, Mr. Cameron," Anne said, extending her hand in greeting.

"I hope we shall meet again," Alex said.

"It would be my pleasure," Anne replied.

"Gentlemen," Alex said, addressing the bankers. "Thank you so much for your advice. It will be very helpful, I'm sure, in my dealings here."

"Feel free to call on us at any time," Mr. Farley said.

He turned as if to go, then paused, and looked at Anne.

"Oh, by the way, Miss Trevor. Concerning your accommodations at the hotel . . . since I'm the only foreigner registered there, it must be I who have taken your suite. I'll see that the error is rectified immediately."

"Oh!" Anne exclaimed, mortified. Before she could say anything further, he bowed in farewell and strolled out of the bank.

"Oh!" she said again, feeling the color burning on her cheeks. And suddenly her embarrassment turned to anger, for she realized that as he'd bowed and turned away, his mischievous smile had opened into a broad, teasing grin.

"What a scoundrel!" she sputtered. "Letting me stand here all this time while he talks pleasantries, knowing full well that I'd put my foot in my mouth."

"I'm sure he was only being a gentleman," Mr. Farley offered, trying to smooth the situation.

"Gentleman be damned!" Anne exclaimed. "He waited till the last minute to throw it in my face."

"Well, at least you'll have your usual suite back."

"Hell!" Anne fumed. "I'd rather sleep in a barn!"

That afternoon when she returned to the hotel, the clerk caught up with Anne on the stairs and informed her that her belongings had been transferred to her regular suite.

"And the person who occupied it before?" she asked.

"He seemed very pleased to be moved to a single room down the hall."

Anne nodded and went on up to the suite. Inside, on the table by the window in the sitting room, stood a vase of red and yellow roses, their fragrance sweetening the air. Tucked amid the foliage was a small white envelope. Anne opened it and read the bold black handwriting.

Please do me the honor of joining me for dinner this evening.

Alex Cameron

At the writing desk, Anne scribbled a note in reply, gritting her teeth at the forced politeness of her words.

Dear Mr. Cameron,

Thank you for your kind invitation to dine with you this evening. However, owing to a previous engagement, I must regretfully decline.

Yr. obt. svt.,
Anne Trevor

She sealed it and carried it downstairs to the desk to be placed in Alex's box.

Well, that's the end of that! she thought. I hope I never lay eyes on him again!

Anne had no previous engagement. In fact, with her business satisfactorily completed, she had time on her hands. The life of San Antonio still moved with the languorous pace of Mexico, and it would be hours before dinner.

Anne strolled outside, and again her thoughts returned to the young girls she had played with as a child. Curiosity as to what had become of them nagged at her, and she decided to seek them out.

Crossing the street she made her way down the block in the direction of the house where the farrier's daughters had lived. She recognized the building at once with its limestone walls pierced by two long rectangular windows flanking a wide archway. On the other side of the arch, she recalled, there was the shady courtyard where the farrier had had his forge and anvil.

But when she got close, she found that the shop had been replaced by a bootery.

"Been gone a long time, ma'am," the bootmaker said in response to Anne's inquiry, "—killed in the war."

"And his daughters?" Anne asked.

"One died of the smallpox, back a couple of years. But the young one . . . named Kathleen, I believe . . ."

"Yes, Kathleen . . ."

"Well, I last seen her living down by the river."

"Can you show me the way?"

"Just follow the river a bit, then ask someone. They'll know her—Kathleen O'Brien. She runs a boardinghouse."

The sun was setting as Anne left, and the sky above was streaked with pink and violet. She looked about for a coach, but the street—narrow and crowded with bird sellers, stonemasons, and candy vendors—had no room for a horse and buggy to pass through.

Resigned to walking, she threaded her way through the browsing crowd and found at last a passageway of steps descending from the street to the river, where the hurly-burly of the street could be left behind. The crystal clear river coursed between its stone-paved banks, and the evening breeze ruffled the pecan trees whose spreading branches met in a canopy mid-river. All was cool beside the racing water. Overhead, mockingbirds trilled their farewells to daylight, and the heady perfume of vining roses sweetened the air.

Anne followed the curves of the river, making her way past squalid adobe shacks built barely a foot above the water and past the substantial stone houses of the rich, with their lush gardens sloping gently to the bank and their muslin-draped bathing huts, floating at the edge of the water.

Though it was all utterly beautiful, somehow the scene disturbed Anne, frightened her. She was used to open space, where her eyes could travel freely from horizon to horizon. Here she was hemmed in by a vaulting tunnel of pecan and cottonwood. The houses on both sides of the river seemed to close in on her like the walls of a canyon. She was accustomed to the *brasada*, to its shifting sands and stunted brush. Here blooming cannas and heavily laden banana and fig trees threatened to overrun the narrow flagged path, and vines overflowed in a tropical tangle that seemed to snare her and cling to her like cobwebs in a barn.

She shivered and hurried on. Visiting Kathleen no longer seemed such an appealing idea. She looked about for a flight of stone steps that would lead her up into the street, but the river took another of its many bends and concealed what lay ahead.

A low sound alerted her and stopped her in her tracks. She knew instantly it was a dog, growling ominously from the shadows just at the curve in the bend.

She froze, hoping it would go away. But the growling continued, a deep, throaty rumble. Slowly she began to back up, to retrace her steps, wishing she were in pants instead of the long green taffeta dress that rustled loudly with every movement she made.

For a moment she thought she was safe. She was about to pivot on her heel and make her escape, but suddenly the huge dog sprang from the shadows and confronted her. Stark fear chilled her spine. She gasped with alarm. Gray-white foam clung to its muzzle; its wild eyes seemed to blaze with an inner fire. It lunged for her, snapping. She jumped back just in time to avoid its bared fangs.

The dog snarled in mindless rage, shaking its head from side to side, flinging off flecks of clotted foam.

Anne's heartbeat thundered in her ears. She had no time to look for a weapon. The mad dog was crouching again, readying itself to spring at her again.

Anne screamed and leaped feet first into the water. Her cry echoed off the stone walls lining the river and mingled with the outraged howl of the rabid dog that cringed on the bank.

Anne tried to swim, but the swirling water filled her boots until they felt as heavy as lead, while the rapid current caught her wide skirt and wrapped it like a shroud around her legs. Feeling trapped by the river, carried along with its swift movement, she flailed helplessly, barely managing to keep her head above water. Again she screamed, a long, mournful, helpless wail against the reaching arms of death.

Then the churning water took her under. Bubbles streamed upwards, catching in her hair that fanned out above her face. Her lungs burned, and she felt they were about to burst. Finally she sensed a sudden grip about her chest, as if an iron band had been slipped around her body and tightened. It forced the last gasp of air from her body. Her mouth instinctively opened, and the instant before darkness overwhelmed her, she felt the rush of water into her throat and knew she was drowning.

Anne remembered nothing of those last few moments. She awoke in a daze, lying on her stomach on a blanket in the flagstoned entryway of one of the grand houses that lined the river. She was dimly aware of a rhythmical, forceful pressure being applied to her back, just below her shoulder blades. A foul mixture of water and vomit gushed from her throat. She gasped feebly and took a breathful of sweet, clean air.

"She's coming around," a voice said. It seemed to reach her from very far away, as if spoken from a mountaintop.

"Don't stop!" another voice said. And she again felt the pressure on her back.

Dizzy and exhausted, she wanted nothing more than to sink back into the heavy unconsciousness that had enveloped her. But deep within her brain, alarm bells were clanging out warning: Don't give up! Struggle! Fight!

She tried to clench her fists, but her fingers merely fluttered feebly. She coughed, and her lungs ached as if they'd been seared with molten lead. But again she swallowed a breathful of air, and she felt her mind beginning to clear.

"She's breathing on her own," the first voice said, a voice that seemed vaguely familiar to her, but which, in her daze, she was unable to identify. "She'll live."

Sometime later she became aware of being carried through a garden. It was night by then, and a crescent moon flickered through the overhanging branches above her. Her lungs still ached, but she took deep breaths, reveling in the gardenia-scented air—treasuring her newfound hold on life.

She was taken into a large stone house and carried upstairs to a bedroom. Two women stripped her wet clothing from her and dressed her in a long white nightgown.

"You nearly drowned, my dear," the older woman said as she plumped the pillow behind Anne's head. "We heard your cry just in time. You're very, very lucky."

Anne smiled wanly and attempted to speak.

"Now, now, my dear. Don't try to talk. You're exhausted and need to sleep. My daughter and I will sit beside you."

She took Anne's hand in hers and stroked it.

"Everything will be all right," the woman said.

"Thank you," Anne murmured. Then, closing her eyes, she fell asleep.

The next morning she awoke to find two Mexican

maids in her room watching over her. On the table beside her was a pot of steaming coffee and a china cup.

"How does the señorita feel?" one of the maids asked.

"Where am I?" Anne gasped weakly, half rising from her pillow to look about the unfamiliar room.

"This is the house of Señor and Señora Buchanan," the woman answered.

"How did I get here?" Anne asked. But before the maid could answer, the harrowing events of the night before flooded back into her memory. "Oh, yes . . . now I remember. I almost drowned. Someone saved my life."

She shivered and hugged herself tightly with both arms. If anything, the memory of her brush with death was even more frightening than the awful event itself.

"Would the señorita care for coffee?" the maid asked.

"I'd like that very much," Anne replied, but when she tried to bring the cup to her lips, her fingers trembled so badly that the maid had to steady her.

The other servant, who had slipped from the room, returned shortly with the older woman whom Anne remembered from the night before.

"I'm Dora Buchanan," the woman said, smiling warmly and taking a seat on the edge of Anne's bed. "I'm glad to see you looking so well. A bit shaky, perhaps, but you're going to be just fine. I've ordered breakfast brought up for you. It'll steady you in no time."

"I want to thank you so much for . . ." Anne began.

"Oh, don't thank me, my dear," Mrs. Buchanan said, shaking her head. "It was a gentleman friend of ours who pulled you from the river and resuscitated you."

"Then, I'd like to thank him personally."

"If you feel strong enough after you've eaten, my

dear, you can do so this morning. The gentleman is downstairs and will be having breakfast with Mr. Buchanan."

"But my clothes . . . I have nothing to wear."

Mrs. Buchanan appraised Anne's figure. "I'd say you're just about my daughter's size. One of her morning dresses will look lovely on you. Dolores," she said, addressing her maid, "fetch something pretty from Sally's wardrobe and help the señorita dress."

Anne was still a bit rocky on her feet after she had eaten and dressed, but clinging to Dora Buchanan's arm she negotiated the long flight of stairs and walked with her to the dining room.

Swinging back the double louvered doors, Dora announced their entry. "Here is our lovely victim, on her own two feet to thank personally the gentleman who saved her life!"

The blood drained from Anne's face, leaving her nearly as pale as when she'd been dragged half-dead from the river. There at the table, looking up at her, was Alex Cameron.

"Y-you?" Anne mumbled with disbelief.

A slow smile crossed Alex's lips, the same smile she'd seen the day before, warm yet containing a hint of gentle mockery.

"Are you the one who saved me?" she asked.

"I am," Alex answered.

Dora Buchanan's eyes darted back and forth between the two. "Do you know each other?"

Anne was too astonished to answer, but Alex smiled again and replied, "We met only yesterday, but for the life of me I didn't recognize Miss Trevor in the state she was in last night." He rose and bowed, brushing her hand with his lips.

Anne felt suddenly giddy. A mixture of embarrassment and gratitude swept over her, and she found it impossible to speak.

Of all people! she thought. Of all the men in San

Antonio, he *would* be the one to pull me from the river.

Alex's blue eyes caught her quandary and sparkled with mischievous delight. "And to think, Miss Trevor, despite all the trouble I went to arrange for you to have your usual suite at the Menger, you didn't spend the night there after all!"

"Oh!" Anne exclaimed in a sudden rush of breath. A flurry of anger at being mocked swept away her previous feelings of thankfulness. Even the embarrassment was gone.

"A bit of teasing goes a long way, Mr. Cameron," she found herself saying. The glitter in her eyes matched his. "You must know how I feel about yesterday, and I would think you'd have the decency to drop the subject."

"Oh, my!" Dora Buchanan muttered, mystified. She dropped Anne's arm and moved back. "I'm sure I don't know what this is all about."

"Ah, look!" Alex said, ignoring Dora's discomfiture. "Miss Trevor's getting a bit of color back—a spot of rosy pink on each cheek."

Anne was too angry to reply.

Dora attempted to calm her. "Please, Miss Trevor, won't you sit down. . . . I'll have Juanita bring us another pot of coffee."

"I'd rather not," Anne said. "If you'll have your carriage sent around, I'd like to go back to my hotel. Thank you very much for all you've done for me. I'll have your daughter's dress cleaned and sent back to you straightaway."

At the hotel, Anne packed in a fury and booked a seat on the morning coach heading south. The coach was crowded and hot, and though the trail was well traveled, the vehicle pitched and swayed roughly, repeatedly knocking the passengers against one another. Anne congratulated herself on having the good sense to wear trousers and a thin cotton blouse, even if it did mean hard, disapproving stares from the two other women who occupied the coach. She gave them both a steady, challenging look in reply, then turned her attention to the dry monotonous landscape rolling slowly by.

The next day, they reached the Agua Verde station, where Anne had left her horse. The station was still operated by the couple who had taken care of her years before when she waited through the night for the rendezvous with Kelly. They knew who she was now, of course, and treated her with the deference they deemed suitable for the *patrona* of the vast Lantana Ranch.

"Oh, Miss Trevor," the woman said, "I wasn't looking for you till tomorrow. I was hoping to have hot buttermilk biscuits ready when you came by. As it is, I ain't got nothing but a pan of cornbread."

"I love cornbread, Mrs. Parker," Anne replied.

"I swan! I didn't know that," Mrs. Parker said, smiling happily at this stroke of good luck. "Well, I got more'n plenty—and just about the best I ever made, if I do say so myself."

She clucked about Anne like a mother hen, placing her at the head of the long table and serving her before the other travelers.

"Nice trip?" Mrs. Parker asked, serving up a brimming bowl of split pea soup.

"Very nice," Anne replied, and for the first time since leaving San Antonio, the image of Alex Cameron flashed across her mind. She swept it away with a shake of her head and attacked her soup hungrily.

Within the hour she was mounted up and ready to ride to the Lantana.

"Good-bye, Miss Trevor," Mrs. Parker said, bobbing a little curtsy. "You come back soon, you hear?"

"I will, Mrs. Parker. Nice seeing you again." Anne spurred her horse and headed for home. It was a long hard ride, and Rudy was waiting in her office when she arrived.

"I'm bone-tired, Rudy," Anne said, taking off her stetson and tossing it atop her desk. "If there are any problems, let's let them simmer till morning."

"No problems, Anne," Rudy said. He was standing just outside the yellow glow of her desk lamp, but she could see the flickering of its lively flame in his eyes.

Silence fell between them, but Anne was fully aware of his desires.

"I think I'll turn in," she said. "I need a good night's rest."

In one swift movement, Rudy caught up with her. His arms went around her, pulling her to him. His head lowered, seeking a kiss. Anne turned her cheek, avoiding his lips.

"Please, Rudy! I'm half dead!"

"I've missed you!" he breathed, tightening his embrace.

She looked up at him. His eyes blazed with the fires of passion. She was too weary to fight him. Her near drowning and the long, hot trip from San Antonio had depleted her reserves. It was easier to submit to him than to try to struggle free. She felt herself sigh heavily.

He maneuvered her to the long leather couch before the cold, empty fireplace and began to pull her clothes from her body. She didn't resist. She lay limply, staring blankly at the darkened ceiling above her. His passion was hot and urgent. He took her without tenderness, intent only on satisfying his need.

She felt nothing—no pleasure, no pain. Time seemed to suspend itself. The weight of his body on hers went unnoticed; his hoarse gasps of excitement fell on deaf ears.

Ever since she had first submitted to him, the night after the battle with Valdez, Anne had tried to avoid further intimacy with Rudy. She knew she didn't love

300

him; there were times, in fact, when she hated him, wished he and Emma and their brood would pull up stakes and move away. She longed for peace, and as long as he was around, she knew she wouldn't find it. Repeatedly she would determine never to let him touch her again. She would tell him so—all the while seeing in his eyes his certainty that he would eventually overrule her. He seemed to have an uncanny ability to come to her when she was most vulnerable, when she was too weary or downhearted to resist or when loneliness flooded her spirit and made her willing—even eager—for the warmth of his arms around her.

Anne feared Emma's jealousy. Knowing that Emma could be vicious—even violent—when aroused, for days after every illicit liaison Anne worried that something in her own face, or something she said, or something she did would alert Emma to the truth.

Anne tried to warn Rudy of the incipient danger, but he brushed it off, saying Emma was a fool. She was too busy, too tied down by her children, too occupied with her chores to be aware that anything was going on. And every time, Anne, her defenses undermined, found Rudy's assurances convincing and allowed herself to be caught once more in his trap.

With a final violent groan, Rudy at last satisfied himself. He rolled off her and sat for a moment in silence on the floor beside the couch. Then he rose, buckled his trousers, and without a word shambled heavily from the room.

Anne lay on her back watching the play of lamplight on the ceiling above the desk. A moon moth spiraled into the circle of light. It fluttered helplessly, snared fatally by the hypnotic flame. She heard its fragile body thump against the lamp's glass chimney. Then, an instant later, its dusty wings caught fire and sent up a tiny curl of gray smoke that dissipated as quickly as it had risen in the heated air above the flame.

That's me! Anne thought. I know the danger but can't help myself, and I too will be singed by the fire.

30

Alex Cameron!

In the month since she'd been back from San Antonio, Anne had never given him more than a passing thought. But now she had in her hand a letter, posted in Corpus Christi three days before, informing her that Alex Cameron would be passing through on his way to Laredo, and begging her hospitality for a night's lodging on the Lantana.

Her first reaction was to have Rudy send Alex Cameron away when he arrived. Then, recalling that he *had* saved her life, after all, she grudgingly gave orders for the guest room to be prepared and for a yearling to be killed for barbecue.

Alex arrived the next afternoon on a prancing roan whose sleek coat exactly matched the color of his hair. He was much handsomer than she'd remembered, tall and well-built, with wide, strong shoulders and narrow hips. A month in the Texas sun had burnished his complexion to a fine bronze patina that contrasted strikingly with his sea-blue eyes.

He bowed and kissed her hand, an action that both thrilled and discomfited her.

"Quite an empire you have here, Miss Trevor," he said, his soft Scottish burr falling pleasantly on her ears. "For the past six hours I've passed nothing that wasn't marked with your famous crown of thorns brand."

"We're getting ready for roundup, Mr. Cameron," Anne replied, leading him up the steps into the hacienda. His complimentary remark pleased her, but she was determined to treat him with correct but cool deportment.

"And what a magnificent house! No one prepared me for such a dwelling in the middle of the brush."

"It's very old," Anne said, "built by my stepmother's grandfather back in the days of the Spanish land grants."

"That would be quite new by our standards," Alex said. "Portions of my father's house date back to Robert the Bruce."

"Well, after all," Anne replied, having no idea who Robert Bruce was but bristling at the imagined slight, "this *is* the New World."

"Indeed it is, Miss Trevor! And quite an exciting world at that. In one short month, I've seen enough to dazzle me for a lifetime."

Once again, he had turned her coolness against her and pleased her with his words.

She paused at the foot of the stairs. "Maria Elena will show you to your room. I'm sure you would like to freshen up from your trip. Afterwards, I'd be pleased to show you around."

Half an hour later Anne was leading Alex on a tour of the ranch. She admired the way he sat in his western saddle, and she could see that his keen eyes missed nothing he was shown.

"The cattle graze freely on the range," she was saying as they watched an outfit of cowboys driving a herd toward one of the many corrals. "Several times a year we round them up and send them up the trail to market at the railhead. In a few weeks this bunch will

304

be going to Newton, Kansas, where they'll meet up with the Atchison, Topeka and Santa Fe."

"If you could keep the herd in one area, you could do away with roundup," Alex offered.

Anne smiled wisely. "If we kept the herd in one area, they'd die of thirst. There's little enough water around. I've seen a year and more go by when the creek beds stayed dry as bones, and there wasn't enough grass on fifty acres to support a single cow. Besides, there's no way on earth to pen up these cantankerous critters for long. I've got a neighbor about fifty miles to the north of me who tried a board fence once. It cost him darn near a fortune and took forever to put up. But he didn't even have time to sit back and admire his work before his bulls began knocking it down. No . . . these are free range animals. Always have been, always will be."

Alex said nothing, but she saw that his eyes were studying every detail of the scene as if he were examining the landscape through a microscope.

They rode down to the tank, a pond of trapped creek water covering more than six acres where the animals gathered to drink.

"I assume you represent a group of British businessmen," Anne said. "Ever since the war, your people have invested heavily in our Texas ranches."

"Nay, not I," Alex replied. And again she remarked how odd, yet attractive, his Scottish burr sounded here in the *brasada*. "I'm my own man, Miss Trevor. I represent no one but myself."

"Then what brings you here?"

"Adventure, I suppose. The chance for excitement." He sat easily in his saddle, stroking his chin thoughtfully and looking out over the gathering herd. "As you said yourself, it's the New World, and I aim to be a part of it."

"You want to buy a ranch?"

"Aye," he said.

305

"Well, the Lantana is not for sale."

"I didn't fancy it was." He leveled his gaze at hers. She held his eyes for a long moment, then glanced away, unable to match his directness.

Their tour lasted most of the afternoon. Alex asked a thousand questions. Anne answered them all politely, correctly, but she held her warmth in reserve.

"If the cows run free on the range, then surely your men must collect animals belonging to other ranchers. What do you do about that?"

"We either return them or drive them to Kansas with our herd and settle up with our neighbors later."

"Is that the law?"

"It's an unwritten law—a code, you might say. We live by fair play. It's the only way to survive out here."

"And do your cowboys really live by that noble code?" he asked.

"Of course they do. They have to. Oh, there's an occasional ruckus, but it's usually settled quickly. We have a saying: 'God made some men big and some men small, but Sam Colt made all men equal.'"

"I don't understand," Alex said.

Anne smiled. "When everyone totes a gun—a Colt—you're mighty careful who you pick on."

"I see, I see," Alex said, and he too smiled.

And so it went throughout the long, pleasant afternoon. Anne showed him the corrals and the stables. Together they toured the bunkhouses and the little village of ramshackle *jacales* where the Mexican families lived. Alex inspected the sturdy mustang horses and the hardy longhorns, and he in turn told Anne about British stock, heavy beefed, short-legged beasts like Herefords and Angus.

"I'm afraid the *brasada*'s harsh conditions would make them roll over and die," Anne said, regretfully thinking how much more money they would bring than the scrawny Texas cows.

As the sun sank low, they returned to the hacienda.

306

Later, around a blazing campfire, Anne feted Alex with a barbecue. Watching him in the flickering light, she observed how quickly he had adapted to this alien land. In appearance he was no different from any of the other men around him. He wore leather leggings and a broad-brimmed Stetson as if he'd been born to them. He attacked his barbecue with gusto and didn't recoil when the cook smashed the yearling calf's skull with a hammer and served him a portion of the brains.

When he spoke, of course, his accent betrayed his origins; yet Anne couldn't help noticing how quickly he'd learned the lessons she had given him during the day. His talk was sprinkled with localisms, words like "wrangler," "remuda," and "hackamore." He talked easily with Rudy about "bulldogging" and "brush-popping" as if he had been doing them all his life.

After dinner, when the campfire had burned down to dull red coals and the stars were bright silvery points, a cowboy pulled out his guitar and sang about death in the streets of Laredo. When he finished, Alex took the guitar and, in turn, sang of Scotland, of brave Highland soldiers and bonny lasses.

His voice was deep and strong, tinged with a plaintiveness that brought stinging tears to Anne's eyes. Watching him closely as he strummed the guitar and sang with his eyes closed and his head tilted back to the night sky, she wondered if perhaps she had misjudged him.

After a while, when she rose to return to the house, she half hoped Alex would accompany her. She would offer him a whiskey and they could sit in the courtyard beside the fountain and talk of things they hadn't discussed during the day. She wondered about his childhood, his family, the land where he was born. He had sung about a bonny lass on the other side of the sea, and she wondered if he had a fiancée.

But Alex remained with the men, and Anne went

inside alone. Later, as she slipped into bed, hearing their deep, hearty laughter, she realized they were telling jokes—racy, manly stories they'd been saving until after her departure, and she found herself able to distinguish Alex's own robust laughter from the others. She hugged her pillow tightly and closed her eyes, feeling lonely and envious.

The next morning Alex told her that he would be traveling on. He was determined to buy land and couldn't afford to stay any longer on the Lantana. To her surprise she discovered that she did not want him to leave.

"I could take you to the Ebonal," she offered, hopefully. Its operation is a bit different from the Lantana's."

But Alex demurred. "I'm going to see a man named Kendall on the Agarita," he said. "I've already written that I would be there today."

Anne nodded, saying she understood, but as she stood alone on the porch, waving farewell and watching him ride off to the Agarita, she ached with disappointment.

31

Anne couldn't erase Alex from her mind. Glancing up from her desk, she would spot a prancing roan, and for a moment she would believe that Alex had returned, only to realize in the next instant that the rider was a rawboned cowboy newly hired for roundup. Or at night, she would hear a man singing to soothe the gathering herd, and the timbre of his voice would remind her of Alex. She tried to recall the words of the broody ballads he'd sung around the campfire. Instead, her mind would conjure up the image of his face, tilted toward the bright summer stars as he strummed his plaintive tunes.

Rudy was suspicious and jealous.

"Don't be silly!" Anne told him indignantly, infuriated that her emotions should be so transparent. "In any case, what has it to do with you?"

"You know very well," Rudy accused.

"I'm sure I don't!" Anne snapped, cutting off the conversation.

During the next several days, Anne tried to avoid Rudy, but the details of the upcoming roundup threw them together time and again. His very proximity pressured her; she responded by being curt and cool.

Then, by chance, she overheard a mention of Alex. The speaker was a cowboy in one of the outfits that had arrived from the south with another herd of longhorns; he remarked that the Scotsman was visiting the Vivian ranch some sixty miles distant.

Anne knew the owners of the Vivian, a lively middle-aged couple named Magee who staged balls—"fandangos," as they were called—and boisterous week-long house parties at the slightest excuse. This year alone Anne had received invitations from the Vivian to celebrate Valentine's Day, April Fool's Day, Vivian Magee's birthday, and the first day of summer. The Magees' hospitality was famous, and ranchers trekked with their families from counties a hundred or more miles away in order to attend their parties.

It surprised Anne that the Magees had not thrown a fandango in Alex's honor. It was a perfect opportunity for a fiesta. And then, in a flash, she saw how she could lure him back to the Lantana.

"Delia, Maria Elena, Eugenia!" she called to her most trusted servants. "I'm going to have a party—a fandango and a barbecue. I want the house cleaned and put in perfect condition. Polish the silver, beat the carpets, and see that every candle is replaced."

In the kitchen, Anne gave orders to prepare breads, pies, and *dulces* for the crowds that would gather. And she sent for Jacinto—the stooped, gray-bearded Mexican who was famous for cooking the best pit barbecue in South Texas.

"You choose the beef, Jacinto," she told him. "Pick the best you can find. And be sure there's enough. I'm inviting everyone I know."

Then she sat down at her desk to scribble letters of invitation, asking her far-flung neighbors to come to the Lantana to help her celebrate roundup and the beginning of another drive up the Chisholm Trail.

The last note she wrote was to the Magees, and

310

she was careful to include the line: "Please come! And bring along any guests who may be visiting the Vivian!"

Summoning a dozen vaqueros, she handed them packets stuffed with envelopes and told them to deliver the invitations as quickly as possible.

When Rudy heard what was afoot, he stormed into her office, his face flushed with anger.

"This is the worst time!" he argued. "We're too busy with roundup for a party."

"I won't be taking any hands from you," Anne countered.

"The men will be drunk for days!" he said.

"I'm counting on you to prevent that," Anne said coolly.

"You know what effect this will have on them," he went on, his face growing redder by the minute. "They'll be worthless, no good, thinking only about raising hell for a couple of days."

"Not if you control them, Rudy," Anne said, rising from her desk to conclude the conversation. "And I'm sure you can do just that. Besides, the invitations are already out. It's too late to recall them. We haven't had a party on the Lantana since before Papa died. I'd say it's high time."

"It's a terrible time!"

"Well, you'll have to make the best of the situation!"

She reached for her Stetson and strode from the room, leaving Rudy behind to fume. She knew the source of his anger. Clearly, he understood that her desire to see Alex again lay behind her sudden decision to have a party, but his disapproval didn't daunt her.

I'm the boss, she told herself as she walked out into the yard to inspect the long, narrow pit Jacinto was digging for the barbecue fires. I'm the *patrona* of this ranch, and no one is going to tell me what I can or cannot do. Rudy has no claim on me! None at all! And it's about time he realizes that!

Within three days, all the riders had returned to the hacienda. Anne noted with delight that all but a small handful of ranchers—those occupied with their own roundups—had accepted. And she could barely suppress a grin of triumph when one of the men reported, ". . . and the Magees said shore they'd come and bring along that Scotch feller that's staying on their place."

One entire bunkhouse was vacated—the cowboys crowded into the others—and made ready for the male guests. The women and children would occupy the series of bedrooms lining the upstairs corridor. Anne made an inspection tour of the rooms.

"I want two pitchers of water on every washstand," Anne said. "And flowers! A vase of flowers beside every bed."

Short, squat Maria Elena, who barely came to Anne's elbow, nodded obediently and made a mental note.

"And put a bag of lemon sachet in every wardrobe."

"Sí, señorita," Maria Elena murmured and made another note.

Anne left the last bedroom and stared across the corridor at the closed door facing her. With a wave of her hand she dismissed Maria Elena. She crossed the hall and knocked.

From within came a voice responding *"Pase!"*

Anne raised the latch and swung open the door. Inside by a window, with a pile of embroidery on her lap, sat Sofia.

As always, her luminous beauty took Anne's breath away. Although she had passed her thirtieth birthday the previous spring, Sofia's skin was still as smooth and milky white as it had been when she was a child. Her hair, braided in two buns covering each ear, was sleek and black without a strand of gray, and she was as slim and lithe as a school girl.

"Buenos días, Sofia," Anne said, approaching and

312

kissing her on the forehead. "How are you today?"

"Muy bien, gracias, señorita," Sofia replied cheerfully, then held up her needlework for Anne's inspection.

"My, that's lovely, Sofia! The finest work you've ever done."

Sofia smiled brightly. "Do you really think so? Do you?"

"I certainly do."

"Do you think *Tía* Natalia will approve?"

As always, a dagger of grief pierced Anne's heart. She clasped Sofia's hand warmly. "*Tía* Natalia will love it," she said.

Anne had long ago given up any hope that Sofia would recover from the horror of her captivity by Valdez. She remained frozen in time—her mind that of a ten-year-old locked within the body of a mature woman. The servants, in their devotion, humored her every childish whim and protected her from the realities of the present. Anne was never certain that Sofia knew who she was. Sofia never called Anne by name, but addressed her always as "señorita." On the other hand, Sofia never asked where Anne came from or why it was Anne who always visited her and not her beloved Natalia or her father Enrique, who lived on in her mind, and were more real to her than anyone actually present. She spoke of them as if they would be appearing at any moment; yet it didn't seem to matter that they never came.

Anne had no idea if Sofia remembered Joel. She didn't have the heart—or the courage—to ask.

As to Carlos, now a beautiful, black-haired, dark-eyed, spirited little boy, Sofia seemed to consider him a doll, a plaything, a toy to amuse her from time to time. She would spend hours dressing him in various outfits, one after the other. For his part, Carlos adored Sofia. She was more playmate than mother—Anne found herself assuming the mother role more and

313

more. And gradually, as the years passed and Carlos grew, Anne realized she had to wean him away from Sofia's influence.

Knowing that Sofia would seldom leave her room without permission, Anne moved Carlos into a bedroom of his own at the far end of the corridor directly across from hers. He pined at first for Sofia, and sometimes Anne had to cross the hallway in the middle of the night to dry his tears and comfort him. Sofia longed for Carlos, as would a child deprived of a cherished plaything. But little by little, each became reconciled to the new order. Carlos still visited Sofia in the mornings and after naps. But he was growing up and was finding so many more things in the world outside to intrigue him that eventually, by his own choice, his visits to his mother became briefer.

Now, Anne bent and kissed her stepmother's smooth white forehead and left her to her embroidery. As she closed the door behind her, Anne's heart felt like a stone in her breast.

32

Anne had been on her feet all day, greeting the arriving guests as they rolled up in coaches and wagons or trotted up on horseback. But as she kissed and welcomed each newcomer, she gazed over his shoulder for the first glimpse of the special coach that would be coming from the Vivian.

The long, hot afternoon dragged on. After greeting Anne, the women hurried with their children to the cool, shuttered bedrooms upstairs, to rest and recover from the journey, which for the hardiest and most determined revelers had taken three days. The men dropped off their gear in the bunkhouse set aside for them and went about exploring the Lantana, for many of them had never visited the ranch before. They checked the stables, the slaughterhouse, and the tanning shed and compared them with their own. They inspected Anne's mustangs and estimated with open admiration the number of longhorns that had been rounded up for the long drive north. And then they gathered beneath the shade of a pair of oaks and traded lively stories as they passed tequila and redeye from hand to hand.

In the yard, Jacinto tended the long pit in which six beefs had been buried to roast among smoldering mesquite coals. Occasionally a feather of blue-gray smoke would puff free from the mounded earth and waft its mouth-watering aroma in the direction of the gathered ranchers.

The sun dropped low in the sky, casting long shadows over the landscape. The women and children, looking remarkably refreshed after a few hours rest, reappeared. Some women congregated in the courtyard around the cooling fountain; others strolled outside to watch the children play and to exchange long-stored gossip which, for those who lived on the most remote ranches, would have to last for another year or more.

It had been two hours since the last coach pulled up at the steps of the hacienda, and by Anne's reckoning, most of those who had accepted her invitation had already arrived. There would be stragglers—there always were—and a few would never arrive at all, held back by some last-minute emergency on their ranch. For those who had made a late start or who had simply misjudged the distance, Anne signaled for two towering bonfires to be lit to mark their destination.

She was worried now, preoccupied. Why hadn't the Magees arrived with Alex? They didn't live that far away by ranchers' standards—not more than sixty miles. They should have been here by now. And even if something had come up that kept the Magees at home, why hadn't Alex ridden over without them?

"Señorita," Jacinto said, hobbling up beside her, "the barbecue is almost ready."

Anne's eyes scanned the darkening horizon. "We'll wait a little longer, Jacinto," she said. "Will it keep?"

"For a while yet," he answered and shuffled off back to the pit.

Darkness settled, but around the bonfires it was bright as day. On a platform built in the middle of the yard, a quartet of mariachis recruited from among

316

the vaqueros entertained the guests with Mexican ballads and love songs.

At last the barbecue would wait no longer. Jacinto
and his crew of helpers dug up the succulent sides of
beef and began carving them on long tables laden with
pots of frijoles, platters of vegetables and fruit, and
large linen-draped baskets containing *jalapeño* cornbread and hot tortillas.

Anne's guests ate as if they hadn't had a bite of
food in weeks. One by one the sides of beef were
carved and served, their juicy bones hauled off and
thrown to a pack of baying dogs down by the arroyo.
The pots and platters were emptied and refilled time
and time again. The laughter and high spirits among
the crowd told Anne that everyone was having a grand
time. Sally Hendricks and Seth Dalton, who every
one suspected were sweet on each other, staged a
lively impromptu dance on the musicians' platform,
much to the delight of the band and their audience.
And old Bill Gilly, who had downed more than his
share of red-eye during the day, performed a rubber-
legged jig despite his wife's mortified protests that he
come down from the platform this instant and go to
bed. The crowd howled and shouted for more, and
Bill Gilly, just working up a good head of steam,
obliged.

Anne moved among her guests, stopping to chat
here and there, smiling at their pleasantries, admiring
their children, warming to the role of the gracious
hostess. And in general she was pleased with the party
and happy that her guests were enjoying themselves,
but part of her was elsewhere. A moon had risen, and
her eyes darted continually into the pale blue distance
in the hopes of catching sight of the Magees' coach.

Once she thought she saw them. But when the
coach rolled up, guided to the hacienda by the flaming
bonfires, she found it was only the Gibson family, late

because their coach had been mired down in a rain-softened creek bed.

She greeted them warmly and steered them to the groaning barbecue tables. But as she turned away, her face registered her disappointment. When she looked up again, she caught sight of Rudy standing by a pillar on the porch, watching her intently. And she saw his lips curl in a smile of satisfaction.

She wheeled about, wishing to avoid speaking to him. It was only after she had gone a few yards that the significance of his smile dawned on her.

Spinning around again, eyes flashing, she called for him.

"What have you done?" she demanded.

Rudy's eyes opened wide with mock innocence. "I don't know what you're talking about."

"You do, indeed!" she accused, her lips pressed tight with disgust and anger. "You've done something to keep the Magees from coming!"

"Not me," Rudy protested.

"You're lying, Rudy!" she snarled, not caring that a nearby knot of people had turned their eyes toward her. "You might as well tell me. I'll find out the truth, you know!"

Rudy took her by the elbow and steered her away from the curious group.

"Don't touch me!" she commanded, wrenching herself free of his grip. "Just tell me what you've done!"

"Anne! Please, you must understand!"

"You sent word, telling them not to come, didn't you?"

"I only did it for your own good. For us, Anne! Can't you see that? For the two of us!"

Anne stared at him with hate. "There is no such thing as the two of us!"

Rudy's face flushed with desperation. "You don't want him, Anne! He'll use you! He'll take this ranch that you and I have built together. He's an opportunist, Anne. I can see it in his face."

"And I can see lying and cheating and conniving in your face Rudy! I've put up with a lot from you in the past—because of what you did for my father and because of Emma and the kids. But I'm through now. I'm sick and tired of your possessiveness, of your sneaking around behind my back. I don't trust you anymore, Rudy."

"Anne . . . Anne, please . . ."

"I want you off the Lantana, Rudy. Right away— the sooner the better!"

"Anne, wait!"

But she had turned and was striding through the crowd toward a group of cowboys sitting among themselves underneath the mariachis' platform.

"Fidel!" she called, summoning one of the men to her side.

"*Sí*, señorita?" the young man asked.

"I want you to ride to the Vivian ranch—ride all night if you have to. Tell Mr. and Mrs. Magee that I'm having this party after all, despite what they might have heard from Rudy. Say that there are still four more days of fiesta. And tell them that I beg them and their guest, Mr. Cameron, to attend."

Fidel nodded his understanding and hurried off toward the stable.

The guests caroused until the early morning hours, and Anne stayed up until the last bunch of diehards staggered off to their quarters. Yet shortly after dawn she was bathed and dressed and moving about the hacienda checking arrangements for the day ahead. She had left the kitchen and was crossing the courtyard when she heard someone call her name.

Glancing up, she saw Emma standing beneath the arch. Clustered behind her were the children—all six of them, from Davey, who at fourteen was already

319

taller and huskier than Rudy, to the baby Sonia.

"Why, Anne?" Emma asked, her eyes wide with desperation. "Why have you told Rudy he has to go?"

"I don't want to talk about it Emma," Anne replied.

"Anne, please! Think it over! Change your mind!" Emma begged, leaving her children beneath the arch and entering the courtyard.

The sight of her depressed Anne. Her lank brown hair was untidy, as if it had never been combed. Her dark eyes, once the best feature in her otherwise plain face, were red and nearly swollen shut from hours of weeping. Her dress was wrinkled and gaped open where rolls of fat strained against the fabric. And Anne saw that her simple Mexican sandals were run-down at the heels and held together with makeshift strands of knotted rawhide.

Emma approached and dropped heavily to her knees.

"Don't do that, Emma. Get up."

But Emma continued to kneel and stared up at Anne, her great puffy face contorted with misery. "I'm pleading with you, Anne. Don't do this thing! Where will we go? What will we do?"

She tried to clasp Anne's hand, but Anne pulled away.

"Don't let it end like this, Anne!" Emma sobbed. "Think of all we've been through together. You helped me birth Davey. You named him. You're his god-mother. And the other children—they look up to you. *Die armen kinder!* They love you."

Anne tried to keep her eyes off the children hud-dling together beneath the arch.

"We went through the war together. Those were hard times, but we helped each other, and we sur-vived. And now you want us to leave! Why, Anne? *Why*?"

Anne's face was a mask. She didn't want to look at Emma, but she couldn't tear her eyes away. Emma looked so pitiful, so miserable and frightened at the prospect of an unknown future. Gazing at Emma's wretchedness Anne thought, God knows she has little enough to live for here on the Lantana, especially now that Rudy no longer loves her. Anne was fairly certain that Rudy had ceased sleeping with Emma. He treated her abominably, ignoring her for long periods or berating her unmercifully in front of servants and cowboys—whoever might be around.

And now here she was kneeling in front of Anne, with her children looking on, begging as she had never begged before.

A wave of pity swept over Anne. How could she tell this poor, desolate woman that she was sending Rudy away because he was in love with her? How could she say that Rudy was insanely jealous of her, that his possessiveness interfered with her life? How could she suggest that Rudy had been constantly unfaithful to Emma and that she—Anne—had been his lover? An unwilling lover, perhaps, but his lover nonetheless!

Anne found herself stooping, reaching for Emma. She clasped her hands and pulled her to her feet, and in that instant she saw a spark of hope flash in Emma's swollen eyes.

"All right, Emma," Anne said softly. "He can stay."

Tears welled up in Emma's eyes. She embraced Anne and sobbed wretchedly against her shoulder.

"Oh, thank God," she murmured. "And thank you, Anne, thank you!"

Anne extricated herself from Emma's embrace. "Go on home, Emma," she said quietly. "Take your children and go home."

Emma backed away, her trembling lips half-formed in a smile of relief, hot tears staining her sallow cheeks. Then she turned, extending her arms, gathering her children around her.

Anne looked away, unable to watch any longer,

thinking, No matter what I feel about Rudy, I won't allow myself to harm Emma more than I already have.

When she looked up again, she saw with relief that the archway was empty.

Rudy was still in bed when Emma and the children returned to their house.

"It's all right," Emma said wearily, pausing in the doorway to brush a lank strand of hair out of her red swollen eyes. "I pleaded with Anne. We don't have to leave."

Rudy's lips curled with contempt. "You stupid woman! How can you go crawling on your belly? Did you really think she would send us away?"

Emma flinched at his words.

"I have her in the palm of my hand," Rudy went on, curling his fingers into a fist. "Tight! Like that! She couldn't get along without me. I know too much about the ranch. I'm too valuable to her. Besides . . ." His voice trailed off and he looked away.

"What, Rudy?" Emma asked, a note of suspicion lacing her tone, "Besides . . . what?"

"Nothing," he answered, brushing her off. "Now start breakfast. It's late and I'm hungry."

Late in the afternoon of the next day Maria Elena shuffled up to Anne's side and told her that a coach had arrived.

Her heart beating wildly, Anne ran through the foyer and reached the porch in time to see Moses and Vivian Magee clambering out of their coach.

"Lordy, Anne, what's this on-again off-again party you're throwing?" Vivian shouted by way of greeting. She was a short, fat woman with silver curls. "I swan, we was countin' on it and our hopes was plumb dashed when we heard it'd been called off!"

"All a big mistake, Viv," Anne assured her, letting herself be pecked on both cheeks. "Howdy do, Moses?

You're looking fit!" But her eyes searched past them for sight of Alex.

The coach was curtained inside against the dust and heat, but she saw a movement inside.

"I hope you meant it when you wrote we could bring any and all who was visitin' on our place," Vivian said.

"Why, 'course I did, Viv," Anne replied.

"Well, good, 'cause we sure took you up on it."

At that moment, Alex stepped from the coach into the sunlight. He looked incredibly handsome, dressed in tight brown gabardine trousers and a fawn silk shirt caught loosely at the neck with a navy blue bandana.

Anne smiled with delight, unconsciously brushing her hair back from her face to present him a better view.

But Alex didn't bound up to greet her as she hoped. Instead, he turned back to the coach and reached inside. Anne's smile froze as she saw a tiny white-gloved hand slip into his and a lovely brunette in sea-green organdy emerge.

"I believe you already know Mr. Cameron," Vivian chattered happily at Anne's elbow. "And now I'd like you to meet my little niece, Flora—visitin' us all the way from Macon, Georgia."

"Well, aren't we lucky," Anne said, feeling her smile further stiffen on her face and noticing that Flora's small, gloved hand was still entwined with Alex's.

"It's a thrill and an honor to meet you, Miss Anne," Flora drawled, making a jouncy little curtsy. "I was just saying to Alex here that I wouldn't have missed this party for the world!"

"I'm so glad you could make it," Anne replied smoothly, but her eyes flashed like lightning in a thunderstorm.

"Ain't she the prettiest little thing you ever laid

eyes on, Anne?" Vivian chirped gaily.

"Oh, hush your mouth, Aunt Viv," Flora giggled, blushing on cue. "You're about to embarrass me half to death!" But she rolled her great, dark eyes up at Alex and fluttered her long, fringed lashes.

"She's absolutely beautiful," Anne murmured truthfully, but she felt her jaws locking as she spoke. Flora, a delicate Dresden figurine, barely reached to Alex's chest. Her lustrous black hair fanned out over her creamy shoulders, and her low-cut, tight-fitting bodice set off her tiny waist and voluptuous breasts to perfection.

For the first time in her life Anne wished she weren't wearing trousers. She knew she wore them well. They revealed the statuesque curves of her tall figure as no dress on earth could possibly do. But Flora looked so soft and feminine—so like what Anne imagined would appeal to Alex—that she wished she could disappear from the steps that very moment.

"Well, honey," Vivian gabbled on, "ain't you gonna ask us in? I swan, after that long trip, I'm so dry I could spit cotton!"

"Oh, yes! Of course!" Anne apologized, feeling her cheeks go red. "Do come in! What can I get you to drink?"

Flora slipped her arm proprietarily through Alex's and followed Moses and Vivian up the steps.

"Why, isn't this simply the grandest house you've ever seen!" Flora gushed as they walked into the foyer. "Who would have thought to find such a mansion— wouldn't you call it a mansion, Alex?—out here in the wilds of Texas!"

"I'm glad you like it," Anne said graciously, wanting to rake her fingernails over Flora's perfect porcelain face.

She ushered them into the courtyard, which was already filling with guests newly risen from their siesta.

"Well, lookee here, Moses!" Vivan shrieked. "If

it ain't Amy Lou Potter in the flesh. Lordy, honey, I haven't laid eyes on you in a coon's age!"

Vivian and Amy Lou Potter charged each other like two wild javelinas and hugged with delight.

"C'mere, Flora, sweetie!" Vivian called. "C'mon over here! I want you to meet one of my oldest and dearest friends!"

Reluctantly, Flora let go of Alex and went to curtsy before Amy Lou. So Anne found herself alone with Alex for the first time.

She stared at him for a moment, then, said, "Well, at least you could say 'How do you do.' You haven't spoken a word to me since you arrived."

Alex grinned, a mischievous light flickering in his eyes. "I was just wondering how long you'd be able to keep that smile on your face."

Suddenly, Anne became aware of the cramp in her jaw brought on by her set smile. Embarrassed and humiliated, she let her facial muscles relax.

"That's better," Alex said. "A counterfeit smile doesn't suit you at all."

Anne stiffened. "It must give you great pleasure to torment me, Mr. Cameron. You almost never have anything agreeable to say."

The teasing mischief departed his eyes, replaced by a strange, almost wild look that swept over him as if he'd been invaded by a sudden turbulent storm. He gripped her arm and drew her away from the gathering in the courtyard. She was too startled by the change in him to resist. She let him steer her across the foyer and into her office. He kicked the heavy double doors closed behind them. Then he took his hands and cradled her face, tilting it up toward his.

"So you want to hear something pleasant," he said. "Perhaps you'll find these words agreeable enough. I find you the bonniest lass I've seen in all my life. I've carried the picture of your face in my mind ever since our first meeting."

325

His face was dark, his eyes as deeply blue as a wind-tossed sea. For a moment, Anne thought he was going to slip his arms around her and kiss her. But he broke away from her instead and moved across to the empty fireplace.

"What is it?" Anne asked, dreading the answer she expected. "Is . . . is it Flora?"

Alex gave a short, surprised laugh. "Flora? Is that what you think of me? Nay, it's not that silly, empty-headed girl. I never knew her until a week ago, and I haven't had a minute's peace since."

"Then what is it?" Anne asked, drawing near to him. "What's troubling you so much that you find it difficult to talk to me?"

Alex turned and faced her squarely. "I left my native soil and came to Texas for one reason—to invest in land, to buy my own ranch. In my travels, I've discovered there's nothing to be had around this area. Oh, there are a few thousand acres here and a couple of hundred there, but nothing really suitable. I want a spread like yours—not that I dare dream of anything so grand! There's not many—perhaps none—that can hold a candle to the Lantana. But I want to be able to stand in the middle of my own ranch and know that even with a full day's walking I won't be able to reach the perimeter. It's my dream, and I mean to make it come true. And, because of that, I find that I must move on. I've heard there's land for sale in the measure that I want, but it's almost a thousand miles from here, in the northern reaches of the state, near the border of the Indian Nation."

Alex smiled at her, and she saw in his expression a mixture of regret and wistfulness.

"So you understand," he went on, "although I find you bonny and fascinating beyond telling, I'll not trifle with you. Where I'm going might as well be on the moon. With so many miles between you and me, there can be no future for the two of us together."

He bent over and kissed her lightly. And before she could stop him, he had opened the doors to the foyer and slipped outside to join the others.

Anne's mind was racing. She sank down on the couch and held her trembling shoulders in her arms. No man had ever treated her that way before. Kelly, whom she had desperately loved, had taken her affection as if it were a casual gift and then threw it away. And Rudy, whom she turned to out of loneliness, had given her nothing but trouble in return. Neither man had had any qualms about sharing her bed, and never once had either of them considered her feelings.

Now this handsome, complex Scotsman had touched her life—a chance encounter that promised to be all too brief. But because he could not promise her a future, he would keep his distance from the outset. Suddenly she understood the roots of his maddening, sometimes infuriating behavior. He teased her and taunted her so that he would not grow close to her. But it had been too great a burden for him to bear silently any longer, and he had broken down and revealed his heart to her.

She rose from the couch and straightened her shoulders. Except for her father, she had never known a man of such honor. And it dawned on her that she might never meet another.

I must keep him here! she vowed to herself. I can't let him leave!

The afternoon was fading into evening. Another feast was set before the guests, and the main rooms on the ground floor were being cleared of furniture for the fandango to be held that night. Anne had hired Major Woodrow's celebrated Society Band from San Antonio. It had cost an extravagant amount, because of the distance they had to travel, but she considered it worth every penny.

It hadn't crossed Anne's mind to dress for the dance, but now, thinking of Alex, she hurried to her wardrobe to search for a gown that would catch his eye. There was the organdy, but she hated the color pink— and besides, Flora had been wearing organdy. For a moment she considered the sea-green silk. It would match her eyes. But it had long sleeves and a high neck, and she wanted to show more of herself than it would allow.

Then she found the dark red taffeta. It was daring, she knew—a deeply cut bodice with a long, tapered waist, which flared into a wide, full skirt and rustled enticingly with every movement. She pulled it on over her head and stood before her full-length mirror as Maria Elena buttoned up the back.

"Qué bonita!" the maid whispered admiringly, and Anne smiled at her reflection with satisfaction.

She twirled this way and that, watching the skirt bell out flatteringly. She reached up to pull the ribbon from her hair, shaking it loose so that it tumbled in soft waves about her shoulders. And she hitched up her skirt an inch or two to reveal the bright tips of her silver dancing slippers.

Pleased and confident of the effect she would achieve, Anne turned to leave, ready to make her appearance at the ball downstairs.

But Maria Elena, calling, "Señorita!" held her back.

"What is it?" Anne asked.

Maria Elena approached carrying the garnet lavaliere that Martha had bequeathed Anne just before she died.

Anne stared at it for a moment as if she didn't recognize it. It had been years since she last wore it— years since she had had an occasion to place its golden chain around her neck.

"Of course," she whispered to Maria Elena. "It will complement this dress beautifully."

She took the necklace and put it on. Its single garnet caught the light and glowed like a blood drop on her breast.

"Bellísima!" Maria Elena breathed.

"Thank you," Anne murmured. And she turned to go, feeling tall and strong and beautiful.

33

Anne paused at the top of the stairs to pull on her gloves. The melody of a sweeping waltz, played by Major Woodrow's band, filled the house and beckoned her.

She descended the steps slowly, regally, as if the music were being played for her alone, an accompaniment to her entrance. Walking directly across the foyer, her silver slippers tapping lightly on the polished tiles, she reached out and swung back the doors to the ballroom. At that moment, dramatically, the music came to an end. Major Woodrow, resplendent in a uniform of forest green trimmed with gold braid and adorned with glittering epaulets, turned to accept the dancers' applause. As he took his bow, he caught sight of Anne's silhouette in the far doorway, and raising his baton, he directed his band in a jaunty fanfare.

All eyes turned toward Anne, who was standing as if she were a queen surveying her court. There was a sudden, spontaneous burst of applause and a dozen old veterans shook the room with the high-pitched shriek of the rebel yell.

Laughing with delight, Anne moved into the room at a regal pace. To every man there, she was the loveliest creature they'd ever seen, and there wasn't a woman in the crowd who didn't wonder if she would have the courage to appear in public in a gown as daring and revealing as the one Anne wore.

Again Major Woodrow bowed deeply before Anne; then straightening, he announced: "Ladies and gentlemen . . . a reel! Choose your partners!"

A flurry of excitement swept the crowd, but no one moved; it was Anne's to make the first choice. She didn't hesitate. She walked directly across the dance floor and extended her hand to Alex. Flora, who had been clinging to his arm, masked her surprised anger with a well-bred smile, but the hard glitter in her eyes only heightened Anne's exhilaration.

The dancers formed a double row, the men facing the women. Major Woodrow brought down his baton and the reel began.

Anne danced as she had never danced before. Her slippers seemed to float inches above the floor. She linked arms with Alex and twirled about as if caught in one of the *brasada*'s summer whirlwinds. Now, arms around each other's waists, they stepped in time to the music beneath an arch of clasped hands. They broke apart—Alex to one end of the line, Anne to the other. Then, after only a moment, they were dancing toward each other again. The music was gay and lively. It seemed to Anne that they had miles to cross before they touched. She felt as if she were in a dream where everything moved slowly—Alex coming toward her, the waves of his chestnut hair rising and falling as he shifted from toe to heel, his smile growing broader as he neared, his hands reaching out to take hers.

Then, suddenly, they touched! The music crashed about her ears. She felt her brain go dizzy with joy and excitement. They were holding on to each other now. She felt the strength of his arms around her. The music rollicked on, calling for them to pull apart once more, but Alex held her close, breaking the formation, leaving the other dancers behind. They circled the

331

room, locked in each other's arms. Nothing existed outside their embrace—the guests, the room, the music itself seemed to disappear. They were alone together, lost in each other's eyes. It was a moment made to endure for eternity.

For Anne, the rest of the evening passed as if in a dream. She danced with others, she saw that everyone's glass was filled, and she chatted sociably with all the wallflowers. But her heart was with Alex.

She would glance across the room and find his eyes on hers. She would wish for something to drink and would discover him at her side with a glass of champagne. She would finish a dance with one of the handsome bucks who had ridden for days to attend her party, then find herself being swept back into Alex's arms to begin another.

She danced and laughed and drank more than she ever had before, and she grew quite lightheaded, whether from exhilaration or champagne she never knew. Nor did she care. All that mattered was that she was in Alex's arms. And she realized, by the way he held her and gazed into her eyes, that he was hers!

The band played on until well past one. Then, when the musicians staggered off, exhausted, Moses Magee grabbed a fiddle and entertained the dancers. One by one the guests drifted off to their beds, weary, happy, filled with food and liquor. Even Moses Magee eventually heaved a sleepy sigh, laid down his fiddle, and staggered out to the bunkhouse. Finally, only Anne and Alex were left.

They made a circuit of the room, snuffing out candles. Shadows grew around them, a deepening darkness that drew them closer together. At last a single candle remained and Alex, wetting his fingertips, pressed the wick. The flame sizzled and went out.

His arms went around Anne's waist and pulled her against his body. His lips found hers and he kissed her ardently. Anne moaned with ecstasy and entwined her fingers in his wavy hair.

"You can't leave here, my darling," she whispered, trembling. "I won't let you go!"

"Even if I wanted to, I couldn't," he replied.

"I need you, Alex. I need your love, and I need your help. Your search is over, my dearest. You don't have to look any further. Everything I own, the Lantana and all it contains, is yours."

"And you?" Alex asked.

"I'm yours, too," she replied.

Together they walked up the darkened stairs and down the long corridor to her bedroom. He closed the door behind them and swept her into his arms. She felt his fingers free the buttons down the back of her dress. She raised her arms and pulled the gown over her head and let it drop to her feet. Quickly Alex slipped out of his clothes, and they fell onto the bed. He kissed her until she was breathless—until she felt exactly as she had when the river dragged her under. She gasped for air and her fingernails raked the length of his muscular back. He cried out with both pleasure and pain, catching her arms and pinning them to the bed.

She squirmed beneath him, not really wanting to free herself but relishing the contest of pitting her strength against his. She caught him off guard and rolled him over onto his back, but his arms went around her and tightened until her breath was squeezed from her lungs and she thought she would faint.

Then, suddenly, he released his grip on her. She straddled his waist, mewing with pleasure as his hands sculpted the curves of her breast and her waist. With his fingertips he delicately brushed the pale smooth flesh of her belly; then his hands slipped between her legs.

She rose on her knees. He was ready for her. With his hands beneath her buttocks he lowered her onto

333

himself. Anne threw her head back, eyes closed tightly, and watched the explosion of a thousand stars behind her lids.

Shortly before dawn a sudden, brief thunderstorm broke over the *brasada*. Anne woke in Alex's arms as lightning crashed violently about the hacienda, silvering the walls of the bedroom. Above the thunder's roar, they heard the nervous bellow from the gathered herd.

"The cattle!" Anne said, making a move to rise. "The storm might stampede them!"

But Alex held her back and pulled her close to him. "They'll be all right," he murmured reassuringly. "The cowboys will take care of them."

Anne lay in his embrace, wide-eyed, staring at the lightning flashes on the ceiling. Soon, as quickly as it had blown up, the storm passed. The rain that had stung the window panes dwindled to a soft patter, then ceased altogether.

Anne heard the soft, soothing voices of the night guard calming the skittish herd; and then a cowboy began to sing:

"Oh, I am a Texas cowboy,
    just off the stormy plains.
My trade is hosses, cinches,
    saddles, ropes, and bridle reins.

Oh, I can tip a lariat
    and with a graceful ease
I can rope a streak of lightnin'
    and ride it where I please.

I love the rollin' prairies,
    with all their joy and strife.
Behind a heard of longhorns
    I've journeyed all my life.

And if I had a little wife,
        how happy I would be,
For the prettiest girl in all the world
        has fell in love with me."

Alex chuckled quietly and Anne felt his laughter with her cheek against his chest.

"Aye, I'd say it's true," he whispered. "The prettiest girl in all the world has fell in love wi' me!"

Just before sunup, Alex rose and dressed. The house was still quiet as he made his way downstairs and through the foyer. Stepping out onto the porch, he paused a moment and took a deep breath of fresh morning air. Off in the distance, the night guard was being replaced by the outfit that would set off on the trail drive after breakfast.

The big day had come, and Alex could feel the excitement in the cowboys who rode up to take charge of the herd.

He watched for a moment, then bounded down the steps and strolled off toward the bunkhouse.

But his appearance on the porch had not gone unnoticed. From his saddle among the cowboys, Rudy stared in outraged disbelief at Alex's retreating figure.

He knew without a doubt what had transpired, and the worm of jealousy and hate writhed within his soul.

Soon Anne's guests were all crowding onto the porch or swarming about the yard. For the dozenth time in seven years, Ben Talley, looking fit and tough, waved his bandana above his head and signaled that the hour had come to begin the trail drive. The cowboys shouted and fanned their hats. The cattle bellowed and began to mill about, raising dust.

"H'yaw! Hee-yaw!" the men hollered from horseback, and the big herd—like a sluggish river—started to move.

"Well, they're off for Kansas!" Moses Magee cried. "Give the boys a cheer!"

And the spectators who were crowded in the yard and perched on the porch railing shouted their salute and farewell. Little Carlos, beside himself with excitement, chased after the departing herd, waving his Stetson and raising his boyish voice in imitation of the grown-ups.

At her window upstairs, Sofia leaned against the wrought-iron grillwork and watched her son—not really knowing he was her son, but deriving pleasure from his childish antics. A smile flickered across her pale lips and she raised her hand to say *adiós* when Ben Talley, high in the saddle, riding beside his pointer, turned to wave good-bye.

The first of the lowing animals were already lost in the cloud of yellow dust before the flank and the drag set out. And behind them came the wrangler, looking out for his horse-herd. Off to the side, some distance away, jounced the chuck wagon, every square inch of its space stocked with provisions for the journey.

Anne watched from the porch, unable to conceal her excitement. Though she had seen many trail drives leave the Lantana, she never got over the thrill of watching the herd spread out and begin its slow, stately march north. Nor could she forget her own journey up the Chisholm Trail. Oh, God! she thought. Suddenly that seemed so long ago!

She blinked back tears and smiled again. She felt a hand clasp hers and she looked up to see Alex at her side.

"I never knew it would be such a spectacle," he said. "It's far more magnificent than anything I ever expected."

"It is a grand sight, isn't it?" Anne asked.

"Aye, that it is," Alex agreed. "Something to tell our grandchildren about."

336

His words stirred her soul and sent a surge of happiness through her—a sense of elation such as she had never known before.

"Our grandchildren . . ." she murmured. "Oh, Alex! Hold me! Hold me tight and never let me go!"

34

"In Scotland, even the sunlight is different," Alex told Anne. "Here it's white hot, so close you feel you could almost reach up and burn your hands. In my country, it's a distant sun we see, a pale disc lying far to the south, casting long shadows and giving out a wan yellow light such as you see here only in the moment just before sunset. The countryside is hilly, covered with grass that is so dark green that at times the hills seem almost black. And when the heather blooms it looks as if a purple mist has settled in the valleys."

He pulled his Stetson farther down his forehead and squinted out at the bleached landscape that surrounded them. Their coach bounced over the rutted trail, and white dust rose like a dry fog behind them.

"I'll take you to Edinburgh one day," he said. "Some people call it Auld Reekie because of the pall of smoke from all the chimney pots, but it's a bonny town. We'll walk the Royal Mile from Holyroodhouse to the Castle, and from there you can look out over the firth and see the Highlands some fifty miles away. And then we'll go to the Highlands itself, to my father's house to meet my family."

"Tell me about them," Anne said.

"My parents are old—I was born quite late in their lives. I have no sisters, but I have a brother named Robert who is my senior by seventeen years. 'Tis he who'll inherit the family house and all my father's lands."

"And nothing for you?" Anne asked.

Alex shook his head. "Nay. It's our custom for the firstborn to take over from the father."

"And you?" Anne asked.

"Why, I'm to make my own way like any other fellow. That's the reason I left Scotland. I wanted to go where the opportunities were greatest. I came across a copy of the *Anglo-American Times* and read of Texas and of the cattle empires that were being created here on land that could be got for as low as ten shillings an acre. I made up my mind to cast my fate with the newest part of the New World. Not for me the choked cities of New York or Boston or Philadelphia. Oh, I visited them all and found them to be very little different from London. I spent as short a time in them as possible. I knew all along that I would end up in Texas. I fancied that with a lot of work and a little luck I, too, could have a barony of my own."

Anne smiled. "And I suppose I'm that 'little luck.' "

Alex laughed. "Aye, that you are, my love. Thank God for your spill in the river. But for that we might never have met again."

"We almost didn't," said Anne. "After that scene in the bank, I didn't want to see you again. You teased me unmercifully. I thought you had the manners of a polecat."

"And I thought you were a fine, bold lass!"

Laughing, Anne linked her arm in his. "And now— what do you think of me?"

"I still think you're a fine, bold lass, and I love you all the more for it!"

Anne closed her eyes and leaned against Alex's shoulder. It had been a hectic, whirlwind week—a dance every night and three veritable feasts each day—culminating in a wild, rambunctious rodeo with Anne's guests competing against her vaqueros.

After the rodeo, coaches began to roll up to the hacienda, to take on their passengers and strike out across the brushland carrying home the tired but happy revelers. Those who lived far away left first; next door neighbors like the Magees and the Kendalls, with only fifty or sixty miles to travel, stayed over one more night. Remaining guests were surprised at breakfast that last morning to see Anne glide into the dining room wearing a high-necked gown of white silk and lace.

She smiled nervously, and when she spoke there was a note of shrill excitement in her voice.

"I'm sorry to disturb you," she said, "but would you all please come with me to the chapel?"

"What's this?" Moses Magee mumbled to his wife. "A prayer meetin'? I knew we shoulda left yesterday like I wanted!"

"Hush, Moses!" Vivian hissed, as puzzled as the rest of the guests but rising to follow Anne nevertheless.

At the doorway to the chapel, Anne paused and said, "Go on in and take a seat."

They arranged themselves in the pews, whispering to each other, wondering what was about to happen, and craning their necks for a glimpse of Sofia who, along with Carlos, sat directly in front flanked by the maids Eugenia and Maria Elena.

Then Reverend Polk, the Methodist preacher who had recently settled in Joelsboro, entered by a side door and took his place behind the lectern. He smiled benignly and peered out over the rims of his glasses at the impromptu congregation.

Behind them, the chapel door opened again, and everyone swung around. Anne and Alex stood for a moment on the threshold; then, arm in arm, they walked slowly down the aisle.

"Well, I'll be danged!" Vivian Magee breathed. "I do believe there's gonna be a weddin'!"

Flora, sitting at her left, first looked stunned and then began to cry. Vivian shoved a handkerchief at her and patted her arm in solace.

Anne and Alex reached the lectern. The preacher cleared his throat and began: "Dearly beloved, we are gathered here together . . ."

Their honeymoon coach waited just outside the hacienda, and the visitors lined the steps to wish them well and to see them off.

"Honey, this has been some party!" Vivian Magee bubbled, pecking Anne's cheek. "We come for a fandango and a bit of ropin' an bulldoggin' and end up at a weddin'! I swan, Moses an' me will never be able to top this!"

"Best of luck to you, young feller," Moses said, wringing Alex's hand. "You got a good woman and a good ranch!"

Flora was still too choked with tears to say anything, but she smiled bravely and managed to kiss Anne on the cheek.

"Where are you headed on your wedding trip?" someone called out as the newlyweds climbed onto the coach.

"San Antonio!" Anne shouted back. "And then New Orleans!"

Alex snapped the reins and the coach lurched forward.

Everyone on the porch cheered and waved, and Anne waved back and blew kisses at her friends until they were far, far away.

They took their time, stopping over at inns and stagecoach stations along the way, arriving in San Antonio in the late afternoon of the fourth day.

"Now, you'll not begrudge me the use of your usual

341

suite this time, will you?" Alex asked as they pulled up at the Menger Hotel.

Anne laughed and strolled arm in arm with him to the desk. She watched as he took a pen and signed the register "Mr. and Mrs. Alex Cameron, The Lantana Ranch."

"Anne Cameron," she murmured at his side. "I like the sound of it."

Alex's eyes lingered on the register book. The Lantana Ranch! he thought to himself. I like the sound of that!

They had barely moved into their suite when a message arrived from Marcus and Dora Buchanan inviting them to a party in their honor at their home by the river.

"How in the world did they know?" Anne asked, reading the invitation again.

"I telegraphed from Yellow Rock," Alex said.

"I imagine the news was quite a surprise," Anne said, "considering the way I acted toward you that morning at their house."

"I don't think they would have thought us likely prospects for marriage," Alex replied, his eyes bright with humor. "What time are we invited for?"

"Eight o'clock," Anne answered.

Alex pulled his watch from his pocket and snapped open the cover. "Well, we have plenty of time."

"For what?"

He smiled and pulled her into an embrace. "To get to know each other a bit better."

Now Anne smiled too. She put her arms around his neck and they tumbled onto the bed.

The Buchanans' party was a gay affair, dinner for twelve beneath the glittering chandelier in their elegant dining room. Anne knew most of the guests, wealthy ranchers and their wives.

"My dear," Lucinda Hambleton advised Anne. "Now that you're married, you really should build a

342

house here in San Antonio. It's so much nicer than being stuck out on a ranch all the time."

"But I like living on the Lantana," Anne objected.

"Well, I like the Palo Verde, too," Lucinda countered. "Still, I'd go out of my mind if I had to stay there day in and day out."

"But there's so much work to be done on the ranch," Anne said. "I really can't see being away from it for very long."

"All work and no play . . ." Lucienda said airily, fluttering her hands as if to wave away Anne's objections. "Just think of all the parties you'll be missing. And the shops! Why the cleverest little Frenchwoman just opened a brand new millinery business near the plaza. Absolutely the latest designs! I must take you there tomorrow."

Anne nodded politely, but decided she'd be very busy tomorrow when it was time to go shopping with Lucinda. Hats! The only hat she was interested in was a curly-brimmed Stetson, but she kept that opinion to herself.

The servants swept away the dinner plates and replaced them with coffee and little saucers of *flan*.

"Look at this," said Gideon Ward, a paunchy, gray-mustachioed cowman from Uvalde County. He reached into his breast pocket and pulled out a small packet. He unwrapped it and tossed the contents onto the table in front of the group.

"What is it?" Marcus Buchanan asked, reaching for the object and holding it up so all could see a coiled strand of wire, about a foot and a half long, studded at intervals with sharp points.

"It's a new invention," Gideon Ward explained. "Called thorny wire, I believe."

"And what's it for, for heaven's sake?" Lucinda Hambleton asked.

"For fencing," Gideon answered.

"Fencing what?"

343

"For fencing in cows, my dear," he said.

"You'd have to have some mighty tame cows," Anne offered, losing interest and returning to her *flan*.

Marcus Buchanan shared her opinion. "Now what fool's gonna trust a puny strand of wire like that to hold in a wild bull? No way in hell!"

"Marcus!" Dora said, afraid her husband had offended Gideon.

"That's all right, Dora," Gideon assured her. "I'm of the same mind as Marcus. I just brought it along for amusement."

Alex reached out and accepted the wire from his host. He turned it over in his hand and examined it, a frown creasing his forehead.

"Where did you get this?" he asked.

Gideon shrugged. "Oh some crackpot down at the stockyard gave it to me. I didn't catch his name. Didn't bother myself to ask."

"Didn't some cowman down around your area try fencing with wire?" Marcus Buchanan asked Anne. " 'Course it wasn't thorny like this."

Anne looked up from her dessert. She had been only half listening, and it took her a moment to concentrate on the question. "Oh, yes," she answered at last. "But he had no luck. The cows just pushed right through it whenever they pleased."

Gideon nodded knowingly. "And it cost him a pretty penny, I'd wager."

"I imagine it did," Anne replied absently, bored by the conversation. She took her spoon and began scraping the last of her *flan* from her saucer.

Alex continued to study the wire, running his fingertips along the heavy strand and delicately touching the wickedly sharp points.

"Do you have anything like that back in Scotland, Alex?" Marcus asked him.

"No, nothing like this at all," Alex replied. "But

344

our herds are quite docile, and we're able to pen them in with stone walls and hedgerows."

"Hell, our critters are so tough even chaparral don't scare 'em. They *like* the dad-burned stuff. Let one of 'em get a hiding place among all those thorns and you'll spend a week trying to drive it out," Gideon boasted.

"Anyway," Lucienda Hambleton piped up, "who needs to put up a fence? The good Lord gave us enough open range to accommodate everyone!"

Anne glanced over at Alex. He had uncoiled the wire and was holding it out in front of him. His *flan* lay untouched at his place. She reached over surreptitiously and took it for herself.

"I wish you remembered who gave you this," he said quietly, addressing Gideon.

"Can't for the life of me," Gideon replied. "But I do recall him telling me he was gonna stage a demonstration in the plaza, right in front of the Alamo. Tomorrow afternoon," he said. "We oughta go over there and take a gander. That's bound to be some sight to see, I'm here to tell you—cows'll be running loose all over the place!"

Everyone but Alex laughed heartily. Then Dora Buchanan rose, signaling the end of dinner.

"Well, gentlemen," Marcus said. "Let's step into the drawing room for cigars and brandy. We'll rejoin the ladies later."

At the Menger Hotel the next afternoon, Alex received a message that Gideon Ward was waiting in the courtyard below.

"Let's go, darling," Alex said to Anne.

"Whatever in the world for?" she replied, a slight hint of annoyance in her voice. "I can look at a wild cow any time I take a notion."

"It's not the cows I want to see," Alex said. "It's the demonstration of the wire."

345

"Wire, wire!" Anne said. She was sitting at the dresser pulling a brush through her hair. "You know what I think of wire fence. It's nothing but some day-dreamer's silly invention. Why, I bet he's never been on a ranch in his life."

"It's worth going to see," Alex coaxed.

"Not to me. I don't want to go."

"Then what do you want to do?" he asked.

She rose from the dresser and slipped her arms around his neck. "I want to stay right here and let you make love to me."

Alex smiled and looked down at her. "We can do that later—we have lots of time for that. But right now I want to see that demonstration." He peeled her arms from around his neck and reached for his hat.

"You're going anyway?" Anne asked, surprised.

"Of course," he answered, heading for the door. "I'll be back shortly."

And then he was gone, leaving Anne standing in the middle of the room, her hands on her hips, her mouth open in a little O of amazement. She had honestly thought she could change his mind and persuade him to stay with her.

"Well, I'll be damned!" she breathed, and immediately her astonishment turned into hurt anger. She grabbed her hairbrush and hurled it across the room, knocking over a vase of yellow roses on a table near the window.

Stepping into the courtyard, Alex heard the crash above him and realized that it came from their suite. He paused momentarily, looking up, then shrugged and went forward to meet Gideon.

The plaza in front of the Alamo was already teeming with gawking spectators. Alex and Gideon pushed their way to the front of the crowd and found that a pen had been erected of upright cedar posts, placed at intervals and connected with strands of the same

346

wire that Gideon had displayed at dinner the night before.

"Keerful!" warned a rangy, sun-baked old codger in a plaid shirt and a tattered straw hat. "Them pricklies is sharp as rattlesnake teeth. Lookit what one of them little devils done to me!" He held out his arm, revealing his torn sleeve and a long red scratch where a barb had ripped the flesh.

Alex turned to Gideon. "What do you think that wire will do to a cow?"

"Hell, if chaparral don't cut 'em to ribbons—and it don't—this puny wire shore won't hold 'em in." Gideon glanced around apprehensively. "I don't know about you, Alex, but I'm thinking we might oughtta move back a pace. Once them critters come chargin' outta them chutes, they're liable to bust right through this fence and trample us."

But it was too late to move. The crowd pressed in on them and held them fast. Then a man strode into the center of the pen and addressed the crowd.

"This here invention will change the face of ranching," he announced. "And we aim to show you how. Now I've been all over the place demonstrating this wire, and everybody falls all over theirselves to advise me that an ornery ole Texas bull will rip this wire right off the posts without so much as a howdy-do. Well, I'm gonna demonstrate that those folks are talking through their hats. There ain't *nothing* that can get through this wire!"

A murmur, mixed with derisive laughter, swept through the crowd.

The man, dressed like a city slicker with a derby on his head, held up his hands for silence. "I hope all you ranchers out there are taking heed. This wire will enable you to keep your herd in one place instead of having them run all over God's creation."

"And what about us farmers?" came a shout from the crowd.

The man smiled. "Well, it stands to reason that what holds something in can also hold something out. Do you follow me? It means for the first time you can fence in your farms. You won't have to put up with a trail herd trampling all over your crops. And it'll keep your own critters out of the cornfield."

There were a few isolated cheers, but mostly the crowd remained dubious.

"It's an old saying that actions speak louder than words," he man went on. "So I'm gonna climb right out of here and get on with the show."

Now the crowd seemed to share in Gideon's fears, and there was a general apprehensive movement backwards, away from the pen.

Without further ado, the chutes were swung open and a dozen bellowing head of cattle thundered into the pen. There were screams from the crowd, and people began shoving, trying to make their way to safety.

For a moment the animals stood in confusion in the middle of the pen. Then one big bull with majestic horns pawed the ground and started for the fence.

"Oh, Lord!" Gideon exclaimed, stumbling backwards. "We're done for!"

Alex watched in fascination, frozen to the spot, as the bull charged directly toward them. Gideon had thrown himself to the ground, curling himself into a ball, covering his head with his arms.

The bull rammed the wire. It bulged, zinging with tension. But it held, and the bull recoiled as if it had been clubbed in the head. On the other side, several feisty cows attacked the fence, only to feel the wire's painful sting. The bull moseyed down the fence, butting it from time to time, and shoving his tough flank against it once or twice. But as Alex watched, he saw that some dim realization had taken place in the animal's mind.

The big bull and the cows milled about, excited by

348

the crowd, but they were staying well away from the fence. With some embarrassment, Gideon had dragged himself up off the ground and was dusting his trousers.

"It works, Gideon," Alex said.

"I can't believe it!" Gideon replied.

The crowd was reassembling now, relatively assured that the critters wouldn't break loose and trample them.

"Look at them," Alex said. "They won't touch the fence."

Someone in the assembly let out a rebel yell. It was picked up by others, and soon the plaza rocked with cheers.

Alex and Gideon went off to have a drink and contemplate the wonders they had just seen.

"It works. Yes, indeed, it works," Gideon said, when he and Alex were settled in the courtyard of the Menger, sipping juleps. "But what are you going to do with it? I reckon it'll prove handy for erecting stock pens to hold the herd during roundup. But other than that I don't see much future in it. The critters gotta run free. They gotta get to grass and water; otherwise they'll starve to death behind that wire."

Alex nodded. From what he knew of the *brasada*, everything Gideon was saying was true. Penned up, without free access to nourishment, the animals would die.

Alex's brows were knit with brooding concentration. The new thorny wire fascinated him. It seemed such a damned fine invention. He had seen it check a wild bull in a matter of minutes. It would be a shame if its only usefulness lay in constructing a few stock pens to be used at roundup.

Gideon broke his train of thought. "I sure would like to have another one of these juleps. Mighty refreshing on a hot afternoon like this! But I promised the missus I'd be home early. Her sister is coming for dinner."

Alex rose to shake Gideon's hand.

"We leave for New Orleans tomorrow," Alex said. "So this is farewell for a while."

"Have a good trip, you hear! Tell Anne good-bye for me. And next time you're in San Antonio, come by and see us."

Alex thanked Gideon and watched him leave the courtyard. Then he signaled for another julep and sat back down at his table. He reached in his pocket and pulled out a piece of paper. After the demonstration in the plaza, he had caught up with the man who had shown the wire and had taken down some information.

Now he spread the creased sheet of paper out in front of him and reread what he had written: "Joseph Glidden. DeKalb, Illinois."

I wonder where that is, he thought. And how do you get there from here?

"DeKalb, Illinois!" Anne cried in astonishment. "We're supposed to be spending our honeymoon in New Orleans. Are you suggesting we go to DeKalb, Illinois, instead?"

Her tone irritated Alex. He turned away from her and stared out the window at the setting sun.

"Not *instead*, my dear," he explained. "We'll go to New Orleans too. But *in addition* . . ."

"No, Alex! No! I don't want to go to DeKalb, Illinois. I've never even heard of it. If you're so all-fired interested in that silly wire, can't you just write a letter to this Mister Giddings?"

"Glidden," Alex corrected. "His name is Joseph Glidden, and he's the inventor of the wire."

"Well, whatever, can't you just write to him?"

"I want to see him personally."

"For the life of me, I don't know why! You know the wire won't work for us. You said so yourself. You know our cows would die if we cooped them all up in

350

little pens. So, please, Alex, please . . . I want to go to New Orleans tomorrow like we planned. Why don't you write to Mr. Giddings and ask him for the information you want?"

Alex left the window and went to the desk. To Anne's immense relief and satisfaction, he took out a sheet of paper, dipped the pen in ink and began to write.

When he finished, he folded the paper and sealed it in an envelope.

All smiles now, Anne glided across the room to the desk where he sat and put her hands fondly on his shoulders.

"What did you say to him?" she asked.

"I told him that we would be in DeKalb next Wednesday."

35

Anne had never ridden on a train before, but even the novelty of this somewhat hair-rising experience failed to dispel her sulfurous mood. She glowered her way across Arkansas and Missouri, hating the inconvenience of having to leave the train every hundred miles or so and travel by stage to a neighboring town where another train waited to carry them onward.

Alex ignored her bad humor. He knew that a word of apology from him, a promise to hurry with his dealings with Joseph Glidden so that they could hasten to New Orleans and resume the honeymoon, would brighten Anne up—and it was obvious that she desperately wanted to brighten up. It was not her disposition to sulk and pout, and he thought she was growing weary of the pose. But he decided to let her stew a while longer—for her own good.

When they reached Illinois, they transferred to one of George Pullman's new sleeping cars, but Anne pretended to ignore this relative luxury. While she sequestered herself in their berth, Alex cheerfully roamed the train, making acquaintances among the other passengers. He dined heartily while Anne picked with feigned disdain at the food on her plate, and he stayed up late playing poker with newfound friends in the parlor car.

"I should think a gentleman would pay better attention to his bride of less than a week instead of carousing around and playing cards till all hours," she snapped when he rejoined her after a midnight game.

"You know I have a passion for poker," he said nonchalantly, pulling off his boots and preparing for bed.

"Well, have you ever considered that I might enjoy a game or two instead of staying cooped up here while you humor yourself?"

"You play poker?" he asked, surprised.

"Of course I play poker," she retorted. "And I'm damned good at it."

"I never knew," Alex mused.

"There's a lot about me you don't know," she reminded him.

"Well, no matter," he said, dismissing her complaint. "It isn't seemly for a lady to sit at a gentlemen's gaming table."

"We could play here . . . in private," she blurted out, astonishing herself for suggesting such a thing. She cared nothing about a game of cards. She was tired and angry and wanted only to go to bed.

Alex discerned all this by the expression on her face and determined not to let the challenge pass. "Very well, my love," he said brightly, reaching into his coat pocket and producing a deck of cards. "Who will deal? You or I?"

It was too late for Anne to back down. She tried to concentrate on her cards, but her mind wandered and she blundered badly time after time. They were using matchsticks for chips, but Alex had suggested that they count for dollars and Anne was too irritated to protest.

They played in almost absolute silence for nearly an hour, speaking only to raise and call. At last, tired

353

and out of matches, Anne threw in her cards and dropped out of the game.

"Had enough?" Alex asked.

"For tonight," Anne replied coolly. She untied the sash on her robe and prepared to crawl into the bed.

"Just a moment," Alex said.

"What's the matter?"

"You owe me . . . let's see here. You owe me two hundred and seventy-six dollars."

Anne's jaw dropped. "Don't be silly, Alex!"

"Don't you pay your gambling debts . . . or is that something else about you I don't know?"

"Oh!" Anne gasped in a fury. She snatched her purse from a hook on the wall and pulled out a fistful of bills. "Here!" she said, counting them out and tossing them across the berth at Alex.

He let them fall at his feet. Suddenly, he reached out and grabbed her by the shoulders, giving her a little shake.

"Anne! Anne! Let's stop this absurdity this minute!"

She blinked as if suddenly released from a spell. Alex slipped his arm around her and drew her close. The train rocked their bodies gently together.

His arm still around her, he sat her down and began to explain. "It's clear to me, Anne, that your way of ranching is going to change. The open range, as noble and beautiful as it may be, is a wasteful way of raising cattle. I know, because I've seen it done differently in Britain. Until now, you've had no choice. The free range and periodic roundups were the only method available. But as of this moment they're antiquated. Overnight, they'll be a thing of the past, a romantic memory. This new wire of Mr. Glidden's will bring about a revolution. Mark my words, Anne, I can see it coming!"

Anne stared at him as if mesmerized, unable to escape his gaze. He seemed to be looking through her, viewing a distant landscape that lay hidden from her eyes. And when he spoke again, his voice trembled with conviction.

"And if we're to survive this revolution . . . nay! if we're going to thrive and prosper, we must get a head start on our competitors!"

He paused for a moment, then spoke softly with his lips close to her ear. "I know you're unhappy. This isn't the honeymoon you dreamed of. Nor is it mine. But it's only an interlude—a brief interruption. In a few days, we'll be on a paddle-wheeler steaming down the Mississippi toward New Orleans. And then we'll have a grand and glorious time, just as we planned. But, Anne . . . Anne! This journey to Illinois is for the good of the Lantana!"

The locomotive whistle wailed into the night. The Pullman car swayed rhythmically beneath them, speeding across the green Illinois farmlands.

Anne clung to Alex and buried her face in his shoulder. Her lips quivered and stinging tears filled her eyes.

"There, there," he murmured gently. "Dry those eyes. There's no reason to cry. We're together and we love each other."

"Oh, yes, Alex! We do love each other, don't we?"

"Beyond words, my dear!"

"Oh, my darling," she said. "I'm sorry. I've been so selfish. I wanted all of your attention. I wanted you to think of nothing but me."

"But don't you see, Anne?" he said, tilting her face toward his. "I *am* thinking only of you. You are the Lantana . . . and the Lantana is you. And there is something else you don't realize—the Lantana is not merely a ranch. It is a barony. You control more land than many European monarchs, and your empire is peopled with subjects who need you and look to you for their well-being. It is not some paltry thing that you're the queen of. It is, in fact, a kingdom!"

Anne gazed into his eyes. Once again, they seemed to be looking out at a faraway landscape, and if she

355

couldn't yet quite see exactly the scene that they beheld, the solemn tremor in his voice stirred her soul and made her wonder.

"Oh, Alex!" she whispered. "You frighten me!"

"Nay!" he said. "There's nothing to fear. You're strong, and together we'll be stronger still. Side by side, we'll take this kingdom and make it supreme! Oh, Anne! It's a glorious venture we have before us!"

His eyelids flickered and his gaze reluctantly left the visionary landscape and settled on her face. Diamondlike tears sparkled on the fringe of her lashes, and color blazed across her cheeks. His lips sought hers, and they sank onto the bed together.

Their visit to DeKalb lasted less than twenty-four hours. They caught the next train to St. Louis where they boarded the paddle-wheeler *Memphis Queen* bound for New Orleans.

The meeting with Joseph Glidden had been a success. He had greeted Alex and Anne warmly and showed them through his mill, where noisy, clacking machines wrapped the sharp barbs along a constantly moving strand of shiny galvanized wire.

Later, back at Glidden's office, Alex had asked, "How much wire is on each reel?"

"Six hundred yards," Glidden had answered.

Alex had taken a piece of paper and scribbled his calculations. "In that case, Mr. Glidden, we'd like to place an initial order of six hundred reels."

Glidden's eyes had grown wide. "My God, man! Do you aim to fence in your ranch or the whole state of Texas?"

"Just the southern third," Alex had answered, not batting an eye. "Just the southern third, more or less."

Now they were traveling on the *Memphis Queen*, living like royalty in the paddle-wheeler's finest stateroom. By day they sat on deck, watching the panorama along the Mississippi's banks drift slowly by. Brass

356

bands greeted the steamboat at every dock. The atmosphere was gay and festive. At night they dined luxuriously and danced until they were ready to drop beneath sparkling crystal chandeliers in the boat's ballroom.

Anne was supremely happy. She banished from her mind the memory of the trip's unpleasant beginning. She thought only of herself and Alex; and she was very much in love—so much in love that she failed to notice the distant look that swept over him from time to time. She missed entirely the air of preoccupation that often took him away from her.

And Alex decided not to trouble her with his thoughts—not yet, not until after they had visited New Orleans and had had their honeymoon.

Waiting at the crowded dock as the *Memphis Queen* steamed into the Crescent City, was Charles LaForet, a prominent banker and the owner of La Rivière, one of the loveliest plantations upriver from New Orleans.

He spotted Alex and Anne at the paddle-wheeler's railing and pushed through the throng in order to be at the foot of the gangplank when the couple alighted.

"Alex, *mon ami!*" he exclaimed with pleasure, grasping Alex's hands warmly. "Welcome to New Orleans!"

"It's wonderful to be here, Charles," Alex replied. "I'd like you to meet my bride. Anne, this is Charles LaForet."

"I'm happy to meet you, Charles," Anne said, smiling. "Alex speaks so highly of you."

"Don't believe a word he tells you!" Charles admonished, laughing, but obviously flattered. He was a tall, well-built man in his early fifties with a handsome Gallic face—high cheekbones, proud, patrician nose, and quick, intelligent eyes.

Anne liked him immediately and was happy that Alex had thought to write ahead, informing his friend of their visit.

"Leonie is beside herself with joy that you've come,"

357

Charles said, adding for Anne's benefit, "Leonie is my wife. She's planning a gala party for the two of you at La Rivière. And of course, the children are dying to see you again, Alex."

"I imagine they're quite grown by now," Alex said. "Let's see . . . it's been four years since we last saw each other."

"Four years!" Charles exclaimed, shaking his head. "Yes, yes, I still call my daughters children, but I suppose they're young ladies to everyone else. Suzanne is sixteen, and Jeanette turned eighteen last St. Joseph's Day."

He led them to his waiting carriage and held Anne's hand as she climbed inside.

"To the Hotel St. Louis," he informed his driver, then climbed into the carriage and settled on the leather seat beside Anne. "Well, Alex, you look extremely fit. Texas must agree with you. Or perhaps it's your lovely young bride. The last time I saw you at your father's place in Scotland, you were quite pale and broody, wondering what to do with your life. It looks as if you've made the right decision."

"I have, Charles," Alex said, smiling at Anne. "I assure you, I have."

"And how is your father?"

"A bit creaky in his old age, and as cantankerous as ever," Alex replied.

"I don't believe it," Charles said, turning to Anne. "Douglas Cameron is as hale a man as you'd ever hope to meet, and perfectly charming! My family and I were guests at his home in the Highlands during our last visit to Europe. I must say, we've never been entertained more warmly. And I hope to repay a small measure of his kindness during your stay in our city."

At first, New Orleans beguiled Anne. She and Alex lived in a splendid suite at the Hotel St. Louis and partook of the delights of the Crescent City, accompanied by Charles and Leonie. They dined on food

358

with exotic flavors that neither she nor Alex had ever tasted before: sweet pompano delicately baked in parchment; thick, steaming gumbo over rice; garlicky *andouille*, soft-shell crab and succulent crawfish—all served with delicious hot crusty bread.

They went to the French Opera House, and Anne fell in love with the music of Haydn and Beethoven, but she found *Le Barbier de Seville* silly and tedious— an opinion she kept from Charles and Leonie, who seemed to revel in every moment of it.

Some nights they danced until they were exhausted; and twice Charles lent them his carriage so they could ride up the River Road and out into the country to picnic alone beneath huge oaks bearded with gray moss.

And every afternoon when the air grew heavy, and swollen-bellied clouds hovered low over the city, Alex and Anne left the LaForets and retreated to the solitude of their suite. They made passionate love while a warm, tropical rain pelted the streets and spattered against their louvered shutters. Then, satisfied, exhausted, and sublimely happy, Anne would fall into a deep sleep while Alex lay beside her, thinking, worrying, with the shadow of a frown darkening his brow.

A week after their arrival, Charles sent his carriage for them, and Anne and Alex rode upriver to a party at La Rivière.

"What a beautiful house!" Anne exclaimed, clutching Alex's hand as they rolled up the long horseshoe drive.

A mellow full moon had risen, revealing a white-columned mansion, encircled by a broad gallery. Lights blazed behind French doors, and the lilting strains of orchestra music reached their ears long before they pulled up at the carriage block.

Leonie was on the steps to greet them.

"Welcome, *mes chers*," she said, extending both hands to greet them. Hearing Leonie's slight French

359

accent again pleased Anne and added a further dimension to the magic of the scene.

"What a lovely gown, my dear," Leonie said. "Paris, no doubt?"

"I'm afraid not, Leonie," Anne replied, amused yet flattered. "It was copied by one of my maids on the Lantana from a picture in *Godey's Lady's Book*."

"*Mon Dieu!*" Leonie exclaimed, truly astonished. "I must have that woman's name!"

Linking arms with both Anne and Alex, Leonie led them up the curving staircase to the gallery and through the French doors into the ballroom.

The LaForets had spared no extravagance. The orchestra played from a dais garlanded with ferns and roses from the plantation's flower garden. Liveried servants circled the room carrying trays laden with champagne, and long linen-draped tables bore platters of food and drink worthy of a bacchanal.

Charles, who had been watching for their entry, was threading his way through the dancers to welcome them. "You must come at once and speak to Jeanette and Suzanne," he said. "They're quite put out that you've been here a week and they haven't seen you yet."

He led Anne and Alex back across the crowded room toward a group of young people gathered near the dais.

"Jeanette," he called over the music, "Suzanne. Here's Alex and his wife."

The younger, Suzanne, turned first. She was a pretty girl with russet hair and a ready smile.

"Oh, Alex!" she cried. "Do you remember me?"

"Of course, I do," he smiled. And he introduced her to Anne. "Do you still love horses?" he asked.

"They're my passion," Suzanne laughed, and Anne could see that behind her carefully coiffed and gowned exterior was a sixteen-year-old tomboy who would rather be busy in the stables than dancing at the ball.

360

Then Jeanette left her group and came to meet them.

Her beauty was breathtaking. She had her father's features—the high cheekbones, the patrician nose. And her raven hair accentuated the milky smoothness of her complexion.

"But you've grown up!" Alex said, taking her hand. "When I last saw you, you were a little girl."

Her cheeks turned the color of the roses that adorned the dais, and Anne saw unmistakably that her lips trembled as Alex took her hand.

"Oh, Alex!" she breathed. "I . . . I'm so happy to see you again."

Alex introduced her to Anne, but the warmth in Jeanette's eyes was reserved only for Alex. She spoke briefly and politely to Anne, then returned her gaze to Alex. "Will you dance with me?" she asked him.

"Please do," Charles said. "That will give me the opportunity to waltz Anne around the floor."

Alex put his arm around Jeanette's waist and they moved away. They danced in silence, circling the ballroom. As they passed the open French doors, Jeanette pulled away and whispered, "Let's go onto the gallery, Alex. Just for a moment."

She held onto his hand and led him outside. The moon was bright and cast a spell over the lawn before them. Jeanette stood at the balustrade, looking out, with Alex at her side.

Suddenly she turned and looked at him. Her dark lashes sparkled with tears.

"Oh, Alex! I've lost you!" she cried, falling into his arms.

Alex held her stiffly, taken aback.

"What are you saying, Jeanette?"

"I love you, Alex!" she wept. "Surely you knew that! Not a day has gone by since I met you in Scotland that I haven't thought of you! And now . . . now. . . ."

Alex tried to pull away, but Jeanette held onto him. "Please, Jeanette, please!" he murmured.

"I just can't bear that you're married!" she sobbed, her shoulders shaking. "Now you're lost to me forever!"

The scent of roses in her hair reached Alex. He looked at her tenderly. His smile was sad, for he understood the heartbreak of youth.

"Jeanette, you'll always be dear to me," he said.

She threw her head back and stared at him with flashing eyes. "I don't want to be dear to you. I want to be loved by you!"

Alex pulled her arms from around his neck. "Let's stop this, Jeanette. Let's go back inside. Listen. The music has ended."

She nodded dumbly, wiping the tears from her eyes. Alex turned to reenter the ballroom, but Jeanette reached for his hand and held him back.

"I'll never forget you, Alex," she said. "And I'll never stop loving you!"

After the ball Anne and Alex returned to their hotel and slept until noon the next day. Anne woke and sent for breakfast to be brought up, but Alex lay abed, worry creasing his brow.

He knew he could keep his plans from Anne no longer. During the last few days, he had noticed an air of restlessness about her. Like a child gorged on chocolate, she had had enough of New Orleans. The Lantana was calling her back. Only the morning before, as they walked down the Rue Royale, she had exclaimed, "Oh, how these buildings crowd in on you! I don't see how a person can live in a place where you can't look out over miles and miles of wide open spaces!"

Crowded cities and verdant byways held only a limited attraction for Anne, and she had observed: "There's too much vegetation here. Everything is so

362

green and mossy and damp. It's almost as if the plants would take over if you turned your back on them for a moment. Look how the trees grow over the streets so you can't even see the sky!"

It was time to leave, Alex knew. But he didn't know how he was going to tell Anne that he wasn't going back to the Lantana with her.

She solved the problem for him that evening when she took his coat to hang it up and found in the pocket a single train ticket from New Orleans to San Antonio.

"Where's the other one?" she asked, fishing in the other pocket. "Oh, Alex, I think you've lost it!"

He'd meant to tell her the next morning, after one last night on the town, but now he could no longer evade the question.

"I haven't lost it, Anne," he said. "There . . . there isn't another one."

She looked up, alerted by the tension in his voice. His coat hung limply from her hand. "I—I don't understand."

He took his coat from her and tossed it on the bed. "Anne, let's sit down. I have to tell you something."

He led her across the room to the sofa and filled two glasses with champagne from a bottle chilling in a silver ice bucket. Anne took the thin-stemmed crystal glass but did not drink.

"What is it, Alex? Tell me. Something's wrong. I can see it in your face."

"Anne, you will be going back to the Lantana by yourself."

"What do you mean, by myself? What about you? What are you going to do?"

"I have to make a trip, Anne—a business trip."

"Well, I'll go with you!"

"No, Anne, I'll be gone far too long. You're needed on the ranch to take care of things. You said yourself you don't trust Rudy, and I fear we've been gone too long as it is."

363

"Alex, I don't understand. What kind of business trip? And where?"

Alex looked away from her imploring eyes. "I'm going back to Britain, Anne."

"No!"

"Yes, I must. I've thought it out very carefully and it's the only way. I'm going to buy breeding stock for our ranch. Your wild cattle can be much improved, but we've got to have good heavy beef to accomplish that."

"Alex, that's a crazy scheme. It won't work!" She bolted from the sofa and began pacing the floor in front of him. "English cows can't survive in South Texas. They can't manage in the brush. They're not built for it. They'll starve."

Anne stopped her pacing and fixed her gaze on Alex. "The wire!" she exclaimed. "The goddamned wire! Now I know why you were so all fired up to go to Illinois. You've had this plan all along—you knew you were going back to Britain, but you kept it from me!"

"I didn't want to ruin this trip for you."

"Oh, aren't you thoughtful!" Her eyes flashed angrily. "So you show me a good time for a couple of weeks, to placate me, then you gallivant off across the ocean by yourself for God knows how long and leave me to go home from my honeymoon alone! Well, I won't have it, Alex. Either you go back to the Lantana with me, or I'm coming with you!"

"Anne, you know that's impossible. You know they need you on the ranch."

"I won't have it!" she cried. "I won't be left by myself! I married you so I wouldn't be alone anymore! Alex . . . Alex!"

He grabbed her hand and tried to pull her toward him, but she wrenched free and resumed her pacing.

"Anne, be reasonable. It's for us—I'm doing this. If those scrawny longhorns of yours have made you a wealthy woman, think what price heavy beef stock will bring!"

"I don't need any more money!" she cried. "I'm probably the richest woman in Texas!" Now she came to him grabbing his hands and kneeling at his feet. "Oh, Alex, I only need you . . . with me, by my side always."

He pulled her up onto the sofa beside him and held her in his arms. She was weeping, so he kissed away her tears. "Oh, Anne, my love! We will be together, the two of us side by side forever."

She was silent for a while, resting against him, feeling safe and secure in his arms, trying to gain control of her voice. At last she asked, "Then you won't go? At least not now? Not when I can't go with you?"

Alex sighed. "I'm sorry, Anne. Believe me, I am. But I sail tomorrow noon."

36

At four the next afternoon, the train with Anne aboard chugged out of New Orleans. She had refused to accompany Alex to the dock to see him off. All morning he had tried to talk to her, but she had greeted his efforts with steely silence. He had attempted to kiss her good-bye, but she had turned her back on him and stared out the window at his waiting carriage on the street below.

"I'll be home as soon as I'm able, Anne," he'd told her, his hand on the doorknob. "A few months, that's all. I promise."

She hadn't replied. She didn't even turn around to see him leave. And when the door had closed behind him, she'd banged the shutters to, so she wouldn't see him in the street.

She wired ahead to the Menger Hotel in San Antonio, reserving her suite, and she wired Rudy at the ranch, informing him that she was coming home alone and that he should send a coach to San Antonio to meet her.

It was the first week in September, and the days were growing noticeably shorter. The shadow of the train racing alongside lengthened until it reached the bleached trunks of the cypresses growing out of the swamp. The sky above ignited as if touched by a red flare. And then it was twilight.

Anne shivered and hugged herself tightly. She had no idea what the future held for her. Alex had sailed on a ship whose name she didn't even know. And for what destination? England? Scotland? She had asked for no address and he had given her none. And how long would he be gone? A few months, he had said. But Anne wasn't so sure.

Sitting alone in the growing darkness, rocked by the swaying motion of the train, she remembered Rudy's warning about Alex. "He'll use you!" Rudy had said. "He's an opportunist. I can see it in his face."

And now Anne was afraid that Rudy had been right. In the few short weeks since their marriage, Alex seemed already to have taken over control of the ranch. He had dragged her to Illinois against her wishes and contracted to spend a fortune for barbed wire that she didn't want and could see no use for. And now he had abandoned her, to sail to Britain to buy stock that she was convinced would weaken and die in the harsh conditions of the *brasada*.

What a fool I've been! she thought bitterly. He *is* an opportunist and he's wasting no time taking over the Lantana.

She sighed miserably and peered out into the ever-darkening swamplands. Now she wondered if Alex really loved her. It seemed impossible that his ardor was counterfeit. He had pleased and satisfied her as no other man ever had. Could his passion have been false, a ruse to make her think he loved her?

Anne's pride rose within her and drove this suspicion into one of the far recesses of her mind.

Impossible! she told herself. He does love me! I know he does! He *has* to!

The night closed in around her, and she fell asleep in the hard, uncomfortable coach chair.

The trip was arduous, with many changes from

367

train to stage to train again. But at last they left the piny woods behind and reached the vast prairie, dotted with oaks and cottonwood, that heralded their nearness to San Antonio.

In less than an hour, with whistle blaring and bell clanging, the train pulled into the depot. Anne was the last passenger off. She stepped lightly from the train and cast a glance around for a coachman to collect her baggage and drive her to the Menger Hotel. Instead, her eyes fell on Rudy. He was standing against a pillar among the throng that gathered for the train's arrival.

"Rudy!" she cried, pushing her way across the platform.

He turned, and when he saw her, he smiled and started forward to meet her. A shaft of sunlight struck his hair, glinting silver. His ruddy cheeks glowed beneath his tan, and the muscles of his broad shoulders rippled beneath the fabric of his shirt.

He held out his arms for her, and she shocked herself by falling into them and allowing him to hold her close. Then, pulling herself together, she drew back and arranged her mouth in a smile.

"Thanks for meeting me, Rudy," she said. "I didn't expect you to come yourself."

"I thought I'd enjoy the trip," he replied. "It's been a coon's age since I been in San Antone."

His wintery blue eyes held fast to hers, distracting her, causing her to stammer. "My—my baggage! There's an awful lot. Do you have some—someone to help?"

Rudy smiled again, his lips turning up slowly at the corners of his mouth. Without taking his eyes off her, he called to two Mexican youths standing nearby. "Amigos! Go get the lady's baggage."

The boys caught the coins that Rudy flipped in the air and shoved through the crowd toward the train.

"Where's your husband?" Rudy asked, still holding her with his gaze.

"He's on a trip . . . a business trip." She seemed unable to break away from his eyes.

"Will he be gone long?"

Anne almost blurted out that she didn't know. But suddenly the spell between her and Rudy was broken and she dropped her eyes. "No," she answered untruthfully. "Not long at all."

The boys returned, staggering beneath the weight of Anne's baggage. Rudy relieved one of them of the largest valise and hefted it lightly onto his back. "I got the coach waiting just outside."

"I was going to the Menger," Anne said. "I didn't expect to head out for the Lantana until tomorrow. But now that you're here, we might as well start for home."

"I was hoping we could stay over a day," Rudy said. "I got some shopping to do. Emma gave me a list."

"Of course," Anne said, shaking her head. "How selfish of me! You're probably tired from the trip up, too."

"Not too tired," Rudy said. "I spent last night at one of the inns just south of town. I got me a fresh start this morning."

"Well, it's all decided," Anne said, climbing up onto the coach. "We'll stay over a day. I'll get you a room at the hotel."

As Rudy hauled himself up beside her, a slight secret smile played over his lips.

That evening they dined together at a little German restaurant beside the river. Since Anne's appetite had not returned, she picked at her food while Rudy ate heartily of baked sausages and boiled potatoes.

"Aren't you hungry?" he asked, indicating Anne's plate, which she had scarcely touched.

"Not very," she answered. "I don't really feel like eating."

"Well, then, have a little more wine," he urged, reaching for the bottle and refilling her glass.

It was a tart acidy white wine, not really to Anne's liking, quite inferior to the expensive French wines she had tasted in New Orleans; but she found herself drinking it quickly, and in a few minutes she again extended her glass to Rudy and asked for more.

He smiled again, the same secret, almost indolent smile she had seen cross his lips from time to time.

He emptied the bottle into her glass and called out, *"Herr Ober, bitte! Noch eine Flasche Wein!"* And immediately a new bottle of wine was set before them. Rudy refilled his glass and toasted Anne.

"Welcome home. It's good to have you back."

"Thank you, Rudy," she said, noticing that her tongue felt thick and lazy. The alcohol seemed to have flowed into her limbs, making her feel warm and limp, and she caught herself swaying from side to side as if she were on a raft at sea.

"Oh my!" she said, unable to suppress a surprised giggle. "I think this wine's gone right to my head."

Rudy smiled again. "You should eat something."

"I couldn't take another bite," she said, and something about the statement struck her as supremely funny. She burst into laughter and held her sides while tears streamed down her cheeks.

Rudy laughed too, a deep baritone that seemed to rumble out of his chest.

Anne dabbed at her eyes with her napkin. "Oh, Rudy, I believe I'm drunk!"

He merely smiled again and topped off her glass.

"No more! No more!" she protested, but she raised the glass to her lips and drank.

When they rose to leave half an hour later, Rudy had to move to her side and support her. She staggered onto the stone walk outside, wondering why such solid

370

paving should undulate so. Rudy slipped his arm around her waist and propelled her forward.

"Oh, steps!" she cried, looking up at the flagged stairs that led from the river bank to the street above. "I'll never make it up!"

Rudy swept her into his arms as if she were a limp rag doll and carried her to the street. She felt warm and protected being held so. She nuzzled close to his chest with her arms linked loosely around his neck, and he heard her murmur, "Oh, thank you, Rudy! Thank you! I could never have gotten up here by myself."

He carried her down the street and across the plaza to the hotel. Ignoring the surprised clerk at the desk, he took the stairs two at a time to the second floor and opened the door to Anne's suite.

He marched with her through the sitting room into the bedroom and settled her gently on the bed. Anne shook her head, trying to dispel the dizziness that swept over her in relentless waves.

"Oh, Rudy," she muttered feebly. "The room is spinning and I can't make it stop!"

She felt his hands behind her, fumbling with the buttons on her dress. His face was close to hers, and she found that by concentrating on his eyes she was able to conquer the spells of dizziness. She looked into them, seeing winter skies and raging blue northers. She felt his warm breath on her cheek and smelled the tartness of the wine on his lips.

He pulled her dress away and she fell back against the pillows. In an instant, he was kneeling over her, breathing heavily, his tongue flicking at the corner of his mouth.

Suddenly the dizziness left her. The double image of him she had been seeing merged into one again. She raised her arms and placed her hands on his chest, holding him back.

"Oh, Rudy!" she whimpered, her eyes wide and dark. "No, please! I'm married now!"

He caught her wrist and pulled her hands away, pinning them at her sides. Lowering his face, his lips covered hers in a long kiss. "You're married," he whispered at last, his breath fluttering like a trapped moth against her ear, "but you're still mine. You'll always be mine. Alex doesn't love you. I've told you that. I can see it in his looks. And now he's gone and left you alone. A young bride . . . left all alone. Can that be love? Answer me, Anne!"

She tossed her head on the pillow. "I don't know! Oh, Rudy! I don't know!"

"I love you, though," he whispered, still teasing her ear with his fluttering breath. "I've loved you for years and years. And I would never leave you, Anne!"

Tears filled her eyes and she sobbed without shame.

"I'm faithful to you, Anne," he went on, his voice a low drone that lulled and consoled her. "I'll always be at your side, Anne. Always . . . always!"

She felt his body cover hers, the strong muscles of his chest pressing against the yielding flesh of her breasts, his golden-downed belly brushing hers, his long legs sliding between her knees and forcing them apart. He took her arms and locked them around his neck; then lowering his hips, he thrust into her.

"Oh, Rudy!" she cried. Her fingers dug into the nape of his neck and she forced his mouth hard onto hers.

1875

37

On the seventh of February, Anne received a letter from Alex. It was postmarked "Naples" and was dated "November 17th." Opening it, she read,

My Dearest Anne,

I am writing this in the hope that it arrives in time to wish you a happy Christmas. My deepest regret is that I am not there to share it with you. If ill health had not intervened, I should have sailed for Galveston in early December, and we could have been reunited in time for the holidays.

However, it seems that the several months I spent in the Texas heat had thinned my northern blood far more than I suspected.

The English chill attacked me almost as soon as I arrived. I ignored it at first but eventually was forced to take to bed with a spell of pneumonia, which left me too debilitated even to advise you of my illness.

Presently, with God's grace and the expert ministrations of one of Harley Street's finest men of medicine, I recovered strength enough to travel. On my physician's orders, I have come here to Naples where, it is hoped, the Italian sun will restore my health.

All this, of course, has set my endeavors back many months. I intend to return to England to complete my project there, but I have been told that the earliest I shall be allowed to travel will be March.

I trust all is well on the Lantana, and I send, across these many thousand miles, my truest love.

Alex

Anne looked up from the letter and gazed into the dancing flames in the fireplace, deeply troubled. It had been five months since she returned to the Lantana from New Orleans—five months during which she had not heard a word from Alex. She had had no way of knowing where he was or what he was doing— and no clue as to his feelings toward her after her harsh and petulant refusal to bid him good-bye in New Orleans.

At first she had watched eagerly for a letter, with an anticipation born of worry, guilt, and regret. She wanted to be able to write to him saying that she was sorry for the way she had acted and that of course his trip abroad was the right thing to do. But most of all, she wanted to hear from him that he loved her, truly loved her—to read the reassurance that would have given her the strength to break finally and completely with Rudy.

But no letter had arrived, no reaffirmation of Alex's love, no reassurance of his feelings. And, as the months passed, as the terrible winter closed in with one blue norther after another blasting across the prairie and bringing rain and sleet until Anne feared she would never be warm again, she had turned more and more to Rudy. His strong arms around her seemed to offer protection, while his kisses and passion dispelled the intolerable shadows of loneliness that haunted her soul.

And finally, now that she had accepted the truth

374

of their relationship—that she and Rudy were indeed lovers, that what they shared was not simply an occasional indiscretion but an abiding affair—the letter from Alex arrived with the words of love she had once so desperately needed to hear.

"Too late!" she thought. She crumpled the letter in her fist and almost threw it into the fire. But at the last moment, something stayed her hand. Perhaps it was the recollection of her bright hopes the morning she and Alex stood in the chapel to be married, or perhaps the lingering, fond memory of the way he had kissed her and made love to her. Or perhaps it was merely the desire to reread the letter one more time, to fix in her mind his assurances that he truly loved her.

At any rate, she smoothed the wrinkled paper and slipped it into a pigeonhole in her desk.

Then, squaring her shoulders, trying to put the whole dilemma out of her mind, she pulled on her heavy sheepskin coat and went outside into the blasting cold.

A new shipment of barbed wire was arriving almost every week. Anne kept her cowboys busy planting cedar posts and stringing wire along the perimeters of the three ranches under her control. When the first shipment had rolled in by wagon, she'd almost refused it and drafted a telegram to Joseph Glidden, cancelling the contract. But Rudy had prevented her from sending it.

"If nothing else," he'd advised, "you'll mark the boundaries of your land, and it'll make it harder for bandits like Valdez to rustle your stock."

Anne had thought about this for a moment, then decided not to send the telegram. The thievery from across the border had increased alarmingly, according to Rudy's figures. Perhaps the barbed wire *would* serve a purpose. She'd conceded and had given orders to begin stringing.

Pulling the lapels of her sheepskin coat close around her neck, she strode into the yard and up to Rudy, who was standing beside a wagon loaded with wire.

"Where is this going?" she asked.

"To the Ebonal," he answered, shouting above the howling north wind. "We're trying to link up its fence with the one on the Lantana. Got to make a trap for all them critters running from the cold."

The bitter winter had driven countless mavericks farther south than ever before. Now Anne's men were working feverishly to construct a barrier across the northern extent of her land, to keep the animals from leaving her property when spring finally came. And she had branding outfits out marking the cattle with the crown of thorns as fast as they could. The weather that had brought death and devastation to so much of the state was a boon to the Lantana, increasing its wealth with every further drop in temperature.

"Another winter like this," Rudy called out cheerfully, "and we'll own every cow in Texas!"

Anne looked at him without responding. She had not missed the "we" in his statement, and she was not at all sure she liked it. She shivered and pulled her coat more tightly around her. She couldn't remember ever feeling so cold. The chill seemed to permeate her body and settle in her bones, and, lately, even when she lay on the leather couch wrapped in a woolen blanket before a roaring fire, she never seemed to feel truly warm.

She turned and strode back into the hacienda, shutting the heavy oak doors against the blasting north wind. Once inside her office, she put more logs on the fire and stoked it until the flames crackled and licked the sooty bricks. Then she turned to her rolltop desk and pulled out Alex's letter. On the envelope was a return address, where Alex would be staying once he returned to England.

She took a sheet of paper, dipped her pen in ink, and wrote,

My Darling Alex,
   Please hurry home. I need you more than ever—more than I can say.

She paused, the ink on her pen drying as she thought again of Rudy and of the way he seemed to be taking control of the Lantana and of her very life. She realized that time was short. If Alex didn't return soon, she feared Rudy's takeover would be complete, and she would lose not only Alex but the Lantana as well.

She inked her pen again and scribbled furiously, reaffirming her love for Alex and expressing her deep worry over his health. She filled four pages with her broad, slanting script before ending the letter:

My dearest, my love! I count the days until your return. Please write and tell me you've already booked passage. I'll be in Galveston to meet you, watching for the sails of your ship to appear over the horizon.

                              Your loving wife,
                                   Anne

She sealed the envelope and called for her maid. "Maria Elena, have Ernesto take this into town and mail it. I want to be sure it gets off today."

"Sí, señora," Maria Elena answered, taking the letter and disappearing in search of the errand boy.

Then Anne took up the business at hand. She flipped once more through the official documents that lay in piles on her desk. Their high-flown legal language made little sense to her, but she was aware of their import and she realized they meant security. The month before, she had made a cold, arduous journey to Austin to register title to the three ranches under her control. With growing frequency she had heard

377

disturbing tales of whole sections of neighboring ranches being taken from their longtime owners and turned over to squatters who were clever enough to present themselves at the state capitol and claim title to whatever unregistered land they desired. She was determined not to let one square inch of the Lantana slip between her fingers, and these documents that now lay before her seemed to guarantee that her ranch—all one and a half million acres of it—would belong to herself and her heirs forever.

Anne's fingertips brushed the legal papers almost affectionately. Gathering them all together, she slipped them into a leather envelope, which she bound with rawhide strips. Then she stuffed the envelope into the small steel safe beside her desk and locked it.

In the fireplace, the logs blazed brightly, but they seemed incapable of dispelling the chill in the room. Anne pulled her sheepskin coat snugly about her shoulders and rose. She intended to fetch the woolen blanket that lay across the back of the leather couch, but halfway across the room she was seized by a wave of dizziness that caused her to stagger and grab the nearest chair for support. She leaned there for a moment, swallowing deep gulps of air, waiting for the nausea to pass; but it persisted, and she had to press her fingers against her throat to keep from being sick. She managed to pull herself around onto the chair and slump down with her head on her knees.

At last the nausea left her and she was able to sit up. Once again, she felt the biting chill of the room, and when she extended her hands toward the hearth, she saw her fingers trembling.

"Something's wrong with me," she said to herself. "I must see Casimiro."

The attacks had first started after her return from Austin. In the beginning, she put them down to exhaustion from the hard, cold journey. But when they returned time and time again, she began to believe they were caused by nerves—brought on by her concern over Rudy and her estrangement from Alex. Now, shivering before the fire, her pale face feeling drained of blood, she wasn't so sure.

"Casimiro," she murmured and got slowly to her feet. She found him in his little *jacal* at the edge of the group of shacks where many of the Mexican families lived. He was brewing a pot of herb tea as she entered. The air inside the hut was gray with smoke from the mesquite wood fire, and his scrawny, ancient dog was curled up on a straw mat before the adobe hearth.

Casimiro bade her good day and offered her a cup of *tisana*. He was stooped; his hair was long, covering his shoulders, and yellow with age. But Anne had never known him to look any other way. Nor had anyone else on the Lantana. No one really knew how old he was—but it was rumored that he was past one hundred. And whenever an impertinent child had the bad grace to ask, Casimiro would wrinkle up his old face in a secret grin and reply, "I remember this land before any man's footprints made a track across its sands. I remember the time when there was no moon and the nighttime sky was empty of stars."

Watching him now, bending over the pottery cups he was filling with tea, Anne almost believed he did remember those ancient times.

"What is it, Doña Anne?" he asked when he had given her her cup and had seen her settled on the only stool in the hut.

"I'm not well, Casimiro," Anne replied, speaking in his patois of Spanish and Indian. "My stomach is like a boiling spring filled with unclean water, and my brain spins like a tumbleweed tossed by a whirlwind."

Casimiro's gaze was on her, his yellowed eyes looking deeply into hers, plumbing her soul. He raised his finger to his lips, ordering her to speak no more. Then he took her hands and held them between his parchment-dry palms. His eyelids fluttered and closed, and he appeared to drop into a trance as he concentrated.

At last, he reopened his eyes and released Anne's hands. He looked closely at her face, reached out to run his hand over her belly.

"What is it?" she asked. "Do you know what sickness I have? Can you heal me?"

"There is no sickness," Casimiro replied, his voice like a thin, cold wind in winter. "And you need no cure."

"Then what's wrong with me?" Anne asked, perplexed.

"There is life within you," he answered softly. "New life."

Anne gasped, and her face went pale. "No! That's impossible!"

Casimiro half-turned, but his face wrinkled in a knowing smile. Her response was familiar. He had heard it countless times from the protesting lips of frightened peasant girls who went on to be delivered of fat, squalling babies while vowing they'd slept with no man.

"Impossible!" Anne exclaimed again.

Casimiro returned his gaze to her. "A child," he said simply. "Before the moon is full again seven times."

"No!" Anne cried, unwilling to accept his verdict, but knowing immediately that what Casimiro said was true. And she didn't need to count the months to realize that the baby was Rudy's.

Her mind reeled and she was afraid she was going to faint. Alex! she thought. Oh, Alex! I've ruined everything between us now!

Quickly, she regained control of herself and leaned toward the old curandero. "Casimiro," she murmured, her voice trembling. "You must help me. I can't have

380

this child. Surely you know some herb, some medicine, that will take it from me. Please give it to me!"

A dark veil dropped over Casimiro's eyes, and he looked away from her. "I know of no way," he said simply.

"Oh, Casimiro! That can't be true! You're wise. You know the power of all the herbs and roots. Please tell me!"

He turned again to her, but she couldn't penetrate the cloud that obscured his eyes.

"I heal. I make whole again. I give life," he murmured. "That is all I know how to do."

He bent over the fire, poking it with a charred twig. He couldn't help her—or he wouldn't. It didn't matter which; it was all the same. And Anne understood that no matter how convincingly she begged, he would have no more to say to her.

She rose and crossed the earthen floor to the door. Already she could feel the cold blast of the wind outside. She turned. Casimiro was watching her.

"Thank you anyway, Casimiro," she told him. And she managed a wan smile despite the torment that churned within her soul. "I understand."

She slipped outside, closing the door quickly behind her.

38

That day and the next were a nightmare for Anne. She was torn with anguish, distraught at what was taking place within her body, and despairing over what was bound to happen to her marriage. For the first time in years she failed to make her daily visits to Sofia, and when Carlos playfully badgered her for a game of dominoes, she sent him howling from the room with a swat across his bottom. The maids flashed silent, intuitive warnings to one another and kept their distance. Working quietly, they avoided her room and her office, keeping to the back corridors and the kitchen.

Her worst moment came when Rudy strode into her office, without knocking, on the pretext of discussing some point of business but actually hoping to bed her down on the couch before the fire.

"Get out!" she said icily.

Stealthily, he latched the door behind him and stood before her, a smile flickering at the corners of his mouth.

"Don't you understand English?" she said, her voice cutting like a knife-edge across the room. "Or do I have to say it in German? *Hinaus!*"

The smile fell from Rudy's face, but he made no

move to leave. She was infuriated by the sight of him standing before her, his hands hooked in his back pockets, his hips cocked provocatively forward, and the cold of the outside still blazing handsomely red on his cheeks. Her eyes narrowed and glittered, and she realized that if she reached for her Colt she could easily aim it and shoot him—without qualms—with satisfaction, in fact.

"Hinaus!" she screamed, rising to her full stature and pointing toward the door.

Her fury caught Rudy off guard. He backed away and fumbled behind him for the latch. She stared at him, her face a frozen mask, until he slipped outside and shut the door.

Then she collapsed against the desk, her shoulders shaking with the great sobs that racked her body. She didn't know what to do or to whom to turn. She was aware of a notorious saloon in Joelsboro where ladies of the line, wearing bright taffeta with peacock feathers in their hennaed hair, sold their favors to cowboys and lonely, far-from-home drummers. "Surely those women know a way to keep a baby from being born!" she thought. "If anyone knows, they will!"

But how could she go to them? How could she ask them to help her without inspiring rumors and gossip that would sweep through the town? And if word spread in Joelsboro, it would certainly reach the ranch. Then it would be only a matter of time, once Alex returned, before he learned the truth.

She went to bed early that night, but sleep wouldn't relieve her of her torment. She tossed and turned, oppressed by the weight of the quilts and winding herself in the shroudlike sheets. Twice she bolted from bed and was sick, weakly hanging her head over her washbowl, groaning with misery, weeping for herself and for her marriage that she was sure was ruined.

At last, when the hands on the brass-faced clock on

her bedroom wall reached midnight, she hauled herself out of bed again and pulled on her clothes.

She had to take the chance. There was nothing else to do. It was unthinkable that she could have this baby. She would have to trust that she could slip into town and meet with one of the women at the saloon without being noticed.

"Money!" she thought. "If I give her money, maybe I can buy her silence!" And she stole into her darkened office and filled a leather pouch with shiny double eagles.

The night was bitter cold and a sleety rain was driven along by a gusty northwest wind. She sneaked her horse out behind the hacienda to mount it and then rode following the arroyo until she was far enough away from the house and the darkened *jacales* to strike out eastward for the little town.

It seemed to take forever to reach the road that led into Joelsboro. The town was quiet, almost deserted. Even the stray dogs that normally roamed the silent streets had sought shelter beneath the board-walks.

Her body was stiff from cold. Her breath froze on her upper lip, and her eyes stung from the wind's icy blasts.

Now that she had reached the town, panic seized her. Everyone was asleep. Even the boisterous saloons were dark and shuttered. After hitching her horse to a post in a shadowed spot, she walked gingerly along the boardwalk, trying to muffle the hollow clatter of her boot heels on the planks. In the distance, she heard a door open and shut, and she flattened herself against the entrance of the dry-goods store.

She peered through the sleety night, hoping against hope to catch sight of one of the prostitutes who frequented the saloon, but the sole passerby turned out to be a drunken cowboy wandering coatless in the

384

freezing wind and singing a barroom ballad in a tune-less, slurry voice.

He staggered by without seeing her, and she remained pressed tightly against the storefront until he disappeared around the corner at the end of the street.

Fresh tears filled her eyes as she once again sank into despair. There was no way out! There was nothing she could do! And the prospect of riding back to the Lantana through the bitter night sapped the last of her resolve.

There's always the empty school! she thought. It'll be cold without a fire, but at least I'll be out of the street. I can rest there for a while.

Bending against the wind, she made her way down the street toward the unused schoolhouse. She slipped around behind it and pulled her key ring from her pocket to unlock the door. But as she fumbled with the keys, her fingers numb with cold, she saw out of the corner of her eye a glow in a window farther down the alley.

She paused, key in the lock, and it dawned upon her suddenly that the lamplight was coming from the house that the drunken cowboy had just left.

She shoved the keys back in her pocket and crept stealthily down the rutted alley. The shack's window was curtained, but the stiff wind penetrated the loosely fitted sill and ruffled the fabric, parting it just enough for Anne to catch a glimpse of a woman's bare back and her long, curly hair, much too blond to be real. The woman half turned, cocking her ear as if she'd heard a suspicious noise, and Anne saw that her cheeks were rouged and her lips were painted.

Anne's courage almost failed her. She shrank back into the darkness, and her heart pounded in her ears. But she gritted her teeth and clenched her fists and forced herself to knock on the door.

"Go on away, you sorry drunk!" came a woman's

385

voice from within. "Ain't you rode this pore ole pony enough tonight?"

Anne swallowed the lump in her throat and knocked again, saying: "Please! Please, open up!"

She heard a rustling in the room, then footsteps crossing the floor. The door opened a crack, and the woman's heavily mascaraed eye peered out.

"Well, look what the cat drug up!" the woman murmured, appraising Anne and frowning suspiciously.

"Please!" Anne begged, feeling the dry warm air from the room against her cheek. "I've got to talk to you. Can I come in?"

"Helluva time to come a-calling," the woman said testily, but she opened the door wide enough for Anne to slip inside.

The room was sparsely furnished, a lumpy bed, a doorless wardrobe stuffed with flashy dresses, and a spindly washstand bearing a cracked pitcher and a white enamel bowl. But Anne felt the warmth radiating from the sooty black wood stove blazing in the corner, and without asking permission, she hurried across to it and rubbed her frozen hands over the heat.

The woman pulled her hastily donned robe tightly around her waist and tied it with its sash. She looked to be in her forties, with impossibly blond hair, heavily-lidded brown eyes, and generous breasts that strained against the cheap fabric of her robe.

"Well, what is it, honey?" she asked. "What brung you here? You lost your way or something?"

"I'm sorry to bust in on you like this," Anne began. "I'm . . ."

"I'm acquainted with who you are, ma'am," the woman said. "You may be froze blue, but I recognize your face. You're Anne Trevor, ain't ya?"

"Anne Cameron," she corrected, suddenly intimidated, her courage slipping away again.

"My name's Mandy," the woman said. "I suppose

386

I'm pleased to meet ya. 'Course I don't know the manner of your business with me yet."

"I'm in trouble," Anne said honestly. "I need your help."

Mandy's eyebrows shot up and she looked askance at Anne. "Sit down, honey," she said. "Sit down before you fall down."

There was no chair, and Anne looked at the bed with qualms, thinking of the drunk cowboy and what must have just taken place there.

Reading Anne's thought, Mandy tossed back her head and laughed. But she reached over and yanked a dingy quilt over the wrinkled sheets and patted it, indicating that Anne should sit.

Anne obeyed docilely.

"Now, Mrs. Cameron," Mandy began. "Just what kind of trouble might you be in, and what makes you think I can help you?"

Anne opened her mouth to speak, but nothing came out.

Mandy's eyebrows shot up again, and she began nodding slowly. "Oh . . . *that* kind of trouble, she said sagely. Her mouth half-curled in a sardonic smile. "Mm-huh . . . I think I know what you mean. And I understand why you think *I* can help."

Anne's eyes were wide. Trying to think what to say, she heard her own voice blurting out, "I'm—I'm pregnant! And I can't—I can't have it."

"Wrong papa, huh?" Mandy said bluntly.

Anne caught her breath and nodded dumbly. "Can you help me?" she asked desperately.

"I reckon I can."

"I'll pay."

"You're darn tootin', you'll pay," Mandy said confidently. She crossed the narrow room and reached the wardrobe, shoving aside a pile of camisoles and pulling out a brown glass jar with a metal lid.

"How far gone are you?"

387

"Three months, I think."

Mandy gave her a sharp look. "What did you wait so dad-blamed long for?"

"I didn't know," Anne replied.

Mandy smiled wisely at Anne's ignorance. "Well, you ain't the first young thing who thought she only swallowed a punkin' seed." She went to the washstand and shook the contents of a nearly empty powder box into the enamel bowl. Then she filled the box with a brown, floury substance from the glass jar she'd taken from the wardrobe. She replaced the top on the box and handed it to Anne. "This oughta do," she advised. "It'll make you sick as a dog for a spell. You'll think you're gonna die . . . but you won't. All you'll do is lose the baby."

"How do I take it?" Anne asked.

"Mix it with cow's milk," Mandy replied. "And drink it down, all of it."

Anne held the box in her hands, staring at it for a moment. Then she brusquely shoved it into her coat pocket and pulled out the pouch of gold coins she had brought. "Here," she said, pushing it into Mandy's palms. "I reckon there's enough here to pay you for your trouble . . . and . . ."

Mandy nodded. "Yeah, I know. And for me to keep my big mouth shut. Well, don't fret, honey. I'll be silent as a tomb."

Anne shuddered. She rose, frantic to leave. She felt dirty and ashamed, and she was unable to meet Mandy's eyes.

"Go on," Mandy said, understanding. "Get on along home before they find out that you're missin'."

"Thank you," Anne murmured, circling around Mandy and reaching for the door.

"Good luck, honey," Mandy called after her.

Anne stepped outside into the cold and heard the lock turn behind her.

She made it back to the hacienda with darkness to

spare. Her absence had gone undetected, and she crept into the kitchen and filled a glass with milk from an earthenware jug in the pantry. In the privacy of her locked room, she pulled the powder box from her jacket and poured the brown substance into the milk and stirred it with a spoon. It was slow to dissolve and clotted in wet lumps around the edge of the glass. With trembling fingers she brought it to her lips and drank.

She gagged at the foul mixture and had to force herself to drain the glass. Then she threw herself on the bed, choking on the bitter aftertaste, and held her throat to keep from retching. Without bothering to undress, she hauled the heavy quilt up over her and curled herself into a ball. Her mind swirled, and her body shook with fear and apprehension. Her bedroom windows had filled with the cold gray light of dawn before her troubled brain ceased torturing her and gave way at last to sleep.

Within an hour, she awoke feeling as though a dagger had been plunged into her abdomen. She sat up in bed and immediately doubled over with pain. Her eyes opened wide with terror, and she felt herself gasping for air.

"Oh!" she cried aloud. "Oh, my God!"

The pain gripped her unmercifully, a tight, hot burning in her belly. Her brow was feverish and slick with sweat, and she shivered uncontrollably.

In the corridor outside, Maria Elena heard Anne's outcry and tried the door, only to find it bolted shut.

"Señora!" the maid called with concern. "Qué pasa, señora?"

Anne pressed her fist into her abdomen to stifle the pain. It subsided temporarily but suddenly returned— more severe than before, knifing through her body, sending blinding lights of agony across her eyes.

She buried her face in her pillow, trying to muffle her scream, but Maria Elena heard and ran, wild with

389

fear, calling for help. The servant's cries reached her sister Eugenia downstairs. Eugenia flew to the door yelling for Rudy, who was saddling his horse to ride over to the Ebonal. He dropped the cinch and sprinted toward the hacienda.

"What's wrong?" he hollered. "What's happened?"

"The señora!" Maria Elena shouted back, joining Eugenia in the doorway. "She must be sick! She cried out, and her door is locked."

Rudy pushed past the frightened women and took the stairs two at a time. "Anne!" he yelled, reaching her door and pounding on it with both fists. "What's wrong?"

A spasm of unbearable pain gripped her belly, and in doubling over, she tumbled from the bed and sprawled on the floor.

Rudy heard the sound of her body hit the tiles. He stepped back, then hurled his broad shoulders against the door. Wood splintered, but the bolt held. He threw himself against the door again and again until at last the bolt ripped from its anchors and he stumbled into the room.

Anne was lying white-faced, glassy-eyed on the floor beside the bed. He knelt beside her and cradled her head in his arms. Maria Elena and Eugenia rushed into the room behind him.

"The señora is dying!" Maria Elena wailed. And Eugenia, convinced it was true, crossed herself on the forehead, the lips, and the breast.

Rudy slipped his arms beneath Anne's body and lifted her back onto the bed. Her head swiveled wildly from side to side as she drifted into and out of consciousness. She was mumbling something, and Rudy had to place his ear close to her mouth to make out her words.

"Casimiro," he said, when he finally heard. "She's calling for Casimiro. Quick! Send for him!"

The maids hurried off, their footsteps clattering

down the corridor. Rudy tried to help Anne to stretch out, but the pain that consumed her kept her knees drawn tightly against her breast. Sweat poured from her body, soaking her clothing, and she shivered as if she were freezing.

After what seemed an eternity, Rudy at last heard Casimiro approaching the door. The old man entered the room. Behind him, carrying his leather pouch of herbs and medicines, were Maria Elena and Eugenia.

Without a word to Rudy, Casimiro leaned over the bed and peered into Anne's eyes. He placed one hand on her belly, exerting just enough pressure to evoke a sharp cry from her lips. Then he straightened as far as his stooped body would allow and looked back into her eyes. He read the truth in them and knew what she had done.

He motioned for Maria Elena to bring his pouch. From it he pulled a thick, gnarled root still dusty with the soil in which it had grown. "Boil this and mash it," he told Maria Elena, "until it is a paste. Then give it to the señora to eat. It will make her well again."

The maids left the room, hurrying to the kitchen. Casimiro retied the straps on his pouch and hefted it onto his thin shoulder.

"What's wrong with her?" Rudy asked, holding Casimiro back.

The curandero looked directly into Rudy's eyes and said, "She is with child."

Rudy's jaw dropped and he took in a sharp breath of air. It was his child! It had to be!

"Will she have it?" he asked.

"Yes," Casimiro said simply. "The poison she ate nearly killed her, but the angels protected the baby. It will not die, and the señora will carry it as God has willed."

He turned to go, but at the door, his eyes once again sought Rudy's. So he is the one, Casimiro thought to himself. So he is the father of her child!

And now he understood the reason for Anne's desperation.

When Rudy returned home late that afternoon, Emma looked up from the stew she was stirring in the fireplace and said with surprise, "I thought you were over at the Ebonal!"

"I didn't go," Rudy said, sitting at the round oak table and struggling to pull off his boots. "Anne is sick and I been at the hacienda all day."

Emma's eyes narrowed and she withdrew the ladle slowly from the steaming stew. "So the duchess is sick and her lackey sat by her bedside!"

"Leave me alone, Emma," Rudy warned, a menacing edge to his voice.

But Emma refused to drop the matter. "When I was ailing a month ago, you rode off and I didn't see you for a week."

"That ain't the same, and you know it," Rudy muttered.

"No, of course, it ain't the same," Emma said sarcastically. "I'm only your wife. I only feed you, and have your children, and look after your clothes. It ain't the same at all!"

Rudy was silent, staring into the fire. Emma dropped the ladle onto the hearth and lumbered over to Rudy. She knelt at his feet, her heavy body pressed against his leg.

"Oh, Rudy, Rudy! What is it? What's gone wrong? Can it be that you love her more than me?"

Her face was upturned to his, but he refused to meet her eyes.

A pain of anguish shot through Emma's heart, and she remembered that harvest time so long ago when she had looked from her mother's kitchen window and had seen her handsome young Rudy stripped to the waist working in the field. And she recalled their walks beside the Comal river, their fingers locked together,

her heart racing with love for the young man who had chosen her for his bride from among all the other girls in the county.

Looking at him now, she still saw him as the sturdy youth she had fallen so passionately in love with. She ignored the passage of time—the sprinkling of gray in the silver blond of his hair, the fine white creases on his forehead and around his eyes, the slight thickening of his waist, and the cloudiness of deceit and disgust in his eyes that were once as clear and blue as a winter's sky.

She remembered him as he had been when they first made love, and she wished she could turn back the clock.

"Oh, Rudy!" she implored. "Don't you love me anymore?" She clasped his hand, but he wrested it free of hers.

"Quiet, Emma," he said tiredly. "Don't talk such foolishness."

Her hands felt empty without his between them. He moved his leg away from her body, and she imagined that her final support had been taken from her. She rose slowly, holding onto the table.

"So it's true," she declared, her voice trembling. "You do love her."

"Nonsense, Emma."

"You're always with her."

"It's my work!"

"It's more than work!" Emma cried. "I can tell it. Women know these things!"

Rudy stood up, heaving an impatient sigh. Anne was having his baby. She had tried to kill it but had failed, and now she would carry it to term. He tried to imagine what this would do to her marriage: Alex is proud, Rudy thought, and if he is a true man, he will not keep a wife who bears another man's child. Surely he will divorce her—that's the only honorable course. They will make an arrangement: Anne will

393

deed Alex the Trevor or the Ebonal— certainly not the Lantana, which she loves as much as life itself. And then . . . and then . . .

Rudy paused. The consequences were almost beyond his imagining.

And then—he considered, his heart racing—Anne will turn to me!

He looked across the kitchen at his wife, thinking, "I'll divorce Emma and marry Anne. Then I'll be *patrón* of the Lantana, and our child will be its heir!"

He turned quickly and headed toward the bedroom, where he could be alone with his dreams, but Emma's voice stopped him in the doorway: "I won't let her have you!" she vowed. "I still love you, Rudy, and I won't let her take you away!"

39

Anne's recovery was slow, and it was further impeded by the knowledge that she had not lost the baby. Whatever it was that Mandy had sold her, had succeeded only in making her deathly ill. It had not killed the child in her womb. And she realized now that she was destined to have the baby. Nothing on earth, not even fear of Alex and the prospect of a ruined marriage, would force her to undergo a second time the agony she had just experienced.

It was days before she was able to leave her bed, and then she could stay up only for a few minutes at a time. Her belly was already beginning to swell, but she wore loose clothes that kept her condition a secret. At times, she almost wished she wouldn't recover. She dreaded the day when she would have to appear in public, and she wondered what she could possibly wear. Her leather pants had always fit her like a second skin, and she knew that even now she wouldn't be able to get into them.

She saw as little of Rudy as she could manage, leaving the job of running the Lantana more and more in his hands, a situation which—considering his dreams of the future—delighted him. The fencing on the northern perimeter had been completed, and she was relieved that he had to be away for days on end, overseeing operations in the more distant sections of the ranch.

Anne would go down the corridor to Sofia's room to sit with her stepmother and watch the progression of spring through the iron bars of the upstairs bedroom. Winter's clouds were swept back north, and a warm blue sky took their place. Mockingbirds sang in the greening mesquites, and yellow daisies blossomed on the prairie. Sofia embroidered altar linens for the hacienda's chapel. She seldom spoke anymore, not even when Carlos came into the room for a visit; but her busy fingers moved deftly, drawing delicate designs with her richly colored threads, and her golden thimble flashed brightly in the afternoon sunlight.

The lengthening days were passed with Sofia in almost unbroken silence. But on the grounds below, preparations began for spring roundup. Anne took scant interest in them; from time to time she heard Rudy's strong, confident voice shouting orders, but she didn't bother to inquire what was taking place.

Nevertheless, it was impossible to isolate herself completely. For nearly a month rumors had swept the Lantana that Valdez was on the move again, and during one of their frequent meetings, Rudy informed Anne that he had taken it upon himself to order a veritable arsenal of rifles and ammunition from the East. Anne was rankled that she had not been consulted over such a tremendous expenditure, and she tried to gather the strength to tell Rudy to cancel the purchase. But the arrival of Vivian Magee that evening persuaded her to let the order stand.

As Anne crossed the foyer, her long robe sweeping the floor, she heard the voices of several of Vivian's servants chattering excitedly with her own maids in the kitchen beyond.

Vivian was waiting alone in the parlor, and when she saw her friend enter, she jumped to her feet and ran to Anne, arms outstretched, near collapse, needing to be held. Her steel-gray hair was bedraggled and tumbled about her shoulders, and her normally jolly face was pinched with grief.

"Oh, Anne! Anne! It's so horrible!" she cried, burying her head in the soft fabric of Anne's robe.

"What is it, Vivian?" Anne asked, a chill of fear racing up her spine.

"We were attacked by Valdez! He had an army with him. They killed so many . . . so many."

Anne eased the distraught woman onto the sofa and held her tightly. "Oh, Vivian! No!"

"And Moses . . ." Vivian sobbed, breaking down completely. "They shot him . . . on the porch of our house. He died in my arms. Oh, my Moses! My poor, poor Moses!"

Tears filled Anne's eyes, and she rocked Vivian in her arms, offering silent comfort, unable to find words to express her feelings. She ached for Vivian, knowing how devoted she and Moses had been to each other, how like two children, delighting in pranks and gossip and parties. They had been a pair, and one without the other was unthinkable. But now Valdez had broken their perfect match; Moses was dead and Anne feared that the future for Vivian was one of hollow despair.

"You can stay here, Viv," Anne said softly, "as long as you like. And I'll send a crew of men to your ranch to guard the place."

Vivian pulled back and looked at Anne with wide, tear-filled eyes. "It's no use, Anne. There's nothing left to guard. It's all gone . . . the house, the barn, the stables. Even the little Mexican shacks! They burned them all and drove away the horses."

"We'll rebuild, Viv," Anne said, surprising even herself with the courage that suddenly welled up in her. "I'll give you anything and everything you need. We'll rebuild and restock."

Vivian shook her head. "I don't want to. I don't

care anymore. I never want to see the place again."

Anne held her friend and stroked her tangled hair. She understood. Without Moses by her side, their ranch would never be the same.

Vivian stayed on at the Lantana. In a strange way, her dependence on Anne served to renew Anne's strength in much the same manner as, years before, Emma's cowardice in the face of Enrique's marauders had matured Anne's courage.

For the present Vivian lacked the will to rebuild, but Anne sent an outfit of cowboys down to her ranch to salvage the scattered herds, knowing that the men's presence on the spread would persuade Vivian's vaqueros and their families to return. And once they were back on the ranch, reestablishing their *jacales* and replacing the barns and stables and the burned-out ranch house, Anne was certain that Vivian could be encouraged to go back and take the reins once more.

As March gave way to April, and Ben Talley departed the Lantana, driving another of Anne's huge herds north to market, Vivian began to recover from her overwhelming loss. She no longer sat for hours at a time in her room contemplating leaving Texas forever and returning to her family in Georgia, and she ceased breaking into wrenching sobs whenever she thought of Moses. Anne could see the change in her as day followed day. Vivian stood straighter. The puffiness around her eyes disappeared, and she began to take an interest again in how she looked.

Her newfound strength somehow seemed to sap Anne's. As Vivian recovered her will to go on, Anne slipped back into lethargy, content to linger in her robe in Sofia's room or in her own, whiling away the hours in a sort of listless daydream.

And now it was Vivian's turn to help Anne.

"Honey, what's wrong with you?" she asked late one afternoon after knocking at Anne's door and being

invited in. "You ain't the same girl I used to know—
loungin' around all day in your robe, hardly eatin'
enough to keep a bird alive. You've always been a
spunky 'un—scrappy and full of fire. What's happened
to you? Or are you just pinin' away for Alex?"

The mention of Alex's name drained the blood
from Anne's cheeks, and she turned her face from
Vivian and stared off across the prairie.

Vivian thought she'd hit on the problem. "Come
on, honey. Try to perk yourself up. He's bound to be
comin' home soon for sure. You got a letter from him
yesterday. Wanna tell me what it said? Did he tell you
when he'd be gettin' back to Texas?"

"I haven't read it," Anne said softly.

Vivian was astonished. "For heaven's sakes, why
not? Seems to me you'd be dyin' for word."

"I don't want him to come back," Anne blurted out,
hot tears filling her eyes and spilling onto her cheeks.

"You can't mean that!" Vivian exclaimed, bustling
over to Anne and seeing her weeping eyes for the first
time. "Why, honey! Honey! What's the matter?"

Suddenly Anne could keep her secret no longer. It
burst from her like a rampaging spring river through
a dam. "I'm pregnant, Viv! I'm going to have a baby,
and it doesn't belong to Alex!"

Vivian was struck speechless, and her silence only
deepened Anne's despair.

"He'll quit me," Anne murmured. "I know he will."

Still unable to find words to comfort her friend,
Vivian merely nodded, as sure as Anne was that Alex
would indeed leave her.

"And the worst part," Anne went on, sobbing
ashamedly into Vivian's shoulder, "is that the father
is Rudy!"

"Oh, no!" Vivian whispered.

"I don't love Rudy," Anne said. "I never have. It's
just that he was the only one I had to turn to. It
seemed that whenever I was lonely or down, or when-

ever there was trouble, Rudy was there at my side. After Papa died, and after Sofia went . . . well, after what happened to Sofia, Rudy was the only link to the past. That meant a lot to me—more even than I realized at the time. He was my security, the only person I had to depend on. He's so strong—too strong, I'm afraid. And so I went to him out of loneliness, out of sadness . . . and because he was there. I didn't want to become his lover, but . . . but I didn't have the strength to resist."

"There, there," Vivian whispered, stroking Anne's hair, trying to comfort her. She wanted desperately to console Anne, to assure her that everything would be all right. But she couldn't. In her heart she knew it wouldn't be.

Later, when Anne had stopped crying and they were sitting together in the window, watching the lowering sun in the west, Anne said to Vivian, "Maybe I could go with you . . . to your ranch—at least until after I've had the baby. You have a lot of work to do there, and I could help."

"Honey, there ain't a soul on earth I'd rather have come stay with me than you. But think about what you're proposin'. You'd be leavin' this fine ranch in Rudy's hands, and to do that is as good as handin' him the Lantana on a silver platter. I ain't nosy by nature, but since I've been here I couldn't help noticin' that he damn' near runs the place single-handed—just like it was his. And if you leave here, like you're thinkin', you might as well write his name on the title papers . . . 'cause he'll take it! Mark my words, he'll take it!"

Anne stared at Vivian wide-eyed. "But he can't! He can't take the Lantana! I won't let him!"

" 'Course you won't, honey," Vivian said, remarking with satisfaction that Anne had squared her shoulders and was sitting upright. "You won't let anybody take this ranch—not if you got a drop of your papa's blood in your veins!"

"Papa!" Anne breathed. And her thoughts flew back to Joel's funeral, when she had stood before the mourners and promised to continue his dream.

"You're gonna have a hard row to hoe, honey," Vivian went on. "It ain't gonna be easy by a long shot. You'll have to take your chances with Alex. If he quits you, like you think—well, there ain't a whole lot you can do about that. But if he's a good man—and let's hope he is—then he'll be like Hosea whom the Lord commanded: 'Go yet, love a woman beloved of her friend, yet an adulteress, accordin' to the love of the Lord . . .' "

Anne shook her head. "That's too much to hope for."

"Maybe so . . . maybe so," Vivian conceded. "You might very well lose Alex, but you'll still have the Lantana."

"Yes," Anne murmured. "The Lantana!" How could she for a moment have forgotten her vow to Joel's memory? This was his land. It had nurtured his dreams. And she had sworn to preserve it, to insure that it lived on after them. How could she have been willing to abandon it, to deliver it into Rudy's grasping hands?

"Oh, Viv!" she cried, embracing her friend. "How can I thank you? You've given me the strength to go on."

Vivian smiled gently and returned Anne's embrace. "Don't thank me, honey. I didn't give you nothin'. You've always had that strength. I'd say you merely forgot where you'd stowed it."

401

40

Anne finally read the letter from Alex. His words were warm and passionate, but his professions of love filled her with dismay and apprehension rather than with joy. The letter ended with his promise that he would be home by the first of summer.

"Two months," Anne thought. "Two short months!" As much as she missed him, as much as she still loved him and yearned to be held once again in his arms, she found herself wishing that there were a way to prolong the interval, to lengthen the days before his ship docked in Galveston.

Nevertheless, she took pen and paper and wrote to him telling him that she waited eagerly for his return, and cringing at her deceit when she added that all was well.

Vivian's encouragement and the reality of Rudy's growing power stirred Anne from her lethargy at last. For the first time since she had attempted the abortion, she began to think about her appearance. Looking for something to wear, she rummaged about in her armoire. Her leather breeches were out of the question. She struggled into a pair and found them impossible to button. But she came across two dark cotton dresses that fit reasonably well.

"Thank God I'm tall," she murmured, standing before her full length mirror and examining her image. She saw that her height helped disguise the thickening of her waistline, and she discovered that by throwing a shawl over her shoulders and knotting it at her middle she could still hide the fact that she was pregnant.

"At least for now," she said, addressing her reflection. "But for how long?"

As she left her bedroom and descended the stairs, she met Maria Elena coming from the foyer.

"Oh, señora," the maid said, all smiles. "It's good to see you looking so well. How do you feel?"

"I'm fine, Maria Elena. Thank you," she said, opening the door to her office and entering it.

Rudy's presence at her desk surprised her.

"What are you doing here?" she asked, not troubling to conceal the irritation in her voice.

"There's work to be done," Rudy replied. He made no move to stand. Rather, after glancing perfunctorily at Anne, he returned his attention to the open ledger book in front of him.

"You have your own office, Rudy," she said. "Why aren't you using it?"

"The account books are here," he answered. "I thought I'd bring them up to date. They haven't been tended to in a long time."

Anne couldn't deny it. She had not looked at them since she discovered her pregnancy. Bills, vouchers, and pay records were crammed to overflowing in the desk's pigeonholes. Still, it infuriated her that Rudy had taken it upon himself to assume her duties. Ever since Joel's death, she alone had been in charge of ranch finances, and it frightened her that now this private information lay exposed to Rudy's eyes.

"That'll do, Rudy," she said sharply. "Just leave the books there. I'll take over."

"I'm far from through, Anne," he said, making it

403

obvious that he had no intention of abandoning the task to her. "There's business here that's months old."

She strode across the room, reached over the desk, and slammed the ledger shut.

Rudy's hand shot out and grabbed her wrist, squeezing it tightly. "Quit fighting, Anne," he said levelly, quite sure of himself. "You might as well get used to me at this desk. We're partners now . . . or we soon shall be."

"I don't know what you're talking about," she said between clenched teeth. Her eyes flashed ominously.

"I think you do," Rudy replied, a slow smile playing across his lips. He released her wrist and sat back, letting his eyes appraise her figure, taking his time, making it obvious that he was studying her. "Why the dress, Anne? Are you going somewhere? Or . . . have you just suddenly taken a fancy to skirts?"

"My clothing is of no concern to you," she snapped.

"But why you wear it is," Rudy said. He rose abruptly and faced her, his eyes level with hers. "I know your secret, Anne. I know you're pregnant, and I know the baby is mine."

Anne flinched and staggered backward as if he'd struck her. "Get out!"

Rudy took a step toward her. "Be smart, Anne. When your husband gets back and finds out, you're going to need me. I'll be the only ally you'll have."

"I'd be safer with a sidewinder for a friend!" Anne said.

Rudy lowered his eyes and shook his head. "You do me wrong, Anne. I love you." His voice was quiet, and the sincerity of his tone threw her off guard. "You've never believed it—not really. But it's true. I love you more than anyone else on earth. I know what you think of me. I know you fear my ambition. Well, I can't deny it. I am ambitious. Ever since I was put out of my father's house as a young man, I've wanted to own something. Working here on the Lantana, first for Joel, then for you, but always for wages, I've kept my dream alive. Someday, I vowed, I'd have a ranch too, and none would suit me better than the Lantana. But, Anne, you must believe this: I'd throw away that dream for you—if only I could have your love in return for mine."

"That day will never come, Rudy," Anne said, moving away from him.

He smiled wistfully, not attempting to pursue her. "That may well be," he said. "But I'm willing to take my chances. I'm willing to wait."

"Then you'll have to have the patience of Job."

Rudy nodded. "I have."

Anne took advantage of his position to circle around him and assume her place at her desk.

Rudy turned and faced her again. "Think about it, Anne. Think about what's happened in the past. When you ran off with that cowboy and rode the trail to Kansas, I didn't say nothing to you, even though I already loved you. And then you married Alex and went off with him on your honeymoon. But after he left you in New Orleans, I was waiting for you when you came back alone. And I'm still waiting . . . and I still love you."

Anne opened her mouth to speak, but holding up his hand for silence, Rudy went on, "Now when Alex gets back and finds out that you're pregnant, we'll see who remains by your side. We'll see whose love is deeper. And maybe then you'll come to me at last."

He didn't wait for her reply. He turned quickly and hurried from the room, shutting the door behind him.

Anne slumped in her chair at the desk and held her head in her hands. Oh, Rudy! she thought. You don't understand! How can hate turn into love? How can fear turn into trust? You just don't understand!

In the weeks that followed, that confrontation was never mentioned again. Yet whenever Anne's and

405

Rudy's eyes met, it was clear that each remembered and that each was waiting, with different plans, for Alex's return. Like the calm within a storm, their dealings with each other were unnaturally still—yet charged with the anticipation of coming violence.

It arrived sooner than they expected—and in a totally different form.

In mid-May, Anne took her carriage and rode into Joelsboro to see the doctor concerning her pregnancy. Jacob Collier, a garrulous old drunk, had drifted into town the winter before and set up practice in a two-room office above the pharmacy. Rumor had it that Collier wasn't a physician at all, that he'd gained his experience doctoring horses in South Carolina, but on his wall he had a framed diploma printed all in Latin that no one could read. That certification, dubious as it was, convinced all but the most skeptical, and on the days when he was sober enough to hold office hours, his waiting room was full.

He was a thin, balding man with a luxurious gray mustache and a hacking cough, and every few minutes as he was examining Anne, he would sneak a snort of red-eye from an amber tonic bottle secreted in his desk's bottom drawer.

"Yes sirree, you're pregnant, all right," he said, wiping the liquor from his mustache and licking his lips.

"I know that," Anne said shortly. "I just want to know if everything's going like it's supposed to."

Dr. Collier's eyebrows shot up and he pursed his lips. " 'Pears to be. You ain't had no trouble or nothin', have you?"

"I was sick a while back," Anne replied, coloring the truth, "but I feel fine now."

"Good, good . . . ," Dr. Collier mumbled, sidling over to his desk and taking another swig from the medicine bottle.

406

Rising from the examining table, Anne fastened her dress and picked up her bag.

"Yep, I'd say you was doin' just fine," Dr. Collier reaffirmed. "You're healthy as a horse."

Anne rolled her eyes, remembering the rumors of his past.

"Now, uh, ahem . . . that'll be a dollar," Dr. Collier added, holding out his palm.

Anne loosened the strings of her reticule and fumbled inside for her wallet.

"Ain't had no bad sickness out at your place, have you, Mrs. Cameron?" the doctor asked.

"Nothing serious," Anne replied, pulling out a dollar and handing it to him.

"We had a spell of whooping cough here in town," Dr. Collier volunteered. "Had half the young 'uns in town here in my office. It must be the night air. I keep tellin' them to keep the little tykes in, but no, they let 'em run wild at all hours. Had a woman in the other day, a Mrs. Pritchett by name, dad-blamedest big swellin' on the back of her neck. Had to cut it right out. Terrible sight to see. . . ."

"I'm sure," Anne said, hoping he wouldn't be more graphic.

"And old Amos Willoughby came banging on the door, scairt he was having a stroke, but all it turned out to be was the results of too much red-eye the night before."

When he broke into a wheezy laugh, Anne took advantage of his momentary glee to back out the office door and pull it shut behind her.

As she made her way through the waiting room, she was surprised to see Emma sitting on one of the straight-backed benches.

"Why, Emma! Are you sick?"

"Hello, Anne," Emma said, not bothering to feign warmth. "It's only this." She held up her arm and showed Anne a festering boil on her left elbow.

"You should have let Casimiro take a look at that," Anne said helpfully. "I'm sure he could fix you up in no time."

"I never had no truck with them Mexican herb doctors," Emma said defensively. "And what's ailing you, Anne?"

Anne hesitated, then said, "Nothing. Nothing really. I just thought I might need a tonic, but Dr. Collier says I'm fit as a fiddle."

Emma smiled politely and nodded farewell when Anne bade her good-bye.

After a moment, Dr. Collier poked his head into the waiting room and signaled for Emma to come in. He lanced her boil, smeared it with thick, yellow salve, and bandaged it with gauze.

"Keep it clean," he advised, handing her a jar of ointment, "and put some of this on your arm every time you change the bandage."

"Thank you, doctor," Emma said, rising. She reached the door, then turned and added, "I see my friend Anne Cameron was just here. I hope she's doing well."

"Oh, Mrs. Cameron's just fine," the doctor said happily, his hand reaching into his desk drawer for his medicine bottle. "Tall, strong woman like that shouldn't have any trouble having that baby."

Emma's expression didn't change, but she drew in her breath sharply.

"You live out on the Lantana, don't you?" Dr. Collier asked.

"Yes . . . yes I do," Emma replied.

"Well, when the time comes, you be sure and call on me. I'll come out and see that everything's done all right. Don't you let her trust them midwives."

"No, doctor. Of course not," Emma said. "And . . . and when do you think the time will be?"

"August," Dr. Collier replied. "Sometime round the middle of August."

He was too busy fishing for his bottle at the bottom of the drawer to notice the paleness that swept over Emma's cheeks. And when he looked up again, she was gone.

That night, Emma lay in bed with Rudy sleeping beside her. She heard the clock strike two, and still she had not closed her eyes. As Rudy's chest rose and fell, Emma found herself resenting every moment of his sound sleep.

So, now I know exactly the manner of your 'work', she thought, watching the dim profile of her husband's face. It's not just fencing and cowboying. It's bedding down with the *patrona* too! I thought so all along, and now I know it for a fact. She's having a baby, and it can't be any man's but yours!

Emma sat up, the anguish in her breast nearly overwhelming her. "Oh, Rudy!" she cried softly. "How could you do it? I'm your wife and I love you! How could you fall for her wiles?"

She slipped quietly from her bed. "I won't let her have you. I'll die first, but I won't let her take you from me!"

She shambled into the kitchen, her mind crazed with jealousy, every fiber of her body crying out for revenge. "I hate her!" she breathed aloud. "She's nothing but a whore! I raised her when she was a motherless girl, and now she's taking my husband from me! I must stop her! I can't let her do it!"

She leaned against the wooden drainboard, breathing heavily, trying to formulate a plan. She wished they could pack up and leave the Lantana, but she knew that Rudy, enthralled by Anne, would never consent to go.

"What am I to do?" she muttered miserably. "What can I do to release my Rudy from that whore?"

Then her eyes fell on a box of matches resting on the windowsill. She gasped at the thought that raced through her mind and tried to turn away. But the force

409

of jealousy within her propelled her hand forward, and her fingers closed around the box.

The night was calm and quiet. No breeze ruffled the fresh green leaves that spring had brought to the trees. The horses slept in the remuda, and the corrals stood empty.

Emma trudged silently across the yard behind the hacienda. The big house loomed before her, a dark, sleeping silhouette. Once, she thought she heard a sound, a twig snapping or the opening of a latch on a door, and she pressed herself against a tree trunk, waiting until she was sure there was nobody about. Then she hurried through the shadows until she reached the hacienda.

She crept slowly until she found the back gate of the courtyard. The rusty latch groaned as she raised it, but the gate swung open without a noise. She stole across the patio until she stood beneath the curving staircase in the foyer. She reached out and pulled over a cane-bottomed chair. Then she took a match from the box she'd carried with her and struck it on the tile floor.

It sputtered, then burst into life. Its light illuminated the entire foyer. With trembling fingers, Emma lowered the match until its flame licked the chair's dry cane seat. A curl of gray smoke filtered through the close weaving; then the cane crackled and caught fire.

Emma stood back, watching her work. The fire spread quickly over the seat and up the cross slats on the chair back. The wood blackened, then burst into flame. With her foot, she shoved the chair against the staircase until the fire lapped the underside of the risers. The old wood caught almost immediately, first smoldering, then bursting into fiery tongues that licked hungrily for the next higher riser. Smoke gathered like dense fog beneath the staircase, then billowed upward into the corridor above.

Emma staggered backward, her fist pressed against

her mouth to stifle a silent scream. Oh, God! she cried to herself. What have I done!

Suddenly the whole wall burst into flame, the intense heat singeing her tousled hair. It forced her back, and she stumbled through the smoke, choking as it filled her lungs, reaching wildly for the door through which she had entered.

She ran across the courtyard and shoved through the wooden gate, not slowing down until she was well clear of the hacienda. Then she turned and looked around.

The house still appeared dark and silent, giving no hint of the devastation that was taking place within.

"Oh, God! Forgive me!" she breathed, gasping for breath. She thought for an instant that she was going to faint. Her mind whirled, and in her sudden confusion, she almost raised her voice in a cry of alarm.

Then suddenly she realized that she had to keep quiet. To summon aid would give her away. She had no choice but to turn around and race back to her own house.

Within a minute she had reached her porch. She hung onto the railing and stared through the night at the hacienda. It was dark against the starry sky. Then, at a window in the middle of the house, an orange glow appeared.

Emma turned her back, not wishing to see more, and stole silently back into her bed. Rudy never stirred. His chest rose and fell with the deep breath of sleep.

Emma waited, tears welling up in her eyes as she stared at the darkened ceiling. Now, for the first time, she thought of the others in the house—not Anne, but of Sofia and Carlos and Maria Elena and the other maids who lived in the hacienda.

She sat upright, ready to wake Rudy, when the nighttime silence was shattered by the frenzied clanging of a bell.

411

Rudy stirred, his sleeping brain jarred by the signal of alarm.

The sudden clamor snapped Emma's nerves, and she cried out, "Rudy! Rudy!"

The alarm rang in their ears. Rudy shook his head clear and reached for his boots. "Valdez!" he said.

Emma almost corrected him, almost said, "No! The hacienda is afire!" But she caught herself in time and watched as he grabbed his Winchester from above the bed and raced for the door.

Emma hauled herself out of bed and hurried from the room. She caught up with Rudy on the porch, where he stood as if frozen, staring out into the night.

The hacienda was ablaze; a torrent of flames rushed through the windows and rose in a fiery maelstrom above the tiled rooftop.

"Anne!" he cried, his eyes glittering with fear. *"Anne!"*

Again the dagger of jealousy pierced Emma's heart, and as Rudy threw aside his rifle and started to bolt from the porch, she reached out for his arm and held him back.

"No, Rudy! No! Let her die!"

He spun about and looked at her. Her twisted face was lighted by the orange glow of the flaming hacienda. She was weeping, her chin quivering and her shoulders shaking with sobs.

But in the flickering light of the blaze, he saw the truth.

"You!" he accused. "You did this!"

"For you, Rudy! For us!"

His face contorted with hate. He wrenched his arm from her grasp and slapped her viciously across the face. She stumbled backwards and fell in a heap beside the door.

"Rudy! I'm your wife!" she cried, holding her cheek.

"You're a bitch!" he shouted at her. "A murderous bitch!"

Then spinning on his heels, he left her there and ran toward the hacienda.

At the first sound of the bell, Anne's eyes had opened wide. She was throwing back her covers and clambering from the bed when the odor of smoke reached her nostrils. *Fire!*

She sprang to the window, gripping the iron bars that now made her room a cell. Old Jacinto was sounding the alarm, yanking on the rope that swung the bell. The yard was filling with cowboys dressed only in long johns, their startled cries reaching her ears, sending a further chill of terror up her spine.

"Miz Cameron!" one of them shouted, seeing her pale face behind the wrought iron. "We'll save you!"

But suddenly the window just below her exploded from the intense heat, and a geyser of flame erupted, sending her reeling across her room.

"Carlos!" she cried. *"Sofia!"*

She ran to the door and threw it back. Dense black smoke billowed through the corridor. She held her breath and ran across to Carlos's room, bursting in on the sleeping child and shaking him awake.

"No!" Carlos moaned, still drugged with sleep. "No, leave me alone!"

"Wake up, Carlos! Wake up now!" she ordered, hauling him from bed and lifting him in her arms.

Suddenly his eyes opened wide. "Smoke!"

"The house is on fire! We've got to get out of here!" Anne said.

Carlos's arms tightened around her neck. "Mama!" he cried.

Anne stumbled to the open door, but the thick acrid smoke forced them back. Panic seized her, and she raced across his room to the window. The entire bottom floor was aflame, the roaring fire already heating the black grillwork that trapped them in.

413

Rudy reached the scene in time to see Anne hurl her weight ineffectually against the wrought iron.

"Gott im Himmel! Nein!" he bellowed in horror. "Anne!"

The cowboys had already formed a bucket brigade, but Rudy knew—as did Anne—that it was useless. Even if by some miracle they managed to put out the fire, there could be no escape from the deadly smoke.

The flames reached higher, and Rudy watched with numb despair as Anne and Carlos tottered backward and disappeared into the room.

A frantic cowboy tried to shove a water-filled bucket into Rudy's hands, but he flung it down and broke into a run for the hacienda.

"You can't go in there!" another cowboy cried, grabbing Rudy by the shoulders and trying to pull him back. "The whole place is burning down!"

But Rudy wheeled around and crashed his fist into the man's jaw, breaking his hold on him and knocking him in the dirt.

Crazed with fear for Anne's life, Rudy bounded up the porch steps and burst through the big oak doors, yelling her name.

Emma, who had followed him to the hacienda, stood breathless from the run from her house, and watched with stunned disbelief as Rudy disappeared into the inferno. She sagged to her knees, tears streaking her cheeks, the light from the flames flickering across her face as she screamed to him, "Rudy! Rudy! Come back!"

Suddenly the roof of the porch collapsed, bringing down tiles and flaming timber, blocking Rudy's escape. Sparks flew upward like a million maddened fireflies.

Emma shrieked—an inhuman howl that split the air—and collapsed in the dirt.

Inside the foyer, Rudy spun about helplessly, trapped in the holocaust. The stairs were impassable; a huge section had collapsed and was replaced by a whirling funnel of fire, and searing flames raged from the parlor and the office. The intense heat singed his hair and blackened the shirt on his back.

He roared with agony, clawing wildly at the smoldering fabric, but the shirt burst suddenly into flame, enveloping him, and he sagged to his knees among the shower of embers falling from the ceiling.

Upstairs in Carlos's room Anne stood frozen with fear, her eyes watching the leaping blaze reach through the window and ignite the curtains. They billowed out from the wall as if blown by a hurricane and sent flying cinders whirling through the room. Carlos flailed in her arms, crying for Sofia.

Then suddenly, his mother appeared in the doorway, a pale ghost emerging from the smoke.

"Come with me," she said, beckoning like a specter in the fog.

"Sofia!" Anne cried. "We're trapped!"

Again Sofia beckoned, her placid face exhibiting an unearthly calm. "Come," she said.

Anne followed dumbly. Sofia vanished into the smoke, seeming to be unaffected by its poisonous vapors.

"Sofia!" Anne screamed, fumbling blindly in the corridor. The noxious fumes gagged her and seared her lungs. Carlos gasped and lost consciousness, his head lolling against Anne's shoulder. Her mind reeled, and she started to fall.

Then suddenly she felt Sofia's cool hand grip her wrist and pull her sideways through what appeared to be an opening in the corridor wall. She sank to her knees, letting Carlos slip from her arms.

It was nearly a minute before her befuddled mind registered that she was no longer breathing smoke. Instead her lungs were filling with damp, musty air like the atmosphere on the banks of a stagnant creek.

Slowly her brain cleared, and she realized she was at the top of a steep flight of stone stairs. Carlos

415

revived and began whimpering as he fought for breath.

From out of the darkness came Sofia's calm voice, "Follow me . . . follow me."

Anne struggled to her feet and hoisted Carlos into her arms again. She could hear Sofia's footsteps just ahead of her, and she followed them, descending the steep, invisible stairway down through the thick walls of the house.

The tunnel! she thought, tears of relief stinging her eyes. Of course! The tunnel! Why didn't I think of it?

The sound of Sofia's footsteps ceased, and Anne heard the scraping of stone against stone. Sofia strained and hefted the weighty cover from the entrance to the underground passage.

Having lowered herself through the opening, Sofia turned and took Carlos from Anne's arms. Anne followed her into the tunnel, too grateful for salvation to care about the repulsive slime beneath her bare feet.

"Oh, Sofia! You've saved us!" she cried in thanksgiving. Sofia didn't reply, but carrying Carlos in her arms, she began to make her way down the long, dark passage. After a moment, a distant memory attempted to form in her mind. She paused for a moment and tried to recall.

As Anne caught up with her, she heard Sofia murmur something under her breath.

"What, Sofia? What is it?"

"A lady is sick," Sofia remarked quietly.

"What lady?" Anne asked, making no sense of what Sofia had said.

Sofia struggled with the memory that flickered just beyond her consciousness. "A lady is sick . . . a handsome *caballero* . . . I must help. . . ."

But the effort to remember was too great, and Sofia ceased to try. She resumed her progress down the tunnel, and Anne heard her reciting to Carlos:

416

"One is for sorrow,
Two is for joy,
Three is a letter,
And four is a boy. . . ."

The cowboys watched in helpless frustration, their empty buckets dangling from their hands, as the raging fire ate through the hacienda's roof beams and the walls began collapsing on themselves. Above the inferno, the sky glowed a baleful orange, and the atmosphere was heavy with the smell of smoke.

"They've had it, boys," one of the men said, his weary voice cracking with emotion. "Ain't nobody coming out of there alive."

Off to the side, Emma sat in the dirt, surrounded by her stunned children. She held herself in her own embrace and rocked from side to side, muttering, "Rudy, Rudy, Rudy. . . ."

One of the cowboys, taking pity on the little ones, shambled up and stammered his sympathy. "I shore am sorry, kids. Yore paw died like a hero, trying to save the *patrona* and her kin."

Emma moaned, her eyelids fluttered, and she slumped to the side in a faint.

From afar came a shout, a yelp of surprise and joy. All heads turned, eyes searching through the lurid light and yellow smoke that enveloped the collapsing hacienda. They saw a distant movement: one figure, two, then three—the last that of a child.

Suddenly someone shouted, "It's them! It's Miz Cameron an' Sofia an' the boy!"

The trio emerged through the fog of smoke. The dumbstruck men gazed upon them as if they had risen from the dead.

"They're safe!" a cowboy cried. "They're safe!"

A jubilant cheer filled the air, and Jacinto set the bell to clanging in exultation.

417

41

Maria Elena, her sister Eugenia, and four other maids had perished in the fire because the servants' rooms were on the first floor behind the stairs. They were buried at noon the next day. Their six graves were side by side in the little cemetery where both Martha and Joel were interred.

There was a seventh grave, lying open and empty, and Anne couldn't keep her eyes off it. It had been dug for Rudy, but Emma had sent word by her oldest son, Davey, that she would not permit Rudy to be buried on the ranch.

After the ceremony for the maids, Anne took a buckboard and drove toward Joelsboro, stopping just outside town at the desolate graveyard the local citizens called Boot Hill.

The afternoon sun was hot and bright in a hard blue sky. A sultry, relentless wind blew from the south and sent a fine mist of sand scuttling over the countryside as Anne climbed down from the buckboard and crossed the dusty field toward the mourners gathered around Rudy's coffin. Reverend Polk was standing at the head of the grave, his Bible already opened to the twenty-third Psalm.

Emma, flanked by her children, looked haggard and

old. Davey stood next to her and supported her, his arm linked in hers. But when she saw Anne coming across the field, Emma pulled her arm away from Davey's and broke from the group. She marched toward Anne and stopped her before she reached the grave site.

Anne held out her hands to take Emma's, but Emma made no move to accept the gesture of sympathy. Her eyes were red and swollen from hours of weeping, but a flame of hate flickered within her pupils.

"You're not wanted here, Anne," she said, her voice flat and hard.

Anne's solemn face paled. "I only came to pay my respects. Surely. . ."

"There's no room for you among us."

"Please, Emma," Anne said. "Let's not have a scene. Not here . . . not now."

"We won't," Emma said, "because you're going to turn and go."

Anne dropped her eyes and nodded quietly. "Very well, Emma, if you insist."

Emma's lip curled with loathing, and she said, "I'll not have my husband's whore mourning alongside us."

Anne looked up sharply.

"You didn't know I knew, did you?" Emma asked, relishing the shock on Anne's face. "Well, Rudy told me everything. We had no secrets between us." She paused, her eyes glittering; then she continued, "Except for you, ours was a perfect marriage. Rudy loved me—he always loved me. And he cared no more for you than any man cares for a common whore!"

"It doesn't matter now, does it, Emma?" Anne said softly.

Beyond them the preacher waited. The mourners watched, wondering what was taking place between the two women.

"Go, Anne," Emma ordered. "Leave us here in peace."

"I'll go," Anne replied. "But whether you believe me or not, I'm truly, truly sorry."

Emma turned her back on Anne and walked off toward the gathering. Anne stood for a moment watching. Reverend Polk's voice reached her: "The Lord is my shepherd; I shall not want. . . ."

Then Anne turned and headed for the buckboard.

Returning to the ranch, she surveyed the devastation. The hacienda had been reduced to a pile of rubble. A few plumes of gray smoke still wafted upward from the blackened timbers, and as she picked her way through the debris, soiling the hem of her dress with the ashes underfoot, the shock of the tragedy began to dawn on her.

"Nothing," she murmured quietly to herself. "There's nothing left." Then she thought of Rudy and the maids and of the horrible death they had suffered, and a wave of nausea caused her to stumble and fall against the burned-out hulk of her rolltop desk.

"Oh, Viv!" she whispered, thinking of her friend to the south. "Now I know how you felt! Now I know why you didn't want to go on!"

But the memory of Vivian's courage helped her pull herself together. She drew a deep breath and lifted her chin determinedly. "I'll rebuild, too! And I'll build it better than it ever was before!"

She walked into the courtyard, which now stood open on all sides, surrounded by the smoking heap of rubble that had once been the house. The gaily glazed tiles were streaked with soot and ashes, and charred hunks of wood floated in the fountain.

Off to the side, Carlos poked among the ruins. She watched as he nudged something with the toe of his boot and then bent to retrieve it.

"Look, Anne!" he called, holding up the object in his hand. "Look what I found."

She made her way over to him and looked into his palm. In it lay the garnet lavaliere that Martha had given her.

"Oh, Carlos!" she cried, tears springing to her eyes. "It survived! It's the only thing I have of my mother's, and it survived!"

"Put it on," Carlos said, handing it to Anne.

She pressed it to her lips, then fastened its delicate golden chain around her neck. The setting sunlight struck the jewel and made it glow deep red.

Anne bent and kissed the boy on the cheek. "Thank you, Carlos. And because you found it, it will be twice as precious to me!"

Hand in hand, they walked from the ruins and joined Sofia who sat on a bench beneath the limbs of a pair of oaks.

"Now where are we going to sleep tonight?" Anne wondered aloud.

"We can sleep in the barn," Carlos suggested.

Anne smiled and ran her fingers through his raven hair. "I don't think that would be too comfortable." Her eyes darted from the bunkhouses to the *jacales* that stood in the distance. "We'll find a place," she said, rising and calling to one of the cowboys who was lingering nearby. "Monte, do you think you can scare up some room for us in one of the bunkhouses? You might hang some blankets around a couple of cots so my stepmother can have her privacy."

"Sure thing, ma'am," Monte replied, ambling toward her. He was a thin, long-limbed man with sandy hair and a sparse blond mustache. "But if'n I was you, I'd put up in Emma Stark's place."

"Well, I don't think Emma would be too happy with that," Anne said.

"She won't care none," Monte replied, taking off his hat and brushing back a shock of hair that fell across his forehead. "She up and moved out."

Anne glanced at him with surprise. "Are you sure?"

"Yes'm. I helped her boy Davey load their belongings onto a wagon early this morning. He said his ma weren't of a mind to stay on out here. They're gonna set theirselves up in Joelsboro."

Anne almost blurted out, "Thank God!" Instead, she caught herself and said, "Well, if that house is empty, we might as well use it. Would you and a couple of the boys take over some cots for us? That's all we'll be needing for the night."

"I'll get on it right away, ma'am," Monte said, turning on his heel and striding off toward a group of men gathered near the stable. "Hey, you fellers!" he hollered, pleased with his moment of responsibility. "Come with me. We got a job to do for Miz Cameron."

Anne had never given much thought to Rudy and Emma's house. She hadn't been in it in years. To her it had been just an isolated stone structure halfway to the horizon, with a low front porch and a shingle roof. Now as she made her way through the empty dwelling she was surprised to see how small it was. She had forgotten. "Where did they all sleep?" she found herself asking. There were only two bedrooms, with a long, narrow living area in between where Emma cooked and the family gathered to eat. Rudy had earned enough money for them to live better than that. He must not have cared, Anne thought. The walls were damp and musty, and when she looked up, she saw starlight through the cracks in the shingles.

After Sofia and Carlos had fallen asleep on the hard cots brought over from the bunkhouse, Anne sat alone on the hearth in front of the empty fireplace and tried to take stock of their situation.

One thing's for sure, she mused, looking about the tiny house—there's no room for maids to live with us here.

It took a moment for the absurdity of this thought to dawn on her.

"Maids!" she cried out loud, clapping her hand

over her mouth to stifle the outburst of hysterical laughter that rocked her shoulders. "My maids were buried this morning! The hacienda has burned down, Rudy's dead, and I'm pregnant. And I'm worried about rooms for the maids!"

She gave in to mad laughter. She couldn't help herself. Tears streamed down her cheeks and she laughed hysterically until she thought she was going to be sick. Then the hilarity turned into racking sobs, and she stretched out on the hard, wooden floor, hugging herself for comfort and weeping uncontrollably.

42

Alex leaned against the ship's railing and scanned the sun-drenched Texas shore as the *Weymouth Star* sailed into Galveston Bay.

"Looking for someone?" said a voice at his side.

Alex turned and smiled at Harvey Larkin, a pudgy congenial importer with whom he had struck up a casual acquaintance on the voyage.

"I was trying to find my wife in the crowd," Alex replied, turning his eyes back to the milling figures on the dock.

The eighteen-day voyage from Liverpool and the bracing sea air had proved the perfect tonic for Alex, and as he sailed into port that bright June afternoon, his complexion was ruddy, his eyes flashed brightly, and his lungs felt strong and healthy.

"She wrote that she'd be here to greet me," he went on.

"That ought to be a happy reunion," Harvey Larkin said, his eyes twinkling with good humor. "I understand you've been away a long time."

"Aye," Alex agreed, "Far too long."

The ship was inching into its berth, and stevedores were grasping for the lines as they were thrown.

"But it's been a successful trip," Alex told Larkin.

"I traveled all over England and Scotland buying good stock to breed with my wife's native cattle."

"And you found what you wanted?"

"That I did. Herefords, Angus, and Brahman with bloodlines longer and more noble than our dear queen's."

Larkin laughed heartily, and his eyes followed Alex's gaze to the dock below. "Well, Mr. Cameron, do you see your little woman?"

"Nay," Alex replied, smiling at Larkin's assumptive description of Anne. "And as for 'little,' she's far from that. She'd stand head and shoulders above you, my friend."

"Why then, she ought to be quite easy to spot in this crowd."

"You would think so," Alex murmured, a frown of disappointment wrinkling his forehead. "Yet I don't seem to see her about."

"Well, she's probably waiting inside one of the buildings. You know how women fear the sun."

"Not my Anne," Alex said. "She's afraid of nothing. Perhaps she's been delayed en route. A million things can happen."

"I hope nothing serious."

"I'm not worried," Alex said, watching as the sailors lowered the gangplank and the first sea-weary voyagers set foot on shore. "Anne can take care of anything."

His eyes swept the dock one last time; then he turned and followed Larkin down the gangplank. As he stepped ashore, he heard a messenger boy shouting his name.

"Over here!" Alex called back. "I'm Mr. Cameron."

"Telegram, sir," the boy said, giving Alex a sealed envelope and pocketing the coin Alex handed him in return.

Alex tore open the envelope and read,

REGRET UNABLE TO MEET YOU STOP AWAIT YOUR
ARRIVAL AT LANTANA STOP LOVE ANNE.

"Damn!" Alex muttered. For months he had imagined their meeting. He had dreamed of sweeping Anne
into his arms and covering her face with kisses. He
had planned to take her to dinner at the lavish Galveston Palace and then to lead her upstairs to their suite,
where they could hold each other in private and make
love again for the first time in more than nine months.

But now he checked into the hotel alone, exchang-
ing the suite he had reserved for a simple single room
on the top floor. And once inside, with his baggage
crowded around him, he sat on the edge of the bed
and pulled out his wallet.

"Nineteen . . . twenty . . . twenty-one dollars and
seventy-three cents," he murmured as he counted all
the money that was left to him in the world. He had
planned carefully before he left, calculating his ex-
penses down to the last penny. But his illness and
the necessity of traveling to Italy to recover had caught
him short.

Still and all, he hadn't worried. What did it matter
if he arrived in Galveston with only a few dollars in
his pocket? He had been certain Anne would be there
to meet him.

Only she hadn't shown up.

"Ah, now, this could be sticky," he thought, riffling
through the dollar bills once more. "The room is
four dollars, and the coach to Agua Verde is sixteen-
fifty. That leaves me a dollar twenty-three." He lay
back on the bed and pulled the pillow beneath his
head. "So . . . that means no supper tonight if I'm
to afford a meal or two on the trip home." Then a
slow smile brightened his face and he sat up, pulling
on his boots and reaching for his coat. "No supper
tonight . . . unless I can manage to separate some
poor bloke from his money."

Finding a poker game was no trouble. At the first saloon he visited, he spotted a gaming table with an empty chair and anted up. Two hours later he rose, collecting his winnings from the green baize cloth, and graciously thanked the other players.

"I seem to have hit upon a spot of luck," he said.

"That weren't luck, Mr. Cameron," one of the men responded. "That was puredee talent. You dang near cleaned me out, but it was a true pleasure to watch you play."

Alex strolled back to the Galveston Palace, a thick roll of bills bulging in his pocket, and feasted on oysters, stuffed flounder, peas, and chess pie, washed down with a bottle of iced champagne.

Four days later, Alex stepped off the coach at Agua Verde. He hired a horse from Cyrus Parker, the station keeper, and galloped off toward the Lantana.

Anne witnessed his arrival. The sight of him riding up on a big bay mare sent an involuntary thrill through her body, and she wanted to cry out to him, to go racing across the pastures and throw her arms around his neck. But she hung back and kept silent, standing behind the railing on the low-roofed porch of the little stone house she now occupied. And her hands unconsciously went to her swollen belly, which no dress nor artfully draped shawl, could conceal any longer.

She saw him rein back the mare as he spotted the destroyed hacienda. And she saw him dismount and confer with a group of cowboys that gathered around him.

"They'll tell him all about it," Anne thought. "They'll describe the fire and break the news to him about Rudy and the maids. They'll tell him everything—except . . . except about me."

Then she saw the cowboys pointing toward the

427

little house where she waited. Alex looked her way, seeing her for the first time. With a quick, graceful motion, he swung back into the saddle and spurred his horse.

"God give me strength!" she said aloud, backing farther into the shadow of the overhanging roof. The moment she'd been waiting for, yet dreading, had arrived at last. She'd played the scene in her mind a thousand times, trying to imagine Alex's face, wondering what he would say and what she would reply in return. But now that the moment was at hand, she could remember none of those scenes. With each passing second, Alex drew nearer, and she realized that unlike her imaginings, which had flown from her mind, the scene that was about to take place would remain in her memory until the day she died.

Alex's horse thundered up to the house, scattering pebbles and dust as he yanked back on the reins. He didn't dismount, but remained in the saddle and looked down at Anne. He didn't understand what was wrong with her, why she cowered in the shadows, but he saw fright and apprehension on her face.

He dropped from the saddle, landing lightly on his feet, still holding the reins in his hand. "Well, bonny Anne, have you no kiss for your husband?"

"Oh, Alex!" she cried, fighting back tears. The sound of his voice seemed to release her from the bonds that had held her paralyzed on the porch. She flew down the steps and embraced him, raising her face for his kiss. But as their lips met, she broke into sobs and turned away.

"Now, there, Anne," he said softly, trying to comfort her. "I'm home at last. I'll take care of you. All your troubles are past."

"No," she murmured. "No . . . they're not past."

"Then what's the matter, my love?" he asked, feeling her break from his embrace.

Silently, she moved away from him, stepping back so he could view her body.

She saw his expression change from that of puzzlement and worry to disbelief and shock. The ruddiness of his cheeks paled, and his eyes narrowed and grew hard.

"Who's the father?" he asked, speaking barely above a whisper.

"It's better if you don't know," Anne murmured.

"I understand," he said. Then he fell silent.

She stood before him, trembling, her breath catching in her throat. She wanted him to do something—to draw her back to him and enfold her in his arms, assuring her that everything would be all right, or to rage against her, to slap her and tell her that he despised her. Anything! Anything but this unendurable silence!

Instead, he took his eyes from her and gazed out at the limitless prairie, shimmering in the afternoon sun.

"Oh, Alex, my dear Alex," she managed to say, stammering at each word. "I'm sorry."

The pallor left his cheeks as anger raged through his blood. "Being sorry always comes too late."

"Don't say that, Alex! It's not too late. I'll make amends!"

He looked at her again, a rueful smile on his lips. "My dear," he said, his voice cold and unbending. "There are some things that once broken can't be mended."

"No!" Anne cried, unable to accept his judgment. She reached out for him, but he turned his back on her and walked his mare over to the hitching post and fastened the reins.

Anne slumped on the steps and held her face in her hands, sobbing. She felt the thud of his boots as he climbed past her to the porch and entered the house. Hauling herself up, she followed him inside.

He glanced around the main room, pausing briefly

429

at a rear window to watch Sofia and Carlos, who were picking wild daisies in the pasture beyond. Then he looked into one of the bedrooms.

"Sofia and Carlos sleep there," Anne murmured, watching his eyes shift to the door of the other bedroom. "That's ours," she said.

He shook his head. "No, Anne. That's yours."

"But what about you . . . ?"

The bitter smile returned to his lips and he shrugged his shoulders. "This room . . . the porch. Anywhere else will do."

They resumed their life together, yet lived as strangers. After a few days Alex took a group of cowboys to the coast to claim his herd of British cattle that had been landed at St. Mary's.

His absence was almost a relief to Anne. His cold but polite demeanor was about to drive her mad. He spoke to her only when she addressed him, and he slept on a narrow cot in a corner of the main room. Their meals were taken in silence.

Yet Anne couldn't raise her eyes and look at him without a catch in her throat and a desperate yearning to feel his arms around her. She found it intolerable—unbelievable—that he would never hold her again, that she would never taste his lips on hers or lie with him in bed.

And so, while he was away, she found herself looking forward to his return from St. Mary's, hoping against hope that something might soften his heart and that he would take her back again as his wife.

But when he arrived with the herd, he spent the remaining hours of the day around the new corral that had been constructed for the animals, not bothering to come to the little house until long after nightfall. Alone in her bed, Anne heard him enter and throw himself wearily on his cot. She lay awake watch-

430

ing the stars between the cracks in the roof until tears filled her eyes and the bright pinpoints of light blurred and swam above her.

43

June passed and gave way to July's blistering heat with no improvement in relations between Anne and Alex. Once, when she could bear his silence no longer, she drew on her courage and asked him, "If you hate me so much, why don't you leave me? I'll give you a divorce."

"There's no question of your giving me anything, Anne," he replied. "I certainly have the grounds. If I were of a mind to divorce you, no court in the state would prevent me."

"If you feel that way," she said, "why do you stay on?"

"Business," he answered. "Strictly business. Every penny I own is tied up in the cattle I brought back to the Lantana. If I left, where would I go? And how could I start again without money to buy a place of my own?" He paused and looked out over the prairie. "Oh, I suppose I could persuade a court to grant me a goodly portion of your lands. Aye, I imagine a sympathetic judge would be amenable."

"Divide the Lantana?" she cried. "Never! It belonged to my father and Sofia, and now it's mine."

"Not yours alone, Anne. 'Tis part mine, as well." He paused and looked at her, seeing on her face the fear that he might very well make good his threat. He smiled sadly and went on, "Not to worry, Anne. I wouldn't do that. I know how much this prairie kingdom means to you. I'll do nothing to diminish it."

Heavy-hearted, she turned away and murmured, "Thank you."

"Don't thank me," he said. "As I told you, it's strictly business." He pulled out his bandana and mopped his brow; then he left the porch and stepped out into the sun. "I'll be going down to the corral to check the animals. Despite what everyone warned, they're thriving here. The men tell me the windmill will be finished in another day or two. If it's true that we can pump water out of this dry land, we'll order more windmills—a dozen or two to start with—and plant them here and there. Then we can divide the ranch into sections and tend the herds as they do in Britain. There'll be no more wild, wandering cattle. We'll know the whereabouts of every head we own. And it should make it a damn sight more difficult for the rustlers to trouble us."

Anne didn't reply. She didn't care. The windmill was Alex's idea, and she wasn't at all sure she believed it would work. Moreover, the sight of it offended her—its angular, upright skeleton marring the clean, flat line of the horizon.

What did trouble her was Alex's mention of rustlers. Only the day before she had received a letter from Vivian Magee, warning that Valdez was on the move again. Vivian was not sure of his whereabouts, but her cowboys reported a rumor that he was moving north through the *brasada*.

Anne turned and went inside, leaving Alex to go to his precious cattle. Sofia looked up and smiled placidly as Anne entered, then returned to her needlework.

With a shiver, Anne remembered Valdez and the horror he'd done to Sofia. She reached above the fireplace and checked the Winchester carbine that

433

hung there. Then she went to her room and examined the deadly Colt Peacemaker that she kept by her bed. It was loaded and ready to fire.

Moving to a window, she brushed back the curtain, and her eyes traveled past the pastures to the chaparral-choked *brasada* beyond. "You're roaming out there, Valdez," she murmured. "Hiding in the brush like a hungry coyote, waiting for the sheep to nod. Well, I vowed once I'd be waiting for you next time. And, by God, I'll be ready!"

A week later, she awoke in the middle of the night, her dreams disturbed by a vague discomfort. Not a breath of air stirred in the dark bedroom, and she tossed back the thin sheet that covered her. Her hands traveled over her distended belly and her swollen breasts, and she shut her eyes, shifting her position, seeking a cooler part of the bed. She had nearly drifted off to sleep again when she was seized by a cramp low in her back. It was sharp and insistent; then it vanished almost as quickly as it had appeared. But it had awakened her fully, and she became aware of dampness between her legs.

"It's time," she whispered to herself. "The baby's coming."

She made no move, but lay there as the hours passed, knowing that the pains would have to worsen and come much more often before there was anything to be done. She tried to return to sleep, but whenever she began to doze, the cramps would grip her again and bring her back to wakefulness. At last, when her bedroom windows were graying with the light of dawn, she heard Alex stirring in the other room.

She called for him and he appeared in the doorway.

"Send for the doctor, Alex," she murmured. "My baby's coming soon."

He turned to go, but she called him back.

"And send for Consuelo. She midwives the Mexican women. She'll be able to help."

Within a few minutes Consuela arrived. She was a short, fat woman, her wrinkled face wreathed in smiles. In her time, she had delivered hundreds of babies, including eleven of her own. By the time Dr. Collier rode up, Consuela had bathed Anne and changed the soiled sheets on the bed. She had collected a pile of fresh, clean towels and laid them out on the table.

"*Agua caliente,*" the old doctor ordered.

"*Ya lista,*" Consuela replied happily, indicating a pot of steaming water on a crackling campfire just outside the bedroom door.

"Well, you done thought of just about everything, señora," Dr. Collier said.

Consuela grinned proudly and nodded.

The doctor leaned over Anne, his breath still reeking with last night's whisky. "How do you feel, Mrs. Cameron?"

Anne tried to speak, but a sudden, sharp pain took her breath away. All she could manage was a brief nod.

"Well, let's see here," Dr. Collier said, beginning to examine her. "The pains are coming pretty quick now, are they?"

Anne nodded again, panting.

"Yep, yep," the doctor muttered to himself. "Everything looks just fine. A woman built like you could drop a foal without batting an eye."

"Are you really a horse doctor?" Anne whispered.

"What's that you say?" Dr. Collier asked, looking up and cupping his hand behind his ear.

Anne smiled despite the pain and murmured, "I was just wondering about something I once heard. It was nothing."

Her labor lasted for another hour. And then, almost before she knew what was happening, she was

435

grunting loudly, and soon Dr. Collier held up a scrawny, slippery infant and slapped it on the bottom.

The baby gasped, then cried out lustily. Dr. Collier handed it to Consuela, who wiped its face and wrapped it snugly in a thick white towel.

"What is it, Doctor?" Anne asked, rising on one elbow and reaching out to take the baby from Consuelo.

"A boy, Mrs. Cameron. A healthy baby boy."

Anne cuddled the child close to her and looked into his face for the first time. "He looks like an old man," she murmured, smiling with joy and pride. "He's red and wrinkled, and he doesn't have a hair on his head."

"He's beautiful, señora," Consuela said, clasping her hands together and grinning happily.

"*I* think so, Consuela," Anne breathed, and she placed her lips lovingly on her baby's forehead.

"Have you got a name for the feller?" Dr. Collier asked.

Anne looked up and answered, "I think I'll christen him Joel—after my father."

"Joel the Second, huh?" Dr. Collier said.

"*Dos,*" Consuela said, uttering the Spanish word for "two."

"*Dos,*" Anne repeated, smiling. "That's probably what we'll call him: Dos."

"I've heard 'em called worse," Dr. Collier said, heading for the door. "Well, I'll just clean myself up a bit and be moseying on. This good lady here can take care of most things. I'd say she knows as much as I do about bringing babies into the world, but if you need me, just holler."

Anne looked up from her baby, her face radiant. "Thank you, Doctor."

Dr. Collier smiled at her and slipped through the doorway. As Anne settled back with her newborn child in her arms, she heard Alex's voice from the porch.

436

"Has she had it, Dr. Collier?" he asked.

"Indeed, she has," the physician replied. "Congratulations, Mr. Cameron. You're the father of a handsome little boy."

There was no reply from Alex. Anne heard him enter the other room, move about for a minute, then leave again. But she didn't care. Nothing—not even his failure to look in on her and the baby—could lessen the overwhelming happiness that filled her spirit.

Consuela brought Anne a bowl of stew and sat with her while she ate. Anne devoured the meal as if she'd been starved for a week; then she held out her bowl for more. She could have asked for a third, but a wave of fatigue swept over her, and all she wanted to do was sleep.

Consuela took the baby from Anne's side and laid him in a cradle next to the bed. By the time she looked up again, Anne was sound asleep, her lips still upturned in a blissful smile.

Consuela tiptoed to the door and shut it quietly. Then she gathered up her shawl and left, heading for home.

The crack of rifle fire wrenched Anne from her deep sleep. She bolted upright in bed and looked over the side to the cradle. Dos stirred, one tiny fist going to his mouth, but he did not wake.

Slipping from bed and standing unsteadily on her feet, Anne shuffled to the window. As she pushed back the curtain, another barrage of gunfire split the air.

An army of horsemen thundered down on the ranch, firing as they galloped. Anne saw three of her men drop where they stood, while another dozen or so scattered for cover, ducking into the stables and the barn.

It's Valdez! she thought, knowing with certainty that her old foe had returned. She saw Alex run from

437

the barn to a stable, carrying an armload of the Winchesters that Rudy had ordered from the East.

The Mexican rustlers swarming over the area were too numerous to count. They felled two more of Anne's men and stampeded a herd of longhorns corraled beside the barn. The animals bellowed with fright and scattered, heading for the brush.

Then came the report of rifle fire from the barn, followed by another fusillade from the stable where Alex was barricaded.

Anne wheeled about, her eyes wide with fear. She thought of Sofia and Carlos. She looked to the cradle. And Dos!

She made it to the door and threw it open. In the main room Sofia sat frozen on her bench by the window. Carlos stood beside her, his hand locked in hers.

"Sofia!" Anne cried. "Come here!"

But Sofia wouldn't move.

"Carlos!" Anne screamed. "Get in here, now! Bring Sofia."

The boy too seemed paralyzed with fright. He clung to his mother, oblivious to Anne's cries, and stared out the window.

Suddenly there was the sound of heavy boots on the porch outside. Anne backed up and slammed her door. Forgetting her pain and weakness, she hurried over to the table beside her bed. She reached out and grabbed the Colt 45, her forefinger slipping over the trigger, her thumb cocking the hammer.

Silently, she moved back to the door. Not a sound came from the other room. She waited a moment, trying to still her racing heart, gasping for breath.

Then she inched the door open.

Valdez stood in the middle of the room, his back to Anne. Sofia sat transfixed on the bench, clasping Carlos's hand. Her face was the color of tallow, and terror blazed in her eyes.

At that moment a great calm came over Anne. She felt her body fill with strength and power.

"Valdez!" she said quietly.

He turned, his expression one of mild curiosity at hearing his name. Anne waited a moment until she saw a flicker of recognition in his eyes, until she was sure he knew who she was.

Then she raised the heavy Peacemaker and fired. The bullet tore through him. His lifeless body jerked backward and fell in a heap next to the hearth.

Suddenly, Sofia leaped to her feet and began to scream. Carlos broke from her side and raced across the room, throwing his arms around Anne's waist. And in the bedroom, Dos started to cry.

"Hush up, Sofia!" Anne ordered. She was still holding the heavy pistol and was trying to unwrap Carlos's arms from around her. "Don't squeeze me so tight, Carlos! You're hurting me!"

But Carlos continued to cling to her, and Sofia's cries rose in intensity. Anne tried to turn, to go back to her baby, but Carlos held on to her so tenaciously that she was unable to move.

"Stop it!" she screamed. "Both of you! Stop it!" Tears sprang from her eyes, and she felt she was about to collapse. "I can't take care of everyone all the time!"

Sofia abruptly fell silent; her large, dark eyes seemed to register understanding. Carlos released Anne's waist and scurried back to his mother. And in the bedroom, as if he too understood, Dos quit crying.

Anne tottered unsteadily, then caught her balance. The pistol fell from her grip and clattered on the wood floor. She heaved a deep sigh of resignation and brushed back the hair that had fallen across her eyes. "Well, maybe I can take care of everyone," she murmured wearily. "At times, it seems I have to."

Then, she noticed for the first time that the firing outside had ceased. Stooping painfully, she picked up the Peacemaker, cocking its hammer, preparing for the worst.

She crossed the room and peered cautiously through the open door. In the field beyond, she saw a score or more of Valdez's men lying dead. In another moment, her eyes caught a movement from the barn. A band of her men emerged, glancing warily about, their rifles poised ready to fire. They shouted a signal, and more men followed them from the barn and other buildings.

It's over, she thought. We've driven them off.

A group of cowboys emerged from the stable, as she watched, her heart in her throat, for sight of Alex. Three, four, five men came out.

"No! Please, no!" she breathed, her hand going to her throat. Then she saw Alex walking out into the sunlight.

"He's safe!" she murmured. "I couldn't have stood it if he'd been killed."

Her knees grew weak beneath her, but she steadied herself against the doorjamb. She could see that Alex was looking toward the house, but it surprised her when she saw him strike out across the field, running toward her.

The wind caught his Stetson and blew it from his head, but he didn't stop. He ran full-speed until he reached the porch. He hung on the railing, gasping for breath, until he was able to ask, "Was anyone hurt? Is everything all right?"

"We're safe," Anne replied.

He crossed the porch, still breathing heavily. "We drove them off," he said, "at least for the time being. But I'm afraid they'll probably be back."

"They won't come back," Anne said.

"How do you know?" he asked.

"Because I killed their leader," she said. She stepped aside and let him look into the room at Valdez's body lying in a spreading pool of blood beside the hearth.

440

That evening, late, Alex came into Anne's room. She was sitting up in bed, holding Dos to her breast. She had no milk yet, but the baby sucked anyway and was quiet.

Alex stood uncomfortably by the doorway until Anne bade him sit down at the foot of the bed.

"You were very brave, Anne," he said, finding it difficult to make his eyes meet hers.

"I killed another man like that," she replied softly. "A long time ago when I was a child. I can assure you, it's no easier the second time."

"He deserved it," Alex said.

"I know that better than you," Anne murmured.

Now Alex looked at her and was deeply moved. Her face was wan and pale, her features drawn with fatigue. The baby at her breast was small and vulnerable. Suddenly Alex wanted to go to her, to hold her and kiss her.

He blinked and glanced away, recalling that only hours before she had dragged herself from bed and saved the household from Valdez. His heart filled with pride and admiration for her bravery, and when his eyes returned to her he saw, almost mystically, the steeliness of her spirit.

Anne lifted her baby from her breast and cradled him in her arms.

"A fine looking boy, Anne," Alex said.

"My son," Anne replied.

And there was something in her voice—a warning, an intensity, a new tone of strength—that kept him seated at the foot of the bed.

Silence stretched between them. Finally Anne spoke. "I'm tired, Alex. I need to sleep."

He rose apologetically, sensing that an important moment had slipped between his fingers. "Yes . . . yes, of course. I'm sorry."

He moved across the room.

"Alex," Anne said. Her voice was cool.

He turned.

"Please close the door behind you."

Alex sat on the edge of the narrow cot in the other room and held his head in his hands. His soul ached with a sense of loss. He wanted desperately to go back in to Anne, but something had changed within her, and he knew he hadn't the courage to knock at her door.

44

Valdez's army of rustlers had wreaked havoc across the ranch. Not only had they killed seventeen of the Lantana's men, but they had cut fence all along the many miles of its perimeter, scattering cattle and horses into the *brasada*. Losses were tremendous. Throughout the next week, one devastating report after another reached ranch headquarters. A thousand head lost here . . . three thousand lost there. Five thousand from the Ebonal alone had been driven off into the wild. And worst of all, for Alex, nearly a quarter of the herd he'd shipped from Britain had been killed by the marauders.

"They hurt us bad," Anne wrote in a letter to Mr. Farley at the bank in San Antonio. "We need to buy new fence, and my husband wants to purchase a number of windmills to provide water for the stock. And, of course, we'd like to build a new ranch house. The other ranch house burned down, as I mentioned in my earlier letter. Please be so kind to let me know how much money I have in my account. As you realize, I have no records, since the account books were destroyed in the fire."

A week passed, then another, while both Anne and Alex waited anxiously for Mr. Farley's reply. But none came. Then, on the sixteenth day after she had dispatched her letter to him, Mr. Farley himself rode up in a coach to the little house that Anne now occupied.

"You didn't have to come yourself," she said, greeting him on the porch.

"I thought it best if I saw you in person," Farley replied, shaking her hand and inquiring about Alex.

"He's down at the corral," Anne answered. Then, turning to Carlos, she said, "Quick! Go get Alex. Tell him Mr. Farley is here."

Carlos sprang from the porch and jumped bareback on his little palomino, clinging to its mane as he kicked it into a gallop.

"Good-looking boy," Mr. Farley said.

Anne smiled. "He's my half brother, but he's like a son to me. You know, I had a baby boy of my own not a month ago."

"You don't say?" Farley replied. "He's doing well, I trust."

"Mean as hell, Mr. Farley," Anne laughed. "He keeps four maids more than occupied. Not to mention his poor mother."

"You seem to have recovered right nicely."

"Well, thank you, Mr. Farley," Anne said.

She had more than recovered. She had bloomed. Her complexion had never glowed as brightly. Her hair was more lustrous than ever. And, if anything, her figure had improved. Not only was she back in the leather breeches she liked so well, but her Mexican cotton blouses fit her as they never had before. She caught Farley's appreciative eyes on her breasts, and made him blush with the knowing smile she gave him in return.

"Ah, here comes Alex now," she said, glancing up and seeing Alex and Carlos riding up together. "I'm sure he'll be extremely interested in what you have to report."

Alex greeted Farley cordially, and the three of them

444

went into the house and drew up chairs around the big oak table.

"Well, Mr. Farley," Alex said. "You see the situation for yourself. We have a lot of rebuilding to do here on the Lantana."

"And on the Ebonal too," Anne added. "Miles of fence were destroyed and have to be replaced."

"So we need to know where we stand," Alex concluded.

Farley unstrapped the battered leather case he'd brought with him and pulled out a set of black-bound books.

"The situation is not good," he said, his face somber and serious. "In fact, your position is very bad."

Anne glanced with alarm from Farley to Alex and back. "What do you mean, Mr. Farley?"

"I'm very sorry to have to tell you this, Mrs. Cameron," Farley said, "But the truth is that you have no money left with us at all."

"But that's impossible!" Anne said, half rising.

"I don't understand," Alex said. "This ranch has always made money."

"I'm sure it has," Farley replied, opening the books and turning them so both Anne and Alex could examine their entries. "But in the past seven or eight months, there were many extremely heavy withdrawals. Here, look for yourself."

Anne's eyes raced over the ledger. In January, there was a draft for $10,000. The next month revealed withdrawals totaling $36,000. And then in March, her account was diminished by $93,000.

She couldn't believe her eyes. "There's something wrong here! I never authorized any of these drafts!" She flipped the pages. Each succeeding month told the same story—only worse. In April, her account dwindled by $166,500. And the last withdrawal, in early May, further depleted her balance by nearly a quarter of a million dollars.

445

The truth struck Anne at once. "Rudy!" she breathed.

Alex looked up sharply.

"It was Rudy," Anne said. "I was sick. He took charge. Then he was killed in May, and . . . look! Look!" Her trembling fingers traced the long line of figures. "Since that time there've been no more of those big drafts."

She groaned and closed her eyes, feeling sick at her stomach. "I've been such a fool. I didn't trust him, but I never thought he'd do anything like this!"

"Emma!" Alex said. "She'll know where the money is."

But Anne shook her head in dismay. "No, not Emma. Rudy never told her anything. Besides, if she had money like this, she wouldn't be living the way she is in Joelsboro. No . . . there's no telling where the money is—in Mexico maybe, or in banks all around here, deposited under false names. Or just buried somewhere out in the brush, in places only Rudy knew, places we can never hope to find."

A stunned silence settled over the table.

Finally Alex said, "Then we've nothing left to us. Is that right, Mr. Farley?"

Farley shook his head. "It's worse than that, Mr. Cameron. In fact," he said, flipping the ledger's pages to the last column of figures, "you're badly overdrawn. Your account shows a debit of $9,377."

Alex rose and paced the room. "So that's why you've come to see us personally."

Farley nodded. "I'm afraid so, Mr. Cameron. Our board of directors is quite uneasy over your balance."

Alex leaned on the table and looked into Farley's eyes. "Then what can we do? Can we arrange a loan?"

Farley's face suddenly turned mulish. He lowered his eyes.

"We've always been good customers of your bank," Anne reminded him. "And the Lantana has always made money. Even back in 'seventy-three and 'seventy-four, when so many ranches went under, the Lantana still turned a profit."

Farley nodded, but she could see in his face that the loan would not be approved. Their losses had been too great, and Farley had seen firsthand the devastation the ranch had suffered. He wouldn't recommend that his bank take the risk.

"I'm sorry, Mrs. Cameron, dreadfully sorry," he said, and it was obvious to Anne and Alex that his sympathy was indeed genuine.

"This is too much," Anne said to Alex later that evening, after Farley had left. "The last straw. I'm sick of fighting and struggling. I'm bone-tired and I don't want to spend the rest of my life like this. I never asked for all these burdens. I'd like to be like those women in Joelsboro with nothing to do all day but cook and raise kids and gossip over the back fence. . . ."

Alex had been leaning against the mantel in front of the empty fireplace, watching her rave on like that for half an hour.

He pitied her, knowing that her anger and despair were directed only at herself for having been so disastrously swindled by Rudy. Her face was drawn and pale, and he saw fine lines of worry etched across her forehead.

"I can't stand any more, Alex," she said wearily, dropping onto a chair at the table and burying her face in her hands.

Alex struck a match on the stone mantel and touched its flame to the tip of his cigar. He sniffed the fragrant blue smoke, then threw the burnt match into the fireplace.

"Then there's only one thing to do, Anne," he said. His voice was calm and reasonable. "And if you do it, you'll be free for life, with never another thought of money or responsibility to worry your mind."

447

She looked up. "What Alex? Tell me! I'll do it."

"Sell the Lantana."

She stared at him dumbstruck.

"Yes! Sell it!" he went on. "You'll find a pack of buyers waiting. And the money will set you up forever. You won't have to live in Joelsboro. You can live in San Antonio or New Orleans. Or even in New York if you so wish. And you'll be rich enough to live like a grand lady with servants and carriages and all the fine clothes you could ever want."

He crossed the room swiftly and raised the lid on the writing desk, grabbing pen and ink and a sheaf of letter paper. He set these on the table in front of Anne and said, "Here! Write to Mr. Farley. Ask him to be your agent. He'll be more than happy to represent you. Tell him you want to sell the Lantana—as a whole or in bits and pieces. Tell him you want to be free of it forever. He'll have it sold inside a month, I'll wager."

Anne sat staring at the writing materials before her. It would take only a few lines—a short note— and all her burdens would be lifted from her.

The Lantana!

Suddenly her face contorted and she swept the paper, the pen, and the inkwell from the tabletop with the back of her arm. They went flying across the room and scattered on the floor.

"No!" she cried, just as Alex had known she would. "No! I can't! I won't!"

Alex stood silently, watching with pride and admiration as her indomitable courage once again lifted her spirit.

"I can't!" she said. "I promised I'd never sell the Lantana. They'll have to carry me out of here dead before I'll leave it!"

The next morning before dawn, Anne heard Alex

stirring in the main room. She left her bed and went to the door. An oil lamp blazed on the oak table, and in its glow, she saw that Alex, who was already dressed, was stuffing shirts into a brown valise. On the floor beside his cot stood another case, already packed.

"Are you leaving me?" she asked.

"Yes," Alex answered.

"For good?"

"Yes," he replied. Then he turned and gazed at her standing just outside the yellow pool of light. "I think it's for the best. We've no real marriage any more."

She closed her eyes and murmured. "I should have guessed."

"But I'm going to save your ranch for you, Anne," he said.

She looked at him again. His expression was serious.

"I married you for love," he said in a voice both solemn and somber. "You must believe that. But I also married you because I wanted the Lantana. I wanted us to reign over a kingdom as great and powerful as this country has ever known. But the fates were against us, Anne, and now it will never be."

He laughed cynically. "I tried to be an opportunist, but there's a flaw woven into my fabric—a thread of honor that I can't rip out. I can't just leave you here with all your troubles. I can't simply walk out, much as I wish I could. When I met and married you, you were a rich woman, and the Lantana was strong and mighty. I'll not abandon you until it is that way again."

He paused and snapped shut his valise. "I'll save your ranch for you, Anne. I'm going to New Orleans, where I can get a loan. I can arrange it through Charles LaForet. It will put you back on your feet. And then . . . I'll disappear from your life forever."

He stood in the doorway, bags in hand. "I've taken some money," he said. "I'll have to appear prosperous in New Orleans."

"Don't leave, Alex," Anne said.

"Good-bye, Anne," he murmured.

Then quickly, before she could call him back, he disappeared into the darkness outside.

45

"Alex, my friend!" Charles LaForet said, entering Alex's beautifully appointed suite at the Hotel St. Louis. "Welcome back to New Orleans!"

The two men shook hands warmly. "Thank you, Charles. It's good to see you again," Alex said. He motioned toward a table arranged with bourbon, Scotch, iced champagne, and several bottles of vintage burgundy. "Will you have a glass with me?"

"Champagne would be nice," Charles replied, settling himself on the settee beneath a glittering chandelier. "I see you've once again taken the finest quarters in the hotel."

"I plan to do some entertaining," Alex said, handing Charles a glass of Dom Perignon.

"Well, we won't allow you to do it all," Charles said. "Leonie has already planned a lavish ball in your honor at La Rivière. She's terribly happy that you're back in town—as are Suzanne and Jeanette." He took a sip of champagne, settled back, and said: "And shame on you, *mon vieux*, for not bringing your lovely wife with you. How is Anne?"

"Very well," Alex said, not changing expression. "She sends you her best."

451

"And mine to her, of course," Charles responded. "Now, Alex, what brings you to New Orleans this time? Business or pleasure?"

"Both, I should say."

Charles smiled approvingly. "*Mais naturellement!* Why not? The Americans always caution one never to mix business with pleasure, while we New Orleans Frenchmen consider such an attitude nothing short of heresy. If we couldn't have a little fun with our business, I'm afraid we'd do no business at all!"

Alex laughed and raised his glass to Charles.

"Now then," Charles went on, "Leonie will take care of your amusement. May I be of any help with your business?"

"As a matter of fact, I was going to call on you at the bank tomorrow," Alex replied.

"Well, you have me here at your disposal," Charles said, holding out his hands in a gesture of generosity. "What do you need?"

"A loan," Alex said. "We're contemplating some major improvements on the Lantana, and we thought we'd use someone else's money rather than our own."

"That's why there are banks," Charles said.

"I'm talking about big money," Alex warned.

"Exactly the type of loan we like," Charles smiled. "Come by my office tomorrow, and we'll take care of everything. I know you well, Alex, and I've been a friend of your father's for years. There'll be no problem, I assure you."

Alex smiled. The ploy had worked. He had chosen New Orleans to seek the loan because of his acquaintance with Charles—and because it was far enough away that news of the Lantana's dire straits would not have reached there.

"Now," Charles said, draining his glass. "Our business is finished. We can seek some pleasure. I know a place with the loveliest quadroons in town. They'll wine us and dine us as if we were kings. You can gamble or dance or . . ." He shrugged pointedly. "Well, let's just say that the ladies are amenable to any suggestion."

Though the evening was spent in pleasure, as Charles had planned, Alex spent the next morning scribbling figures on paper, calculating the sum Anne would need to pay off the Lantana's debts to Farley's bank and to repair the fences that Valdez's men had destroyed.

"Anne can manage with that," he thought, folding the paper and slipping it into his coat pocket. "The money will be enough to see her through. This autumn she'll send another herd of cattle up the trail, and the profit should relieve her of any further worries."

He left his suite and descended the stairs, heading for his appointment with Charles. He had almost reached the lobby doors when he heard someone call his name.

Looking around he saw Jeanette rise from a sofa situated beneath a leafy palm.

"Oh, Alex!" she said, hurrying across the lobby toward him. "I couldn't believe my ears when Papa said you were in town!"

She wore a tight-fitting gown of watered silk with a matching hat. Her black curls framed her delicate face, setting off the creamy whiteness of her skin, and her eyes sparkled with pleasure at seeing him again.

Her beauty took Alex's breath away, and for a moment, he couldn't speak. He raised her hand and kissed it, then stood back gazing at her, marveling at the loveliness of her features.

"Are you staying long, Alex? Papa said you were here on business. Please don't finish it and race off before we've had a chance to see more of you."

"I shan't be leaving soon," Alex said. His voice was husky and he seemed unable to take his eyes off her.

"Merveilleux!" Jeanette cried. "Then you're coming to the party at La Rivière?"

"I wouldn't miss it for the world."

"And will you dance with me?"

"Every dance."

Jeanette laughed with pleasure. "I'll hold you to that promise, *Monsieur*."

"Do you have plans for the afternoon?" Alex asked. "Or will you have lunch with me?"

"I'd love to have lunch with you," Jeanette said, smiling mischievously. "As a matter of fact, I've already reserved a table for two at a little restaurant I know, not two streets away."

"Then what are we waiting for?" Alex smiled. And he went to the cafe with her, forgetting completely about his appointment with Charles.

They were soon seated at a charming little table with brightly colored linens and fresh flowers, but Jeanette was too excited to do more than pick at the pompano that adorned her plate. She couldn't believe that she was actually sitting across from Alex—just the two of them alone—without Anne, without her sister Suzanne, and without her mother as a chaperone.

"I must confess that I'm being extremely naughty," she said. "I'm supposed to be running errands with Suzanne. *Maman* would kill me if she knew I slipped away to see you. But I threatened Suzanne that I would tell all about her and Andre Desmoulins at the Comus Ball last Mardi Gras if she hinted a word about what I'm doing."

"Would your mother be so terribly unhappy that you're having lunch with me?" Alex asked, amused.

"You're a married man, Alex!" Jeanette breathed, thrilled by the wickedness of the situation. "It's just not done."

"Ah, but it is," Alex said. "You're doing it."

"And loving every moment of it," she said. "I'm

454

afraid I'm not the dutiful *jeune fille* my mother thinks I am."

"You're no longer a *jeune fille* at all," Alex said. "You're a beautiful woman." His fingertips touched hers across the tablecloth.

Jeanette's hand drew back as if she'd been burned, and Alex heard her breath catch in her throat. Her dark eyes grew wide and her cheeks turned pale.

"Oh, Alex," she said, her voice barely a whisper. "I know it's wrong, but I've dreamed of you every day since I last saw you. I can't get you out of my mind. You see . . . I'm still in love with you."

Alex's face was solemn. "But as you said, Jeanette, I'm married."

She dropped her eyelids and nodded sorrowfully. "I know. And that brings me to the awful part—I don't care. It doesn't matter to me at all. I still love you."

Suddenly Alex wanted to hold her in his arms. He wanted to feel her lithe body next to his and taste her lips.

"Let's go," he said. Tossing some money on the table, he rose quickly, reached for her hand and pulled her up with him.

They hurried through the streets to a stable where Alex hired a carriage. Arm in arm they rode out of the city until they found a grassy field sheltered by gnarled moss-bearded oaks.

Alex stopped the carriage and lifted Jeanette down. Together they strolled through waist-high grass until they came into a tree-shaded clearing.

Then Alex took her in his arms and kissed her. She went limp in his embrace as if she had swooned, but the pressure of her lips on his laid bare her passion. They sank gently to the ground and held each other tightly. Their lips parted, and they kissed until they both were breathless. Alex's hands caressed her

455

breasts, and she threw back her head and gasped for air.

"Make love to me, Alex!" she cried. "I want you!"

Later, they sat together beneath an oak. Alex was shirtless and Jeanette rested her head aginst his bare chest.

"I'm not sorry," she murmured. "Not sorry a bit. I've wanted this to happen ever since I first met you years ago in Scotland. I'm not even sorry for Anne's sake, although I know I should be."

"There's no reason to be sorry about that," Alex said, running his fingers gently through her hair. "Anne and I are no longer together."

Jeanette looked up into his eyes. "You've left her?"

"Aye," Alex replied softly. "It's for the best."

"Oh, Alex," Jeanette said. "Are you . . . are you getting a divorce? Then maybe we. . . ."

She couldn't bring herself to utter her hopes aloud. But Alex anticipated them by saying, "Yes, I'll be getting divorced, Jeanette, but your family would never approve."

"I don't care about their approval," she said quickly. "I only care about you, Alex. I love you and I want you."

"It just can't be, Jeanette," he replied.

"Don't say that, Alex!" she cried. "I don't believe it!"

Then she slipped her arms around his neck and kissed his lips. "Make love to me again, Alex," she whispered into his ear. He could feel her racing heart against his naked chest. "Make love to me!"

Anne had just put Dos back in his cradle after nursing him and was buttoning up her blouse when she heard the sound of a horse's hooves outside. Going to the door, she was surprised to see Ramiro Rivas riding up to the little house. She hadn't seen him in years—

not since he had run the cotton train for Joel during the war—but she recognized him immediately. Though his black hair was faintly touched with gray, he looked as strong and sturdy as ever.

He reined his horse to a halt and dropped lightly from the saddle.

"Ramiro!" she called out, rushing down the steps to greet him. "What a pleasant surprise!"

She grabbed his hands and shook them warmly.

"Then you remember me, señora?" he asked smiling with pleasure.

"Well, of course I do," she said. "How could I ever forget my father's old partner? And what is this 'señora' business? I've always been Anne to you!"

Ramiro's smile transformed to one of deference. "But times have changed, señora," he replied, "In the old days, I was an *hacendado* like your father. Now I am merely one of Mr. Kendall's vaqueros. And it's only proper that I should address you as 'señora.' "

"That's nonsense, Ramiro," Anne said sharply. "And I won't stand for it."

He smiled again and nodded, but she could see in his eyes that he would have it no other way.

"Come in out of the sun," she said, still holding onto his hand and leading him up the steps. "I'll get you something to drink."

"No, señora," he said, drawing back. "I must not stay long. No one knows I've come here."

His tone alarmed her and she looked at him for an explanation.

"Mr. Kendall has found out that you owe a great deal of money. He has written to your bankers in San Antonio, offering to pay your debts. He hopes, of course, to take your ranch."

"Never!" Anne cried.

"He's a smart man, señora," Ramiro said. "And greedy. It would please him to own every acre in South Texas."

457

"Well, he'll never get it," Anne vowed, but the precariousness of her situation was very clear to her. If Kendall picked up her debts, then he could foreclose on her, taking everything she owned except this pathetic stone house where she lived.

"I've come to warn you," Ramiro went on. "My friendship with your father was deep, and I would not like to see you lose the Lantana the way I lost the Agarita."

"My father tried to help you," Anne said. "You knew that, didn't you?"

Ramiro nodded. "Yes. It was too late for me, but you still have time." He reached into his vest and pulled out a sealed white envelope. "You see. This is Mr. Kendall's letter to your bankers. He ordered me personally to take it to San Antonio. I'll delay my journey. But sooner or later, I'll have to deliver the letter and carry the answer back to Mr. Kendall."

"How long do I have?" Anne asked.

"A week?" Ramiro ventured.

Anne thought of Alex's promise to save the ranch for her. She'd had no word from him since he left, and now she wondered whether she would ever hear from him again. "I hope that's time enough, Ramiro," she said.

"I have to go now, señora," he said. "I don't want anyone to know I was here."

"Thank you, Ramiro," Anne said clasping his hand and kissing him on the cheek. "If I can ever help you, please come to me."

Ramiro hesitated. "After I lost the Agarita, your father asked me to come work for him on the Lantana. I declined because the Agarita was the only home I'd ever known, but things are not the same there anymore."

"In that case, I'd like to renew my father's offer," Anne said. "I need a foreman. The job is yours if you want it."

458

"*Gracias,* señora," Ramiro said. "But first, the Lantana must be saved."

He backed away and bowed. Then he swung onto his horse and spurred it away.

Suzanne LaForet lay awake in her bed at La Rivière. Only a minute before, she had heard the big grandfather clock at the end of the hall strike four, and now she picked up the sound of stockinged feet padding stealthily down the corridor outside. In another moment, the door opened, and she saw the silhouette of her sister slip into the room.

"Jeanette," Suzanne whispered.

"Suzanne!" Jeanette breathed, startled. "You should be asleep!"

"So should you! Where have you been?"

"It's none of your business," Jeanette replied sharply.

"You've been with Alex again, haven't you?"

"What makes you think that?" Jeanette asked, trying to mask the guilt in her voice.

"It's perfectly obvious," Suzanne replied, propping herself on her elbow and watching her sister undress in the moonlight that filtered through the window's sheer curtains. "You practically threw yourself at him all during the ball, hanging on his arm, laughing at everything he said, making it clear as day you didn't want to dance with anyone but him. I was mortified," she announced, although she was nothing of the sort. As a matter of fact, her older sister's shameless flirtation with Alex had fascinated her, and she was dying for details of what went on between them. But she put on a reproving voice and added, "Everyone was talking."

"Let them talk," Jeanette said impatiently. "What do I care for their gossip?"

She threw her ball gown on the floor and climbed into her bed.

"Well?" asked Suzanne, expectantly.

"Well, what?" Jeanette replied, feigning annoyance.

"Tell me! Tell me everything!"

Jeanette turned on her side and faced her sister across the space that separated their beds.

"I love him!" she said breathlessly. "And he loves me. We're going to be married."

Suzanne was taken aback. "But you can't!"

"Why not?"

"He's married."

"He's left Anne. He's going to get a divorce."

"That's even worse! No one will receive you."

"I don't care a fig about that," Jeanette said. "But you'll come see me, won't you, Suzanne?"

"I don't think *Maman* will let me." Suzanne bit her bottom lip and fretted. "Oh, Jeanette, you *can't* marry a *divorcé*. It's a mortal sin!"

"I don't care! I love Alex more than I love God."

"That's blasphemy, Jeanette. You'll burn in hell!"

"I won't mind as long as Alex is with me."

After a moment, Jeanette spoke up again. "I've just come from him," she said. "I crept into his room after everyone was asleep, and we made love for hours. Oh, Suzanne! It was marvelous!"

Suzanne lay on her bed, her eyes wide, staring at the ceiling. She was too shocked to respond.

His affair with Jeanette troubled Alex. He was not sure if he was in love with her, but he couldn't deny his fascination with her. There was a fierceness about her that intrigued him, and he couldn't help being excited by the danger associated with their illicit meetings.

They met as often as Jeanette could manage— sometimes only for an hour, making love with quick, intense passion in a deserted barn in a secluded section of La Rivière. At other times they had an entire afternoon or evening, for Jeanette had found a sympathetic friend who discreetly looked the other way while the lovers stole into her Garden District house and sequestered themselves in a bedroom upstairs.

But always, when he left Jeanette and returned alone to his suite at the St. Louis, Alex felt a gnawing guilt. As yet he'd sent no word to the Lantana. He'd still done nothing about the loan he promised to secure for Anne, and he realized, with an uneasy conscience, that the longer he delayed, the easier it was becoming to put it out of his mind entirely.

He stood at his hotel window looking down into the narrow rainswept street, watching a lonely carriage roll by, its oil lamps glowing yellow in the midnight darkness.

"I must take care of Anne tomorrow," he said to himself. "I made her a promise, and I'll not go back on it."

Lightning flashed in the sky, and the image of Anne's face appeared before him in his mind. She was pale, but her chin was lifted proudly, and her eyes stared steadily at something in the distance.

Alex shook his head and rubbed his brow as if to erase the picture. But when he looked back into the darkened street, the vision of Anne returned.

"What is she looking at?" he wondered. "What is she seeing?"

But he knew.

In the rumble of thunder that rattled the windows, the memory of his own voice returned. The words he had spoken to Anne on the train carrying them across the Illinois farmlands to DeKalb echoed through his mind: *Side by side, we'll take this kingdom and make it supreme! Oh, Anne! It's a glorious venture we have before us!*

Swearing, Alex slammed the shutters and turned back into the room. He crossed the carpet and poured himself a stiff shot of Scotch whiskey. It burned his

461

throat, but he refilled his glass and slumped down on the settee, the bottle at his side.

The next day at lunch, he sat with Jeanette at the same restaurant where they had first dined.

"What's the matter, *mon cher*?" she asked. "You've hardly said a word. And you look as if you didn't get a wink of sleep."

Alex tried to avoid her eyes. "I had a bad night," he said.

"It must have been the storm," Jeanette proposed. "It kept me up too—but I was thinking of you."

Alex smiled and let her take his hand.

"I was thinking, Alex darling, after we're married, if things are difficult in New Orleans, we could go to Scotland to live."

Alex shook his head. "Nay. I like it here."

"Then here it'll be," Jeanette said. "Whatever you want is all right with me."

Alex withdrew his hand from hers and pulled out his watch.

"I must go," he said. "I have some business to attend to."

"Oh, Alex, no!" She frowned and bit her lower lip. "I've arranged to be away all afternoon. It was hard, but I convinced *Maman* I *had* to see my dressmaker."

"I'm sorry, Jeanette, but I really must keep this appointment."

"Oh, all right!" she said, tossing her head angrily. "Go on about your business. You've been no fun at all today. I've never seen you so moody!"

Alex didn't attempt to reply. He paid the bill and escorted Jeanette to her carriage.

"Don't bother to call on me, Alex, until you're in a better humor," she said.

But the look of pain on his face frightened her, and she reached from her carriage and clasped his hand. "Oh, Alex! I didn't mean that. I'm sorry. Can we meet tomorrow? Anywhere—you name the place."

"We'll see," Alex said. "I'll send you a note."

He signaled her driver, and her carriage lurched forward. He watched after it until it turned and disappeared into Dauphine street.

Then he hailed a carriage for himself and directed the driver to take him to the Delta Bank.

46

It was October when the first mild, wet norther of the season swept across the rugged prairie of the Lantana. Sofia lay abed with congestion, and Carlos fretted at having to stay indoors. Dark circles ringed Anne's eyes, the result of her walking the floor all night comforting Dos, who was suffering from colic.

Old Ben Talley, veteran of every Lantana cattle drive since Joel sent the first herd up the Chisholm Trail, sat at the oak table and gave Anne the latest bad news.

"We lost a dozen more hands today, ma'am. I just can't keep 'em from leavin'. We've missed four payrolls already, and I can't, in all conscience, bring myself to tell 'em we'll make the next."

"I don't blame the boys, Ben," Anne replied wearily, shifting Dos from one shoulder to the other. "They can't work for free."

"What's gonna happen, ma'am?" Ben asked. His coffee cup was empty, but he refrained from asking for more, knowing that Anne could no more afford the luxury than he could.

"I don't know what'll happen, Ben. I've tried not to think about it."

But she had thought about it, and she hated what

she considered to be inevitable. William Kendall had assumed her debt, and only the day before she had received a letter from him. She seethed as she read it but continued reading until she came to the third paragraph:

I would be willing to accept only the Lantana and the Ebonal as payment of your debt. In other words, you could keep the Trevor. I know—considering the memory of your father—what it must mean to you. I will call on you personally so we can talk it over.

Those words had made Anne explode! She ripped up the letter and threw it in the fire. Now, looking at Ben Talley, she said: "That carpetbagger Kendall is coming tomorrow—to feast like a buzzard on the pickings. I wish I had the guts to shoot him between the eyes!"

The next morning she met Kendall outside her house. He smiled with oily politeness, but she saw the stealth of a coyote in his eyes.

"How do you do, Mrs. Cameron?" he inquired.

She stood, holding Dos, with Sofia and Carlos just behind her.

"What's your business?" she asked him.

He removed his hat and leaned against the porch railing. "Like I wrote you, Mrs. Cameron. I've taken up your debt."

"I'm aware of that."

He smiled again and shrugged. "Well, I'm afraid I have to call it due."

"You just try," she challenged.

Kendall's eyebrows rose in surprise. "Now what do you mean by that?"

"Turn around, Mr. Kendall," she said. "But turn slowly. Don't make a sudden move—not if you value your life."

Kendall pivoted cautiously on his heel. As he turned,

Anne's cowboys stepped out into the sunshine, their Winchesters loaded and pointed at his chest.

"Well, this must be some kind of a joke," he stammered. "You can't be serious."

"Deadly serious," Anne responded.

"Do you mean they'd actually shoot me?"

"If I so much as raise an eyebrow," Anne replied.

"This is crazy," Kendall said.

"Try me."

Kendall thought better of it. "Well, maybe I can let the debt ride a while longer."

"Maybe you can forget it altogether," Anne said.

"I can't do that! I paid over twelve thousand dollars!"

"Write it down to neighborliness, Mr. Kendall," Anne said, her voice hard as steel. "Now get off the Lantana!"

"I'm going."

"Now!"

Kendall grabbed his reins and swung up into his saddle.

Anne glanced off to her side, spotting Ramiro Rivas among her cowboys. She nodded, but so slightly that only Ramiro caught her gesture. Smiling in understanding, he raised his rifle to the sky and fired.

Kendall's horse reared back, whinnying wildly, and shot off across the prairie. For a moment, it looked as if Kendall would be thrown, but he held on and disappeared over the horizon.

It was a beautiful autumn day at La Rivière. The sky was an umbrella of blue silk, and the evergreen oaks rustled in the caress of a gentle north breeze.

The LaForet family was gathering—as they did every Sunday—on the sweeping green lawn in front of the imposing plantation house. Long tables, draped in crisp white linens, had been arranged beneath the trees, and servants were parading from the mansion

466

with platters and baskets laden with food, roast turkey and smoked ham, biscuits and brioche, apples, pears, and strawberries with whipped cream, and a dozen deep pecan pies just out of the ovens.

The LaForet women, resplendent in their Sunday finery, gathered in groups, gossiping happily beneath the oaks or strolling arm in arm about the beautifully tended lawn. Some browsed in La Rivière's magnificent garden, picking roses for their hair; others watched proudly over their children, who played on the banks of the fish pond or took turns riding the tame little ponies that the stableboys had led over from the stalls.

The men lounged about in morning dress, sipping juleps and milk punch, conferring about the races. They discussed cotton prices and the virtues of their newest hunting dogs. And, when they were certain their womenfolk were out of earshot, they talked about the latest lovely quadroons they'd been with in the Vieux Carré's sporting houses.

It was an honor, Alex knew, to be a guest at a LaForet *matinée*. It was a family gathering, not ordinarily open to outsiders. But the day before, he'd received a note from Charles inviting him to attend.

As his landau rolled up the long horseshoe drive, Charles himself was waiting at the carriage block to greet him.

"I'm very pleased you could honor us today," Charles said.

"The pleasure's all mine," Alex replied.

"Come. Let's find you a drink," Charles said, taking Alex's elbow and leading him toward a table set with bottles and crystal glasses. "Then we'll stroll around a bit so you can meet everyone. As you can see, the LaForet family is rather numerous—over a hundred of us, I'd venture to guess, although I don't think anyone's ever taken the trouble to count. But that's precisely the reason I asked you here today. It seems these garden parties are the only time we're all gathered together."

A maroon-jacketed servant mixed fresh mint with sugar in the bottom of a glass and filled the tumbler with bourbon. Then he poured the mixture into a frosty silver julep cup, packed with ice and decorated with a sprig of mint, and handed it to Alex.

Charles took a milk punch; then he and Alex began to make the rounds, meeting family as they walked.

"My cousin Sylvie and her husband Antoine," Charles said, pausing only long enough for Alex to shake hands and murmur greetings. "My aunt Celestine, and another aunt Clotilde. And, ah! Here is one of my favorite nephews. Bernard!" he called. "Here's someone I'd like you to meet."

And on it went as they circled the vast lawn, the names crowding into Alex's head: Felicity, Roger, Aunt Berthe and Uncle Maurice, Jean-Luc, Genvieve, Michel, David, Jules, Madelaine, Louise, Isabelle, Philippe, Lawrence, and Camille. And any number of Andres, Francoises, Maries, and Pierres.

Alex was puzzled. Charles seemed driven, as if bent on introducing him to everyone as quickly as possible. Every now and then, as they strolled from one group to another, Alex glanced about, looking for Jeanette, but she was nowhere to be seen. Still more members of the family appeared from time to time through the wide French doors of the mansion, and Alex hoped, with every new group that emerged onto the gallery, that Jeanette would be among them.

At last, he and Charles had come to the farthest reach of the lawn and were retracing their steps back toward the mansion. As they passed beneath a mossy oak, Charles paused and offered Alex a cigar from a silver case he pulled from his coat pocket.

"Quite a family, isn't it?" Charles asked, striking a match and holding it out to Alex's cigar. "One of the largest in the parish. And very closely-knit. We all enjoy each other's company. That's why these *matinées* are so faithfully attended. Even old Bertrand is here. He's the fat, bald man helping himself to a bowl of strawberries. He's the black sheep of the family. He lives with his mistress in the Vieux Carré, but every Sunday, like an old swain, he calls for his wife in his carriage and rides out here. He wouldn't miss it for the world."

Alex's glass was empty and he was eager to head back toward the house. His eyes still searched the gallery in front of the French doors, hoping for sight of Jeanette. But Charles seemed in no hurry to move on. In fact, it appeared to Alex that he was intentionally keeping him at a distance so he could view the scene as if from a box seat in a theater.

A silence had developed between the two men, and it was moments before Charles spoke again.

"I'm afraid," he said at last, "that my daughter Suzanne has been indiscreet. She passed on to me a bit of news that saddened me, I must say."

Alex looked at him inquiringly.

"She says that she heard from Jeanette that you and Anne are being divorced."

"It's true, Charles," Alex replied. "I should have told you myself, but . . ."

"I understand. It's a private matter. There was no need to tell me." He fell silent momentarily, his eyes sweeping the lawn, pausing here and there on family members. Then he spoke again. "Suzanne also tells me that Jeanette is in love with you."

He knows, Alex thought. He knows everything!

"I have to tell you, Alex, fond as I am of you, that any relationship between you and Jeanette is simply unthinkable. It would not do for a LaForet to become involved with a person who's been divorced."

Alex smiled wryly. "You Catholics are a strange

breed, Charles," he said. "You wink at infidelity as in the case of the old gentleman you pointed out a moment ago. Yet you won't tolerate divorce. It's strange to me."

"There's a method in our madness, Alex," Charles explained. "The heart of the matter is the family—the stability of the family. That's why I invited you here today. I wanted you to see the LaForets gathered together in closed ranks."

"And none among you is divorced?"

"None," Charles said. "And not because divorce and remarriage is deemed a sin. Nothing so ethereal would enter our minds. But we avoid divorce because it is divisive. It would split the family. And we're strong and rich and successful because we stick together. Oh, one might stumble and fall, but the others are always there to help him up. Then together we move on, forgetting and forgiving the indiscretion."

"I understand what you're telling me," Alex said.

Charles drew his eyes away from his family and looked at Alex. "No. I'm not sure you do, yet."

Alex made a move to go, but Charles held him back.

"Wait a minute, Alex. Look. Look up there on the gallery."

An ancient woman, dressed in gray silk, appeared at the balustrade.

"My grandmother," Charles said. "She was ninety-six this summer. Look how she smiles! How happy she is to be surrounded by her family."

The elderly woman raised her hand and waved to the gathering on the grass. It was the regal gesture of a queen.

Then another woman joined her at her side. It was Charles's mother. And in a moment, Charles's sister Veronique appeared on the gallery, followed by Suzanne and—at last—Jeanette.

470

"Look at that, Alex," Charles said. "All those generations! Think of the continuity!"

And as he spoke, Jeanette stoped and lifted up a little girl, a niece no doubt, for her hair and skin were the color of Jeanette's.

It reminded Alex of the royal family appearing on the balcony at Buckingham Palace.

"All those generations!" Charles repeated softly, and Alex could not mistake the tone of reverence in his voice.

After a moment, Charles looked over and said, "Well, Alex. I see you need another julep. Shall we walk back to the house?"

Alex stood rooted to the spot, his eyes on the women gathered at the balustrade.

"Alex?" Charles said.

Alex turned slowly and faced his friend. "I'll be leaving, Charles," he said quietly.

"Are you sure you won't stay? The *matinée* has just begun."

Alex shook his head. "No, thank you anyway. I'm going. I believe I understand at last what you've been telling me."

Charles's face softened, the faint trace of a kindly smile on his lips.

"You didn't really invite me here to meet your family, did you, Charles?" Alex said. "You've not been presenting me to the LaForets. You've been giving me an example instead. You've been showing me the Cameron clan—or at least what the Cameron clan could be, given the years, the sacrifice, and the discipline your family has gone through."

"I think you do understand, Alex," Charles said. "Return to Anne. Don't give up your dream so readily. Whatever the reason that made you leave her, it can be only a small thing in the grander scheme. The two of you started out to build a dynasty. You'll never achieve it by running away, by breaking it apart before

471

it's even had a chance to flourish. If you destroy it now, you'll regret it for the rest of your life."

Alex nodded. He understood.

47

The following Friday, Anne received news of the loan from the Delta Bank in New Orleans. The funds had already been transferred to her account in San Antonio.

She summoned Ramiro, whom she'd hired as foreman, and told him the news. "Tell the boys they'll be paid," she said. "I've got the money now. And though it galls me to do it, I've written a draft to Kendall, taking care of my debt to him."

"Then the ranch is saved?" Ramiro asked with relief.

Anne nodded. "Yes. The Lantana is free and clear again."

"I'm happy for you, señora," Ramiro said.

"Thank you, Ramiro. Now go spread the word. I don't want to lose any more cowboys."

After Ramiro left, Anne pulled on her leather jacket and saddled up her roan. She rode out across her domain. Her eyes scanned the land from horizon to horizon, and everything she saw was hers.

"I should be happier," she thought. But the pain of loneliness and loss pervaded her heart.

She rode past the little cemetery where her parents

473

lay. The lantana bush she'd planted on Joel's grave
had flourished, and despite the autumn coolness, it
still bloomed with flowers of rust and gold.

Tears stung her eyes.

"What's the matter with me?" she thought. "I should
be jubilant. I've kept my vow to you, Papa. The Lantana has been saved."

But the tears spilled from her eyes and glistened
on her cheeks. Within her was an immense void, and
it astonished her that emptiness could be so painful.

Gently she spurred her horse and moved on, wandering without direction, not caring where she went.

Her house and the barn and stables disappeared
behind her. Ahead was nothing but the vast *brasada*.

She rode for a long time, the cool north wind drying
the tears on her face. At last she approached the
barbed wire fence that stretched in either direction for
as far as the eye could see. She rode up to it and followed its length until she arrived at the main gate. The
big, wrought-iron archway straddled two massive limestone pillars. In the iron was written:

LANTANA

and above it was her brand, the crown of thorns.

She stopped her horse and sat a minute beneath the
arch. Her mind was blank. Her body felt numb all
over. She heaved a deep, slow sigh of resignation.

With her gloved hand, she tugged the reins to the
left, preparing to leave. But as her horse turned and
started away, she caught a glimpse of a dark speck
appearing on the horizon.

"I hope it's one of the cowboys coming back," she
thought to herself, and she decided to wait at the gate
for him to arrive.

When she looked up again, she saw that the horseman was galloping. He was spurring his steed unmercifully and sat low in the saddle, his face nearly
buried in the flying mane.

474

Anne watched and waited as he grew nearer, and she wondered what his hurry was, for he seemed almost pursued as if he were desperate to make it to the gate.

Then suddenly she felt a tingle on the back of her neck, and she sat straighter in the saddle and stared out at the rider who was so swiftly closing the distance that lay between them.

Now he was nearly upon her, and her heart jumped in her breast.

"Alex!" she cried.

He reined up in a scattering of gravel, breathless from the ride.

They sat facing each other, separated by the big iron gate. Anne heard her heart drumming in her ears. Alex gasped for breath, trying to speak.

"Anne," he said at last. "Anne . . . may I come home?"

She watched him for a moment, not trusting herself to talk. He waited for her reply.

After what seemed like an eternity to him, she swung down from her saddle and raised the heavy latch and pulled back the gate. Alex dismounted and walked his horse through.

They stood gazing into each other's eyes, neither daring to reach out and bridge the distance between them.

Alex spoke again: "I told you once, Anne, that there are some things once broken that can never be mended."

"I remember," Anne murmured.

"I was wrong," Alex said. "My love for you is stronger now than it ever was before. I'm sorry. Can you ever forgive me?"

Anne's lips trembled and her eyes brimmed with tears. She reached across for his hands and drew him to her. His arms went around her waist and held her tightly as they kissed.

"Oh, my bonny Anne," Alex whispered into her ear. "I've missed you so!"

Anne looked into his eyes and breathed, "Welcome home, my love!"

THE BEST OF THE BESTSELLERS
FROM WARNER BOOKS!

THE BEST OF THE BESTSELLERS
FROM WARNER BOOKS!

REMEMBER IT DOESN'T GROW ON TREES